PALE WOLF

Bad Wolf Chronicles - Book 2

TIM McGREGOR

Perdido Pub
TORONTO

Perdido Pub
6 Lakeview Avenue
Toronto, Ontario

Publisher's Note: This is a work of fiction. Names, characters, places, and incidents are a product of the author's imagination. Locales and public names are sometimes used for atmospheric purposes. Any resemblance to actual people, living or dead, or to businesses, companies, events, institutions, or locales is completely coincidental.

Book Layout & Design ©2013 - BookDesignTemplates.com

Pale Wolf/ Tim McGregor. -- 1st ed.
ISBN-13: 978-1484946992
ISBN-10: 1484946995

For Ginger and Ruby

I'm a goddamn force of nature.

–KAREN WALTON, *GINGER SNAPS*

I

IN HIS DREAMS, SHE CAME BACK.

The nightmares too.

John Gallagher sat up and wiped a forearm across his brow. The same thing almost every night, waking up with the sweats, heart banging in his chest. This night no different from the rest but this time, she came back.

Lara Mendes had stepped warily from the trees into an open meadow. Gallagher's former partner in the homicide detail, missing and presumed dead these last three months. In his dream, he searched the dense forest looking for her. Sometimes he found her, dead at the bottom of a ditch, her remains torn apart by wild dogs.

This time was different. She came back. On her own.

He was scrambling through the thicket, hands scratched raw from the brambles, knees dirty from crawling through the loam. He dropped to his knees in exhaustion, wanting to give up. He looked up and there she was, stumbling out of the trees.

Her eyes wide with fear, her dark hair wet and plastered against her face. He ran to her. She startled at first, then hurried to meet him. There were tears in her eyes as she limped forward.

He almost had her, almost touched her when the wolf took her. It slammed into her from behind like a freight train and dragged Lara back into the dark trees. Her eyes bald with terror, fingers clawing the dirt.

And then she was gone.

Gallagher heard her screams, cutting through the air to him from the inky darkness. All he could do was listen.

And then the wolf came back. Enormous and powerful, a giant in its proportions. Its maw opened and the monster's big, big teeth closed over his throat and there was a snap as his neck broke and then he woke.

He rubbed his eyes until the numbers on the alarm clock came into focus. Almost five. No getting back to sleep now. He swung out of bed, pulled on the clothes left draped over a chair and headed downstairs. Stepping quietly past his daughter's bedroom door.

Gallagher sat with his feet propped on the desk in his small office next to the mud room. He clicked through all the police monitoring sites and RSS feeds for the fourth time this morning but there was nothing new. No reports of dog attacks, no wolf sightings, no unusual homicides under the parameters he had put in place. He reached for his cup but his coffee had gone cold.

A thump overhead, the creak of the floor from the upstairs bedroom. His daughter was up.

He was brewing a fresh pot when Amy came downstairs. A bleary-eyed seventeen-year old shuffling like the walking dead in ratty slippers. She flopped onto a stool at the kitchen counter and Gallagher slid a bowl of fruit and yogurt under her nose. "Morning sunshine. Sleep well?"

Amy looked down at her breakfast then up at her dad. "Can I have some coffee?"

"It'll stunt your growth."

"I'm tall enough." Amy tried a smile but it came out like a disturbed leer. Mornings were not her strong suit. "Please."

"Half a cup." He slid the cup across the counter to her and watched her lace it with a lethal dose of sugar. "Do you need a lunch today?"

"No. I'll pick up something." She sipped her cup, watching him clean up. "You must be tired. I heard you get up at four."

"I'm all right."

"The nightmare again?"

He threaded a tie under his collar, ignoring the question. Code for 'change the subject'. Amy didn't pursue it, already knowing the answer. Her dad suffered nightmares, almost every night since the incident. He got by on three, maybe four hours of sleep. That it was affecting him was plain to see but he never acknowledged it, claiming he didn't need much sleep anyway. "Don't go with that tie," she said.

"It's my best one."

She pointed at it with her spoon. "It's still got that stain on it."

He flipped up the end, saw the offending blemish. "Damn." He stripped it off and tossed it onto the back of a chair. "Where's the blue one?"

Amy munched away then nodded in the direction of his office down the hall. "Anything new on the search front?"

"Same. Big fat nada."

She offered a conciliatory smile. Maybe tomorrow. During the incident that had left her dad in the hospital with a shredded ear and two cracked ribs, his partner, Detective Lara Mendes, had disappeared without a trace. When he recovered, he began searching for her. Obsessively. She'd helped him those first two months, calling every hospital in Portland for the missing detective or any Jane Doe matching her description. Her zeal had waned when it became clear they were not going to find her. She'd started skipping days, calling hospitals every second day, then once a week until she stopped altogether. Her dad didn't say anything about it, he just took on the calls himself. Part of his morning routine now. She had been conflicted about it at first, not wanting to let him down but, at the same time, not wanting to prolong his delusion that Lara would be found. It seemed cruel, like giving a drunk a drink. She had hoped that he'd pick up on her cue and start to accept the reality that his partner was, tragically and hopelessly, gone.

It hadn't.

Gallagher fished his keys from the bowl and grabbed the holstered gun from the countertop. Clipped it to his belt and leaned in to kiss her goodbye. "Will you be home for dinner?"

"No." Amy wiped her chin. "Gabby and I going for dinner after work. Indian."

"Again?" He frowned. "How are you supposed to save money with the way you eat out?"

"Dad? Unclench."

"Okay." Another peck and then he levelled his eyes at hers. "Home before dark. Right?"

Amy tried not to roll her eyes but couldn't help it. "Sure," she said. He left and she stifled a sigh. What part of 'unclench' didn't he understand?

THE river was almost frozen over, forcing the woman to walk farther each day to find a break in the ice where she could toss a few lines in. She had set out three lines past the ice and hunkered down to wait for a bite. She had been here all day without a single tug on any of the lines.

The sun was going down over the trees and unless she got lucky soon, it would be another day of going hungry.

The river at her feet was wide, with sheet ice growing from each bank. Beyond that, a wall of dark forest and solitude and no sign of any other living person. She had chosen this spot for its seclusion. A modest hike back through the trees stood a small shack that she had been living in for over a month. Before the snow fell, the fishing had been good. The trout and steelhead she had pulled from the river provided plenty of meals for one person. She didn't have to risk travelling into town for supplies. The spot had been ideal.

Now she watched her lines trail into the dark water, still and undisturbed for hours.

When the last of the sun fled behind the pines, she packed it in. Another day of rice and beans. Even those supplies were dwindling and she'd soon be forced to walk into town. She'd have to be careful, the money was dwindling too.

Threading her way back through the dense trees to her little hovel of a shelter, she tried to remember how many days it had been she'd suffered an attack from her particular affliction. Thirty days? On a wall in the shack, she had tallied the days with a nub of charcoal from the stove, like a prisoner marking time in a cell.

Today would be thirty-one days. A personal record. The longest she had ever gone without an attack. A point of pride, for sure, but it might also mean that she was long overdue.

2

THERE WAS BLOOD EVERYWHERE. Splattered onto the scuffed walls and pooling out onto the grimy floor where it grouted the tiles. He couldn't get close to the body without stepping in it. It was bad luck to step in a vic's blood. You don't want to track that stuff home. Detective John Gallagher, Homicide Detail, Portland Police Bureau, checked his gut and got to work.

Gallagher tucked his tie into his shirt to keep it from dangling into anything nasty and knelt down at the edge of the blood pool. The vic was male, middle-aged and pale as snow from blood loss. Face down but with no visible wounds, which meant that the wounds were on his front. A neighbour had reported gunshots in the house. The patrol officers who responded found the front door wide open and a body on the kitchen floor.

"I think I see the problem here," Gallagher said, nodding to the detective on the opposite side of the body. "This guy's got a slow leak."

"Damn. My money was on an aneurysm." Detective Rueben Wade studied the body from his angle. Wade was primary here, Gallagher backing him up. Murder calls were rotated through the detail as they came in, every detective grabbing a call as the rotation dictated. Except Gallagher. They hadn't allowed him primary on a body since the incident so here he was, backing up someone else's file. "Maybe they can patch that up," Wade said. "Dude can tell us who killed him."

"I dunno." Gallagher moved around the body for a different angle. "He doesn't look like the chatty type to me."

Gallagher didn't care about being denied primary investigator. He would have once, but not any longer. He was grateful to simply have his job back, his pension in place. His daughter's future. He'd been put on leave following the incident and, unable to satisfactorily answer questions about his lieutenant's death, fully expected to be sacked. His pension would be snipped with a trim pair of scissors and his daughter's future suddenly thrown into question.

To his surprise, he was reinstated three weeks later. The Homicide detail was down in numbers, specifically seasoned homicide detectives and they simply couldn't afford to get rid of him. They brought him back in, read the riot act and gave him his job under a few ironclad conditions.

Stay in the background.

Everything by the book.

A single complaint, the tiniest deviation from procedure, and he would be turfed.

He could live with that. What else was he going to do? There were bigger things to consider, like the house. Barely keeping his head above water as it was, he'd lose it for sure if forced to start over in some other line of work. The house he shared with his daughter would be forfeit. If the house was gone, he'd be forced to find some smaller place and feared Amy would want to stay at her mother's place for good. He couldn't endure that. Not now.

Returning to work hadn't been easy. He had few real friends at work before everything blew up but when he came back, he found even less. His involvement in the death of his former Lieutenant, the whispered suspicions, hung over him like a plague and people stayed away.

He could live with that too. Going back to work meant having access to all the resources of the Portland Police Bureau and more. Resources he needed if he was ever going to find his AWOL partner.

A uniformed officer entered the kitchen and handed something to Detective Wade. A wallet. Wade dug through it, pulling pieces of ID. "Raymond Arbuckle. Thirty-four."

Gallagher squatted on his knees and studied the body on the floor. The victim's hands were dirty and the arms snaked with tattoos. The clothes were grubby and dark with stains. Work clothes. The face was raw and weathered, like life had kicked him around the block and come back for more. He looked out of place in this quaint bungalow. "This guy lives here?"

Wade scrutinized the vic's drivers licence. "Address here says Verlaine. That's ten minutes from here."

Gallagher rose and crossed to a stack of mail on the counter. "Then whose house is this?"

"It belongs to a Mrs. Ines Brakken," said the uniform who was first on the scene. "According to the neighbors, Ines ran screaming from the house right after the shots and hightailed it down the street."

"Jesus." Detective Wade shook his head. "She shot the guy and bolted."

"Is Raymond here the husband? Or the ex?" Gallagher looked back to the body on the tiled floor. "And why did she light him up?"

"Yo, detective?" The uniform pointed at the floor under Gallagher's feet.

Gallagher looked down. He was standing in the pool of blood.

Bad luck.

MRS. Brakken was found halfway down the block at a friend's house. The gun lay on the coffee table with the tang of gunblack stinking up the room. She was incoherent to questions and Wade had her driven to precinct to cool off in the box. Gallagher drove to the house on Verlaine and regretfully informed Mrs. Arbuckle that her husband was dead. He advised her to call someone to come over but Mrs. Arbuckle insisted on going to the precinct to find out more and Gallagher drove her and her two boys there. The grieving woman also had a teenage daughter but she'd been staying at a friend's house for the week. Gallagher let it go, figuring the kid was better off there then crying in the hallways of a police station.

By the time he settled the family into an office to wait, the shooter, Mrs. Brakken, had calmed down enough to answer questions. Detectives Gallagher and Wade entered the box and softballed questions to the woman to get the story out. Did she know the man she had shot? Why was he in her house?

Ines Brakken stated that she had never seen the man before in her life. The deceased, Raymond Arbuckle of 3312 Verlaine Avenue, had busted down her door with a crowbar in his hand, screaming for her husband, Mr. Troy Brakken. Ines tried to call 911 but Arbuckle had slapped the phone from her hand and slammed her into a wall. He was out of his mind with rage, screaming at her that her husband had raped his daughter and that he was here to kill him. When Ines told him her husband would never do such a thing, Arbuckle flew into a rage and told her he would take his revenge on her unless she told him where he was. He struck her, she fought back and fled to get the gun her husband kept in the cupboard near the cereal. She shot the man in the chest but Arbuckle kept coming and she fired a round into his neck. He dropped and a sickening gush of blood gurgled out of his destroyed throat. She ran.

"Holy shit," said Wade as they exited the box. They brought Mrs. Arbuckle into interview room B and gently asked her questions. Mrs. Arbuckle said that she and her husband had found a used pregnancy test in their teenage daughter's room and confronted her with it. The daughter, all of seventeen, denied it all but eventually broke under questioning. She confessed she was in love with a man and they were planning to run away together. The man, fifteen years her senior, was married. Her father flew into a rage and forced his daughter to give up the man's name. Raymond Arbuckle got a crowbar from the garage and peeled off in his car. That was the last Mrs. Arbuckle had seen of her husband.

Gallagher and Wade stepped out of interview room B and took a deep breath. Wade leaned on a cubicle, crushing the plastic Christmas holly strung along the border. "So the dead guy goes off to lay a beating on the scumbag who was screwing his teenage daughter and winds up dead. Mrs. Brakken, attacked by a crazed man she had never seen before, shoots the guy in self-defense."

"Jesus." Gallagher eased a kink in his neck. "How the hell do you frame this mess?"

"Manslaughter?" Wade said. "Let's talk to the lieutenant about it."

Detective LaBayer popped up out of his cubicle with the phone cradled against his shoulder. "G? The husband just walked in. He's in the lobby."

"LOOK, Goddamnit, I need to see my wife. Now!" Troy Brakken stood about six-five and he towered over the uniformed officer he was berating. Demanding to see his wife and openly slandering the officer's intelligence when he didn't get his way.

Detective Wade tried to talk him down. "Sir, if you could follow me. We need to ask you some questions."

"No! Not until I see my wife. How many times do I have to tell you people?"

Gallagher strode past his partner and shoved the man into a chair. Brakken blustered and cursed about his rights until Gallagher snarled, nose to nose. "Your wife shot the father of the girl you're screwing, chump. Take a pill."

"I don't know what you're talking about."

He snatched the man's necktie and twisted. "You just destroyed two families, you piece of shit."

"Leave it, Gallagher." Wade stepped in and pulled Gallagher back. "Ain't worth it."

Wade was right. Gallagher had to watch his step. He turned away from the man, leaving Wade to deal with the man but then stopped cold. Lieutenant Cabrisi stood near the elevator, watching the whole thing. He did not look pleased.

The Lieutenant waved at him to follow. "My office," he said.

"I don't need to remind you of your probationary period, do I?" Lieutenant Cabrisi settled back into his chair with a slight wheeze. He looked every inch the cop, from the mustache to the belly tipping over his belt. Cabrisi had been brought in from Sex Assault to steer the Homicide detail. Gallagher barely knew the man but was willing to bet Cabrisi had an AA chip in his pocket and a shiny Harley in his garage that ne never rode. Some clichés you settle into, like quicksand. Others you buy into. The Lieutenant looked like the buying kind.

Gallagher didn't take a seat, knowing when he was about to get chewed out. Take an earful, let the Lieutenant feel better for doing so and get out. "I was just making a point with the man, that's all. Read the incident report, you'll understand why."

"No I won't, detective. I don't care if you got Satan himself in cuffs, you keep your hands to yourself. Especially in precinct."

"My mistake," Gallagher said, eating it. "Won't happen again."

Cabrisi frowned and let out a sigh, the end of which trailed into the tell-tale wheeze of a smoker. "How are your therapy sessions?"

"No complaints."

"Obviously." The Lieutenant pushed some papers around. "You've missed the last three appointments."

"Yeah. Homicides keep getting in the way."

"Those sessions are a conditional part of your reinstatement here. They're mandatory, not optional."

Gallagher fought the urge to look at his watch. *Just play nice so you can get the hell out of here.* "I'll make the next one."

"The staff therapist is in precinct today. And she's got time this afternoon. Be there."

"Can't. Got plans."

"Detective, make me happy and just frigging be there."

"I'll make up my sessions, don't worry." Gallagher gave in and checked his watch. "But I got to pick up my daughter. She's got practice."

The Lieutenant frowned deeper but let it go. "Basketball, right?"

"Something like that."

3

AMY BROUGHT THE GUN UP in both hands and sighted her eye down the bead. Beyond the sight lay the target, a standard body silhouette at twenty-five yards. Amy steadied her hand, held her breath and pulled the trigger. The Glock kicked a little but nothing she wasn't used to now.

"Again. Six rounds."

Amy fired again, six quick rounds. Remembering what she'd been taught. Don't overthink it, just find the target and go with your gut. The spent casings spit from the chamber and tinkled at her feet and she lowered the gun.

Gallagher hit the button on the wall and the target swung forward. He looked at Amy and gave a thumbs up. "That was better. No hesitation that time."

Amy lifted the earmuffs. "I dunno. I'm still thinking too much."

"Give it time, it'll come." He nodded to the gun in her hand. "Take it apart."

She hit the release and slid the magazine out then racked the slide back. A glance down into the chamber to ensure it was empty. She shook her hand to dispel that weird tension she got when shooting, then she dismantled the piece.

The target dangled before them and Gallagher pulled down the paper silhouette. Four hits on the sheet, two of which were in the eighth and ninth markers. The third puncture was in the blank void in the head area, the fourth had landed outside the silhouette entirely. Gallagher clucked his teeth. "You went for a head shot?"

"My gut told me to."

"Cute. But for the millionth time, forget the fancy headshot and go for the trunk." He pinned a fresh silhouette on the target and punched the button, trailing the piece back to the twenty-five yard line. He thumbed the second pistol on the deck. "Pick up the fifty and load it."

Amy wiped her slick palms down her jeans and took up the second gun. The Desert Eagle was big and heavy in her hands and Amy didn't like the awful kick it gave. Its weight and size made it harder to aim properly and she had to grip it tight to keep the recoil from snapping back and hitting her in the head. She didn't know why her dad insisted she learn to shoot the thing. It was too much gun, overkill unless she suddenly found herself facing down a charging rhinoceros.

They used to shoot hoops in the driveway. Now they shot guns, here on a firing range just off the Banfield Expressway. Things changed. Before the incident, her dad didn't let her even see a gun, locking up his service issue when he came home from work. Now he was teaching her how to shoot the damn things. At his insistence, she'd enrolled in a self-defence class. She had wanted to take Tae Kwon Do but he pushed for something harder and more practical like Krav Maga, a military mixed martial art. At home, there was an intricate alarm system and three bolt locks on both the front and back doors.

The term 'paranoid' often sprang to mind but she had yet to utter it aloud. Give it time, she told herself. Things will settle and her dad would come back to normal. That was three months ago and he had only gotten worse.

"Whenever you're ready."

Amy brought the gun up, arms straight but even with her left hand supporting the weight the gun was too unwieldy. A slight tremor rippled down her biceps, throwing the bead off the target. Be still. Aim. Fire.

Boom.

The recoil jerked her back and she knew it was a bad shot the second she squeezed off the round. Amy snapped the safety on and clunked the heavy thing back to the counter.

"I can't shoot this. It's just too much kick."

Gallagher picked up the Eagle, hit the safety and held it out to her. "You learn to compensate. All it takes is practice."

"It's not practical. I'd never get a clean shot off if I ever had to." She made no move to take the weapon. "Why can't I stick to the Glock? I'm so much better with it."

"Are you quitting on me?"

That was unfair. He always knew how to goad her into something. "I'm just saying it's impractical and too heavy gauge to be of any use. The Glock, or any nine millimetre, is enough to bring down any creep. The fifty cal is just show-off and overkill." She took the gun and resumed the stance.

He watched her slip the muffs back over her ears and said; "There are worse things out there."

THE Siberian, like all dogs, displayed a sixth sense at its owner's approach. It lay curled into a ball on the porch, its tail wrapped over its legs and its eyes closed. The ears twitched and angled for the street, picking up the timbre of the Cherokee's engine among all the other vehicles stinking up the roadway. It rose and trotted down into the yard to wait.

The Cherokee rumbled into the driveway, Amy the first to disembark.

"Here boy." Amy nickered and the dog came to her. Tail wagging and nose pressing her palms until she dug her nails into its ruff. She cooed to it and scratched behind its ears.

The moment her dad swung out of the truck, the dog left her and trotted to his feet. It sat on the cold ground and looked up at Gallagher as if awaiting instructions. Gallagher patted the dog's head and spoke softly to it. "It's okay. Go on."

Amy watched the dog bound back to her with its tail wagging. The dog was a mystery the way it acted like a puppy around her but was oddly obedient to her father. The husky was another lingering effect of the incident, having belonged to a crazed suspect her dad was tracking at the time. The dog was supposed to have been destroyed but her dad pinched it from the animal shelter and brought it home. Not with the intention of adopting it however. For two months, he had taken the dog out to the area where his partner had disappeared, hoping the Siberian could track the scent and follow Lara Mendes's trail from where she had vanished into thin air. For two months, they had come home exhausted and empty-handed.

He had told Amy not to get attached to the dog. It's not a pet and it's not staying. It was funny now, the way the husky leaned into her knees and licked her hands. It was like the dog had always been here.

While the dog nudged her for affection and wagged its tail, it constantly glanced back to her dad, looking for approval or waiting for his lead. When her dad went up the steps to the front door, the Siberian trotted at his heels and followed him inside. That's how it was. The dog played with her but kept an almost spooky vigil at his side. More than once he had had to shoo it from the bathroom.

"Batman and Robin," she said and went up the porch steps after them.

4

THE WOMAN KNELT BEFORE the corroded wood stove, feeding a fresh log into the flames. Sparks roiled out of the grate door, incandescent before winking out into pale ash. She closed the iron door and pushed the vent all the way open to kindle the new wood faster. The day spent fishing had dropped her core temperature to dangerous lows. Her feet burned they were so cold, a hair away from frostbite. How soon did gangrene set in once frost killed one's appendages?

Warming her hands before the grate, she looked over the tarpaper shack she had called home for the last month. A hunter's shack, judging by the makeshift construction and lack of any amenities. One room containing an old woodstove, a few crates and a wobbly table. An army surplus bedroll pushed against the wall and two ancient fishing rods hanging on hooks. No running water. In the clearing out front stood a picnic table and down near the river, a tree stump stained with fish blood and scales.

As crude as it was, it suited her and she remained grateful for the shelter it provided. Deserted for the season and remote. There wasn't even a road, just a rutted track running half a mile from the dirt road. A serious outdoorsman type of place, she was surprised the walls weren't decorated with centerfolds. A small stack of newspapers in a bin to be used for kindling the stove. She had worried that the owner might come back for whatever was still in season this time of year until she rifled through the newspapers. Nothing newer than 2006. She'd be safe here for a while.

More importantly, no one else would be at risk if she lost control again.

When the pain in her toes receded to a tingle, she looked through the crate where her provisions were stacked. A few canned goods and a sack of dried beans. Not much left. She'd have to go into town. A two hour walk. Shorter if she hitchhiked but thumbing a ride could lead to questions. What's her name? Where she's from? She couldn't afford the risk.

The crate was pushed aside to reveal a patch of bare wooden floor. She dug her fingers into a seam and a length of floorboard popped out. Reaching down into the crawlspace under the shack she withdrew a leather wallet sealed inside a clear plastic baggie. An evidence bag in fact, a small vestige of her old life before the misery. Back when she'd had a job. And a home. A life.

She opened the wallet and counted through the meagre bills. Sixty dollars, some loose change. Since vanishing from her old life, she had lived like a hobo. On the move and off the grid. She hadn't a dime on her when she decided to run but she couldn't access any of the money she had. Her bank accounts, her car, all of it had to be left untouched if she was going to make a clean break. If it was going to work, everyone she knew had to conclude she was missing for good and presume her dead. As horrific as that was, as cruel, it was better than them knowing the truth.

But you can't get very far with empty pockets. She had made one stop before leaving Portland for good, an address off Sumner. Jacob Weaver was a scam artist with a major in credit card fraud and minor in dope peddling. She had busted him twice during her time with Robbery Detail but both times the shitheel got off. She paid him a surprise visit and took all the cash he had on the premises before leaving the city of roses for good. A little over four grand in fifties, a portion of which she was certain were counterfeits but Jacob's work was top notch and she never did spot the bogus bills. That meant no one else would either.

She was smart with the money too. Making it last, squeezing every penny tighter than a Scottish millionaire. But it only went so far and for somebody on the run, it burned off too fast. She had found odd jobs here and there, day labor stuff. More than once, she had passed herself off as a migrant worker. Her Spanish was almost rusty next to the seasonal farm workers from Chihuahua and Guatemala. It was December now and that work had shut down for the year.

In Del Norte, a greasy little foreman had tried to cheat her out of her day wages, assuming her to be another illiterate Mexican. She dropped him like a sack of dirt, fished his wallet out and removed her pay.

She had fallen a long way down from the police detective she used to be. And there was still further to fall if it came to that. Her money was running down fast and she had no idea where to scrounge some more or what she was going to do when it ran out.

"Cross that bridge when you come to it," she said and shimmied the loose floor board back into place.

GALLAGHER stirred the guacamole with a fork, mashing the chunks of avocado smooth, while the fish fried in the pan. Sticking a finger in the mess he tasted the guac, seemed satisfied, and set the bowl on the table next to the salsa and jalapeno slices. Fish tacos, one of Amy's favorites. His too.

He just didn't like cleaning up all the bowls of condiments they had with it.

He turned the fish in the pan, watching it sizzle and reached for his beer but it was empty. Got another one from the fridge and lowered the heat on the pan. A dull ache had crept into his shoulders earlier in the day and now it flared up again. It stoked the weariness he'd been fighting all evening. A solid night's sleep might fix both but he knew better than to hope for that. The nights were never good.

Flipping the fish fry onto a plate, he hollered at his daughter to come to the table.

After a brief inquiry into each other's day, they ate in silence. Amy picked at her dinner, distracted and unenthused. He should have picked up on that. She usually attacked tacos with gusto until stuffed.

"You feeling okay?" he asked, spooning beans onto another tortilla.

Amy shrugged. "Gabby and a bunch of others are going to the movies tonight. She wanted me to come. It's her birthday."

He glanced over to the kitchen window. Early December and it was already dark. "Sun's gone down."

That meant no. Amy laid her fork onto the plate. She wasn't giving up that easy. "It's just the movies, Dad. Lots of people around. Crazy bright lighting."

"Sorry." He half-shrugged, then took a conciliatory tone. "We can watch a movie, if you want. You still haven't seen *A Fistful of Dollars*."

He watched her push her plate away. Digging in her heels. There was going to be a fight this time. There had been others.

Amy took a breath, said: "I really want to go. It will be safe. And I think I've earned it."

"Honey—"

She cut him off. "I *know* I've earned it."

The dog lay on a mat, chin on the floor. One ear twitched at the sudden cut in her tone.

Amy watched her dad lean back and take a pull off the beer bottle. No hurry. He could dig his heels in too. "You know the rules," he said. "Home after sundown. No exceptions."

"I can't do this anymore, Dad. It's too much. I've gone along with it to keep you happy but— Enough already."

"I know this is tough. And it doesn't seem fair—" he stopped, reconsidered. "It isn't fair. But things are different now. It's for your own good."

"What are you afraid of?"

He tilted the beer. Said nothing.

Amy folded her arms. No retreat, no give. "I know what's going on here."

His brow arched. A reaction at least. She wasn't sure but did a bolt of fear just flash across his eyes?

"Yeah?" he said. "And just what do you know?"

"It's pretty obvious, isn't it? The curfew and the triple locks on all the doors. The gun practice, the paranoia."

He held up a hand. "Stop."

"There's a name for what's happening."

"Is this about a boy? Is there a boy you want to see tonight?"

Amy's mouth set into a grimace but remained locked. A trick learned from the old man.

"Fer Christ's sakes, Amy. Boys can wait."

She leaned in, elbows back on the table. Eyes on his. "P.T.S.D." She watched him roll his eyes, went on. "Post traumatic—"

"I know what it means," he barked. The husky lifted its head off the linoleum and looked at them. He evened his tone. "Put that thought out of your head."

"What else is it then? These are all the symptoms, dad." Her hand came up, counting off fingers. "The nightmares, the lack of sleep, the paranoia. The anger—"

"The anger ain't new."

"But it's gotten worse. Your control issues with me, like this ridiculous curfew." She nodded to the drink in his hand. "And your drinking. Classic signs. You can't deny that."

Amy paused, waiting for some response. An acknowledgment. Hell, a grunt would do. Nothing. Keep pushing. "All of this goes back to that night in

September. The night Lara disappeared and you wound up in the hospital."

He flinched. A chink in the armour. Neither spoke, some thin thread of wire pulled taut across the table. The Siberian watched them from its nest, eyes darting from the girl to the man and back again.

"What happened that night?" Amy softened her tone. She had tried before to coax it out of him. "Something bad happened and you've never said anything about it. Tell me."

Gallagher rose and gathered up the dishes. "We're done here."

"No. We're not. Tell me what happened."

He ran the faucet, keeping his back to her. "Clear the table please."

It was so easy for him, to just shut it all down and turn it off. Shut her out and become an iceberg. Amy took hold of her plate, ready to do what she was told but then she stopped and sat back down. Not tonight. She slid her plate across the table until it teetered over the edge and fell.

Crash.

He spun around. Saw the mess on the floor, the shards of china everywhere. "What the hell?"

Amy looked her father in the eye. "I'm not a kid anymore. Just trust me. It's okay."

His face reddened but his jaw muscles twitched as he swallowed his outburst and kept his mouth shut. With a quiet grumble, he said; "Clean that up."

Amy got to her feet and stepped around the mess on the floor. "You're right, this isn't fair. I'm supposed to trust you implicitly. With everything. But you won't trust me? We're family for Christ's sakes."

She watched his hands bunch into fists. Knuckles whitening. Silently counting off the seconds to cool down. "Watch your language."

Amy walked away but fired back over her shoulder. "Some family we are."

Retreating into her bedroom, Amy opened every drawer in the dresser, loathing everything she owned.

No matter, she'd find something to wear.

HE was draining the sink when she came back downstairs. Jeans that were too tight and hair straightened pin sharp. The makeup around her eyes wasn't a lot, a little mascara, but it was jarring to see. Gone was his little girl. Gallagher didn't know who this young woman was.

Amy took her coat from the rack and slipped it on. "I'm going out to see my friends. We'll be safe. I'll be back around eleven."

Gallagher flung the dishtowel away. "Don't do this."

"You can't stop me."

The Siberian sat by the door, waiting to go outside. Its eyes roamed back and forth between them. He stood and wagged his tail as Amy approached. She rubbed its head and reached for the door knob.

"I'll be safe," she said. Then a parting shot. "Trust me."

"Do you have your phone on you?"

"Yes."

He didn't try to stop her. What was he going to do, send her to her room? The dog scuttled out with her and the door slammed shut.

He finished cleaning up and then took down a rocks glass from the cupboard. Found the single malt and poured a ploughman's share. He pulled on his boots and coat and then went out to the front porch. Settled into the old wicker chair and watched the street. A car went past and then it was quiet. The husky trotted up the steps and sat at his feet.

Gallagher set his glass on the weathered floorboards and contemplated going back inside to fetch his gun.

5

"LITTLE LATE IN THE SEASON for fishing, isn't it?"

The woman looked up from the items she had placed on the counter. "Pardon?"

The man behind the register, big-bellied with a broad smile, held up the spool of fishing line she'd chosen.

"Fishing season's over, is what I mean." The man behind the counter smiled, holding up the spool of fishing line she'd chosen. He rang it in. "At least for trout and whitefish. You don't want to be caught by the game warden. It's a hefty fine."

"I just like to be ready for next season," she said. The shop owner nodded, seemed satisfied with the answer. Truth was, she did plan to fish out of season. These days, the only protein she got came out of what she could pull from the river near the shack. And that wasn't much, she had never been that much of a fisherman.

She watched the man ring up the rest of her supplies. A few cans and a sack of lentils. Dried chili peppers to give it some taste. Soap, the cheapest and smelliest the shop had to offer. She looked back over the aisles, wondering if she'd forgotten anything. The shop was a bona fide general store, selling everything from groceries to sporting goods to locally made crafts on consignment. A Podunk charm all its own.

"Eleven-twenty," he said, totaling it up. "Say, are you staying down at the Hatfield's place? The cabins on the lake there?"

"No." She paid and loaded her purchases into the backpack. "Thanks."

"My pleasure." He seemed to take no offense at her blunt answer. He looked at his watch and said; "If you hurry over to the Salty Pine, you can still catch the happy hour. Chilli and beer for two bucks. Can't beat it."

She slung the backpack onto her shoulders, thanked him and went out the door.

A battered pickup truck rumbled past her on the road and disappeared behind the post office. No other traffic. The town of Weepers was small and remote, the kind of place that flourished in the summer and curled up and went to sleep in the winter. That might be a problem now. With the tourists gone and only the locals around, she might be noticed. People would want to chat, ask where she's from or where she's staying. Like the shop owner.

She hated the thought of packing up and moving on again but it might come to that. Where would she run to this time?

Cinching up the shoulder straps, she started walking when she heard a door open and music spill out into the street. The Salty Pine tavern was just up ahead on her left, a neon sign glowing in the window. She watched an older man hold the door open for his wife and she took his arm as they ambled to their car parked out front.

She listened to the sound of music and people talking. The door swung closed and the sound muffled to a low murmur. An ache swelled up in her chest at the sounds. Civilization. Life. Community. She'd been alone so long now, isolated and on the run. The rumble of afternoon drinkers nestled inside was a siren call hard to ignore.

"Two buck chili and beer," she uttered, reading the sign on the door. It was a luxury but today, she'd splurge.

THE chili was hearty if bland. Hunkered down at a table near the back, she kept her distance from the happy hour crowd and spiked the chili with shake after shake of tobasco. She wolfed it down and tore the biscuit in half and wiped the bowl with it. The beer, a tall glass of draft, she sipped slowly.

Three tables were occupied with afternoon drinkers, a few older guys propped up on the bar. The TV flickered with the sound muted. She didn't speak to anyone, avoiding eye contact with even the waitress. Still, it felt good simply being around other people. The seclusion took its toll, this exile she'd forced upon herself shredding her nerves raw until she wanted to scream out for someone, anyone. Sometimes just being around other people like this, listening to them talk, took the sting out of her seclusion. The claustrophobia of being trapped inside her own head.

Sometimes it brought trouble.

Four tables over three men leaned over their beers. Ball caps and workboots, hunting knives in leather sheaths hung from their belts instead of cell phones. They argued with vigor, waving their hands about and talking over one another. Lara picked up words here and there, trying to decipher what the argument was about. Words like 'bear', 'bait-traps' and 'hunting party' popped up out of the racket of the bar. She leaned in to snatch more scraps of conversation.

"...two head of livestock that McFarland's lost already..."

"...coyotes don't go for animals that size. It's a mountain lion, if it's anything..."

"Care to add to the class, ma'am?"

She startled, realizing the words were addressed to her. The man with the tattooed forearm squared his eyes straight on her. Unlike his portly friends, he was trim and solid. He smiled at her, a flash of white teeth. "You're more than welcome to join us," he said, pulling out the vacant chair next to him. "Add to the conversation?"

"I'm fine." She dropped her eyes to her bowl. "Sorry."

"Nothing to be sorry about." He got up, took his beer with him and sauntered over.

Damn. She should have left sooner. Now this.

"Mind if I sit?" He pulled out a chair and flopped down without waiting for an answer.

"I was just leaving."

"Can't leave an unfinished drink on the table." He nodded to her half-finished beer. "It's bad luck."

"I've never heard that one before." She picked up the glass and knocked it back.

"You walk away from it unfinished, people here think you're rich." He smiled, gave a wink. "Then when you ain't looking, they stick you with the tab. See?"

She looked him over quickly. He seemed harmless. Friendly even, without the boring swagger of a guy on a pick-up. A few short words would shut him down and he'd slink back to his friends, tell them she was a bitch to cover his strike-out. Then why was an alarm bell ringing somewhere in her head? He didn't look dangerous. "Can I ask what you guys were talking about? Sounds like a hunting trip."

"Predator," he said. "Couple of bossies on a farm near Weller got killed. Taken down and eaten."

"I heard someone mention a bear."

He shrugged. "It's possible, but unlikely. No one's seen a bear round here in twenty years."

"Coyotes?"

"That's what Todd thinks. He don't know shit."

"What do you think it is?"

He shrugged again, as if the answer was obvious. "Wolves. Them big timber wolves, wandering down here from up north."

The alarm rang at full volume. That one word like a fist shattering glass to yank the fire alarm. Along with the clanging bells in her ears, her heart ticked up a notch. Sweat broke down the small of her back. It felt just like—

"Hey, you all right?" The man leaned back, as if she was about to lose her lunch. "You look a little green."

The front door was all the way across the bar. The bathroom three paces to her right. "Excuse me," she said, bolting for the washroom.

It was empty. Thank God. She looked at her reflection in the mottled mirror. Her pupils had already dilated to pinpricks. A faint glow of yellow overlapping the brown.

Not now. Why now?

She pushed into a stall and bolted the door. From an inside pocket of her jacket, she produced the knife. Slipping it from its sheath, the blade gleamed. Silver plated. Clamping it between her teeth, she shrugged off the jacket and pushed the sleeve up past her elbow. The blade, kept sharp from constant honing with a whetstone, pressed into the flesh of her forearm and she pushed in until it bit. Blood welled up in the hairline cut and dribbled down. The effect was almost instant. Her heartrate dropped and her breathing evened out. The smells in the room, amplified from a boosting olfactory sense, dimmed from acute to dulled.

The spell passed, the change averted. She lifted the blade away and watched a single drop of blood fall and bloom on the dirty floor. Lara Mendes looked at her ravaged arm. Crisscrossed with the marks of cutting from elbow to wrist like drunken railway tracks.

6

"EARTH TO AMY."

Amy turned away from the window and looked at her friend. Gabrielle waved her hand, flagging Amy back to the here and now. Amy swatted the hand away. "What?"

"Where'd you go just now?" Gabby said. "You just drifted into outer space again."

"Sorry."

Gabby rolled her eyes and slurped the dregs of her iced cappuccino through a straw. She was a new friend in Amy's world. Unlike the friends she'd grown up with, Gabby was a bit out there. She dressed strange, had weird ideas and was always trying to shock people. She was obsessed with dead rock stars, tabloid magazines and smoked too much weed as far as Amy thought. She had known Gabby since ninth grade shop class but they'd never clicked until this Halloween when Gabby had wandered onto Amy's front porch dressed as a suicide bride. White veil and fake blood dripping from fake slit wrists. High as a kite and having lost her friends, Gabby had snaked her arm round Amy like a life preserver and helped her dole out candy to the trick-or-treaters. They'd been inseparable ever since.

Gabby made a racket with the straw and then flung the plastic cup away. "So, lame-o. Did you even talk to 'Date-Rape'?"

"Would you stop?"

"See? You're such a chicken-shit."

'Date-Rape' was the nickname Gabby had labeled Dan Raylan with when Amy confessed to liking him. A bunch of them had gone out to the movies to see a cheesy horror flick at the Laurelhurst. Dan was there too and Gabby kept pushing Amy to talk to him. For Gabby, talking to boys was no problem. Especially ones she liked, which never failed to flabbergast Amy at how easy she made it look. Gabby would cajole and tease and hurl abuse at whatever boy she was crushing on at that moment. She made it look so easy and pushed Amy to do the same. As if. Amy discovered that her brain didn't work when faced with some boy she thought even remotely cute, floundering like a spastic in gym class.

"Time to man-up, chickie-shit." Gabby thumbed towards the back of the too-brightly lit cafe they were in. Dan Raylan slouched on a small bench near the back with his friends. They'd all gone to the movies and wandered here for coffee afterwards. Amy had picked the table furthest from Dan and had been excoriated by Gabby for it. "Go talk to him already."

"Give me a minute."

"You said that ten minutes ago. Tag." Gabby belched and blew the effuse across the table. "What the hell are you afraid of?"

"Nothing."

"Bullshit. You're scared of everything."

"I'm not like you." Amy rolled her eyes this time. Why didn't Gabby get that?

"What's the worst that's gonna happen, Amy? He's either interested or he's not. If not, then you suffer a tiny humiliation. It's character-building."

"Easy for you to say."

"The world ain't gonna blow up if you embarrass yourself. Hell, no one is gonna notice at all. Not even 'Date-Rape', the lobotomy candidate."

She had a point. Amy pushed her chair back and prepared to march over to Dan and his dumb friends. But then she hesitated, her resolve crumbling and she dipped her shoulders. Already shot down. What time was it anyway?

"Don't check the time. God, you make me puke."

It was way late and there was going to be hell to pay going home. She got up, taking up her bag. "I gotta go."

Gabby sneered. "Amy, please. What's the worst your dad's gonna do? Stick around."

"I can't."

"You can do anything you want," Gabby said. "You don't always have to do what's expected of you."

Amy said goodbye and waved to Dan as she shouldered the door open. He wasn't even looking and she withered at her open display lost on the boy yammering to his friends.

SHE hadn't done anything really wrong. So she'd gone out. Stayed out after sundown for the first time in three months. Was that really so bad? Then why was she tiptoeing up the porch steps praying her dad had gone to bed early?

She should have known something wasn't right. The dog sat up when she approached, tail swishing across the boards, but didn't run to greet her. She reached out and scratched the ruff on his flat head. Then she froze at the sound of his voice.

"Well, what do you know." Her dad sat on the railing. With the porch light off, he remained hidden in the darkness. "You're still alive."

"I just went to the movies," she said. "Nothing bad happened. The world didn't end."

"Yup. Maybe I'm just paranoid after all." He tilted off the railing and stood. She saw the drink in his hand, heard the gravelly timber in his voice. How much has he had?

"Dad, I—"

"Get inside."

The kitchen was cool when she entered, as if a window had been left open. Amy poured a glass of water and turned towards the stairs. "I'm going to bed."

"Sit down."

Here it comes. The speech, the fight. She wasn't up to it. After the foul up with Dan and Gabby's nagging, all Amy wanted to do was curl under the covers and forget the whole night. She set her glass on the counter but remained standing.

He stood near the table, the expanse of floor between them. "I know this has been tough on you. I appreciate that. But you gotta stick to the rules. I let you go tonight cuz I figured you needed it. But that was a 'gimme'. We're back to routine now. Okay?"

For a lecture, it was mercifully short and she could have left it there. She wanted to leave it, to just capitulate so she could escape to her room and marinate in privacy over this disaster of an evening. But why should she? "You can't keep me locked up like this, dad. It's not normal."

"This isn't about normal. It's about being safe."

"I am safe. I'm always aware of my surroundings. I know where the exits are. Everything you taught me, I do. Nothing bad is gonna happen."

"Bad can always happen." He set his glass on the table and reached for the bottle. Spun the top off. "Just humour me, okay?"

Amy chin-wagged the bottle. "Is that gonna help matters?"

"Don't lecture me."

"God!" She fought the urge to hurl her glass at him. "Don't lecture you? Humor you? I have to bend every time but you won't tell me anything. You won't trust me with anything."

"This isn't about that," he said, pulling out a chair and easing into it. "It's about being safe. That's all."

"Safe from what? I can handle myself. I don't get into stupid situations."

He swirled the drink in the tumbler. Irish whiskey, his poison. He cocked his head as if to say something, then changed his mind and kept his mouth shut. "I know, sweetheart. But there are bad situations and then there's worse. Way worse."

Amy watched her father take a drink. His hand shook a little as it tilted the rock glass. And he looked so old now. The dark rings under his eyes, the sag in his shoulders. She used to think of him as tall but he seemed to have lost a few inches as if unable to stand straight anymore. As tight-lipped as he was, one of the few real things her dad had confided to her was the rage he harbored for his own father who had given into the drink. How he had just given up and crawled into a bottle to inure himself from the world. And here he was doing the exact same thing and Amy could barely bite down the rage burning up in her own guts. How stupid can a grown man be?

"You need help, dad." She took a breath, wanting to get it out without losing her temper. "You're in trouble and you need to talk to someone."

"I'm fine."

"Wake up!" The water glass in her hand flung across the room and broke against the wall. To his credit, he at least looked startled. "You're paranoid! And I don't mean in a jokey sense, I mean the clinical sense. You suffer debilitating nightmares. You don't sleep. You drink way too much!" Amy paced this way, that way, trying to burn off the rage but it stoked hotter. "Don't you see what's going on? It's post traumatic stress disorder! A blind man could diagnose this!"

His hand went up. "Enough."

"No, it's not enough. You've been spinning down since that night you ended up in the hospital. The night Lara disappeared. And you won't confide in me about it? You won't trust me enough to tell me the truth?" She put enough spin on the word 'trust' to make a wicked curveball and it hit hard. She went on. "Fine. If you won't talk to me then talk to someone else. Get help, before this gets any worse."

"I can't."

"Yes you can. All you have to do is pick up the phone." She rubbed her eyes then leveled her gaze back to him. "And if you don't, I will call your boss and tell him that you're suffering from extreme post traumatic stress."

He blew out his cheeks in a sigh and then fetched up the bottle and poured a lethal length. Said nothing.

Like a slap in the face, Amy thought. He doesn't care. Doesn't even hear a word she's saying. She needed to get out of here. Get to her room, figure things out. She marched for the stairs.

"You remember the night you were chased by a pack of wild dogs?"

She stopped. Not looking at him but not walking away either.

"Those dogs belonged to a suspect Lara and I were tracking. His name was Ivan Prall."

Amy looked at their dog curled up by the front door, watching them with baleful eyes. "He was one of them," she said. "Wasn't he?"

"Yep. Lara and I tracked that son of a bitch hard. Got close to collaring him a few times even. But Lara studied the guy and found out something unusual. This guy thought he was a monster. And not in the figurative sense. Ivan Prall believed he was a werewolf." He sipped his glass. "That in itself wasn't unusual. I see every kind of crazy. People convinced their Jesus Christ or Judy Garland. The thing is, what we learned the hard way was that Ivan Prall wasn't crazy. He was telling the truth."

Amy didn't move. The clock on the wall ticked away.

"You remember Lara got attacked by the dogs? Ended up in a coma and we all stayed with her. You were there when she woke. Well, the dogs didn't attack her. Prall did. The wolf chewed her up."

Now more than ever Amy wanted to flee. To get out before she heard anymore but her legs didn't work. Her muscles rebelling against her brain.

"Lara got the curse," he said. "Or infected or whatever the hell it is. She started to change. The night we took Prall down, the night we killed the wolf, Lara was too far gone. She went all the way and changed into one of those damn things. Once Prall was dead, she... or it... ran off. And I've spent the last three months looking for her."

The Husky sat up and nosed the door, whining to be let out.

"So, you're right. I am traumatized and going round the bend. But hey..." he threw up his hands. "I got good reason to be."

Amy forced her legs to move and walked away. Plodding up the steps with slow robotic movements. Her dad was off the deep end. Way worse than she could have imagined. Damaged, unstable and crazier than a shithouse rat.

7

THE CUTTING WAS LOSING its efficacy. When she had first stumbled upon this trick, it had been a merciful relief. Like a mosquito buzzing near her ear that she couldn't swat away until that first time she had cut her flesh. The silver slicing into her skin was like squashing the mosquito, its excruciating buzz finally silenced. And then peace. The purifying silver a blinding wash of light that burned everything off.

It was almost manageable after that, this thing inside her. When her pulse spiked and her heart twanged like a piano wire being plucked, she dug out the knife and cut like a teenage girl with a razor blade. She had always assumed that the consensus about teen cutting was true; that it was a cry for help. Now she wasn't so sure. A sharp twinge of pain brought the moment into fierce clarity and made you feel alive. Part rush, part relief.

Yet like any garden variety junkie, the more she used the less its potency. She had to cut deeper to attain the wash of relief and each cut lessened its power as a balm. When she ran out of room on her forearm, the skin crisscrossed like she'd been keeping score on it, she cut into her thigh.

She wiped the blade clean and put it away. Elbows on her knees, she stared at two little droplets of blood on the grimy floor. How much longer could she keep this up? Hiding in a bathroom stall like some two-bit user. Like the creeps and smokehounds she had busted so many times in her old life. How long until the silver edge gave no release at all?

Get up. Get out. Quit the pity-party.

She cleaned up at the sink, averting her eyes from the mirror but gave in at the last moment. She looked ghastly. Unbrushed hair pulled into a ponytail, dark hollows under her eyes. Shabby clothes that, while warm and dry, made her look like a homeless person. Thin too. Way too thin, given her unstable diet now. Her cheeks had a sallow pull to them that made her look old. Or was that just the grime?

Watching the blood run thin and circle the drain, she wondered what had triggered the change just now. There was always a trigger. Fear or danger. The chatty guy in the bar was no threat. Was he?

The bar had filled in when she came out of the bathroom. More seats occupied by men in workboots and women who'd left their name-tags on, hoping to catch the tail end of happy hour. The hunting party, along with the man who had chatted her up earlier, were mercifully gone. The waitress, bless her, had left her unfinished glass on the table, slipping the bill under it.

She put the money on the table and drained the glass. A small fortification before the long walk home.

"Not much fun, is it?"

A man stood near the table. Tall and lean with short buzzed hair. Flecks of grey whiskers in a three-day beard. He smiled. "Scraping the bottom of the barrel. Rock bottom and all that. It's tough."

Lara shrugged. "I wouldn't know."

He took a chair from a nearby table and spun it backwards. Sat down, propping his elbows on the backrest. "Sure you do. The hard part is admitting it. Pride gets in the way, trips us up."

"Whatever you're selling—," she said, reaching for her gear. "I gotta go."

"I'm not selling anything." His hands went up, to show he wasn't hiding anything. "I just recognized a kindred spirit. Keeping to yourself, trying to be invisible. Clinging to the edge by your fingernails. It isn't much fun, is it?"

A patron passed between them, cutting for the bathrooms. He leaned in, stealing a confidence. "I've been where you are. Down. Out. Game over. It doesn't have to be this way. I can help you."

His eyes fixed onto her glass as she killed the beer. That's what this was about. An AA lifer, reaching out to help what he thought was another alcoholic on the downward spiral.

"There's no relief in that." He nodded to the drink, confirming her suspicion. "I know, I looked."

He was harmless, she decided. A do-gooder. But if that was so, why was the hair on her nape standing up? Something about the man wasn't right. A smell or just a gut reaction, she couldn't tell. Maybe it was just the ragged scar on his jaw, cutting a line through the stubble.

She rose, hauling the backpack to her shoulder. "I have to go."

"Oh? You got somewhere to be? Somebody waiting at home?" His smile was cockeyed but genuine. He chin-wagged her chair. "Come on and sit a spell. We both know you got nothing to go home to. Talk to me."

"You know all that, do you?"

"An educated guess." He got up from the chair and held out a hand. "Where are my manners. I'm Edgar. Edgar Grissom."

She turned towards the door. "See you around, Ed."

"At least tell me your name."

"Lois Lane," she said, walking away.

She disappeared. He snorted and then sank back into his chair. When the waitress swung past, he touched her arm and asked for another beer.

THE small hamlet of Weepers trailed off at the main road, the buildings fewer and farther between until there is just blacktop hemmed by forest on both sides. The last sign of civilization was a gas station, homey in its old roll-up doors and chipped stucco. On the far side of the pumps stood a phone booth.

She stopped as she came alongside it, staring at the scratched out plexiglass door, the graffiti scrawled over the metal frame. A temptation that snagged her nerves before but always shunned. Not this time. Not with the stranger's words pinballing around inside her head.

We both know you got nothing to go home to.

How did he know? He didn't. That line probably applied to every defeated drunk he had ever reached out to. It wasn't even a guess. Then why did it claw at her nerves like a rusty fishhook? There was something off about the man and it set her inner alarm ringing. Her heart was banging up the charts and her skin had that clammy itch whenever the change was coming on. Jesus, she just cut with the silver but already the curse was coming back? What the hell.

How long before her little cutting schtick didn't cut muster anymore?

Nothing to go home to.

She elbowed through the glass door and felt the stifling air inside the booth. The receiver was rank with an awful tang, as if fouled by all the crying or yelling that had been emptied into it. No one used payphones to chitchat. These things were only ever used for harsh and unpleasant calls. Desperation or fury, shamed apologies or righteous vitriol.

Pleas for help.

Her call would be no different. Another unpleasant ring from a refugee with no option but a public payphone. She plugged quarters into the slot and waited and, when prompted by a metallic sounding voice, slotted more silver in.

Two rings, then three. Any rehearsed dialogue she had imagined went out the window expecting to hear his voice. The low timber of it, the stunned silence at his end when he realized who was calling. What she hadn't anticipated was hearing his daughter's voice.

"Hello?"

Stupid, stupid, stupid. Why hadn't she thought of that? Panic set in and she thunked the phone back onto its cradle. Out the door of the piss-rank booth, she hurried back to the road, walking as fast as she could.

There was little to be done in the Brakken file. Gallagher spent the morning talking to the few witnesses in the incident, going over their statements again to catch any missing detail and dot every 'i'. Ines Brakken was released on bail and went home to a husband she now knew was cheating on her. Traumatized, she hadn't slept, unable to scrub the image of shooting her assailant from her mind. Carol Arbuckle and her daughter remained at home with the drapes closed, mourning. Gallagher couldn't be sure but the steely tension between Mrs. Arbuckle and her daughter made him wonder if the teenage girl's pregnancy test had come back with bad news.

Christ, what a mess. Two families destroyed and for what? Because Troy Brakken couldn't keep his hands off some girl twice his junior.

The thought of the Arbuckle girl being pregnant sent a shiver down his spine. He couldn't help but think of his own daughter and what he would do if caught in the same scenario. His gut response was that it simply wouldn't happen. He and Amy talked about everything, the lines of communication were always open and Amy simply didn't date. But doubts chipped away at that resolve. How would he know? No teenagers told their parents everything. And after last night, his daughter seemed determined to keep any communication to a minimum.

She had barely spoken at breakfast, keeping her responses to *yes* or *no* before retreating back upstairs. He had wanted to ask what she thought about their discussion last night, what he had told her, but she had fled before he could broach it. How could he have been so stupid to blurt all of it out? She must be scared, thinking her old man was certifiably insane. He wouldn't be surprised if she was gone when he got home, packing up her stuff to go back to her mom's.

Back at precinct, Gallagher finished up the statements and added it to the open file, sending copies to Detective Wade. Putting the sordid business away, he turned to the mess of open files on his desk. A back alley shooting in No Po and a John Doe fished out of the Willamette two weeks ago. Nothing to work with in either case, stone cold whodunits that only a lucky break or an act of God could crack open now.

He pushed himself away from the desk and made for the stairs. Other cops, plainclothes detectives and uniforms chatted and joked all around him. No one said hello or even nodded. His 'untouchable' status remained firmly intact.

Two floors down, he made his way into a dimly lit galley of empty work stations. The bureau's servers hummed away, stacked up on shelves near the wall. Gallagher threaded through the tangle of dead monitors and stripped motherboards to the back where the room's sole occupant sat with his feet propped on a desk. Taylor was one of the techs who maintained the bureau's systems, a flabby mouth-breather who spent too many hours in sunless rooms. Gallagher disliked the kid, cringing at his nasal whine, but he had put him to work on what he deemed a 'special investigation'. If nerdo knew it was bullshit, the kid never let on.

"Detective Gallagher," Taylor groaned. "Here I thought you'd forgotten this week."

"No such luck, Chuck." Gallagher rolled up a chair, the castors crinkling through a mess of empty chip bags and candy bar wrappers. "Jesus, Taylor. You gotta get off this shit before you drop dead."

"What? I'm chained down here for the whole shift. Farthest I can get is the vending machine before something pops here."

"Then ask your mom to pack a lunch." He flopped into the chair and chin-wagged the screen on the desk. "What do you got for me?"

"Not much. Closest thing I got to a hit was this." He punched the keys, bringing up a new screen. "Dog attack in Tacoma. Couple a pitbulls got loose and tore after some kids."

Gallagher read the details on the screen and dismissed it. The dog's owner was found two blocks away. He had kept the dogs locked up and neglected in the garage. He was arrested. Just an idiot of a dog owner, not the kind of animal attack he was looking for.

Taylor had set up a program to monitor all police and emergency bands throughout the northwest, from Washington State south to California and Nevada, east to Montana. There were even feeds from jurisdictions north of the border, police bandwidths from British Columbia and Alberta. The program filtered the data through certain criteria, pinging only incidents of animal attacks or homicides due to animals. Bears, coyotes or mountain lions, anything of that nature or suspected thereof. The primary criteria were dogs and wolves. When a hit came in, it was logged and Taylor checked it and emailed the results to Gallagher. Taylor preferred it as a way of keeping him off his back but Gallagher insisted on coming down to the dungeon once a week to rattle his cage and keep him honest.

There hadn't been a significant hit in over three weeks, every incident knocked out of contention by the subsequent police investigation. In October there had been one big hit that rang out to his ears as exactly what he was searching for. A hiker had been reported missing in the Mount Hood area. A park ranger found the body being sniffed over by three feral dogs. The details had spliced a finger of ice down his marrow, the incident bore so many resemblances to the Prall case that had haunted him since that September night. He had gone home, packed up his gear into the Cherokee. A few hours drive from Portland to the scene. He had arranged for Amy to go to her mom's place that afternoon and planned his route when the whole thing fizzled to nothing. The subsequent police investigation found that the dogs were neither feral nor had they devoured any part of the remains. The coroner later determined that the hiker had fallen down a slope and died from an impact to the skull. Nothing mysterious or strange, just a sad calamity of circumstance. A brief spike of hope in his search, felled by the crushing tedium of banal happenstance.

He'd almost given up after that. The manic way he had shuffled his daughter to safety and blew off work to go chase a hunch. Worse than a hunch, a wispy tendril of hope that faded to nothing in the cold light of the next morning.

Almost.

"Close but no Monte Cristo." He swatted a palm across Taylor's back, causing the young man to spit up a Dorito. "Keep at it."

8

THE DOG LAY ON THE FRONT porch waiting for him to come home. It stood and wagged its tail, heedless to the cold wind sweeping over the yard. Gallagher went up the steps and nuzzled the Husky and the dog leaned into his knees. Although wary of the animal when he'd plucked it from the shelter three months ago, he had come to love it now. Especially coming home. Dogs were always happy to see you, no matter how bad their day was or yours. The husky followed him inside, thumping its heavy tail along the wall.

The smell of fried onions and garlic hit him when he entered the kitchen. Amy hovered over the stove, stirring something with the battered wooden spoon. He lingered in the doorway, speechless for a moment but grateful she was here. He had expected her to be locked away in her room, unwilling to come out. "Wow, look at you," he said. "What's the occasion?"

"Just thought I'd get dinner started." She didn't seem angry or upset but she didn't smile either.

He dropped his stuff onto a chair. "Thanks, honey. I can take over if you want."

"This is almost ready. Grab some plates."

He quickly set the table, gauging the temperature in the room. Civil and polite but there was still tension in the air, things left unsaid. The awkward post-fight niceties. The dog padded around the kitchen, obliviously whacking its tail against the cupboards.

He asked about her day, she said it was fine and then they ate in silence. He chewed over his thoughts too, grasping for a way to broach what he had stupidly blurted out the night before. Maybe he didn't need to, both of them choosing to ignore it. Pretend it didn't happen.

Amy looked up from her plate. "Have you thought about what I said? About talking to a doctor?"

"Doctor?"

"To diagnose the PTSD. I think you have to start there, then they send you to a psychologist or whatever."

"Can't do it. A doctor would report the PTSD to the bureau, then I'm out of a job."

"They wouldn't fire you over it."

"They'd pull me out of the field, stick me in a cubicle. Same thing."

The dog whined, standing over its bowl and waiting for someone to fill it. Amy rose and took up the bowl. Scooped it into the kibble bag and set it back on the floor. The dog looked at it with disinterest, clearly wanting the wet stuff.

Amy took up her fork. "Bottom line, you need help."

"I know," he conceded. "I'm on the case." He looked over at the dog then turned back to his daughter. "You haven't said anything about what I told you last night."

"I don't know what to think about it. If it was a joke, it wasn't very funny."

"Wasn't a joke."

Her eyes finally lifted from her plate and met his. "Then you're worse off than I thought. And it scares me."

One of the things John Gallagher admired about his daughter was her knack for speaking directly. It might sting, it might ruffle feathers, but it was real. He used to wonder where she got it from until he realized it was a result of his divorce from her mother. Things got nasty, angry words shouted back and forth. That certain kind of insane, pointless bickering that failing couples give into. Amy had learned early on to cut through the noise and just get to the point. "Fair enough," he said.

The dog sighed again. Amy went to the fridge for the opened can of wet food and spooned some into its bowl.

"Have you spoken to your mom?" He set his fork down, appetite waning. "I need to talk to her about the holidays."

"She wants to go to Spokane, spend Christmas with Norm's parents."

"You sound thrilled," he said, grateful for the change in topic.

"You haven't met Norm's parents."

"When did you speak to your mom?"

"She called earlier. Right after the crank call. I almost didn't pick up."

"What crank call?"

"I dunno, some creep who didn't say anything. A long distance ring too."

He scratched the stubble on his chin. Distracted, something buzzing through his head. "They didn't say anything? Did you hear anything on the other end?"

"Some noise. Sounded like traffic."

"What time was this? Precise as you can remember, what time?"

"I dunno. I had just started making dinner so...five?"

He got up, marched down the hall to his office. Amy looked up. "What is it?"

"Nothing. Finish your dinner."

IT took five minutes to cut through the redirects but he finally got through to a live human being at the phone carrier he used for the house. Another few minutes explaining to a service agent that he was with the Portland Police Bureau and needed a call traced, if possible. After being passed off to another agent and explaining it all again, he gave the details as precisely as he could. This second agent warned that the trace would take a little time to complete, if it at all. Gallagher admonished the agent to call as soon as it was done and gave his cell number if there was no answer at the house.

When he came back to the table, the dishes had been cleared and Amy was gone. He could hear her upstairs. She had left the dishes for him to do.

The husky, curled up at the front door, was already asleep.

WHEN he arrived at Homicide Detail, Wade was already wiping the Arbuckle file off the big board. Divided into columns on a large whiteboard, every column topped with the name of active homicide detectives. Below each detective were the cases assigned, designated by a number and the victims names. Open files were marked in red, closed cases in black. Detective Wade cleaned the red marked name 'Arbuckle' from the big board and wrote it again in black marker. Closed.

He spotted Gallagher coming in and, pointing to the board, gave a cheerful thumbs up. No one else even acknowledged his presence. Gallagher waved back and wound around the maze to his desk. With another glance at the board, he noted that Wade had not flipped the same name in his own column. Maybe Wade figured he wanted to do it himself. Or maybe he was marking his territory, reminding everyone he was primary on the case.

What case? The whole thing was a slam dunk, the kind of file that required little real work but still padded your closure rate.

With the Arbuckle mess cleared off his desk, Gallagher reached for his murder book and flipped to the two open files fouling up his closure rate. Hopeless whodunits that hadn't had a shred of movement in weeks. Torture.

"Santa came early for you guys." Detective Jeff Kopzych leaned over Gallagher's cubicle wall, thumbing at the big board. "Same day open and shut. Shit bro, I could use an easy-peasy like that."

Gallagher grumbled. Kopzych was a big chinned guy with too much product in his blonde hair. Your basic All-American who had made homicide two months ago. The lack of bodies in the homicide detail was so acute that even screwhead golden boys with a pathological need to groom every five seconds like Krapshoot Kopzych made the cut.

And the kid didn't know when to quit. "It's gotta feel good though, huh? Flipping that so fast without working it," Kopzych said. Two months on the homicide floor and the kid acted like he knew everything.

"You tear yourself away from the mirror once in a while, you might just find some real work under your nose," Gallagher shot back. "You never know, green-as-shit rookies do get lucky sometimes."

Kopzych bristled but put up bluff. "Luck seems to like you, Gallagher. You hiding a horseshoe in your cheeks somewhere?"

"Krapshoot, go back to the play area. Let the grown-ups get some work done."

Charlene Farbre, another detective pinched from Assault to work homicide, laughed from one cubicle over. She despised Kopzych.

Krapshoot stomped off but fired back over his shoulder. "You tired, man. Tired."

No fucking kidding, boyo.

Back to the murder-book, flipping to the first open file. A street kid named Anton Levalle, lit up in a back alley with two gunshots to the head. Nine millimetre slugs, ballistics still pending. Anton was a homeless twenty-something who sometimes worked as a runner for local peddlers. No known family and no friends. The body was found by the garbage crew. Canvasses turned up zilch, nobody heard or saw a thing. Hell, no one admitted to even knowing who the guy was.

He pushed the mess away, deciding he needed coffee. Maybe a donut, something with lots of sprinkles. He stood, thinking he'd ask Charlene if she wants to take a walk, but his desk phone went off. Crap.

It was a manager from his phone carrier, calling back with the results of the trace.

Gallagher scrounged his desktop for a pen, oblivious to the fully functioning workstation right in front of him. Old habits, ink beat pixels any day. "Thanks for getting back to me. What do you got?"

"Weepers, Oregon."

Gallagher had him spell it for him. "Where the hell is that?"

"No idea," the voice said. "But I'm guessing it's pretty remote. Took me forever to trace it down the line."

"And where'd the call originate from? Residence or business?"

"Payphone. Guess they still have those out in the boonies."

"Thanks. You've provided an invaluable service to the Portland Police Bureau."

"No prob. Is this for a big case or something?"

"Oh yeah." Gallagher rolled his eyes. Civilians always got so nosy. "The biggest." He thanked him again and hung up.

Typing the name into a map search, he leaned forward to see what would pop up. The guy wasn't wrong in his guess at the boonies. Weepers Oregon was no more than a flyspeck on the Google map. Toggling the zoom revealed little more than a clutch of buildings flanking a road in the Ochoco mountains. A second general search spit up little more than a few hunting and fishing outfits. He couldn't even find a population number for the tiny village.

Toggling back the zoom on the map, he took in a wider view of the area. Mountains and forest ranges, a little farmland here and there. One main road that scrawled through the forest like a child's scribble, the closest town outside of Weepers was more than an hour's drive north.

Isolated and remote. Closed off to the world by a mountain range and deep pines. It looked like a good place to hide.

JIM McKlusky geared down as he hit the switchback on the dirt road. A light snow mottled the air, dotting and melting against the windshield of his truck. A dancing Elvis toy jiggled from the rearview mirror, shaking its hips as the truck barrelled over the rippled dirtwash road. McKlusky had been finishing up work when his phone rang. It was Jigsaw. He and Roy were out on Bear Lake road, looking at something nasty. "Better get out here," Jigsaw had said. "You're gonna want to see this."

Ten minutes outside of Weepers, the cut off for
Bear Lake road was little more than a gap in the
brush. Blink and you miss it. Another ten minutes
down the winding road, slowing over the gravel
wash and packed dirt, McKlusky wondered how far
in his friends were. He glanced up at what little sky
was visible through the trees. The sun was going
down.

Cresting a rise, Roy's Jeep came into view,
parked tight to the side of the narrow road. Roy
himself was leaning against the box, smoking a cigarette. He waved as the truck pulled in behind.

"What's the emergency, Roy?" McKlusky said as
he swung out of the truck. "I was shutting down for
the night."

"It's grim, Jim." Roy laughed at his little rhyme.
"Nasty stuff."

"Don't tell me..."

"Come on. Best you come see for yourself."

Roy led the way down a rutted track until the
trees gave way to a clearing bordered by a rusty
wire fence. Twenty paces beyond the fence, a man
knelt over a dark lump of something prone in the
weeds. "Jig!" Roy called out. "Jimbo's here."

The man rose to his full height and nodded. Jigsaw Briggs was a big man with long hair and a
scraggly beard. He always reminded McKlusky of a
mountain man, half wild and all the way crazy. Jig-

saw pointed down to the mass at his feet. "We got another one."

As he got closer, McKlusky could tell the lump was once an animal but exactly what kind he couldn't tell. It was that bad. The thing's entrails were spilled out and strewn over the snow. The animal's trunk was torn completely open, the ribs stripped of meat. There were hooves but with the head missing, McKlusky honestly couldn't tell if the carcass was horse or bovine. "Jesus. Who found it?"

"Old Archie," Jigsaw said. "It's one of his horses. Or what's left of it."

"That's worse than the last one. Torn up like this. Jesus."

Roy flicked his cigarette away. "Damn thing barely left anything at all this time."

"This thing is getting nastier." Jigsaw prodded the carcass with his boot. "Or hungrier."

McKlusky knelt down for a closer look, holding his nose against the stench. The brutality of the attack was what struck him, the ferocity. He'd seen kills before; goats taken down by coyotes and such. They ate what they could and left the rest. But this thing, it was like it was personal, the way the horse had been ripped completely apart. He looked up, across the meadow to where a decrepit looking house stood with smoke billowing from the chimney. "Damn things getting bolder too. Not fifty yards from Carthew's place. Shit."

Roy shifted his weight from one foot to the other and then turned away from the damned thing. "What do we do? Call the rangers?"

"What are they gonna do?" Jigsaw spit onto the snow-dusted ground. "Issue it a fine? We need to take care of this thing ourselves. We bait it, lure it in. And then we kill it."

Roy remained skeptical but felt the glaring pressure of his compadres. He nodded in agreement with a caveat. "I hope you know what you're doing."

9

A DUFFEL BAG FLOPPED ONTO the bed, clothes tossed in. Cold weather gear, extra sweaters and long johns. Gallagher zipped it up and dragged it downstairs. Rummaged through the hall closet for the green parka he never had use for. It would come in handy now. He hauled it out to the Cherokee and tossed it into the back. The husky followed at his heels and circled the truck. Ears up and tail wagging, the dog picked up on Gallagher's frenetic packing. Something was up. It followed him back into the house.

In the garage, he pulled out a camping tent from the rickety shelf where it had lain unused for the past three years. A sleeping bag and the box of dented pots and pans. He tried to remember the last time they had gone camping. Tofino, back in 2008? Amy used to love camping and he scolded himself for skipping out on it for so long. The dog sniffed about the corners as he scrounged up any other camping gear he could find. The kerosene lantern, the Coleman stove.

He was hauling the rest of it into the truck when Amy came home. The husky ran to her, circled her and leaned into her knees to be petted.

"We going camping?" She looked into the back and saw the gear. "Bit cold for that, isn't it?"

"I have to go out of town for a few days." He closed the rear door.

"What for?"

Gallagher looked at the dog nuzzling his daughter's hand. He could tell her it was work. That he had to trace some suspect who'd vamoosed. That would be easier. No questions, no fights. He looked up at his kid. "I found her."

Amy blinked. She wanted to ask who but the question would have been rhetorical. She knew exactly who he meant. Before she could say anything, he turned and went back into the house.

The basement bulb popped on and Gallagher crossed the room to a tall metal locker. Unlocking it with a key, he swung the doors open and reached for the big handgun. The Desert Eagle remained sheathed in a holster. He placed it in a green duffel bag, along with a brick of ammunition. He slid the Mossberg off the shelf and pumped the action twice to ensure it wasn't loaded. The black shotgun was the same one Lara had used when they went up against Ivan Prall. The finish was parkerized and the serial numbers filed off. He slid it and a box of hulls into the bag. Last to go in was the big Kabar knife.

Hauling the duffel onto the workbench, he tossed in a few last tools. Duct tape and pliers. Plastic restraint ties and a set of handcuffs. Rope and two flashlights. He zipped up the contents, ready to go.

"Damn it." He stopped, almost forgetting it. Back to the gun locker, where he fetched up a box of rounds for the handgun. 50 calibre magnums he had had specially made. Cost a good hunk of money too. He opened the box and inspected the tips of the rounds. Solid silver.

A creak on the stairs made him turn. Amy sat down on the bottom step, watching him . "How did you find her?"

"The crank call," he said. "I put a trace on it. The call was placed from some backcountry town two hundred miles from here."

She draped her arms across her knees. "That could have been anyone."

"It was her."

"So what, you're gonna drive five hours for a hunch? All based on a wrong number?"

"She finally broke. Called for help." He jammed the ammo box into the bag and clocked the skepticism etched in her face. "Let me guess, you think this is more of the post-trauma? My denial?"

"She's gone, Dad." It just came out and Amy immediately shut her mouth. She hadn't meant to blurt it out like that. So blunt. She saw him bristle as if struck. Too late to take it back, she pressed the matter. "Just face it. Lara's dead."

He slammed the locker door so hard the whole cabinet rattled. "Don't you ever say that. Ever." He clomped up the stairs, forcing her to scoot aside.

A few last minute items pulled from the cob-webbed shelves in the garage. A canister of kero-sene and a package of road flares. Tossed into the back of the truck, the husky shadowing his every step. The dog nickered and whined, refracting his mood back to him. He scratched it behind the ears and the Siberian licked his palm. The regret over yelling at his daughter was eating his guts so he trod back into the house.

Don't leave it like this, whatever you do.

AMY was in the kitchen, rifling through the cupboards and tossing things into a cardboard box. Her backpack sat slumped on a chair with hastily packed clothes spilling out the top.

"What are you doing?"

"Packing some food." She pulled down a box of granola bars, waved it for him to see and dropped it into the box. "Road trip snackage."

"Oh. Thanks." He swung his eyes to her back-pack. "Why is your bag packed?"

"I'm going with you."

"No, you're not."

"You said two days, right? School is done for Christmas break. You drive, I'll navigate."

"Not this time."

"I'm sorry about what I said." Her hand instinctively went to the dog, skiffling its ruff with her nails. "That was wrong. It'll be better with two of us looking for Lara."

"No, I'm sorry. I shouldn't have hollered at you like that. But honey, you can't come with me." He cut short her protest by showing her his palm, like a referee in one of her basketball games. "No discussions. That's just the way it is."

"So I have to go stay with mom and the wet blanket?" Her demeanor shifted, from outrage to pleading. "Don't do that. The two of them are in full Christmas meltdown."

"You can stay here," he relented. "I can trust you to stay here alone, right?"

"I'm gonna have a huge party the minute you're gone. Trash the place."

He cracked a smile. "I'll call you tomorrow. If I'm going to be longer than two days, you go to your mom's, agreed?"

Amy nodded. "You know she's gonna freak if she finds out I'm here alone."

"I know. I'll deal with that when it comes." He put his arm around her, kissed her forehead. "Don't sleep past the alarm. I won't be here to holler at you."

"How long is the drive?"

"Six, maybe seven hours."

"Take this." She handed the box of food to him. "Keep me posted, okay? I want to know what happens."

"Okay." He reached into a pocket and held out a small key for her. "Here. The service issue is in the cupboard. You're not going to need it but, well, just in case." He turned to go.

"Wait a minute," she said. "What about the dog? I can't take him to mom's place. She hates dogs."

"He's coming with me." Gallagher whistled and the husky rose and trotted out the door after him.

GETTING out of the city was a pain, as always, but thirty minutes on the highway and traffic thinned out. The plan was to spend the night driving, taking advantage of the lesser traffic to cover most of the distance. Once he got into the mountains, he'd find a motel somewhere and catch a few hours of sleep. He wanted to enter the little town of Weepers with the sun up and without bleary eyes from driving all night.

The headlights of oncoming cars flared past, the whoosh of traffic on a wet road. The blush of excitement had burned off and the dim prospect of endless highway hypnosis settled in. Doubt crept in like a damp chill. Amy was right in her assessment;

this might be a total wash. Tearing off on little more than a hunch. He'd have to gear down his expectations, gird himself for disappointment. More than anything, keep his emotions dulled to clear his head. He had to remember what he was chasing. That Lara Mendes was no longer just Lara Mendes. She was something else now. Something dangerous.

And what if it really is her? What then? He hadn't a clue. Any scenario he imagined seemed ridiculous and false.

Three hours on and the dog was getting restless. Pacing back and forth on the back bench, wedging its nose out one window and then the other. Gallagher hated stopping. Once settled behind the wheel, he'd just keep going until his daughter groaned and cajoled him to stop somewhere, anywhere. And now the dog was doing the same thing, like a second child clamouring to get out of the stifling cab.

He pulled into a roadside diner, a gas station adjacent to it. The husky bolted from the cab and beelined for the grass, sniffing crazily and peeing over tree trunks, rocks, a fence. He whistled and the husky looked up. "Stay here," he said and went inside.

Coming back outside with a foil-wrapped sandwich and coffee, he looked around but the dog was gone. He whistled once, sharp and loud. The brush behind the diner stirred and the Siberian came bounding out to him, tongue lolling from its jaws. Its fur was slick with wet and its paws muddy.

"What the hell have you been into?"

The dog sat, mouth agape and panting.

"Forget it. I don't want to know." He settled onto the picnic table in the grass and peeled the foil off his dinner. The dog followed, its eyes glued to the crinkling bundle. Annoyed, he was about to shoo the animal away but then leaned back. "Oh shit..."

He had completely forgot to bring food for the mutt. How could he have been so stupid? The dog stirred, thick strands of drool already trailing from its chops. He unwrapped the sandwich, slabs of roast beef sliding from the bread, and tore the thing in half. Put one half on the ground. "Be warned, it's got plenty horseradish on it."

The Siberian attacked it, head jerking back as it swallowed the damn thing whole. Gallagher took a bite of his and looked up to find the husky's eyes looking back at him. Big, sad and pleading. "Get lost. This half is mine."

The dog didn't move a hair. Still as stone. If anything, its eyes got bigger.

"Oh for Chrissakes." He held it out and the dog snapped up the sandwich and he went back inside to order another. Or three.

10

THE TRAPS WERE EMPTY, the snare lines untouched in the snow. She had placed seven of the traps throughout the dense thicket where she had spotted rabbit trails and grouse tracks. All seven were undisturbed, as if the critters had sensed them. Annoyed, she went back to collecting firewood. The sun had just dipped below the treeline and all that was left of the day was a dim haze that darkened by the minute. Her boots were wet from tramping the snow all day with nothing to show for it. She ignored the hollow pit in her guts and faced the fact that she simply wouldn't eat today. She'd come back tomorrow and reset the snares in different locations.

Stupid rabbits.

She climbed the creekbank to the trees and threaded her way through the scrub pine and cottonwoods towards home. This wouldn't be the first night she'd gone to bed hungry and with winter settling in, it wouldn't be her last.

It didn't have to be like this. Sitting on the bank of the creek, she had heard plenty of game in the brush around her. Smelled it too. Hell, she could almost triangulate the position of any animal through its scent and sound. A moment's release and she could have pounced and bagged a grouse or rabbit with ease.

She had done it once. Never again.

A late November day, spent gathering wood and drawing water back to the decrepit little shack. She had worked up a sweat despite the chill air and her hunger came on in a rush, powerful and unrelenting. Hunger the most base, most raw of urges. Sex and fear and anger ran a close second but none of them held a candle to the stripped need of an empty belly. Hunger atuned all of her senses, making each one sharper and alert for the tiniest hint of possible consumption. Her ears had prickled, picking up a jagged, uneven crackle along the pine needle forest floor. Her nose flared, roaring at the scent of a jackrabbit. Before her conscious brain had time to process anything, she was off like a shot, tearing through the brush like a bloodhound. The jackrabbit scampered, thumping through the loam for a nook to hide in. She tracked it down, her heart pumping and her muscles flensing with unknown power. She dove through a rack of fern leafs, snatching the lupus from its flight. She snapped its neck and the thing flopped to the ground like a wet sock.

It took all she had just to calm her heart and push the monster back down into its hole. She swore to never do that again, to never use the heightened senses and powers of the wolf hiding inside her heart to track and kill game. Fearing she would turn then and there she ran for the silver knife and cut.

Her pulse had slowed. The monster sealed inside her heart had, after a brief taste of freedom, been forced back into its wallow. Back to the dark corner where she kept it imprisoned. Any ground, no matter how small, given to the beast brought it that much closer to the surface. To overwhelming her.

Tracking her way back through the brush to her shack, she moved deftly through the lengthening shadows and clutching brambles. She would fix up a small mess of rice and beans. Tomorrow she would try again and if there was no—

She stopped cold. Something was wrong.

Climbing up a rock face, she crested the rise and the tarpaper shack came into view. But so had the smell. The breeze had been blowing north all day and she was upwind of the camp. Blind to whatever had trampled through her home.

The door stood wide open. The little table set up outside was knocked over. The lantern and spare fishing pole lay strewn in the cold weeds, kicked around carelessly. But the smell of it was the thing that froze the marrow in her bones and set alarm bells ringing in her head. That musky, earthen scent she had encountered only once before.

Lupus

Wolf

Werewolf

Whatever it was that had ransacked her solitary refugee camp was not human. It wasn't a bear or a coyote or fox. It wasn't of the natural order. Just the opposite, it was a blasphemy to the natural order.

Like herself.

Since her exile, she had wondered if there were others like her. Like Ivan Prall, the deranged drifter who had cursed her. She figured there must be more, had to be, but the others must keep themselves hidden, or stayed far away from any humans. How could such monsters exist without anyone knowing? Ivan Prall, she figured, had to have been an exception.

Today, she had her answer.

One other than herself existed and had come calling. Had tracked her down all the way out here in the middle of nowhere and tore through her home. Her nose singled out the places where it had marked territory as clearly as if she could see them. Was it challenging her for territory? Was it a message, one she couldn't decipher?

She remained still but her ears opened, catching every sound within a fifty yard radius. Her nose filtered out every smell within the same area. Was it still here? Was it waiting for her?

Was it here to kill her?

Nothing stirred in the underbrush, no telltale sound of pads on pine needles. The trills of a few winter birds and nothing more. She moved forward, silent as she could across the frozen loam, to her tinderbox home. The inside was ransacked also. Her few possessions kicked around, her bedroll torn up and flung into a corner. She held her breath to listen but no sounds hooked her attention. She pulled free the loose board and reached down into the crawlspace under the floor. Her bundle of essentials was untouched. She felt for the oilcloth bundle and pulled it up. Unwinding the cloth to free the gun. A Sig Sauer she'd taken off a drunk in a bar in Tacoma. Full metal, reliable and sturdy in her hand. She slipped the magazine in and snapped the slide home.

Back outside, her ears peeled for sound, her nose tuned to the wind and the scents it carried. Something felt wrong but it took a moment to realize that there was no sound outside of the breeze. The birds had silenced their calling.

And then the sound of the thing itself.

A low grumble, guttural and menacing from deep inside the trees. Her ears prickled and she rotated her head to pinpoint the location but it kept changing, kept moving. Dead ahead at twelve 'o clock. Then three. Six. Her arms raised up, levelling the gun and then she realized what it was doing. The thing was circling her.

One step backwards toward the shack but then the grunting changed direction, ringing behind her. Trying to cut off her retreat. What the hell did it want?

The grip of the Sig slacked in her damp palm and then the sensory information overloaded. Signals crossing; the sharp scent of it was coming south, from behind her but her ears clocked the growling as dead ahead. When it finally broke, the thing burst into the open from the east. She swung the gun round and fired blind at the massive bulk rushing breakneck at her. Her hand tapped off one more round before it slammed into her.

Her mind went blank, the pain white hot. Its jaws closed over her, plowing her across the snow. She fired again and again, no time to aim. Just blast it. A blur of massive teeth swung into view and then bristling pain as those teeth closed over her forearm, molars biting to the bone until the weapon dropped from her hand.

Kicking out like she was on fire, she fought it but the wolf's bulk pressed down on her. Its musk suffocated her until she gagged. She clawed at its eyes, seeking to gouge them out. It roared, the massive head swung to and those teeth locked over her throat. Yet it held back the killing blow, its jaws and weight pinning her down.

There was nowhere to look but its eyes. An iridescent bloom of yellow punctuated by a black pupil. She steeled herself for the violence to come, the brutal jerking back and forth of the wolf's attack that she had experienced once before. But it never came, the monster simply held her still.

There was no way out, no other option save the thing she feared the most. To change and become the wolf. It wasn't difficult. All it required was to let go, to unclench the awful thing locked up in her heart.

So she let slip the monster. It flooded her marrow and cracked her bones. And in the last lucid moment she had, she realized with horror that this was what the lobo had wanted after all. It wasn't here to kill her. It wanted her to change.

ROY and Jigsaw drove over to McKlusky's to organize a hunting party. McKlusky's place was outside of town on Clapton Road, a quarter mile from where they had found the first kill. McKlusky would have preferred they met up somewhere else. His wife didn't much care for his friends, 'the trolls' as she referred to them, and absolutely hated when they came over. But he couldn't argue with Jigsaw's point that his place was closest to the kill sites and made for a practical base to work from .

Jenny told him that if the trolls were coming over, they would have to stick to the garage. She wouldn't put up with them leaving mud on her floors at this late hour. That's where he was when he heard the truck roll into the driveway. He rolled up the garage door and felt the wind bite into him.

Roy and Jigsaw climbed out and fetched the gear from the back and McKlusky waved for them to hurry. "Come on. I ain't heating the outdoors."

He rolled the door back down when they came inside and nodded to the table he had cleared off. "We can set up over there."

Roy unfurled a map and smoothed it out over the workbench, using McKlusky's tools as paper-weights while Jigsaw went back to the truck and hauled in a cooler.

"So," McKlusky said, handing out beer from the garage fridge. "What's the plan?"

"The kill sites are here, here and here." Leaning over the bench, Jigsaw pointed to three small cir-cles crayoned onto the map. "All fairly close to the road. Ten bucks says this thing is coming south out of the hills to kill and then retreating back north. I say we pick two spots north of the road, some-where in this thing's territory. We hang bait and set traps."

"And just hope for the best?" McKlusky looked at the other two.

"No," said Roy. "We wanna get this thing, we ought to rig up a duck-blind and wait it out."

"At night," Jigsaw added. "This thing's a night feeder. That's when we'll get it."

McKlusky nodded and sipped his beer. The thought of spending the night not only outdoors but deep into the brush didn't sit well. They still had no idea what they were hunting and in this weather, they'd freeze their nards off. "What kind of bait we using?"

Jigsaw went to the cooler and pulled up something heavy in a clear plastic bag. Blood and what-all dripped onto the floor. "Finest cuts of offal from the butcher's. Couple days old too so it's got that nice tang to it."

McKlusky winced at the sickly sweet stench of rotting meat. "Put it away, man."

Jigsaw laughed and then Roy unzipped the duffel bag he had brought in. A clink of metal rang and he hauled a bear trap onto the bench. Heavy gauge and springloaded, lethal looking teeth on the iron bands. "I got three of these. Big enough to catch a Kodiak."

McKluksky lifted the metal trap, feeling its heft. He couldn't help but imagine his own leg caught in the medieval-looking device. How bad would that hurt? "You think that will do it?"

"The traps are more insurance than anything. Our best chance is waiting it out, see if it goes for the bait. When it does, we put it down."

McKlusky nodded and slugged back on his can. Jenny wasn't going to like this and she'd be sure to let him know. Plus he'd have to get a few days off work. No way could he spend the night freezing in the trees and then put in a shift. "All right. When do you want to start?"

Jigsaw grinned and bounced on his heels. "Tomorrow night."

11

HE HADN'T SPOTTED A MOTEL in over an hour.

"Hell with it," Gallagher said to the dog.

He pulled off the highway at the next stop, rumbling around to the side of a diner with its lights long gone out. He only had a few more hours to log before hitting Weepers but he didn't want to arrive dazed and sleepy-eyed. Two hours till sunup. Enough time to sleep and grab breakfast when the diner opened and get back on the road.

He got out and stretched and let the dog run before whistling for the husky to hop back inside. "Scooch over," he scolded the dog as he climbed into the backseat and pushed his things onto the floor well. Pulling the parka over his shoulders, he stretched out as far as he could and closed his eyes. The dog whined and then hopped into the still warm driver's seat and curled into a ball.

He woke to the feel of the Cherokee trembling and jerked up. The deafening rumble came from the tractor trailer groaning up beside his vehicle and hissing as it shut down. A man in an Astros ballcap clambered out of the cab and waved at him as he shuffled for the diner. Gallagher yawned and saw sunlight burning the dew off his windows. He had slept later than planned.

He let the dog run free while he went inside and cleaned up and chowed down the sunriser special. He got two tall takeaway coffees and another order of bacon and eggs to go. The Siberian slathered it up in seconds and licked the Styrofoam container clean and then they got back on the road.

The road narrowed as it wound deeper into the forest, the treeline hemmed right up to the ditch as if ready to close in and swallow the blacktop. A light snow began to fall, adding to the ground cover and dipping the pine boughs. By the time he saw the first buildings of the town, the snowfall was steady and he turned the wipers on.

An old service station keeled up on his left and he let off the gas, coasting past. He clocked a battered looking phone booth and wondered if that was where the call to his home had originated from.

He drove on, keeping his eyes peeled for a road sign welcoming him to Weepers, Oregon. Every town had one. When the first outbuilding of the town appeared, it was apparent that there was no welcome sign here.

A grocery store, sporting goods shop and the post office. A liquor emporium on the left, kitty-corner to a bakery. All one-story bunkers of cinderblock with little adornment and no fuss, relaying the fact that this was a working town and if you're looking for frilly tourist bullshit, then just keep driving cause we got no use for you.

"Podunk," he grumbled, trundling past a lumber yard that couldn't even bother to hang a sign out front. "A one-horse Podunk, don't ya think?"

The dog didn't respond, too busy letting its tongue flap out the open window.

He drove past it all until the buildings thinned out and then he spun around and rumbled back. Parking the truck on the street, he ordered the dog to stay and crossed into the grocery store. Brightly lit and barely stocked, a few shoppers pushing carts around. He went over to the lone cashier, a girl in her twenties wearing too much make-up. She saw that he held no groceries and gave him a quick once-over.

Gallagher tried his best smile. "Hi."

"You forget your groceries, sir?"

"No. I'm looking for a friend of mine. I think she's living in the area. Maybe you've seen her." He fished the photo of Lara from his pocket and held it out to her. In a different pocket was the official missing persons flyer but he didn't want to start with that. Too many alarm bells to set off. "Her name's Lara. Have you seen her?"

The girl glanced at the photo then back at him, her eyes suddenly cooler. Alarm bells already rung. "No, sir. I haven't seen her. She your girlfriend?"

"Take another look." He waved the photo, the way you get a toddler's attention. "She may look a little different now. Please. It's important."

A man appeared from behind a display of cereal boxes and stood watching them. A customer or another employee, Gallagher couldn't tell. He looked back to the girl, saw her half-lidded eyes dim with boredom. "I ain't seen her. And I know just about everybody around here. She run off on you?"

Gallagher slid the picture away and thanked the girl. Pushing through the exit, he saw the man scuttle over to the cash and titter to the girl, sharing some secret. "Nice detective work, dumbass," he scolded himself. "Now everyone in town's going to know."

The dog crammed its nose through the gap in the window and whined to be let out. He opened the door and watched it scamper back and forth across the sidewalk. "Come on, dog. We got some work to do."

He left the truck where it was and set out on foot, the town was that small. The snow on the sidewalk was a grey slush dotted with puddles. He imagined the town probably looked welcoming in the summertime but now it just seemed dead and barren. Two or three pickup trucks barreled down the main drag, the drivers turning to look at him as they passed.

At the post office, he showed the man behind the counter the photograph and asked if maybe she came in here to post mail. Or maybe she rented a P.O. box. The postmaster, if that's what he was, didn't recognize her nor could he think of anyone who matched the woman's general description. It was the same story at the sporting goods store and the hardware. The dog dutifully trotting at his heels, waiting outside each door until he came back out. Each time more crestfallen than the last but he tried to hide it and then wondered who he was putting up a front for. Did he not want to disappoint the dog? Ritual behavior from being a father, keeping bad news from your kid until you can't anymore.

Of the locals, he saw nearly none on the street. Everyone drove, even in a town this small. There was one man who stepped out of his taxidermy shop and stood with his fists on his hips. Had a portable phone in his hand and he stood watching Gallagher from across the street, as if waiting his turn for a visit. Someone had already phoned and told him about the stranger asking a lot of fool questions. Gallagher turned around and headed back to the truck, not giving the taxidermy man his due. He would get nothing out of these people. Even if they had seen Lara Mendes, no one was going to talk to strangers.

For the first time since leaving Portland, he questioned his gut. Amy had been right, tearing off like this with so little to go on. Opening the passenger door, he pulled out the map of the area and stood studying it in the street. There was the town, no more than a dot on the map, and there was nothing. Miles of dense forest and scrub all around. A river to the north.

He looked at the dog and said "You got any suggestions, I'm all ears."

The husky looked at him and then lifted a leg to mark a post.

"That's what I figured. Go on, get in."

He fired it up and rolled out slowly, tapping his fingers on the dash as he trawled through the little town of Weepers. The name fit. Up over the next block, a glow of red neon shined in the window. The Podunk watering hole. He drifted over onto the gravel apron and parked out front and looked at the dog. "May as well be thorough."

The interior was dark. They always are. The few patrons looked up at him and then down at the husky heeling behind but no one said anything. Gallagher took a stool at the bar and snapped his fingers for the dog to sit.

When the bartender wandered back from the kitchen, he ordered a pint. The barkeep wore a T-shirt one size too small, the words KISS ARMY kerned badly across his belly. He pulled the draught and set it before Gallagher and then leaned over the bar. "You can't bring your hound in here."

"He won't bother nobody."

"Still," the man shrugged, indicating that it was out of his hands. "House policy."

"Tell you what. If anyone complains, I'll put him outside."

The barkeep shrugged again, not caring either way and turned to go when Gallagher called him back. He snapped the photo onto the bartop. "I'm looking for a friend of mine. Maybe she's come in here."

The man held the picture up to the light. "Haven't seen her before. Sorry."

"Are you sure? Take another look."

He did. "Nope. Girl that pretty, I'd remember." He passed the photo back. "What'd she do? Jump bail?"

"Excuse me?"

"You're a cop, right? What's she wanted for?"

Gallagher wiped the foam off his lip. He was about to ask this upstanding member of the Kiss Army how he knew he was a cop but kept his mouth shut. After a certain time, the job just seeped into your bones and oozed out your pores. "She's in trouble and needs help."

"People need help, they usually ask for it. If you gotta hunt 'em down first, well maybe they don't want any help."

"Izzat so?"

"Truth. Gene Simmons once said 'Life's too short to have anything but delusional notions about yourself.'"

Gallagher drained his glass and pushed it back across the bar. "Far be it for me to argue with a guy in dragontooth boots. Fill that up." He watched the bartender hook the glass under the tap and pull. "Where can I find a motel in town?"

"There's one just down the road, past the church. But it's closed."

"Well, I need one that's open. You got a Motel Six or something?"

"Nope, just the one. It closes right after hunting season's over."

Damn. He had packed the tent but didn't expected to actually use it. No way he was gonna camp with snow falling. And the thought of sleeping in the truck just seemed, well, goddawful. "I'm guessing nobody runs a B and B in town, huh?"

"A what?"

A loud hooting noise cut off his response. Gallagher looked over at a far table where the drinkers were causing a commotion. The dog was sniffing around under their table. He hadn't noticed it wandering off during his chat with the Kiss Army guy.

"Mister, can you get your dog outta here?" A bearded man in a flannel jacket shot Gallagher a dirty look, lifting his knees out of the way as the husky sniffed and cavorted under their table.

He whistled at it, snapping his fingers for it to come away but the dog kept sniffing and nosing its way through the patron's legs. It zeroed in on one patron and stuck its snout into the man's nether regions. The man bolted up and yelled at the stranger to get his damn dog out of here.

Gallagher cursed and tossed a bill onto the bar and went over to pull the dog away. He apologized to the men at the table and gripped the husky by the ruff and marched him to the door.

Sunlight broke through the clouds and washed the street with a pale light. No heat to it but it made even this drab stretch of town seem marginally cheerier. He looked at the dog. "What the hell's the matter with you?"

The dog jerked out of his grip and scrambled away, nose to the ground like it smelled a rabbit. Gallagher watched it pace forward then scramble back like it had lost the trail.

Damn.

He flung open the truck door and whistled for the dog to get in. "Good boy. Let's go to work."

12

SHE LIMPED HOME SHUDDERING against the cold, gathering up stray articles of clothes left cast off in the brush like a breadcrumb trail. Everything hurt, every muscle in her frame bruised and raw and each step stung to the bone.

Her forearm was bloodied, the skin punctured with teeth marks that only now had begun to scab over. The bruising mottled the arm all the way past the elbow and there was another ring of teeth in her left thigh like a giant set of dental records left seared into her flesh.

She wondered if she would freeze to death before reaching home, if she had wandered too far in that state. The cut of the trees and forms of rock began to look familiar and she sighed. The shack wasn't too much farther.

What had happened? She remembered the wolf charging at her. An enormous grey lobo, bigger than a grizzly. All teeth and gaping chops. It had mauled her, of that she could see, but it hadn't killed her. Had she killed it? Anything that happened after the change was lost, like trying to recall a dream. She never remembered her dreams, even as a kid. Why would she be able to recall this?

By the time she found her coat tangled in a cedar branch, her feet had lost all feeling and her legs tingled. Like walking on stilts and it was all she could to do to plant one foot before the other. She stumbled on and the little tinderbox hut came into a view.

On the picnic table out front, sat a man.

She stopped. Unsure that what she was seeing wasn't a mirage.

The man watched her come up, his elbows leaning on the table and his legs stretched out before him like he was enjoying the day.

She slipped the coat over her shoulders and lumbered on with stiff joints until she was ten yards from home and then stopped. The man smiled, as if pleased to see her but didn't move and didn't stand. She studied his features, the close cropped hair and grey patch in his stubble. Familiar but she couldn't place him anywhere.

She was too tired to speak and in too much pain to think so she said nothing. As if waiting for the man to explain himself.

He cocked a thumb towards the shack. "I lit the stove. Better get in there and thaw out."

She limped past without looking at him and went inside.

The man leaned back and crossed one ankle over the other and cast his eyes up at a crooked wedge of blue sky breaking through the clouds.

THE Cherokee turned into the gas station lot and stopped before the phone booth. The dog trotted away as Gallagher opened the back and he called for it to come. A clear plastic bag was pulled from the duffel, an article of clothing sealed inside. A blue T-shirt he had pinched from Lara Mendes's apartment. He drew the shirt from the plastic and pressed it to the dog's nose. "Time to earn your keep."

The dog's tailed wagged brightly and he snuffed and circled the man. He knew the routine, they'd been through it so many times before. He led the Siberian to the booth and coaxed it inside. "In here. Here."

The husky sniffed the floor and the corners of the cracked glass, the phone. Its tail slowed, wiping back and forth with waning enthusiasm. Gallagher's heart sank as the tail stalled and stopped altogether. Nothing.

Strikeout. His daughter was right.

The husky snorted and then the tail sprang up, whacking loud off the glass. Its nose darted about the confined space, huffing it all up. Gallagher bit his lip, afraid to hope but the dog just became more animated until it turned and jumped up on him.

"Good boy," he cooed and scratched the Siberian's ears. Wrassling with and praising the dog. "Come on, out here. Out here."

He led the dog out of the booth to the road and knelt again. "Find her, boy. Find her for me."

The husky nosed the ground, jerking its head this way and that in a zigzag pattern. Its tail slowed as it focused and then swung madly as its nose stuck as if caught in a hook. It scampered forward, nose to the ground, following some invisible line. He called after it, urging it on and the Siberian trotted out twenty paces, thirty. It ran on without a backward glance.

He ran back to the truck and pulled onto the road. Rumbling slowly, he kept back a good ways from the dog, not wanting the noise or stink of the truck to interfere with the dog's tracking. After a while he stopped and slid the stick into park and watched the dog trot forward down the road and then he trundled forward to catch up and stop again. They continued this pace, this weird game of catch-up for two miles.

The dog stopped and hewed left then right and then left again. It turned and looked back at the truck then dropped its nose to the cracked asphalt again. Gallagher leaned over the wheel, watching the husky waver as if lost. "Come on, dog" he said. "Don't lose the trail now."

The husky circled back until it found the scent and trotted forward, nose skimming the snow.

Another mile. Gallagher kept an eye on the odometer as it clicked over and then the dog veered off the road into the ditch and back up the bank, disappearing into the thick tangle of scrub. He slowed where the dog had vanished and his eyes could barely make out the path leading off the paved road. Little more than a tunnel through the dipping branches. He turned the Cherokee onto the rutted path, following the paw prints in the clean snow. The outstretched branches of the trees scraped and clawed at the roof.

He crawled forward, the wheels dropping into ruts and the old truck dipping and bobbing as it negotiated the bad road. The husky little more than a glimpse ahead, tracking further into the white unknown.

HER feet stung as the warmth from the wood-stove crept into them and the dead numbness in her hands receded. She pulled the coat tight over her shoulders and tried to remember. A few broken images blinked in the tape loop of memory. The wolf, its teeth. The gargantuan maw closing over her neck. Beyond that, nothing. A queasy sense of dread that something had happened and she needed to focus. Wake up.

The wolf was outside the door.

A shadow fell over the threshold. The man stepped inside, knocked the snow from his boots and closed the door. He righted one of the upended crates and sat down. Arms propped on his knees, he watched the little fire in the open grate of the stove. He seemed in no particular hurry. The two of them sitting there waiting for the bus.

"You think you know what you're doing," he said. "But you don't."

She turned her head a degree and looked at him. The firelight flashing against his dark eyes. "I know you," she said.

"I tried to talk to you before but you scampered."

At the bar. The man she'd mistaken for an AA do-gooder. Her shivering ceased and with it, the numbness in her head. The man's stink was filling the little room, jagging her nerve endings. Instinct preceded thought and it took a dozen heartbeats to process what her nose was screaming at her. "You did this." She nodded at the trashed room. "You're the one from last night."

"Yup."

The fire cracked and popped in the stove.

"Why?"

"I needed to get your attention," he said.

"By trying to kill me?"

"What's your name?"

She turned away.

"I know the absolute worst thing about you and you want to keep your name a secret?" He shook his head and let out a chuckle. "Fine. You tell me when you're good and ready."

He looked over the shack, as if some clue to her name lay buried there. "So mystery lady, what do you plan to do?"

"Pack up. Move on."

"Yeah. Where's to? Some other remote place where the wolf can run free with a minimal chance of killing somebody?" He leaned forward. "You're kindly running out of country for that."

Her eyes unlocked from the fire and swung his way. "What do you want?"

"I'm here to help you. Barring that, I need to ensure you don't make a mess out here and start a panic."

"I don't need your help."

"You don't have a clue what you need." He picked up an empty can from the floor and looked at its crusty dregs. "Not exactly thriving, are you?"

"Where did you come from?"

"Clay County, Missouri."

"No. How did you become a wolf?"

He shrugged. "Same as everybody. Got bit, survived, then the change come and the wolf turned me inside out." He rose and reached into the woodbin for another log and slid it through the grate into the stove. "Everybody thinks the circumstances are important. That first time. But they aren't. It's like losing your cherry. The specific details may vary but the thing itself is always the same. People sure do like to attach significance to it. Don't know why. Arrogance maybe. Everybody thinks they're special."

Lara couldn't tear her eyes from him. Here was someone like her but he shrugged and scratched his chin like it was nothing important, nothing out of the ordinary. Like he was talking about their zodiac sign and not the fact that both of them could transform into monsters. She straightened her back. "What's your name?"

"Told you."

"Tell me again."

"Edgar Grissom."

"That's your real name?"

"Don't have much use for it these days." He shrugged. "But yeah, that's the one I was born with."

She twisted round, tucking her feet under her and studied the stranger. He seemed calm but her brain felt scrambled by some other sense. A warning signal buzzing inside her ear, a threat she could taste on her tongue. "What do you want from me?"

"I want you to be careful. You're at a critical stage now. Things can go very bad if you're not careful."

"They're already bad."

"Listen, your—" he frowned, as if failing to find the right word, "your condition is getting worse. The change is coming on stronger, triggered from nothing at all. And it's coming more frequently." He took a step closer and knelt down. "Not many of us survive to the point where you are now. But what happens during this next stage is critical."

"Next stage?"

"I can help you through it."

"What happens at this stage?"

"Sink or swim. You become the wolf or you don't. See, most folks, and I mean the few that get this far, can't take it anymore. They tried everything to stop it, slow it. Hell, some even look for a cure but right about now, the truth sets in and it hurts. There's no way out. They go crazy. Or they put a bullet in their head."

"They go crazy," she repeated.

"They go plumb batshit crazy. And that's when they get dangerous. Put the rest of us at risk. See, our kind we got to stay hidden. Don't cause too much fuss. It won't do to have the general public know we exist."

She watched him as he spoke, studied his movements, the fall of his eyes. Batshit crazy. "How many of 'us' are there?"

"More than you'd think."

"What happens to the ones that go crazy?"

"Well," he said. "They have to be put down."

"And that's why you're here. To put me down if I go insane."

"I told you. I'm here to help you. It don't have to go the other way."

He had moved closer during this. He could reach out and touch her if he wanted. She studied his hands. Big and knotted with veins. Grime was worked into the knuckles, dirt encrusted under the fingernails. Or dried blood.

Yet, if he could reach her, then she could reach him. Her arms were folded round herself and her left hand closed over the weapon tucked into a pocket. She swung out, the blade zinging through the air. But her muscles were still cramped, the movement slow.

He leaned out of her arc and stepped back. She rolled to her feet and held the blade high. "You stay the hell away from me."

His eyes caught the glint of the blade, the unmistakable sheen of silver. "Now look what you done." He feinted left.

She swung. He became a blur. Something punched a hole in her mid-section and drove her hard into the wall. The tinderbox shed rattled on impact. A jar fell from the sill. She hit the floor in a heap, lights popping in her eyes. Where was the knife?

His boots stepped into her blurred sightline. Hands gripped her by the collar and jerked her

clean into the air, her feet dangling. His face loom-
ing into view. Teeth gnashed, an unnatural light
burning in his irises.

"Wake up, sister. You don't have time for this."
He let go and she slid down the wall. "Think about
what I said. I'll give you a day, then I'll be back for
an answer. Now, if I were you—"

His head tilted and he crossed to the door,
pushed it open. "Damn."

Lara touched the throbbing pulse in the back of
her head. Her fingertips came away bloodied.

"Look alive, sunshine," he said. "You got company."

She lifted her gaze from the blood to the open
door. Edgar Grissom was gone.

Gripping the wall, she pushed herself up but
everything went seasick and she hit the floor.

13

TENDRILS OF PINE THWAPPED against the windshield as if the forest itself wanted to keep him out. The road winnowed to a thin wedge, forcing Gallagher to snail along in low gear. Of the dog, he'd lost sight completely.

Rounding another crazy turn, the paw prints vanished. A snake of unspoiled snow before him. Not even bird tracks dotted in the white trail.

Gallagher stopped and killed the engine. Stepping out, he walked back the way he'd came, eyes searching the snow for the tracks. He found them fifteen paces back, scooting east off the pathway and straight into a thicket of dead brambles. Jesus. Did the scent move off the path or had the dog spotted a grouse and given chase?

He called out to it and then listened. Wind rustling the pines. Birdsong. Nothing.

"Damn it, dog. You better be right."

He laced his boots tight and zipped up his coat and unlatched the rear door of the Cherokee. The backpack was slung on and he fastened the waistbelt. He opened the black case and took up the big nickel-plated handgun, hitting the latch to spring the magazine. This he fitted into the case and pulled up the mag with the expensive rounds and slotted it home. The weapon slid into the holster under his coat and he pulled the shotgun from under the floor panel and swung the reardoor shut.

The brush was thick and the dried stalks of branches clawed for his face. He pressed on, following the tracks of the dog through the snow and brambles. Pushing past a stand of wintering hemlock he came into a clearing and stopped to listen. The hush of his breath and nothing else. The birds had gone quiet and even the wind had stopped. He clucked his teeth, softly nickering for the dog.

A rustle and then the pounding of paws on the frozen ground. The husky burst out from the thicket on the far side of the clearing and bounded towards him. Tongue flapping from his open jaws, the dog thudded into his knees and circled him twice. Tail swiping fast.

"Good boy," he cooed, rubbing its ribs. "Show me. Find her."

The Siberian snorted and bounded off. East, southeast. He jogged after it, bootheels crunching and forearms shielding his face from the tangles of branches ahead. The ground was bad and he stumbled and slipped in the slick snow. He cursed the dog for a halfbreed mix of a hellhound and crashed onwards. The dog appeared around the bend of a tree stump, its back to him, nose pointing straight ahead and down.

The earth fell away down a steep grade and there, through the trunks of juniper and ponderosa pine, he spotted it. A ghost of woodsmoke twisting from the pipe chimney of some throwup shelter. No bigger than a single car garage. One small window in the north flank, glazed with weathered plastic sheeting instead of glass.

Gallagher felt his heart bang in his chest. He squatted down to one knee and studied the little shack for a long time. No movement in the plastic-sheathed window, no one came in or out. Everything around him was still and hushed. He dabbed his brow, surprised at how badly he was sweating in this chill air. He snapped his fingers and the dog came and he hissed at it to be still.

"If she's in there, then she already knows we're here. No way to sneak up on it."

The husky whined, eager to run. Its tail sweeping the snow.

He rose and marched forward. The dog bolted ahead, cutting this way and that with its nose to the ground. He hissed at it, snapping his fingers for it to heel but the animal was lost in the hunt. The hut remained silent as he approached and he studied the slat door and the table out front. Footprints in the snow going in and out the stoop.

He stopped before the door and called out. Nothing. No response or stirring from within. Gripping the shotgun in his right hand, he pushed the door open and stepped inside. Called her name.

Dark but warm. A flicker of light from the open grate of the woodstove. No one inside.

A bedroll on the floor near the stove. Cans of food stacked against a wall and a mesh bag of dry goods hanging from a nail in the unfinished ceiling. The husky scampered through the hobo shack, nosing every corner.

The fire in the stove. Little puddles of water on the floor where snow knocked from boots had melted. The occupant was just here. She couldn't have gone far. He went back outside and studied the footprints in the snow. Two sets of tracks; one heading due west towards where he thought the road should be, the second veering southeast. These tracks were staggered, as if the strider was drunk, and led straight into the trees.

He followed the second tracks, matching the steps and noting where the person had fallen and gotten up again. Dots of blood appeared in the snow, turning pink against the frozen white. He pushed on, through a stand of spruce and he could hear the sound of running water. A creek or river nearby. The ground dropped, dipping into a valley knotted with oak and scrub and further out, a dark lump collapsed against a tree trunk.

He ran, boots pounding the snow, but the dog outpaced him. It beelined to the dark mass and then skidded and sideswiped away. The figure moved, struggling to get up. The husky circled round the figure, sniffing and springing back.

The figure stood shakily, hidden beneath a tattered parka. Gallagher slowed to a stop.

"Lara?"

The dog trotted sideways and growled and he hissed at it to shut up. He looked back to the figure in the heavy coat, reeling as if drunk. "Mendes? It's me. John."

"Go away." The voice a cracked whisper. "Just go away."

"Look at me." He stepped closer, moving around to see her face. "Don't run."

It was her. God, she was so thin. Lara Mendes. Her face drained of color, raccooned with dark hollows under her eyes. Droplets of blood spackled over her lips. Some pale shadow of the woman he knew.

"Easy." His hand went up in a gesture of caution. "Are you hurt?"

She turned away, hiding her face. "Go away, John. Please."

"You called me."

"That was a mistake."

"For Chrissakes, Lara. I've looked for you everywhere."

Her eyes dropped to the shotgun in his hand. "Why? To put me down?"

"I didn't know what to expect."

The Siberian whined and sidestepped around him. He barked at it to sit. When he looked up he clocked her staring at the dog, squinting in concentration as if trying to pry loose a memory. She shook it off, refocusing on him. "Go home. There's nothing here, so just go."

"You're bleeding."

Her hand shot to her busted lip, came away red. She smeared it on the coat. "It's nothing."

"Enough." He marched on her, exasperated. "Come inside, let's clean you up." He hooked her arm around his shoulders and all but carried her towards the shack. Good God. She weighed nothing.

"Stop." She tried to shirk out of his hands but he tightened his grip all the more.

"Just march," he barked. "Before I change my mind and shoot you."

The dog snorted and fell in line behind them.

THE bag of meat turned slowly in the breeze, slung from a branch overhead. The iron bear trap was set below it. McKlusky had used a sledgehammer to stake the chain into the frozen earth and

Jigsaw torqued the springload and covered the thing with snow and leaves.

The meatscraps from the butcher's had been dumped into a mesh bag and Roy watched it twirl on the rope, dripping all over the ground. "Jesus, that's ripe," he said.

"No shit," McKlusky said. "That thing is gonna attract all kinds of animals."

"We'll end up with a skunk or raccoon in this trap, you wait and see."

Jigsaw brushed the dirt from his hands. "No. They'll stay clear of it."

"The hell you talking about?"

"Anything smaller than a bear knows there's something big out here," Jigsaw said. "They'll stay the hell out of its way."

McClusky picked up his rifle and slung the strap over his shoulder. "Let's go."

They trudged up the hill, breath steaming against the chill. The throw of the flashlights leading the way, the men blowing hard as they climbed uphill to the blind. It was no more than a few boards tacked together and dressed with branches and twigs for cover. Up on a hill that overlooked the bait and the trap in the gulley below. An opening in the boards for them to peer through without letting themselves be seen.

Jigsaw reached for the supplies he'd tucked under the slats and unfurled a tarp for them to sit on without getting their asses wet. The men hunkered down on it and laid their rifles across their laps. Jigsaw opened a small case and retrieved the binoculars. Night vision. He set the glass to his eyes and then adjusted the settings and looked downhill to the trap.

After a while he handed the glass to Roy. "Here. We'll take turns."

Roy peered through the eye-piece. "You sure this is gonna work? That thing, whatever it is, is gonna smell us a mile away."

"That's why we're up here," Jigsaw said, his voice low. "The wind should carry our scent off but the stink of the bait ought to just hang there in that gulley."

McClusky took up the binoculars and looked out into the green-tinged world. "That thing's going to hear you two jawing before it smells us."

They shut their mouths and sat taking turns glassing the valley below. They had dressed for the weather, each man in a heavy parka and layers of clothing and good boots but it didn't take long for the cold to set in, sitting on the frozen ground as they were.

An hour ticked by. It was Roy who broke first. "This is stupid. We ain't gonna see nothing."

"Shut up."

"We're gonna freeze to death before anything shows up." Roy unfolded his legs, his knees popping under him. "They'll find three dead jackasses frozen like popsicles come morning."

McClusky lowered the binoculars and squinted at the settings. "I can't see shit. How do you adjust this thing?"

"Hit the button then use the slide."

McClusky tweaked the slide and raised the glasses and peered out and then lowered them again. "That made it worse."

"Then don't fuck with it," Jigsaw griped. "Give it here."

He handed them over and Jigsaw fiddled with the settings and then they heard it.

A snap, sharp and metallic.

"Holy Jesus."

Jigsaw raised the lenses and glassed the gulley. Green trees against a black night, sweeping the ground. The trap was sprung, the iron jaws closed shut. There was nothing in it.

"Did we get it?" Roy huffed, peering through the slat.

"It's empty," Jigsaw said. He glassed up to where the bait was hung. The mesh bag was gone. A strand of rope swinging from the tree. "Damn thing took the bait too."

"Let me see."

He handed the glasses over and McClusky surveyed the territory. "Son of a bitch. How the hell did he pop the trap? How did he even know it was there?"

Roy wheezed. "That's messed up,"

McClusky scanned the night-vision over the terrain, sweeping past trees and scrub and more trees in a greenish ghost world. Something lumbered past a tree then vanished. Big. "Shit. I see it."

"Where?"

"What the hell is it?"

"It's gone." McClusky lowered the glasses and peered out and then brought them back up to his eyes. Green tree trunks, darkness. "I don't know what it was. It was big."

"Gotta be a bear," Jigsaw said. "What else has got the reach? He musta bumped the trap without stepping into it."

Another noise. Low and animal. To their left and not far away. Every man froze.

McClusky swung the glasses towards the sound. Jigsaw and Roy took up their rifles.

"Do you see it?"

"No."

"What the hell was that sound?"

It came again, sounding off from the darkness. A grumbling animal noise, but now it came from behind them.

"That sure as fuck don't sound like any bear," Roy said. They held their breath to listen. A rustling in the dark, twigs snapping. Coming up on their right flank.

"Holy shit. It's circling us."

The rifles came up, shouldered. Barrels pointing at the darkness, at nothing but night. Jigsaw hissed at McClusky. "Mac, the glasses. Do you see it?"

McClusky brought the glasses up and then lowered them and raised them to his eyes again. "I don't see anything."

"Come on, man." Roy tried to keep the rifle barrel from trembling but could not. "It's right there in front of us."

"Screw it. Lose the glasses. Just listen for it." Jigsaw laid his cheek to the stock and sighted down the barrel. "Next time it sounds, shoot it."

Stillness and the dark. Then a crunch of snow.

The rifles erupted, all three men firing in unison and the collective crack of gunfire echoed off the treetrunks and went peeling off into the night. The hunters looked one to the other.

"Did we hit it?"

The roar, when it came, was a guttural volcano of rage unlike anything they had ever heard. The thing, what it was or was not, bounded up from the low darkness and bowled into them. They saw outsized teeth and an enormous frame. Too fast to be a bear, too monstrous to be anything comprehensible at all. It knocked them about and Jigsaw landed on his back and blasted his rifle blind. The thing roared and pounced and vanished.

He raised up on one elbow. "Roy? Mac, you guys okay?"

McClusky had sprawled into the brush and he scrambled the snow for his weapon and he clawed it up and vowed to never let it go. "I'm here."

"Roy, where are you?"

Roy could be heard hollering and crashing into trees. Already halfway down the hill and falling and still running on, hauling ass in the blind night for the road.

They ran after him, calling out to him to stop. McClusky remembered the flashlight in his pocket and hit it and the two of them chased the spotlight dancing crazily over the trees and the snow. Slipping down the slope and crashing through the brush, raked and clawed by piny spines.

Jigsaw tumbled through thicket, his friend crashing into him. They staggered on and then stopped when the sound came back. That godforsaken roar. The men froze, balls shrinking at the sound.

Then the high lonesome sound of their friend, lost out there in the dark. A single rifle shot. Then the screaming, the naked terror in the man's cries for help.

Silent again. They looked at each other, then pressed on without a word.

They found Roy not ten feet from the truck. Half of him, at least. The throw from the flashlight picked out the dark trail of blood in the snow and followed it along to where it disappeared into the trees.

McClusky felt his legs buckle under him. He felt a tugging and looked up to see Jigsaw dragging him towards the truck and screaming at him to get in, get in and get the fuck in.

14

"AFTER THAT FIRST TIME, I knew right then and there that I could never go back. Never." Lara opened the grate on the stove and dropped in a length of wood. Sparks roiled up as it hit and she closed the metal door.

Gallagher sat on a wooden crate with the shotgun laid crosswise in his lap and watched her. Her movements were slow, her hands shaky. She was weak, that was plain enough. Malnutrition, exhaustion. He scanned over the hovel and its meagre contents. He watched her ease slowly onto the bedroll, her face wincing in pain. "Are you hurt?"

"It always hurts." She looked around the debris on the floor. "There's a jug of water around here somewhere."

It had rolled into a corner. He brought it to her and went back to the crate. The vent on the stove threw firelight over her face. She had lost so much weight the veins stood out. Her eyes dulled from running on an empty tank too long. "Go on," he said.

"I thought it was the day after. Thought I'd been gone just that night, you know. I found a newspaper, saw the date. It had been three days." She sipped the water and it spilled down her chin. She didn't notice or didn't care. "I found my way back home. Saw the police tape across my own door. Do you know how weird that was? I've seen taped doors a million times but to see it across my door, my home? It was like seeing your own headstone. I had been missing for three days and, in all likelihood, presumed dead. Fine. I waited until dark, broke in and took what I needed."

He took the shotgun from his lap and stood it against the wall. Then a deep breath to stifle the anger rising in his throat. "Why didn't you call me?"

"And say what?"

The crackling of the fire filled the silence. "I could have helped." His hand clenched into a fist. "You didn't have to run."

"How could you have helped?" Her gaze flit to the shotgun and then she closed her eyes and rubbed them with the heel of her hand. "What day is it?"

"Wednesday. December nineteenth." He watched her head dip and her shoulders sink but he went on. "What happened then?"

"I made a few stops, gathered all the cash I could manage and left."

"For where?"

"I didn't know. Somewhere remote where there were few people around. I didn't have a plan, other than to get out of Portland." She straightened her back and turned to him. "I knew I was leaving you in a bind. Left to answer what happened but I couldn't do anything about that."

He grunted. "A bind. Yeah."

"What happened to you?"

"They suspended me. The murder of a police lieutenant is no small thing. They didn't like my answers to their questions so they fired me."

"I'm sorry," she said. "What did they make of the Lieutenant's death?"

"Pretty much what I told them. That he'd been attacked by Prall's dogs."

"There were other officers on scene that night. Some of them must have seen how the... seen what happened to Vogel."

"Only one. You remember Bingham? He saw it but by the time the sun came up he was drooling. He's been hospitalized ever since."

"What about Prall?"

"We found him. Or pieces of him anyway. But we found him, the man. Not the other thing. They cremated the son of a bitch and dumped him in a ditch."

"I can't believe they fired you. Were you a suspect?"

"Hell yeah. As were you but you had gone missing so..." He shrugged. "They put together a little task force to find you but nothing turned up. After a week, the assumption was you were dead and the file on Vogel's death couldn't be pushed any further."

"That must have been hard. Under suspicion, getting fired. What did you do?"

"Got drunk. Stayed that way for a week. Then they gave me my job back."

"They did?"

"Homicide detail was bleeding detectives. You remember the rash of retirements they had, just before you made the detail? Well, you were gone. Vogel was dead and Bingham had lost his wits so they quietly brought me back on. Hell, they were so desperate even Kopzych made homicide."

She almost laughed and he tagged it. A tiny light coming into her eyes and for a brief second, Lara Mendes looked liked how he remembered her. It didn't last long.

She scrutinized his face. "You look tired, John."

"Me? You seen a mirror lately?" He reached down to a stray bottle lay near his boot and he picked it up and turned it in his hands. "It's been a rough go since you vanished. Everyone gave up on you, assuming you were dead and gone. Not me. I've spent every day for the last three months looking for you."

Her face, drawn and expressionless as it was, changed and he saw her wince. Like something inside her cracked. He could almost hear it in the quiet of the room. How rough had this been on her? Scared and alone and on the run.

Her hand fanned the air as if shaking loose whatever had bitten home just now. Her eyes cleared and swung back to him. "Why?"

"I had to. I knew you weren't dead." His eyes darted around the walls, the window. Anywhere but her eyes. "What was I supposed to do? Just leave you out there?"

The dog rolled onto its side and went to sleep.

"I'm sorry." She stared into the fire. "I was so desperate to disappear but later on, I was kind of sad or disappointed that no one found me. That I could be forgotten about that quickly. Dismissed. Like I was never there at all. Or I had made no impact on anyone." She shook her head. "It's crazy I know, but. Well."

"You weren't forgotten." He straightened up, turned to see her better. But I still don't understand why you ran like that. You should have come to me. After what we'd gone through with Prall? Hell."

"You're the one I had to stay clear of the most."

"I'm the only one who knew."

"Do you think I can control this? Turn it on and off? I was afraid I would hurt you. Or your daughter."

He shut his mouth after that. She was right, plain and simple. His own safety he could take care of but Amy? Amy was a different story. And so Lara Mendes had fled alone into the wilderness and let the world think she was dead to protect him and his daughter. It was his turn to crack and he felt something snap inside and could not look at her.

Lara brightened. "How is Amy?"

"She's good. Growing up too fast."

"She's a great person, John. I don't just mean a good kid but a good person. You know?"

He nodded. Sometimes he forgot that. Shame on him. He straightened up, looking to change the subject. "I'm starving. You hungry?"

"Constantly."

"I got some stuff in the truck. We can heat it up on the stove." He got to his feet and plucked the flashlight from his pocket. "If I can find my way back to the truck."

"Follow your footsteps," she said and then wavered, remembering what was out there. "Take the shotgun with you."

"What for?"

"We're out in the boonies. There's animals out here."

"Animals?" He cocked an eyebrow at her, unable to tell if she was fooling with him. He snatched up the gun and pushed the door open.

The tinsel was tangled in knots, three runs of it mixed together in a barber's twine of silver, gold and red. It should have been wound up separately before being put away, instead of tangled together like this, and Amy had a suspicion that she herself had done this. She loved decorating the house for Christmas and putting the tree up but she absolutely hated pulling it all down and packing it away. She found it depressing and was prone to just toss everything into the boxes and be done with it. A silver ornament tumbled out and rolled under the couch.

It took ten minutes to untangle the tinsel strings without snapping them and she laid them over the back of the couch to keep them straight. They didn't have a tree or a wreath on the door and Christmas was less than a week away. Dad had said that he wasn't much in the spirit this year and asked if they could leave the decorations packed in the garage. Amy told him she was fine with that but in truth, she wasn't. The neighbors had put up their lights and strung up tinsel and her own house seemed drab and depressing in comparison. She never looked forward to the season until it got close and now some of that old glee she felt as a kid crept in every time she heard an old Christmas tune or saw another porch strung with twinkly lights. Unable to take it anymore, she had fetched up the boxes from the garage and broken them open. What a mess.

She unpacked the tacky Santa that always went on the table in the front hall. Then there was the wreath she had made in the third grade. It wasn't much to look at now, the pieces of tinsel had fallen away, but her dad insisted on hanging it up every season. Most of the stuff in the box was for the tree which they didn't have and, without the truck, she couldn't get.

"That blows," she muttered. The tree was the most important part. If only for the smell of it wafting through the house. That pine scent triggered memories of every Christmas she could remember. But the truck was gone and she was stuck without a tree. Merry frigging Christmas.

She tried his cell again. Three rings before clicking over to an automated voice informing her that the customer was not available at this time. Meaning wherever he was, there was no signal or service. It was the boonies, she reminded herself. He wasn't crashed in a ditch or anything else her mind conjured up.

Still, he was alone, he wasn't himself. Traumatized and delusional and chasing some ghost of a chance over someone who was, in all likelihood, dead.

The banging on the door scared her witless. She marched to the hall, ready to unload on whatever unlucky Jehova's Witness was bothering her this late.

Gabby beamed at her when the door flung open. "Looky here, it's the shut-in." Gabby marched past her, kicked off her shoes and dropped her coat to the floor. "Can I come in or is the pitbull gonna attack me?"

"It's a husky, not a pit." Amy closed the door and followed Gabby into the kitchen. "What are you doing here?"

"I was bored. Thought I'd come rescue the princess from her fortress of solitude." Gabby opened cupboard after cupboard until she found a bag of nacho chips and popped it open. "Dad's away, time for Amy to come out and play. Hey, you got any salsa?"

Amy watched her friend cram a handful of nachos into her mouth, crumbs spilling all over the floor. Gabby was just like that. Messy, bossy, brash. But that was part of the reason why Amy liked her. The girl was an unapologetic bull in the china shop of life and her unstated philosophy was that anything that broke under her bulldozing charm wasn't worth it anyway.

She took the bag from Gabby's hand and scrounged up a bowl and emptied the chips into it. "Some other time. Try eating over the bowl."

"Fussbudget. Listen, there's no harm in it if he doesn't know, Amy. It's okay to get in trouble and break rules. If you get caught just act like you're all in turmoil and confused. Parents eat that shit eat up, you walk."

"I can't believe your folks fall that." Amy opened the fridge and hunted down the open jar of salsa. "First couple times, maybe. But after all this time? How dense can your 'rents be?"

"Dude, they're a Xanax away from being comatose." Gabby crunched away with her mouth open, spewing chip bits everywhere. "But I knew you'd shoot me down. So! Considerate pal that I am, I came up with the perfect solution. A no-holds win-win. Ready?"

Amy twisted the lid off the salsa jar and sniffed it. "This is like, two months old. Finish it off, would you."

"Hello? Did you hear what I just said?"

"Yes but perfect plus plan plus you equals a triple negative."

"Don't math me, bitch. Okay listen... We have a party! Isn't that brilliant?"

"It's the worst idea ever."

Gabby tilted her head, as if speaking to the mentally dulled. "No, it's a practical solution to your exiled status. You stay home, thereby not breaking any of Dad's rules. We come to you."

"And trash the place."

"Do I look that mean? No, we throw a small party. See? Just six of us. You, me, Maggie, Walty, Bridgette, Alex and Griffin. Plus one special guest appearance by..." Gabby mimicked a drum roll. "Date-Rape! Yay!"

Gabby finished her drum roll and waited for Amy to react.

Amy rolled her eyes. "No."

Gabby groaned and then yanked the fridge door open. Helped herself to a beer. "Think about it. Just a small group, negating any trashing or destructive behaviour. Right? No mess either because we don't serve any beer. Just Bloody Mary's. They're veggie-smoothies so you can, like, drink that shit all night and not get drunk."

Amy could already picture the tomato-colored puddles of vomit trailing from the hall to the bathroom. "Did you honestly think I'd go for that? You're losing your touch."

"Withhold thy judgement. Think about it. You'll see the brilliance in my plan."

Amy took the beer from her hand and, gripping Gabby's arm, pulled her friend back to the front hallway. "Put your shoes on."

"I just got here."

"We're taking a walk."

Gabby leaned back in mock surprise. "The prisoner is leaving the compound?"

"I want to get a Christmas tree." Amy slipped on her coat and fetched her keys from the bowl. "You're gonna help me."

"But your dad took the truck."

"The grocer's down the way is selling them. We'll carry it back."

Gabby tilted her again. "Carry it? What, like, in our hands?"

"It's like three blocks, you wuss."

Amy locked the door behind. Gabby stood on the stoop and pulled her coat closed against the chill. She scowled at the wind cutting the drafts in her clothes and said, "You know, sometimes, it's work being your friend."

15

JIGSAW AND MCCLUSKY SAT shivering in the back of the police unit, not saying a word. Their eyes singed by the sight of all that blood on the snow. What had once been a man named Roy Webb, now no more than tangled meat and gristle dusted with the spore-like stuffing of his coat. What is there to say after bearing witness to such a thing?

The sheriff, a lanky-boned woman named Cheevers, had told them to sit tight when she answered McClusky's panicked call. Don't move, don't touch anything, she had said. Standing in the cold and looking away from the wet gore, they had done as told, forgoing even the warmth of the truck nearby. Sheriff Cheevers was no stranger to the torment the human body could endure, especially in her county. Boating accidents, hunting mishaps, extreme misadventure with a Husqvarna Special Torque chainsaw. McClusky watched in slow motion as Sheriff Cheevers marched onto the scene with her face a mask of stone only to pale and fumble at the sight of that butchery.

It was simply that bad.

She told them to warm up in her Bronco while she paced the scene and waited for the ambulance and deputy and fire crew to arrive. Jigsaw fogged the window as he watched the incoming vehicles and avoided the eyes of his friend. After a while Sheriff Cheever hauled back into the truck and put the stick in gear and pulled away from the horror, bound for the police bunker out in Willowbrook, fifteen miles down the 40. A metropolis compared to the village of Weepers.

Questioned separately, each gave a written statement about the events but neither man had any idea what it was that had attacked their friend. Sheriff Cheevers had a deputy drive the men back to town.

On his way out the door, Jigsaw stopped and turned back towards the Sheriff. "What are you gonna do about that thing," he muttered. "Whatever it is."

Cheevers looked up from her paperwork. "Hunt it down. We'll get someone from Fishing and Game up here to tell us what we're dealing with. Maybe some Park Rangers too. Then we'll take care of it. You two, go home and stay out of the way."

McClusky watched Jigsaw sneer at the officer's words as he brushed past him towards the police unit waiting to take them home. He had barely spoken a word since the incident and, dumb with shock, he wanted nothing more than to get home. But the sneer on his friend's face was a bad sign and he knew Jigsaw wasn't about to leave the matter to the authorities.

THE snow was falling again and Gallagher retraced his tracks through the dark until his footprints filled in and he lost his way. Blundering on, he kept going straight with the husky running ahead and bulldozing its nose through the white stuff. He found the logging trail but his truck was nowhere in sight and guessed that he came out somewhere north of where he'd left it. Trampling snow south, the Cherokee's headlights twinkled as they bounced the throw of the flashlight.

Opening the back, he rifled through the food he had packed. Dry goods and canned stuff, a box of power bars and bags of trail mix. He gathered it into a bag and shifted around some of the gear to pull out the sleeping bag. Something shiny rolled out from the compartment and dropped into the snow. He retrieved it and held it up to the flashlight. A red ornament for a Christmas tree, a stray from the box of decorations in the garage for a tree he had neglected to get. A ritual he had always savored with Amy, corny as it was. A ritual that he had completely forgotten in his obsessive drive to track down Lara Mendes.

A week from Christmas and his daughter was alone in a house with absolutely no holiday cheer. How pathetic was that? The guilt of it burned off the lining of his stomach and he dug his cell from his pocket to check in with her. The phone roamed but found no signal.

"She's fine," he grumbled to himself. "Just make it up to her when you get home, dumbass."

The Siberian twitched its ears at the sound of his voice and bounded over to swipe his knees. He thrummed its ribs with his hand and shooed it on. He slid the red plastic ornament into a pocket and threw the rear door home. Trudging back through the snowdrift, he tore a branch from a pine sapling and pressed on towards the tarpaper shack.

LARA Mendes sat on the floor and considered her options. The one overriding urge was to run but the pain in her ribs was too much. Every breath made her wince and she wondered if any were broken from the thrashing that Grissom had given her. Broken ribs were the worst, nothing you could do but try to be still.

The initial shock of seeing John Gallagher had started to burn off. Her guts had roiled from joy to terror and then relief when she had looked up to see his face. Too much and too fast, she couldn't put anything in order but left alone, her gut settled and the cool temperament that had served her so well as a police detective returned. The obvious course of action was to run and to do it now while he was gone. Even more clear was the means to do that. To let go, to unclench the muscle in her heart that she kept constricted and allow the change to come. Become the wolf and run. It was so easy it was almost stupid.

Yet that held its own perils. What if the wolf doubled back and went after Gallagher? What if she opened her eyes in the morning, after reconstituting back into herself only to find the torn remains of her old partner splattered through the snow?

How far could she get on her own power, stitching up in agony under every intake of breath? Not far enough. So what now?

The door banged open and Gallagher marched in, kicking the snow from his boots on the sill. His dog ambled in and shook its coat, spraying snowdust across the room. Its nose twitched in her direction and then turned away, tail down like a scolded puppy.

He dropped a bag into the wedge of light cast from the woodstove, shrugged off his coat and hung it on a nail. His eyes studied her as he unpacked the supplies onto the uneven floor. "You okay?"

"Fine," she said, brushing her hair behind her ear.

"You keep wincing. What hurts?"

"My ribs. Just banged up, that's all."

"Uh-huh." His tone was one she'd heard before, in the interrogation room when a suspect was lying his ass off, but he let it go. He slid something across the floor to her and said, "I don't feel like cooking. You okay with cold camp food?"

She took up the power bar and tore the foil wrapper away. After living on rice and beans for so long, she devoured it in two bites. She looked up to see the dog watching her. It hovered around Gallagher and twitched its nose at her warily. She didn't sense any aggression from it, just an alertness. It was scared of her. She studied the husky, trying to place its familiarity. "When did you get a dog?"

He twisted the cap from a bottle of water. "You don't recognize it?"

She shook her head.

"It was one of Prall's dogs." He thumped the dog's ribs then shooed it away. "He helped me find you."

Lara bristled at the name and regarded the dog again. Ivan Prall, the suspect who had infected her, kept a number of feral dogs. A ragtag wolf pack with himself as the alpha. She remembered the Siberian now. It was Prall's beta. Intelligent and aggressive while it was under Prall's control, the husky seemed docile and almost domesticated with Gallagher. Still, she remembered what the dog was capable of. "So he's a pet now?"

Gallagher shrugged. The dog nestled into a corner but kept its eyes on her.

"Can you trust it?" she asked. "It was practically feral. And it's tasted human flesh, remember?"

His face darkened. "He's all right. He's a hardheaded sonovabitch but he hasn't eaten anybody."

Lara guffawed. A sharp sting laced her ribs at the movement. She tried to hide it.

"That looks bad. Better let me see."

"It's fine." She waved off his concern but he was already kneeling before her.

"Lift your sweater, tough guy. Let me see."

"John, It's nothing—"

"Quiet," he grunted. He reached under her arms and gingerly peeled up the hem of her sweater. He was gentle but even that light touch stole her breath in a sharp intake of pain.

He shifted to get the light from the stove and she watched his brow knit as he studied her ribs. She couldn't bend to see herself. "How bad is it?" she asked.

"It's bruised pretty bad. How the hell did you do this?"

"Just an accident," she lied. She was still wary of her old partner and clung to some hope that he would give up and go home. Telling him the truth would just complicate matters.

"Hold still," he said. "This might hurt."

She felt his hand fold over her ribs. It stung at first and she felt him ease off, his hand hovering gently over her skin. The pain cooled, replaced by the warmth of his palms. More than warmth, it was confusing until Lara realized what it was; simple human contact. Skin on skin. She hadn't touched another person in over three months. Deprived of that simplest of needs, she was overwhelmed by the feel of his hand. Like a crumb of food after starving for so long.

He looked up at her. "I think they're just cracked."

"How can you tell?"

"Just a guess," he said. "You'd be in a lot more pain if they were broken."

His palm flattened against her skin and slid round to the small of her back. She tried not to shudder. His face inches from hers and all she could smell was him. She wondered how she smelled, having not bathed in days. But then his nose wasn't sharpened the way hers was. She touched his arm and nudged him back. "Okay," she whispered.

He leaned back. "I could wrap it but—"

"It's fine." She tugged her sweater back into place.

"Sleep on it. We'll see how you feel in the morning." He reached for the sleeping bag he'd brought in and undid the clasps.

"You're staying?"

"Yup." He unfurled the sleeping bag across the floor and then straightened up and looked at her. "Let me ask you something. How many times have you changed?"

"Changed?"

"You know, gone all wolfman?"

She stalled. "Couple of times." Another lie. "Why?"

"Assessing the risk."

She watched him stretch out on top of the sleeping bag. "Are you worried I'm going to change in the night?"

"Yup."

"Then you shouldn't stay, John. It's not safe."

"I'll be all right. The dog will wake me up if you go all twitchy." He sat up, reached over for the shotgun and laid it on the floor next to him. "Fair warning? If you do wolf out on me, I'll blow your head off."

Lara blinked. "Okay."

Gallagher got up and crossed to his gear. "I almost forgot." He pulled up the pine branch he'd brought in and looked around the shack for somewhere to place it. Fitting it into a slot in the top of the woodstove, he reached into his pocket and produced the red bulb. Hooking it onto the branch, the ornament swayed and shone in the firelight.

"What's that for?" she said, watching the bulb sparkle.

"It's almost Christmas," he said, stretching out on the floor again. "Get some sleep."

She eased down onto her bedroll and listened to the fire pop in the grate. She glanced over to the dog. Its chin rested on the floor but its eyes sparkled in the light, watching her.

She heard Gallagher stir, getting comfortable on the hard floor and then heard him speak. "I'm glad I found you," he said.

She turned away from the fire and tried not to cry. There was no need to, her tear ducts no longer worked as they once did because wolves don't cry.

16

MCCLUSKY SAT NEAR THE WINDOW in the Sagebrush Diner, looking out over the faces at the other tables. Every booth occupied, every patron jawing and speculating over the death of Roy Webb. They had peppered him with questions but he waved them off, saying he didn't want to talk and they let him be.

After the questioning at the Sheriff's office, he'd gone home but was too geared up to sleep and stared at the television for an hour. He didn't want to be at home so he drove around for awhile and landed at the diner. He didn't want to be here either but he couldn't think of anywhere else to go.

The bell over the door rang and he saw Jigsaw enter. He too was beset with questions, to which he grunted away and plunked down across the table from him. "You all right?"

"Nope," McClusky said. "And I never will be."

"That makes two of us."

The waitress clinked a cup of coffee before Jigsaw. A man named Rowling leaned forward and removed his hat. "Fellas," he muttered softly, "I'm sorry for your loss and I know you've been to hell and back but we gotta know what happened to Roy."

Jigsaw didn't even look at him. "Not now."

Rowling straightened up. "We ain't being nosy, Jig. If there's something nasty out there, nasty enough to kill a big man like Roy, we need to know. We all got kids, families. What the hell are we dealing with?"

A low rumble of agreement and nodding of heads rippled through the rest of the diner. Jigsaw looked up at his friend and McClusky nodded, conceding the point. "We don't know what it was. We didn't see it."

"You must have some idea," badgered Rowling. "A mountain lion or somesuch thing?"

McClusky shook his head. "Wasn't that and it wasn't no bear. We heard it, circling around us in the dark and I will tell you this; I have never heard anything like the sound that thing made."

"A bear maybe?" Rowling offered, trying to be helpful. "Kodiak?"

"It was huge, whatever the hell it was."

"Fast too," Jigsaw said. "Roy was out of our sight for maybe two minutes. This thing tore him apart in less than that."

"Jesus Christ," someone in the back said. A cough.

Rowling checked Jigsaw and turned to the people behind him. "Sheriff said she's bringing in people from Fish and Game. Rangers too. They'll get it, whatever it is."

A momentary reassurance went through the diner before Jigsaw cut it short. "You kidding me? You honestly think Cheevers can find this thing? And don't even talk me about the state people. Even if they could find it, what're they gonna do? Tag its ear and relocate it? Jesus H."

"Can't trust the government to protect you," said a voice in the back. "They don't care."

"That's right," Jigsaw bellowed. "We want to protect our own then we got to do it. The way it's always been. This time's no different."

"What do you want to do?" asked Rowling. The million dollar question.

"Organize. Set up a patrol here in town, to keep everybody safe. The rest of us mobilize into hunting parties and we stalk this thing and blow it to Kingdom Come."

"Sheriff ain't gonna like that."

"She'll just have to mind her business until we're done." McClusky peered out over the gawking faces. "Who's in?"

Every seat emptied as the patrons huddled around Jigsaw and McClusky's table, waiting to hear the plan.

GALLAGHER stared up at the bare joists of the ceiling. His back was stiff from sleeping on the floor but he felt good. Rested. For the first time in three months, his sleep was not broken by the nightmares. He had found Lara and she was, if not exactly safe, alive at least. And he was going to bring her home.

The dog's snout zoomed into view, giving him a full bore blast of dog breath. He pushed the Siberian away and sat up, groaning against the ache in his back and turned to Lara's bedroll.

She was gone.

He pulled on his boots and swung up, wincing as his back flamed. He took the dog by the snout. "Where is she?" Clomping out the door, he was hit with the cold chill of morning and called out her name. Everything was still, no birds, no breeze. Fresh tracks in the snow. He followed them as they tacked south straight into the treeline.

Cresting a rise, he scanned through the dark trunks of oak and ash and saw her further down the hill. Sitting on a deadfall tree with her back to him. He called again but she didn't stir. He marched on, the dog trotting before him.

"Lara? What's wrong?"

No answer. He swung over the fallen tree and looked at her. Her eyes were open but lifeless, staring blankly ahead at the creek further down the slope. He gave her shoulder a gentle shake and waved his palm before her eyes. Nothing.

She was sleepwalking. Amy had gone through a spell of it when she was young but nothing like this. It was like Lara wasn't even there.

"Lara," he said. "Wake up. Please."

She didn't even blink. Her arm was wrapped around her, clutching the injured ribs and he wondered if she had made it worse walking here. He took her wrist and slowly peeled her hand away, not knowing what else to do and then stopped cold.

Her hand was covered in blood.

Panic flooded in as he looked her over, searching for the source. Had she cut herself? Was there some other wound he didn't see last night? There was more blood on her sweater and he lifted to check her banged-up ribcage. More blood, trickling slow from angry red slices in the skin. He took her hand and inspected the fingernails. Rivulets of flesh under them. Lara had clawed her torso bloody in her sleep.

"Okay, Lara. Wake up now." He tapped her cheek. "Come on, you're scaring me. Wake up."

Her head wobbled as he shook her but that glassy wash never left her eyes. How badly had she hurt herself? Enough to bloody the snow on the deadfall under her.

"Okay, we're going to get up now." He put an arm round her and lifted. "Come on, we're walking back." He got her up and walked her slowly back towards the shack. His boots slid on the incline and she fell under him but he pressed on until they reached the shelter.

He got her settled onto her bedroll and opened the grate on the woodstove. A few glowing embers from last night's fire. He threw in a few splinters of kindling and eased a good sized log onto it and blew the embers until they rose and took the kindling.

The claw marks were bleeding fresh, torn open from the walk back. He rifled through his backpack, found a clean shirt and packed it against the raw flesh. He spotted a roll of gaffer's tape among Lara's supplies and tore off strips to tape the shirt down.

He'd have to clean the wound properly but the one thing he'd forgotten to pack was a first aid kit. How stupid could he be?

He tried to wake her again but her response was the same. He had to force her eyelids shut and was thankful to not have to look at that eerie stare. The town wasn't that far away. If he hustled, he could drive back, get some antiseptic and gauze and be back within the hour.

What if she went sleepwalking again?

He stomped outside and whistled for the dog. It came bounding from behind the hut and looked up at him with its tongue swinging from its jaws. "Inside," he barked and shooed the husky into the shack and ordered it to 'stay' and closed the door.

Kicking the snow from a pile of wood stacked against the shelter, he rustled through it until he found a pine board that wasn't too rotten and wedged one end under the door latch. The dog whined from within and he ordered it again to stay and then trudged off through the snow to find the truck.

Checking his watch, he wondered if there was a drive-thru in town where he could get coffee.

THE town of Weepers, which had felt almost empty when he first arrived, seemed to have woken up overnight. Slowing the Cherokee to the speed limit as he rolled onto the main drag, Gallagher surveyed what appeared to be a thriving little town. People stood around talking on street corners or leaning against their cars. One man, sitting on the lowered tailgate of a pickup, held a rifle across his lap. At the gas station across the way, two pickup trucks had full gun racks in the back window. Gallagher stopped in front of the drug store, trying to think what could still be in season that had brought these hunters out. Another truck trundled past him and the three men sitting in the box turned their heads in unison to him as they rolled past. All of them were armed.

Hunting down the right aisle of the drug store, he scooped every package of gauze on the shelf into a basket, followed by four rolls of tensor bandages.

Two bottles of antiseptic, a bottle of iodine and three packages of Advil. Lara would probably need antibiotics but that would have to wait until they got back to Portland. Maybe something more rustic to fight infection, like garlic? What his dad used to call Russian penicillin.

Would that even work, given her condition? Wasn't garlic poison to someone who was...? He dismissed the crazy notion and marched for the cashier. He'd seen too many stupid horror movies for his own good.

The druggist was leaning on his cash register talking to a customer. Gallagher caught scraps of their conversation; *animal attack, slaughtered livestock* and *a dangerous animal on the loose.* The two men stopped talking as Gallagher came to the counter. He tried a little small talk, something about the weather. The two men were polite but cold, wary of strangers. He paid and left the store.

Outside, he found a hubbub on the main drag. A Bronco with the words Sheriff's Department emblazoned on the door was parked next to the Cherokee. The sheriff, a tall woman in her fifties, was talking to two men in workboots and parkas. She stood with her hands planted on her hips, clearly displeased with the two men.

Gallagher unlocked the back, listening to the sheriff dress down the two men. "Listen to me Mr. McClusky," she said, "you need to take your firearms home and stay there. All of you. End this nonsense before someone gets hurt."

"Hurt? Someone's already been killed by this thing," said McClusky. "What do you expect us to do, wait for it to kill somebody else?"

"You let the proper authorities handle it," said the policewoman. "Or you can be charged. Your choice."

"That's wonderful that is. My friend gets killed by this dangerous animal and you bust us for protecting our own."

Gallagher's ear snagged on their words. He stepped towards the group and nodded to the sheriff. "Excuse me, Sheriff" he said. "Can I ask what's going on?"

Sheriff Cheevers turned a stone face to him. "Everything's fine, sir. Please go back to your vehicle."

Gallagher moved closer. "Did you say something about an animal attack?"

"Sir, please. Back to your vehicle."

"Hold on, Sheriff. I'm a police officer."

Sheriff Cheevers maintained her stony scepticism until Gallagher passed his ID across. She examined it and handed it back. "You're a long way from home, detective."

"Just passing through." Gallagher folded the ID away and glanced at the two men. "What kind of animal attack was this?"

"We don't know yet. But it was big, whatever it was."

"And it attacked someone?"

"Killed," said McClusky. He nodded to his companion. "Friend of ours. Fucking monster tore him to pieces."

Something cold sliced through Gallagher's insides. "Was it a wolf?"

"Wolf?" McClusky guffawed. "Ain't been wolves here in a hundred years."

"You sure?"

Jigsaw spit on the sidewalk, eyeing the stranger. "What's it to you?"

Gallagher looked at the Sheriff but her expression remained stone. "Just offering my help, if it's needed."

"We're fine, sir," she said. Cold and abrupt. "But thank you."

Gallagher tried for congenial. "I work homicide back home. Sometimes it's good to have a second pair of eyes. Maybe you could show me the remains, walk me though it?"

"Remains?" sputtered McClusky. "There wasn't anything left."

Jigsaw spat again. "The hell you want to see it for?"

Sheriff Cheevers took Gallagher by the arm and walked him back to his vehicle. "I appreciate it, detective. I really do, but we'll handle it just fine."

"Course. No disrespect."

A pickup truck trundled past on the road. Two men clutching shotguns bouncing along in the back. "None taken," she said, nodding to the passing truck. "But as you can see, I got other fish to fry."

"I was wondering what that was about. Thought maybe you had extended the hunting season."

"It's going to be open season on dumbasses if I don't get these Rambos to put their guns away. Have a nice day."

Gallagher climbed back under the wheel and turned the key, a cold chill roosting in his gut. What are the odds this was a coincidence? A lethal animal attack that left the victim in pieces? It sounded all too familiar.

Mendes. How far gone was she? Had she tipped over the cliff the way Ivan Prall had?

He needed coffee. Clear his head and think straight. He pulled away from the curb, unconvinced by his own expedient dismissal of the facts.

JIGSAW and McClusky leaned against the pickup, watching the Cherokee drive away. "Nosy son of a bitch," muttered McClusky.

Jigsaw spat again. "What cop isn't?"

"Who was that?" A voice, behind them . They turned to see Rowling crossing towards them, nodding at the Cherokee driving away.

"Cop. Not local."

Rowling looked on. "Cop? He was here yesterday, asking a bunch of questions."

McClusky straightened up. "What about?"

"Said he was looking for someone. Had a picture of some women, asking all over town if anyone's seen her."

"What woman?"

"That weirdo chick. Dark hair, pretty," said Rowling. "Comes into town once in awhile. Doesn't say shit to anybody."

"What did he want her for? Bail jumping?"

"Just said she was missing is all."

"No shit," Jigsaw said. He pushed himself off the truck and opened the driver's side door. "Mac, get in."

McClusky slid into the cab, watched Jigsaw fire the ignition. "Where we going?"

"Got some questions of my own I want answered."

17

STOPPING FOR COFFEE WAS A MISTAKE. He had already wasted enough time jawing with the locals while Lara was alone and injured and here he was getting coffee to go like it was Monday morning.

A group of men stood around his vehicle, waiting for him when he came out of the diner. The two hunters he had spoken to earlier and two other men. Rifles slung over their shoulders, their faces grim and unfriendly.

Gallagher zeroed in on the most belligerent-looking. "Can I help you?"

Jigsaw scratched at his gut. "What's your name, friend?"

"What do you want?"

Jigsaw glanced at his friend and then back to the stranger. "You had a lotta questions back there. What do you know about it?"

"Wanted to know why half the town was loaded for bear. Excuse me." He marched for the Cherokee but the men closed ranks, cut him off.

"What makes you think it was a wolf?"

He didn't answer. Jigsaw nodded to one of the armed men. "Rowling here said you was asking all over town about some woman. Who is she?"

"A friend." Gallagher stepped close, matching the man's belligerent stare. "Get away from the truck. Please."

"This girlfriend of yours, you find her?"

Gallagher marched for his truck, on a collision course with the man named McClusky and a taller man. They would crash or give way. The taller man stepped aside and Gallagher swept past him to unlock his door. He heard the one named Jigsaw barking at him. "I need an answer, friend. Now."

"I got nothing to tell you."

"Bullshit. You know something—" Jigsaw grabbed Gallagher's arm. A cup dropped from the tray and hit the ground. Hot coffee steamed up from the snow.

Gallagher lashed out fast and dropped the big man. Jigsaw belly-flopped onto the wet pavement with a thud. He moaned once before Gallagher dropped a knee onto his back and growled in his ear. "Listen to me, friendo. I'm sorry for your loss but it's got nothing to do with me." He stood and stomped towards the other men. "Anyone else?"

The others glanced around, waiting for someone else to do something. No one did. Jigsaw moaned and rolled over.

Gallagher climbed into his truck and drove away.

THE dog barked. Lara rose up on one elbow and immediately regretted it when the pain rippled down her side. Her hand went to her ribcage, found the material packed against it. Peeling it away she saw the blood crystallized dark against the wadding. What happened?

The dog stood at the door, yammering away. Lara held her breath and swung up to her feet. A few unsteady steps towards the door and she smoothed the dog's head to quiet it. "Okay, okay. Let me get the door."

The door didn't open. She pushed against it harder but all it did was rattle against the frame. Blocked from the outside.

"Gallagher!" Her voice rang loud inside the shack. The dog stuck its nose to the draft under the door. "Gallagher, open the damn door!"

Not a sound. Why had he locked them inside? Where had he gone? The dog whined, scratching at the floor as if it could dig its way out.

She turned to the window in the far end. Sealed with plastic sheeting, it would be easy enough to tear away but she didn't relish the idea of climbing out. Her ribs hurt just standing up.

The husky suddenly yelped and sprang away from the door as if stung. It withdrew to the far corner, lips curling into a snarl.

Her ear tingled at a faint sound coming from outside the hut. Footsteps crunching snow. A shadow broke the thin band of light under the door.

"John?" The moment she called his name she knew it wasn't him. She took a step back. The door shook, then a small scrape of something falling away. A thud. The shadow under the door receded and all was quiet again.

The husky paced faster, its throat alternating between growls and whines. Lara put her palm flat to the wooden slats and pushed the door open. A glare of white after the gloomy interior of the shack.

She stepped outside into a void of white vapor. The temperature had risen sharply and the snow was evaporating, misting up into a thick fog. Three paces out the door and she could barely make out the shape of the shack in the opaque mist. The air was still, no breeze at all.

The sound of crunching snow, somewhere out in the foggy depth.

The dog circled her, ears twitching crazily at every sound. It barked, the sound cracking sharp into the void. Then nothing, not even birds.

Not good.

The voice, when it came, riffled through the cotton opacity. Coming from everywhere and nowhere. "Time's up."

Lara spun around, trying to locate the source. The dog growled low, bumping into her knees. "Who's there?" she called out. Stupid question. She knew perfectly well who it was.

His hoarse voice croaked in the mist. "I need an answer, Lara. What's it gonna be?"

"Leave me alone, Grissom." She turned back to the shack but it wasn't there. Nothing but whiteness. She couldn't have wandered that far from it.

"You're outta time, honey" Grissom's voice rattled. "The locals are hunting you down. Time to move."

Ten paces, she thought. That was how far she'd stepped from the hut. But she had spun around so many times trying to pinpoint his voice, she had no idea which direction her hovel lay.

A snap. Behind her, a hazy silhouette against the fog. "You've been bad, Lara. You can't go around shitting where you eat. Don't you know that yet?" Grissom took shape against the haze as if materializing from thin air. He stood easy and relaxed, like he did this every day.

"What are you're talking about?"

"You been keeping busy. At night. Putting down livestock. But you went too far. Killing some local fella? Bad business."

"No..."

"Yes you did. Nasty job of it too. Not much left of him."

"You're lying." The response was instinctual but didn't feel that way. There was no way she had killed someone. She hadn't before. Not once. If pressed, she couldn't explain exactly how but she knew. Didn't she? "It was you. You killed someone."

Grissom took a step closer. "The first rule is to stay hidden. Invisible. You don't leave a footprint and you sure as hell don't leave a corpse behind. Not one that can be found anyway. Newbie fuck-up, Lara."

He was lying. Had to be. And how had he learned her name?

"I'm even giving you a second chance here. Now if you honest-to-God want to be left alone, I will go. But you know what that means. You go rogue too early, you can't adjust. You go crazy. You keep changing until, at best, you decide to kill yourself. Worse case, you go all the way and the wolf slaughters everyone around you. It don't care. First people it kills will be the ones you care about. Like that boyfriend of yours."

"Shut up." Lara backed up. How did he know Gallagher was here?

Grissom scratched the stubble on his chin. "Who is that guy anyway?"

She didn't answer.

"Prince Charming rides in to save the princess? You signed his death warrant the minute you called him. You know that, right?"

"He's got nothing to do with this."

"Then the poor bastard will never know what hit him. When you change and you tear his guts open, maybe then the schmuck will realize that his princess is a monster. Kinda funny when you think about it."

The husky, silent until now, jerked forward. Snapping its teeth in a guttural rumble. Lara held it back.

"Do you really want to live like this?" he said. "We're not solitary animals. But you can't go back to your people. That's over. Join the pack, be one of us. It's so much better than you can imagine. You don't have to be alone anymore."

She stumbled back but her legs felt sluggish. She didn't want to be alone anymore. It was too hard. She was doomed anyway. How bad would it be to give in and become part of his world? What exactly was she clinging to? Her old life?

Please...

Her indecision writ large in her eyes. Grissom reached out his hand. "Come."

Lara flinched. Like sticking a wet finger into a socket. No. She pulled back.

He wouldn't let go. "Come." A growl to underscore the command.

She slammed her fists into him, enough force to break his ribcage. All she had to do was lock her grip round his throat and squeeze—

He knocked her back with the force of a bulldozer. She hurtled away, tumbling over the snow.

Her vision blurred. The gauzy form of the husky leapt at Grissom and was knocked back. It yelped, rolling away. When she looked up again, Grissom had vanished into the fog.

An unmistakable roar thundered overhead, heavy enough to rattle her insides. The dog withered, cowering under. Grissom had become the wolf. And it was going to kill her for refusing it.

She could change too. All she had to do was let go and release the pale wolf. At least then she'd have a fighting chance. The husky trembled under her.

No. She wasn't going to give in. But she could let go a tiny bit, enough to open her ears and smell the air the way the wolf does. She whispered into the Siberian's ear to shush it and held her breath to listen. Picking out the smallest scratch of sound, something big padded the snow to the west of her. How far away, she couldn't tell.

Taking the air, she filtered through the smells for the acrid tang of woodsmoke and ash. The shack. South, maybe southeast.

She tugged the dog up and bolted for shelter. Sprinting over the snow, pulling the dog along, she hoped she'd see the shack before running smack into it.

Another roar, unnatural and deafening. The sound of it thundering over the ground, haring after her in the fog.

The shack rose up from the haze like a ghost and she sprinted for it, the monster at her heels. The husky outpaced her and vanished inside the door and she hated it for being safe. Teeth chomped behind her, snapping her hair. She leapt for the open door.

The floor was hard as she rolled and tumbled inside. The wolf crashed into the doorframe, too big to fit, and the entire structure tilted off its flimsy foundations. Beams and studs snapped around her.

The monster popped its enormous teeth, pushing through the frame. The dog gnashed its teeth and looked for an exit that wasn't there.

She clawed out the loose floorboard and plunged a hand into the hidden recess. The wolf forced its way inside, snapping apart the door frame.

Lara swung up with the Glock in both hands and blasted a round into the thing's face.

18

THE FOG VAPORED OVER THE ROAD, forcing Gallagher to a crawl to find the unmarked logging trail. Mist congealed to soup as he turned onto the trail, barely able to see the pathway at all. Maddeningly slow until he found the spot where he'd left the truck the night before.

Gathering up his supplies, he left the Cherokee behind and stalked into the trees. Head down, following his footprints. The snow was melting and, had he been any later, they would have disappeared altogether, leaving him to grope blind through the fog. As it was, he lost the track a few times, stumbling around until he found it again.

He called out for the dog. What answered wasn't the husky. An unnatural roar rippled out of the fog on all sides. A malevolent sound he had heard before and prayed he'd never hear again.

The wolf.

His knees locked, ice in his joints. He was too late. Lara had changed and was loose out here in this godforsaken fog. Dropping the bag to the snow, he unholstered the big handgun. A click and the magazine slid out of the grip and he stuffed it into a pocket. From another pocket he produced the magazine of rounds he had had specially made and slapped it home. The moisture in the air made the grip slick. Taking up the supplies again, he willed his legs to move.

Ears cocked for any sound but all he could hear was the crunch of his own boots. When the trees disappeared he knew he was in the clearing. He could just make out the picnic table out front but the shack wasn't there. Like it had vanished.

Three paces on and he saw that it hadn't disappeared; it was flattened. Knocked completely on its side, the roof had snapped and the walls broke apart and splayed in the snow. A wisp of smoke snaked from the upended woodstove.

No Lara. No dog. Nothing.

He hadn't planned for this. Hell, he hadn't planned at all, just blundering in here thinking he'd find her and walk out. How stupid could he be? Had she killed the dog, the same way she had killed the local man? The livestock?

He dropped the bag at his feet and locked the gun with both hands. If Lara was too far gone, he'd put her down with silver capped 50. calibre rounds. If he was injured in the fray, meaning bitten by the goddamn thing and thus cursed the way she was, well, he'd save one round for himself and stick the barrel in his mouth. Simple, neat.

Amy would be confused, not understanding why her father had driven two hundred miles into the Oregon forest to simply put a bullet in his brain. But she already suspected his mind was crumbling. She'd rationalize some kind of explanation. Everyone does. Didn't matter. As long as she was safe.

He called out her name, bellowing into that white haze.

Nothing. Just the thrum of his own heartbeat in his eardrums. What if it was gone, tearing across the valley towards town? Out of earshot and him standing here like a fool, hollering to the trees.

A sound. Heavy pads drumming hard across the ground, pounding the snow towards him. He brought the gun up, his elbows locked and drew aim at the sound crashing towards him in the opaque wall. He could already see its form. Too small, too lithe—

The dog. Bounding breakneck with its tongue flapping loose, it banged into his knees and whined, its rear end wagging. Terrified. Whether she had spared it or it had simply gotten away, he didn't know. It didn't matter.

He dug his fingers into the nap of its fur. "Where is she? Show me."

The abominable sound came again, a guttural roar that rumbled his breastplate. Coming hard on his leeside, its weight shuddering the ground under his feet. A dim form emerged, dark against the haze. Good God... it was enormous.

Correcting his aim, he locked his elbows and squeezed down on the trigger. Held off, something not right. This lobo was dark, with a grey razorback pelage. He had only seen Lara change once, a frantic exchange all those nights ago, but her lobo was pale. White as birch. Had she changed coats? Was that possible?

The alternate answer was almost worse. This dark monster was some other lobo.

A crack of gunfire settled the matter. The wolf recoiled from the impact and spun around and roared like the sound of hell grinding open. Gallagher lowered his weapon with the round still in the chamber. The shot came from elsewhere.

Lara.

The thing skulked back into the fog like a bad dream. Gallagher hollered at the void. "Lara! Where are you?"

Another blast from a barrel, the shot cracking through the pine branches. He ran at the sound, calling out her name.

"Gallagher!"

Her voice filtered from the void. Disembodied, drawing him in like a sonar ping. She was on her knees in the snow and swung her firearm his way when we crashed towards her. Her face was bloodless and she was heaving like an asthmatic.

He tumbled to her side. "Where the hell did that thing come from?"

"Long story." Her breath staccato and gasping.

"Jesus. I thought it was you."

Her hand clutched his arm to stop herself from keeling over. Her grip so strong it made him wince. "Don't count that out just yet," she gaped.

How far gone was she? He searched her eyes for that telltale glow he had seen before. A red flag that preceded the shitstorm of transfiguration.

"Where's the truck?"

He looked east then west. All the same, a curtain of cotton mist. "I can't tell which way is up in this soup."

The thing roared, everywhere and nowhere at the same time. The husky bristled at the sound, ears rotating to all points of the compass.

He looked at her. "Can you find it?"

"What?"

"The smell of exhaust or gas or whatever."

She scowled and he knew she hated him for asking that. What other option did they have? All the same, he saw her nose wrinkle.

"This way." She clenched his arm, leading the way. The dog followed at their heels.

"I'm sorry," he said, tripping after her. "I know you hate that but—"

"Shut up."

He shut his mouth, following as Lara threaded her way through the trees. She pulled ahead and he struggled to keep up, watching her bound effortlessly over deadfall and dart through the underbrush with lupine grace.

Lara stopped and turned back. "There," she said, pointing the way ahead. The hazed hulk of the Cherokee took shape before them. He pressed on, the dog trotting ahead and then the roar echoed around him. The wolf, coming back.

She barked at him to run and he saw the terror in her eyes. The thing was right behind him. She raised her gun at him and he ducked and she fired. He caught a glimpse of the monster crashing away into the foggy trees.

They scrambled into the truck and Gallagher fired it up, cranking the wheel hard to turn the Cherokee around on the narrow pathway. The front end mowed down saplings and the rear wheels spun in the snow. The spindly fingers of dry branches scraped down the windows, clawing at them to stay. Lara leaned over the seat and looked back.

"Move."

He clocked it in the rearview mirror, the wolf breaking towards them. Gallagher slammed the brakes and the monstrous lobo glowed red in the taillights. Slamming into reverse, he punched the gas and barreled backwards. The wolf had no time to react and the impact was loud. The rear window cracked and metal crunched with a dead thud. Gallagher floored the accelerator, pushing the damn thing back along the road.

He geared up and gunned forward, fishtailing through the bends in the pathway. With visibility poor, the truck hammered through brush and sideswiped the trees. The mirror on the passenger side sheared off and tumbled away behind them. Lara leaned over the seat with the pistol in her hand, eyes peeled for any sign of the thing.

The thicket of trees gave way and Gallagher allowed himself to breathe as the logging trail opened up onto the main road. He spun the truck out but immediately hit the brakes to avoid careening into the object before them.

A green pickup truck blocked the entrance to the road. Headlights burning up at them, two darker figures standing sentry on either side of the vehicle. Rifles in their hands.

Gallagher's Cherokee skidded sideways and thunked loud as the tail end took out a sapling. Gallagher swung out of the door and bellowed. "Move that damn thing! Now!"

The two men raised their rifle barrels at his face. Both looked familiar. The hunters he had scuffled with in town. The one named Jigsaw spoke. "Turn it off."

"What the hell?" Lara climbed out, eyes wide at the raised weapons. "Put the rifles down! And move the pickup."

McClusky arced his rifle to meet her. "Step outta the truck," he said. "Over here."

Gallagher marched on Jigsaw, walking straight down the barrel. A vein throbbed on his brow. "Listen dumbass, the thing that killed your friend is hauling ass right for us."

Jigsaw's eye was swollen but the venom folded in that purpled flesh was unmistakeable. Pure murder. "Get on your knees, asshole. Do it!"

Gallagher glanced at Lara. "It's coming," she said.

They all heard it. The sheer weight of the thing quaking the earth, crashing and tearing through the trees towards them. McClusky eyed his friend, wary and alert. "What the hell is that?"

As if in answer, an inhuman roar washed over them. McClusky and Jigsaw knew the sound, that same goddawful noise from the night Roy was killed.

With the paramilitaries distracted, Lara hollered at Gallagher to cut and run. He didn't need to be told twice. Shifting into gear, he barrelled the Cherokee forward, clipping the rear end of the other truck, pushing it out of the way. Jigsaw cursed at him, swinging the rifle his way. Gallagher floored the pedal but his rear wheels spun in the snow. He backed up to take a run at it.

"Oh God..." McClusky said.

It came on straight down the trail, charging in like a toro and simply swallowed McClusky. Frozen at the sight, Jigsaw watched the monster whip its maw back and forth violently. The man shrieked as he was rent apart. The snow spackled red.

Gallagher bellowed at the other man to run and gunned the vehicle forward. The front end crumpled into the pickup, knocking it back a foot and Gallagher kept flooring it, spraying slush and gravel out the rear wheels.

Lara looked back out the cracked glass of the rear window. The lobo dropped the dead man, swung its foul snout up in their direction and leapt. Its mass filled the window, slamming the vehicle like a wrecking ball. Lara aimed her weapon and fired but the gun clicked on an emptied magazine.

"Here!" Gallagher thrust something at her. A big handled automatic. She took it and swung it up in both hands as the lobo came on again for a second assault. The gun kicked hard in her hand, the boom deafening inside the cab. The window exploded. The monster backed off as if on fire and howled in pain. Gallagher stomped the pedal. Lara watched the thing flop around and swing its massive head in agony. Maybe its death throes.

The engine groaned as Gallagher pushed it hard and didn't let up until he had put four miles between them and that thing on the road. Maybe the other man made it out, maybe he didn't. In the moment, he didn't care either way.

Lara leaned back against the dashboard, eyes still scanning the road behind them for any sign of the wolf. She looked at the gun in her hand. "What is this, fifty caliber?"

"Yeah." Cold air blew around them from the shattered window. "Capped with silver."

19

GALLAGHER JUST KEPT DRIVING, rolling through town and catching a few odd looks at his dented bumper and shot-out rear window. The main drag gave way to the highway and he sped up without a glance back at the Podunk village. Goodbye Weepers. They drove for an hour without saying anything. The Siberian curled up on the backseat and went to sleep. When Gallagher spoke, it was only to ask that she fish out the map from the door pocket and check their route.

Night fell and they drove on before he pulled off the road at a dingy roadhouse whose neon had all burnt out. He asked her to order for both of them while he fed and watered the dog. The food was tasteless but it filled the gap and they both ordered more coffee when the plates were cleared away.

Lara spooned sugar into her cup. A luxury after all this time on the run. "Do you want me to drive for a while?"

"No."

"You don't trust me?"

"No. I just can't sit in the passenger bucket of my own truck."

They watched the other patrons eat and then Gallagher set his cup on the formica top and looked at her. "Where did that thing come from?"

Lara warmed her hands around the steaming mug. "He said his name was Grissom. He showed up day before you did."

"And he's a... you-know-what?"

"Yes."

"What did he want?"

She kept it brief, about how Grissom told her she was doomed unless she joined him. How rogue wolves don't survive. How the change, according to Grissom, was a gradual descent into full wolf. Into madness.

He pushed his cup away. "Do you believe that?"

"Sounds plausible but, considering the source, who knows?"

"What did he want with you?"

"He wanted me to go with him. Join his pack."

"There's more of them?"

"He claims there is." She rubbed her eyes, looking exhausted. "Where did you get silver rounds for that cannon?"

"Had them specially made. The gunsmith thought I was crazy."

"What did you say they were for?"

"Hunting werewolves."

A tiny smile broke over his face and rebounded in her eyes. It faded quickly. "Do you think it's dead?"

She shrugged. "Let's hope so. You ready to go?"

They settled up and went outside to rout the dog back into the vehicle.

AMY knew this was a bad idea. Every scheme Gabby dreamed up always turned out to be a clusterfutz waiting to happen. Sneaking out of the house after dark, jimmying the lock on Gabby's parent's booze cabinet, skipping last period to smoke cigarettes with boys. All of it went spectacularly south and dropped them both into a world of trouble. Gabby never learned, plunging ahead with yet another mental-case plan, oblivious to common sense and past results.

Apparently, Amy concluded, she herself was no better. Gabby assured that a small, impromptu party would be a snap without the risk of crashers getting wind and blowing down the door. A small affair, no more than a handful of people to celebrate the holidays. Born with the bloodhunting instincts of a salesperson, Gabby appealed to Amy's need to get into the Christmas spirit and decorate the house even further. "We've already put up the tree," she derided, "and there's no one here to appreciate. We can make appetizers and sweets, all Christmas stuff. Like a grown up party."

It cut straight to Amy's beating heart but when she demurred further, Gabby closed the deal by stating that they would just have people over to watch a movie and hang. She'd even let Amy pick the movie.

It all sounded so innocent and tinsel-draped, how could she resist? There were six guests in all. Maggie, Bridgette and Walty from their mutual clutch of friends. Their oddball pal Griffin Dunne and Alex, a senior with a pallor like death and attitude to match. The last guest was Gabby's coup de grace; Date-Rape Dan Raylan. That bit was a surprise. "Oops," Gabby feigned, "didn't I tell you he was coming?"

Sneaky bitch. It was hard to think straight with everyone here and Dan draped over the easy chair. The more the merrier, right?

The movie Amy had chosen was her second-most, all-time holiday fave; *A Christmas Story.* Who doesn't love that flick? If that went over well (how could it not?), Amy had a second one queued up if everyone was up for another movie. She knew they would groan when she brought out *It's A Wonderful Life* (so what if it's black-and-white?) but she knew that if she got them to endure the first half-hour, they'd be hooked and all would be sobbing when

George Bailey's friends come to his rescue at the end.

So much for that idea. Everyone showed up but no one was watching the movie, not even when little Ralphie dropped the F-bomb on his dad. The mocha truffles and shrimp dip that she had laid out was devoured in minutes and everyone decamped to the kitchen for more. Alex, a reprobate at 17, was the first to plunder the fridge for her dad's beer. Within seconds they had all helped themselves and Bridgette was making smores in the toaster oven while Griffin sniffed out the liquor cabinet and announced that he was making margaritas. The blender whirled and green slush drizzled down the cupboards.

Now Amy was stuck in a no-win situation. If she let it ride, as Gabby kept hissing at her ear to do (be cool!), the party would spin out and the mess would be gigantic. If she blew the whistle and kicked everybody out, she'd be ostracized as a puckered-up killjoy. The only solution was to convince everyone to go somewhere else, somewhere more fun but the few suggestions she hinted at were declared lame and unimaginative.

Gabby smelled Amy's shit-fit coming on and headed it off at the pass. Uncapping the last two bottles of Sam Adams, she thrust them into the hands of her best friend and Dan Raylan.

"Gracias," Dan said and chugged a third of it back.

Gabby turned to Amy. "You know, Date-Rape was just telling me he was thinking about police work. Maybe a possible career choice, right Dan?"

"Yeah!" Dan smiled at them, a lethal grin that was known to evaporate any panties in his path. "That shit they do on CSI? How awesome would that be? Solving crimes and toolng around in a Hummer."

Gabby laserbeamed Amy. "You know Amy's dad is a cop, right? Homicide detective. Dead bodies and killers and shit. Amy, why don't you show Danno your dad's office? His medals and shit."

"It's just an office," Amy sputtered apologetically. "No big deal."

"Sure it is." Gabby cocked an eye at her with all the subtlety of a mime.

"Cool. Where is it?" Dan wandered out of the kitchen and Gabby shoved Amy after him.

She hit the light switch in the small office and Dan looked the room over. An old computer on an ugly desk, two filing cabinets and a wall of framed commendations. Dan bobbed his head in approval, as if he'd seen dozens of homicide detective's home offices before. "Cool. So your old man solves murders and stuff?"

"Yeah. But it's not like stuff on TV. Dad says ninety percent of it is tedious work." Amy tried hard not to stare at him. The last thing she wanted to talk about right now was her dad but her brain seemed to scramble, unable to come up with any other topic to discuss. Think! "So. What's the interest in police work?"

"Just seems cool, ya know." His mouth hung open, even when he wasn't talking. Amy hated mouth-breathers but chose to ignore it. He poked through the debris on the desk. "You get to carry a gun and shit. Whoa... what's this?"

Dan's eyes snagged on a police truncheon hanging from a peg. He snatched it up and swung it around. "Now this is the shit. Imagine busting somebody's head with this."

"Do you know what cops call that?"

"It's a truncheon."

"A fuckstick."

His eyes lit up, clearly impressed. He swung it again, busting imaginary skulls.

"So." Amy picked at the wet label on her beer bottle. "You need some college for police academy. To start, anyway. You picked one yet."

"Still looking."

This was hopeless. Dan seemed more interested in snooping and had barely even looked at her. Okay, better shut this down before she embarrasses herself. She glanced back towards the kitchen. "Maybe we should check on the others."

"What's the rush?" Dan leaned back in the office chair. He lifted his shirt and started undoing his belt. "Let's get busy."

"Whoa... What are you doing?"

"Gabby said you were dying to give me a blow-job." The belt flopped free and he started popping the button fly. "Close the door."

Amy gaped, speechless. Her turn to be a mouth-breather. "So you just drop your pants? How con-genitally brain-dead are you?"

"Wha...?"

"Do your pants back up. You think I'm gonna just drop to my knees for you? Seriously?"

"Gabby said—"

"Gabby is extremely disturbed. And a chronic shit-disturber." How bad could this have gone? "God!"

"Okay, okay." He struggled with the belt loop. "Touchy."

Amy felt her cheeks flush, anger bubbling up so fast she considered hitting the doofus. Her rage was cut short by the sharp crack of a gunshot.

She sprinted for the kitchen. Griffin stood rigid with the Glock in his hand and a stupid expression on his face. The acrid smell of it hung in the air and Amy scanned a panicked headcount. Everyone accounted for. Nobody lying on the floor. A small hole in the backsplash, two tiles broken.

Alex hoisted her margarita glass. "Wicked."

Dan sulked. "Why does he get to shoot the gun?"

Amy yanked the gun from Griffin's hand. His eyes remained popped, as if he couldn't believe what had just happened. "It just went off," he said.

"It didn't just go off, you released the safety!"

"I just wanted to see it."

"You coulda killed someone."

"Chill, Amy. Nobody dropped."

She slid the clip out and racked the slide forward to eject the round in the chamber. It rolled across the floor and Dan picked it up, entranced as he watched Amy disassemble the gun in seconds.

"You're such a dink, Griffin," Gabby screed. "But hey, nobody got shot—"

"Stop." Amy cut her off with a look. "Everybody out. Now."

"It was an accident," Griffin stuttered. "Don't be so lame."

Amy clawed back the urge to throttle the useless bastard. She spoke slow and clear to the assembled partygoers, warning them to leave immediately before she shot one of them.

"I'd almost forgotten how pretty it is at night."

Lara gazed out the window as the Cherokee glided back through the streets of Portland. The holiday decorations strung along Powell made her wistful, drab and plain as they were. She hadn't seen the city in so long. It felt different. It felt the same.

Gallagher took the phone from his ear and glowered at the screen. "It's not like her to ignore the call."

"Maybe she's out."

"Not this late. What day is it?"

Lara wrinkled her brow. "You're asking me? I barely know what month it is."

"It's late. She should be home." He dropped the phone into the cup holder, resisting the urge to dial again.

"Maybe she's out with a boy," Lara said, watching him bristle at the notion.

"Amy's not like that." He turned north onto 39th and swung west onto Franklin. "She knows better."

"She's seventeen, John. Don't be naive."

"I'll have to get her out of the house before you come in. You can wait at the coffeeshop on the corner or hide in the garage while I drive Amy to her mom's."

"Garage," she said. "I doubt I'd run into anybody I know but why chance it."

The dog woke up the moment Gallagher turned onto his street, tail thumping against the window. Lara felt the dog snuff her ear but when she reached back to pet it, the Siberian shied away. Still wary of her.

Gallagher gunned the homestretch and swung into his narrow driveway only to find it blocked by a strange car. "Who the hell is this?"

Lara looked up at the house. "She must be home. Every light is on."

The front door shot open and he watched a gaggle of good-for-nothing teenagers file out of his house. "What the hell...?"

Lara ducked for cover as Gallagher swung out of the cab and marched on the kids. "Who the hell are you people?"

They rabbited, all save Gabby. Frozen to the spot, she paled. "Hi Mr. Gallagher!" Piping up loud enough to warn Amy inside. "We're just leaving."

"Gabby?" A volcanic rage rumbled inside and he fought to stifle it down. "Tell me you two didn't have a party..."

"A small one." Gabby mustered her sweetest smile. "It was all my idea." Least she could do was shoulder the blame in an attempt to mitigate Amy's punishment. "I talked Amy into it. It was small. We watched Christmas movies."

"Go home," he growled and stomped inside.

The dog slid past her knees as it trailed behind him. Gabby bit her lip, wondering if she should go back in to help explain. Amy's dad was a little scary. And a cop. She'd make it up to Amy some other way, she decided, and booked.

IT went about as bad as she imagined. Dad was apoplectic that she had thrown a party in the first place but to let those shitheaded little peons (his words) run riot through their home was beyond belief.

Amy listened to his rant without uttering a word. Anything she said right now would just infuriate him further so she sat attentive and waited for him to blow off. But then, just as he was winding down, he clocked the broken tile in the backsplash and he started back up again. For her own self preservation, Amy lied about what had happened. Telling him that her dumbass friend not only found the Glock but let a round off in the house, well, her dad would probably drive her to juvie that instant.

Gallagher turned his back to her and caught his breath. "Go upstairs and pack your bag."

"What?" Amy startled. Was he was taking her to juvie hall after all. "Why?"

"You're going to your mother's."

"But—"

"Go."

HE listened to his daughter stomp every step on the stairs and waited for the slam of the bedroom door. Boom. He hustled through the door in the hall and crossed into the garage. Lifting the rollup door, he found Lara leaning against the truck.

"I could hear you hollering from out here," she said, ducking under the door. "How bad is it?"

"Bad," he conceded. "But it saves me from coming up with some lame excuse to drop her at Cheryl's." He lowered the rollup and crossed the floor to go back into the house. "Soon as we leave, go on inside."

Gallagher disappeared back into the house and the garage went dark. Lara leaned against the workbench and listened to her former homicide partner escort his teenage daughter out to the truck, scolding her the whole way.

20

THE SMELL INSIDE THE HOUSE was so overwhelming that Lara retreated into the dank garage to catch her breath before venturing back inside. Tiptoeing through the house, she smelled Gallagher everywhere. And then Amy. Both scents so strong they were steeped into the walls and floors. She nosed up a week's worth of dinners cooked in the kitchen.

The dog was strong too. She could close her eyes and still pinpoint the corner where the husky bedded down each night.

Smell triggered memory. A fact she was vaguely aware of before her affliction. Now, with her heightened senses, it was a blaring siren. These comingled smells of people and food and shelter and pets gushed forth her own memory banks. If there was an underlying motif, it was simply home. This foursquare craftsman house was home to a family. Shelter, safety, belonging.

It was impossible not to contrast this with her current rootless exile. Her gut had ached for this for so long and here it was but she was simply a guest here. Enjoy your daypass.

She was drawn to the kitchen, the center of any home, but was distracted by the twinkling lights from the living room. A Christmas tree stood against the bay window, its evergreen perfume drifting dully through the house. The strung lights reflected off the ornaments and tinsel and there were even a few wrapped presents sitting under it.

She couldn't resist and knelt to check the tags on each gift. Judging by the names, Amy had finished most of her Christmas list. The biggest gift was marked *Gabby*, the smallest was tagged simply *Dad*. Two other presents were labelled *Mom*.

Lara stepped back and sank onto the sofa but the cushions felt too soft. She slid off and sat on the floor and gazed up at the Christmas tree. Such a simple thing, the pine smell and the lights and tinsel, but it punched a bruise into her heart.

Exhausted from running for so long, from hiding, Lara Mendes melted in the warm glow and promise of good cheer. Hokey as it was.

THE kitchen was back to normal when Gallagher returned home. He told Lara to leave the rest, he'd get it in the morning. She could take Amy's room, he'd said, he just needed to change the sheets. She told him not to bother, she'd change them in the morning. Lara said goodnight and was halfway up the stairs when she turned back. "How are you fixed for hot water?"

"We're good," he shrugged. "Unless those kids ruined that too. Why?"

"I've been bathing in cold riverwater for three months. Tomorrow, I want to stand under a scalding shower for as long as the hot water holds out. Fair warning."

Gallagher smiled. "Knock yourself out."

HE rose early the next morning, his back still stiff but otherwise rested. A second night without the nightmares. Looking out the kitchen window as he made coffee, he watched a light snow fall, shrouding the hedges in the yard.

It was going to be a beautiful day.

Cleaning up the mess soured his mood, only because it meant he'd have to have a 'little talk' with his daughter. He always felt like a fraud when he sat Amy down to discuss something stupid she'd done. It didn't happen very often and when it did, it was nothing too terrible. Still, he never felt comfortable as the booming voice of good judgment. His own record was far from unblemished and he had a sneaking suspicion Amy knew it too.

Aside from a lecture, he would have to lie to her about finding Lara. Could he tell Amy the truth or was it too risky? He was flipping the idea back and forth when he heard the the shower come on and run for almost an hour.

When she came downstairs, Lara was wearing his old robe, the one that hung unused behind the bathroom door. She seemed lost in it, draped over her small shoulders with the sleeves turned up. Her wet hair hung loose but it was combed straight and as she settled into a chair at the kitchen table, Lara Mendes almost looked like her old self.

He placed a cup of black coffee before her. "Feel better?"

"Like a new person. But don't use the shower until I've scrubbed the tub. It wasn't pretty what I scoured off."

He watched her wrap both hands around the mug and heard a sigh as she sipped. It was strange, seeing her like this. She had been a ghost for so long and here she was, sipping coffee at his table like it was an everyday occurrence. Draped in that thin material he could see just how much weight she had lost over the last few months. Still. He had almost forgotten how pretty she was and when the fall of the robe plunged too deep a neckline, he had to force his eyes to look away.

Lara didn't seem to notice, lost in the simple luxury of warmth and hot java. "Can I use your laundry? My clothes are pretty grubby."

"Sure." He went back to the counter and cracked two eggs into the frypan. "You can borrow some of Amy's clothes too. She won't mind."

"Will you tell her? About me coming back from the dead?"

"I don't know yet. I hate lying to her." He flipped the eggs onto a plate with some toast and brought it to the table. "She'd want to know but... Here, eat. The bacon's almost ready."

"This is more than enough. Please."

"You're skin and bones, detective. Need to get some weight on you."

She pulled the robe tighter, suddenly conscious to her state, and tucked in. "Have you thought about what's next?"

He stopped pushing the bacon round the pan and looked at her. "Lie low for the time being. Take it slow." He scooped the bacon onto a paper-toweled plate and joined her at the table. His face clouded. "Lara, when it happens, the change, do you know it's coming or...?"

"I can feel it coming on. It's not like a sudden seizure or anything." She put her fork down. "Are you worried?"

"I'd be stupid not to." He dumped too much bacon on her plate. "How do you know it's coming? Is there a trigger, like the full moon pops out of the clouds and bingo?"

"It has nothing to do with the moon. You know that."

"Too bad. Least it would be scheduled. Once a month, we could work around it."

She mopped up the eggs with the last bit of toast. "You're confusing it with a whole other monthly curse."

"Sorry. So is there a trigger?"

"Adrenalin. Fear or anger. Danger. I'll feel my pulse spike, heart speeding up. If I'm not careful, it will kick over and trip the change."

"What do you do? Just calm your breathing or something?"

"If I catch it in time. If not, well, silver works."

"Silver?"

She pushed away from the table and crossed to the hall where her parka hung on a peg. Patted down the pockets and came back, placing something on the table before him. A pearl-handled knife, sheathed in a scabbard of leather with white stitching.

Gallagher unsheathed the gleaming blade and scraped his thumb across the edge. "Solid or plate?"

"Solid."

"Where'd you get it?"

"A silversmith in Del Norte. Old Tiburcio claimed he forged it using the finest silver from Tasco."

"Hell of a craftsman. He made this for you?"

"No, it was sitting there in his display case. He said a man paid him to forge it years ago but he never came back to collect it."

He slid the blade back into its sheath. "Somebody else had wolf problems?"

"That's what I wondered. Maybe the problem got to him before he could pick it up."

"What exactly do you do with this?"

"I cut." She frowned, as if unsure of what to do, then she pushed up the sleeve on her left arm. The skin crisscrossed with thin white scars. "The silver has to draw blood, otherwise it doesn't work. But once it does, it's like being doused with cold water. Puts out the fire."

"Every time?"

"No." Her shoulders sank. "Only if you to catch it in time."

"So how many times have you, you know, changed?"

She fussed with her napkin, stalling. "Four times. Not including the night I disappeared. So that's five."

"First round doesn't count," he said. His fingers drummed the table top. "Four, huh? I don't know if that's good or bad."

"Four times in ninety days?" Her voice sharp, defensive. "Basic math says that's barely an occurrence."

"When was the last time you changed?"

"Three nights ago. The night Grissom showed up. He changed, attacked me as a wolf. No stopping the adrenalin in that situation. I lost."

"Same night that local guy in Weepers got torn apart," he said.

Lara watched him straighten his back, assuming a posture reserved for questioning suspects. Cold and impassive. "Not to be cruel, Lara, but... who did the deed? Was it him or was it you?"

She pulled the robe tighter and crossed her arms. "Don't question me like a suspect, John."

"Okay. Sorry. But I gotta know."

"It wasn't me."

"How do you know? Are you aware when you're the... in that state?"

"No."

"Then how do you know it wasn't you?"

"I can't explain it. Just a gut feeling. But killing someone in that state? It crosses some line in the sand. I'd know."

"That's still just a gut feeling. Nothing solid."

"You're the one who claims detective work is ninety percent gut." She rubbed the bridge of her nose, trying to put in words what she'd never said aloud. "Think about it this way. If you kill someone while in that state, it's like killing the human inside yourself. Giving in to that part. There's no coming back from that. If I had done it, you and I would not be sitting at this table right now."

His coffee had gone cold. "Seems kinda crazy but... okay. Let's work with that for now."

Stillness settled across the table, neither said a word. The dog rose from its bedding and clicked nails across the floor. Its eyes fixed Lara for a few moments before it dipped its snout to its bowl.

"I'm going to get dressed." Lara rose and went up the stairs. When she glanced over her shoulder, she saw Gallagher unsheathe the knife again and test the blade against the pad of his thumb. As if pondering its effectiveness.

21

TINSEL WAS STRUNG ALONG THE cubicles of Homicide Detail and a wreath shed needles onto the industrial pile. Kopzych wore a Santa hat, cocked at a jaunty angle and some fool was piping Christmas tunes through his computer. Gallagher nodded hello to Detective Farbre as he returned to precinct. Everyone else ignored him.

Good.

After informing the Lieutenant that he was back, he checked with Wade about their case load. Nothing to report, nothing to move the needle on any of the open files stinking up their desks. "Everybody's too busy doing their last minute shopping to lift a finger," Wade said, leaning back in his chair.

"Don't worry. Christmas Eve will roll in, and just when you think you might cut out for home to be with the family, the phone will start ringing." Gallagher patted Wade on the shoulder. "Murder loves Christmas."

"It is a time for family."

"That's the spirit." Gallagher was pleased to see some healthy gallows humor creeping into detective Wade's unassailable good nature. Maybe the guy would thrive in Homicide after all.

A handful of memos were waiting for him on his desk, policy changes and internal alerts, which he swept into the recycling bin. His inbox was choked with bullshit but there was an email from Taylor, alerting him to a hit on his search parameters. Headlined 'Bingo', the message read; *Sounds like what you're looking for.* A news report from something called The Beacon Express, a small news affiliate in southeastern Oregon. A police report was attached. Both items reported the death of Roy Webb in Weepers. The incident that had sent the locals patrolling the town with guns. After printing off the police report, he started searching the news feeds for reports about the two men who had stopped them at the road. Nothing pinged.

He called down to Taylor, thanked him for the report and then asked him to look again for any news from that same area. Taylor emailed back two minutes later with a missing persons report. Sheriff Cheevers was searching for two men; Jim McClusky and Robert Jigs. Their truck had fallen through the ice on Snake River, four miles outside of town. Cheevers suspected the two men had also ended up in the river but no bodies had been recovered. A small hunting shack nearby had been destroyed and, according to Cheevers, there was a possibility the two men had been drunk at the time. After destroying the shack, the Sheriff surmised that the men had driven their truck onto the ice when it went through.

He emailed Taylor back, asking him to monitor the item and forward any updates to him. Gallagher read the report again and found it even more disturbing the second time around. He picked up the phone to call home only to realize that Lara wouldn't pick up. He'd have to wait until he got home to discuss it with her.

"Hey partner, slow day?" Wade sauntered up, cradling a thick file under his arm. "We need to give these tips another call, see if anyone's remembered anything."

Gallagher sneered. "What file is that?"

"The Lelander case. 'Member that one?"

Gillian Lelander was a 16-year old girl found dead on the bank of the Willamette which Wade had been primary on. The file went nowhere and remained open. It happened to all of them, a case that a detective couldn't leave alone, couldn't stop obsessing over. Lelander had been Wade's personal haunt for six months now, the detective opening the murder book on it and reading through the file for the umpteenth time. Sometimes he'd enlist Gallagher in his latest tilt at the windmill.

"Do yourself a favor and send it down to cold cases," Gallagher said. "Don't be an Ahab."

Wade scowled. "Says the guy who's spent three months looking for his missing partner."

Gotcha. Gallagher grunted and watched Wade split the paperwork in half. It took a Herculean effort to not blurt out that he had in fact successfully closed his open file and found his missing partner, thank you very much.

"Get through that pile," Wade said, bopping Gallagher on the shoulder, "and I'll spring for donuts. The kind with sprinkles too."

Bastard.

LARA sat on the living room floor looking out the window. A sprinkle of snow fell over 22nd Avenue, melting as it hit the ground. The husky came up and joined her at the window.

"Bored?" She dug her fingers into its fur. "Me too."

She had kept herself busy for most of the day. She stripped the sheets from Amy's bed and bundled them into the washing machine along with her grimy clothes. Borrowing a T-shirt and jeans from Amy's drawer, she was distressed to find the waistband fell loose. Her now bony hips jutted out sharp but not sharp enough to hold up the pants. The junkie look, not attractive.

She made more coffee (with lots of sugar) and helped herself to a container of leftover tandoori chicken. Watched the news. She felt bloated and sick afterwards, her stomach not used to the onslaught of spice and calories. The chatter of the news anchor on the TV was noxious, the news of the day holding no interest for her. Her eyes kept straying to the window until she clicked off the boob tube and took to staring out at the street. She considered taking the dog out for a walk but decided against it, fearing she'd be seen or recognized.

Back to the window and the falling snow, she realized she was trapped here. She couldn't leave the house, despite the fact that every stitch of her muscles ached to go outside. This house, that had seemed such a safe refuge just last night, now felt small.

She laid down on the floor and curled into a ball, her guts rumbling and roiling. Her eyes closed and oblivion came fast.

WHEN her eyes opened, everything was blurry and her teeth were chattering. A hand on her shoulder, shaking her awake.

"Lara?"

Gallagher was leaning over her. Behind him, the street and the snow drifting down. It was dark.

"Are you okay?" He waved a hand before her eyes like she was blind.

"What?"

"Why are you on the stoop? It's freezing out here."

She was sitting on the cold porch stoop, shivering in the thin clothes pilfered from his daughter's drawer.

Her knees ached and her legs were stiff as she rose and they went inside. Gallagher cast his eyes up and down the street, wondering if any of his neighbors had seen her. "How long have you been out here?"

"I'm not sure."

"You get spooky when you're like that."

"Like what?"

"That trance you're in. It's like you're not there." He followed her into the kitchen. "Is that part of it? Like a symptom?"

"I don't know."

She retrieved a blanket from the living room and wrapped it around her shoulders. Gallagher made tea to warm her up but the shivering in her hands didn't subside for the better part of an hour.

HE had splurged and bought rib eye steaks, grilling them over the barbecue despite the weather. They talked about their day over dinner like any couple. She asked about the precinct, who was working the bullpen in the homicide detail. He told her about Wade's obsession with the Lelander case.

How he felt sorry for the guy, knowing the unanswered questions in that file would haunt him for a long time. He ladled seconds onto her plate, urging her to eat some more. Lara pushed her plate away, feeling a bit woozy from a full belly.

He asked her to fix them a drink while he went to fetch something from his office. Said he had something he wanted to show her. She looked through the liquor cupboard, partially decimated by Amy's friends and found a bottle of red. It had been forever since she'd had wine. She uncorked it, found glasses and brought it to the living room. The sofa felt odd under her so she slid to the floor and crossed her legs.

Gallagher came back, a few sheets of print-out in his hand, and stopped. "Something wrong with the couch?"

"Too soft." She pushed a glass of wine towards him. "Guess I've just gotten used to not having furniture."

"Okay." He joined her on the floor, grimacing as he folded his legs the way she did. "What do you know about this guy who attacked you?"

"Not a whole lot. No idea where he came from or even if he told me his real name." She reached for the printout on the coffee table. "What's this?"

"Police report about the incident on the road. When we escaped. You shot that thing with the fifty-cal, didn't you?"

"It wasn't a clean shot." Her eyes scanned the document. "But there's no mention of a wolf attack here. Or bodies. How did the truck end up in the river?"

"Grissom must have survived."

She looked up, piecing it together. "He pushed the truck into the river. Made it look like an accident."

"Dropped the bodies in the ice after it. They won't be found till spring."

"Covering his tracks," she said.

Neither spoke. They could hear the dog in the kitchen, crunching kibble from its bowl. Gallagher puffed out his cheeks. "If he survived, could he track you back here?"

"I don't know. Portland's a long way."

"But he found you the first time. From wherever he was, he tracked you down then."

Lara's eyes drifted to the floor. "Or I tracked him down."

"That doesn't make sense. How do you find someone you've never met before?"

"When I fled, I just needed to get away from here. Away from the city, away from people. I didn't have a destination in mind, I just pushed on. But..."

Her voice trailed off. He waited a hearbeat, then two. "Go on."

"There were choices. This road, not that one. I needed some safe place to hunker down for the winter. I stopped in a dozen places that would have suited me, a few better than where I ended up. But I kept going, something nagging me to keep pushing further." She shrugged. "Without realizing it, I may have tracked him down. Drawn to his territory."

None of that made sense to him. "Why would you do that?"

"Wolves are pack animals. Maybe lycanthropes are no different. Ivan Prall certainly thought that way."

Gallagher bristled at the name, the memory of it. "I don't want to go through that again. If this guy shows up, would you know? I mean, pick up his scent or smell him coming?"

"If he got close." She nodded at the kitchen. "The dog too. But I don't think he'd risk coming here."

"Why's that?"

"Too populated. He said the only way to survive as a wolf is to stay hidden. Avoid busy places where things could get messy."

"Easier to clean up said mess." Gallagher looked at the police report again. "Like staging an accident."

The dog padded in from the kitchen, looked at them both and whined. Gallagher rose, creakily, and crossed to the door to let the dog out. When he came back, he saw her face darkened with worry. "What's on your mind?"

"I don't know if I should be here." She looked the room over. "Cooped up like this. Afraid to go out, afraid of being seen. I'll go stir crazy."

He tapped a finger against his lips, pondering that. "What if you came back? Publicly, I mean."

"And say what? I went on vacation and forgot to leave a note?"

"What if it was memory loss? You suffered a head injury that night, wiped your brain clean and you've spent the last three months living in a homeless shelter? Speaking nothing but Spanish."

"Who's going to believe that? Think about the grilling I would get. From people we know, other detectives." Lara shook her head. "It'll never work."

"I'm grasping at straws here. You got any better ideas?"

"Nope."

"What about a small town? Somewhere outside the city where you wouldn't have to worry about running into someone you knew."

She shook her head. "Just another type of exile. What would I do?"

"Start a new life. Make new friends. I'll come visit you."

"Wow. The highlight of my month would be a visit from grumpy Gallagher."

"Easy." He made a face at her. "Grumpy Gallagher saved your butt, Mendes."

"Right. Thank you Prince Charming." She batted her eyes mockingly and trilled her best Valley-Girlese. "I was, like, sooo in need of saving."

"Ingrate." He elbowed her ribs. She shoved back. Sly smiles on both ends. "Seriously," he went on, "haven't you ever daydreamed about starting over. Chucking everything and reinventing yourself?"

"Not like this."

"Then stay here, with me. You can reinvent yourself here." Gallagher leaned in to her, formulating his cock-eyed plan. "You look different now. We'll tell people we met when I was, I dunno, up north on vacation. Up in B.C., fishing or something. You can say you're Canadian, which means you're from anywhere. We met and yadda-yadda-yadda and you came to live with me. Me and Amy," he corrected.

"And tell Amy what?"

That stymied him. "The truth. She's smart. She can handle it."

"No one would believe that. It's too crazy."

"Then some other story." He shrugged, looked at the floor. "You can't just leave. I won't lose you again."

She looked up. His eyes locked onto hers and wouldn't let go. Her first instinct was to pull away but she didn't. Staring back bold as brass. A giddiness, like vertigo looking down off a rooftop.

"For a long time, I told myself it was my duty to find you. My responsibility," he said. "But it's more than that. Always has been."

Something singed her hand like a hot coal. She broke the spell and looked down, saw his hand close over hers. Alarm bells clanged in her head, warning her to break off but some other part refused and her fingers clamped around his.

"John..." she said. There was more to it but the words evaporated like smoke. It was important but at this very moment, she couldn't remember why.

She felt a squeeze. Her hand folded in his. How small her hand looked. How thin her arm next to his. How could he look at her like this, so scrawny. She tried to shake the notions from her head but they wouldn't leave and when she looked up again, he kissed her.

Everything fell away. The world, the worries, the wolf. Lost in the dark, the only thought was her lips touching his. Her hand found his arm and held on tight, the way a drowning woman clutches a buoy. Something stirring up deep inside, something she hadn't felt in a long time. And by the way he clutched her, he hadn't felt it in a while too. Those old reactions. Gasping for air between kisses, her heart banging away. An ache so acute it stung. Wanting more, wanting it all. To envelop him and devour him, clutch and swallow him whole if she could...

A roar inside her ears. Far away at first, and then blasting as if someone jacked the volume all the way up. She tore her mouth from his. "Stop. John..."

He pulled her back in. His hands on her. His lips on her neck. But the roar returned too, louder than bombs. Something unfolded its wet limbs in that hidden corner of her heart.

She pushed him back. He blinked, eyes sobering up fast. "What is it?"

"I can't."

"It's okay."

"No. It isn't."

"Easy." He pulled her back in. "Lara, ease up."

Her hand still gripped round his neck. He winced and she pulled her hand away. There was blood on her nails.

Her fingernails had elongated, turned coarse. Her heart banging faster and faster. The change had been triggered.

"Lara, what's wrong?"

"John...get out."

22

GABBY WAS A HOLY TERROR on the road. Having nearly rear-ended two other cars and sideswiped the mirror on a parked car, Gabby drove on obliviously, fiddling with the radio and chatting away. Amy sat in the passenger seat, wondering who in their right mind gave her friend a passing grade on the driving test.

"If you want, I can come inside with you," Gabby said. "Your dad probably won't yell too much if I'm there too."

"That's okay. I'm just gonna grab a few things and blow." Amy suddenly bolted back in the seat. "Gabby, STOP!"

"What?"

"The stop sign!"

Gabby focused her attention on the road just as the red sign blurred past. She hit the brakes and the nose dipped and bounced, coming to a stop in the middle of the intersection. Gabby checked for other cars then hit the gas. "All clear. So you didn't get grounded or anything? How is that possible?"

"Don't know," Amy shrugged. "He seemed distracted or something. Whatever. But he ran me outta there so fast I forgot half my clothes. Slow down."

"You're lucky." Gabby turned into the Gallagher's driveway, almost colliding into the parked Cherokee. Gabby squinted at the truck's mangled bumper, the rear window covered over with plastic sheeting. "What happened to your old man's ride?"

"Said he had an accident." Amy opened the door, tripping the dome light. "Hang tight. I'll be two seconds."

Gabby watched her friend run up the porch steps and disappear inside the house.

THE dog was barking and Lara was shaking bad. Not a shiver but a quake so deep her hands were vibrating. Gallagher wrapped his arms around her, trying to hold her still. "Breathe through it," he urged. "Ride it out."

Her eyes flicked up. A warm amber glowing around the iris. Not good. He gripped her tighter, like that would do anything. "Lara, what do I do?"

She was losing color fast, her face and hands a cold shade of pale. What if he knocked her out? Just cold-cocked her into next week? It was harder than it looked, punching someone into unconsciousness. And what if it made the wolf come on faster?

"The knife." Her voice had altered. "Get the knife."

He bolted for the foyer, where her parka hung from a hook. Slapping the pockets until he felt its shape. He dug it out and unsheathed the gleaming blade.

"Dad?"

Amy stood in the open door.

Gallagher froze. Knife in hand, gaping stupidly at his daughter. "Amy...what are you doing here?"

Her face set hard, expecting a fight. "I came to get some stuff. What are you doing with a knife?"

"Honey, you can't be here."

"I know. Gabby's outside, waiting to drive me home."

Her dad came at her, pushing her back out the door. He was out of breath and sweat beaded his face. "Not now. Go back home. Now!"

A loud racket was banging around from deep inside the house. The dog barking its head off. Amy planted her feet, refusing to go. "What is going on? Why is the dog going crazy?"

Another sound. At first Amy wasn't even sure it was a voice but it called out again. A woman's voice, calling out her dad's name.

He sprinted for the living room. Who the hell was this woman in her house? And why was she screaming? Amy marched through the kitchen and turned the corner into the family room. She stopped dead, not comprehending what she was looking at.

There was a woman thrashing around on the floor. She was thin and she was shaking like a junkie. She was wearing Amy's clothes. Her father was on his knees, holding the woman down. Pinning her flat with one arm, clutching the knife in the other hand. Like he was going to stab her.

Oh God, he was going to kill her.

The dog barked and barked.

"Dad, stop!" Amy grabbed his wrist.

He turned and snapped at her to let go. The look on his face. Amy had never seen her dad so scared. She let go. He turned back to the quaking woman. "Where do I cut? Lara, look at me! Where do I cut?"

Amy felt her jaw fall open. This wasn't real. It didn't make any sense but the more she stared at the strange woman, the more it gelled into reality. Lara Mendes. Back from the dead. Even though Amy still couldn't get a good look at her face through the tangled hair, she knew it was Lara.

How?

Lara lifted her shirt. Amy's shirt. Exposing her stomach. "Here." Her voice sounded so strange. "Cut it deep."

Gallagher pressed the blade onto the pale flesh of belly and sliced across. Blood welled up under the knife's edge.

"Dad, stop!" Amy felt her own hands shaking, needing to do something but not having a clue as to what was going on. The whole world had gone crazy. "You'll kill her!"

The quaking didn't stop. He snapped at Amy to back off and cut again, drawing more blood. Another shudder and the woman stilled. Gallagher brushed the damp hair from her eyes and Amy studied the woman's face. It was Lara Mendes, but it wasn't either. Her face so unnaturally white the skin was veined with blue. The eyes were yellow and iridescent as bulbs. And her teeth were all wrong. She had fangs. Jesuschrist, she had long sharp fangs.

Amy dropped to her knees. That crazy story her dad had told her. It was true. But that was crazy. *This*, right here on her living room floor, *this* was crazy. She couldn't stop staring at Lara's face and those weird yellow eyes rose.

Gabby.

Gabby was waiting outside. Amy staggered up and ran back through the house, almost tripping down the porch steps.

Gabby lowered her window. "Is everything okay?"

"Yeah. I'm gonna stay. Bye."

"What's wrong? You're white as a ghost. Is it that bad?"

"It's fine. Go home. I'll call you tomorrow."

"Hold on... Amy!" Gabby hollered but Amy ran back into the house. "Crazy frakking family," she said and backed out of the driveway.

RUSHING back into the room, all Amy saw was the blood. On the floor and on her dad's hands. Lara thrashed and jerked, covered in it. She had never seen so much blood before, not in one place. The room swayed and Amy felt her knees jelly again. Don't pass out, she told herself. Not now.

"Amy!" Her dad's voice snapped her alert. He jostled against the spasms. "Amy. Hold her legs!"

Amy couldn't move, too busy trying to keep the floor from flip-flopping.

"Amy! Help me hold her down!"

Like always, his bark snapped her out of it. She rushed in and sat on Lara's legs, pinning them flat. Her dad leaned down hard onto Lara's chest. She was crazed, gnashing and popping her teeth like a rabid animal. He lowered the blade into the open wound.

"Dad, don't. You're going to kill her."

"It's okay. Cross your fingers and pray this works."

Amy fought the urge to pull his hand away. "Why are you doing that?"

Lara's thrashing subsided a little as the blade bit into her flesh. Almost incrementally, the more the blade cut, the more her frenzy burned off.

Her dad looked up at her. "Got to my office, get the handcuffs from my desk. Second drawer down. Then run upstairs. There's a gun on my nightstand. The eagle. Get that too."

"The big gun? Why?" Amy balked at the thought. "You can't shoot her."

"Just go!"

She ran, colliding into walls as she sprinted through the mud room to his office. The dog chased her. Rifling the drawer, she pulled up the cuffs and ran for the stairs. The big handgun on the nightstand, heavy and lethal in her hand. Hammering down the steps, back to the living room. "Here."

Her dad caught the bracelets and spun one cuff around Lara's wrist. Yanking her arm flat across the floor, he snapped the second cuff around the leg of the old radiator. The second he let up off of her, Lara roared and clawed at him but was jerked back, wrist taught against the chain.

Amy passed the gun to him. He double-checked the safety and kept the barrel trained on the floor and then backed away.

Lara thrashed and chomped and pulled against the restraint with rabid ferocity. A wolf in a leg-trap. "Is that..." Amy stammered. "Is it really her?"

"Fraid so." He was still catching his breath.

Lara jerked and flailed against the bracelets.

"I can't look," Amy said. "It's freaking me out."

"Go in the other room."

Good advice but Amy couldn't tear her eyes away. The thing chained to the radiator was in no way Lara Mendes. It coiled and jerked. Popping sounds emanated from it. Amy watched the woman's hands morph, the knuckles buckle and pop under the skin.

She looked at her dad. "Can't you do something? She's in pain."

"I don't know what else to do."

Fresh blood spattered onto the carpet. The open wound on Lara's belly ran and spilled. Amy ran to get a handful of towels and then approached the thrashing figure on the floor.

"No. Stay away from her."

"She's going to bleed to death!"

Amy felt herself shoved aside. Gallagher bore down fast and cracked the butt of the gun across Lara's temple.

A fresh dribble of blood. Lara Mendes's eyes rolled over white and her body went limp.

Amy jolted forward, pulling back the woman's eyelids with her thumb. Oh shit. Did he just kill her? The woman's head flopped loose in Amy's hands, lifeless as a sock-puppet.

AMY sat at the kitchen table, eyes blasted from what she had seen. Trying to make sense of it. The husky brushed her knee and she startled. She looked into its blue eyes and hesitated before scratching its ears. It was just a dog, not the thing she had seen in the other room. Still, something seismic had shifted in the world and nothing felt solid anymore.

Gallagher came back from the living room, pitched the bloodied towels into the sink and washed his hands.

It was a moment before Amy found her voice. "Is she all right?"

"She's out cold."

"Yeah but is she..." Amy groped for a word, "...normal?"

"Yes." He dried his hands on a towel and looked at his daughter. "You okay?"

Her eyes looked raw, her expression blank. He knew that look, having seen it in the mirror months ago. A stupid, gap-mouthed expression of trying to make sense of the impossible.

When Amy spoke, her voice was hushed. Sharing a secret. "I didn't believe you. When you told me about Lara. I'm sorry."

"Who would?"

"I can't believe she's still alive. How did you find her?"

He outlined the events as briefly as possible. About how Lara had been on the run all this time, hiding, moving on. He left out any mention of the man Lara had called Grissom. Or the other wolf, the incident at the roadside. When he finished, Amy stared down at the table and didn't speak.

He got up and turned the kettle on. "Do you want some tea?"

"This is crazy," Amy said slowly. She had yet to shake the thousand-yard stare. "I mean, werewolves? How can they exist and no one knows?"

"I don't know, sweetheart. I guess they know how to hide."

Amy turned her head towards the living room. "And Lara. On the run all this time. Alone. She must have been so scared."

"She's tough."

The clock ticked on. Amy looked up at her father. "What do we do now?"

Gallagher came to the table. Folded his hand over hers. "We help her. Hide her. Protect her from herself if we have to. Beyond that, I don't know yet."

Amy's eyes darted around the room, slowly turning things over in her head. "What if she changes? I mean, all the way, totally wolfs out?"

"If it comes to that, if she, or it, turns on us? We protect ourselves." He crossed to the counter and laid the big handgun on the table. He thumbed the latch and slid the magazine out. "These rounds have silver loads. They'll do the job."

She took up the magazine and inspected the first cartridge. "You can't..."

"Don't rule out anything."

"I still don't like this gun."

"But you know how to handle it."

She clunked it down onto the table and looked at him. "Is this why you taught me how to shoot?"

"I used to think I knew what was out there. On the street, the bad people. I was wrong." His eyes drifted down to the weapon between them. "I needed you to be prepared."

23

AMY ROLLED OVER AND BUMPED her nose on something hard. The laptop lay where her pillow should be. The light was on and she was still in her clothes. The laptop was open but the screen was dark. Next to it was a notebook and a pen, pages of scribbled notes.

After saying goodnight to her dad and ensuring that Lara was comfortable on the sofa, Amy had gone to bed too wound up to sleep. So she did the one thing that always made her sleepy: homework. Firing up the laptop, she had spent the night researching monsters. Werewolves, lycanthropes, wolfsbane, silver weapons, full moons and ancient curses. Dutifully taking notes, she had hoped to find some consistency within the tangled web of folklore and pop culture, something she could use. There was little consistency among the sources, no consensus on what constituted a werewolf or how to cure someone afflicted with it. Was it supernatural or biological? Curse or disease?

She must have fallen asleep taking notes. She closed the laptop and lowered it to the floor. Rooting through a drawer for some clean pajamas, she heard the dog whining downstairs.

Creeping downstairs, she sidled to the living room to check on Lara. The sofa was empty, the blanket in a heap on the floor. The dog whined, nosing the bottom of the front door. Lara's heavy parka was gone from the hook in the hallway. Her boots too.

No.

She hurried to the front door and flung it open to a cold blast of air. The dog ran out.

Lara Mendes sat on the front stoop, pulling her boots on. She turned and looked up at Amy and then bent back to tighten the boots.

The porch was frigid against Amy's bare feet. "Lara? Are you all right?"

"I have to go."

"Go where?" Amy folded her arms against the cold. "Please, don't. What's Dad gonna say?"

Lara stood, looked at Amy and then looked away. "I'm sorry you had to see that."

"It doesn't matter. Come back inside."

The muscles under Lara's cheek clenched and her eyes hardened, clamping down what was roiling up under the surface. "I could have hurt you tonight. Your dad. I couldn't live with that." She turned and staggered down to the walk.

Amy snatched the woman's arm. "No. Not after all this. I thought you were dead, you can't just disappear now."

"I can't. I'm sorry."

"No. Do you know how long he searched for you? Don't do this to him, Lara. Not after all this." She shuddered, buffeted by the cold wind. "It would kill him."

Lara wavered, her resolve vaporizing as fast as her breath on the air.

Amy linked her arm around Lara's and coaxed the woman back up the porch. "Come on. Before I freeze out here."

Back inside, Amy helped her ease out of her parka. "Does it hurt?" she asked, making a slicing motion across her stomach. "The cut?"

"It's okay. But my head is killing me. What did your dad hit me with?"

"Gun butt." Amy rooted through the cupboard over the sink for a bottle of aspirin. Shook a couple out and poured a glass of water. "Here."

Lara accepted the pills. "Go back to bed, Amy. Get some sleep."

Amy cocked an eyebrow, wary of being hoodwinked. "Promise me you won't run?"

Lara crossed her heart. "Scouts honor. To be honest, I don't think I could make it past the driveway right now."

"Okay." Amy bit her lip, stalling. Something on her mind. "Lara, I'm sorry."

"For what?"

"I gave up on you. I thought you were gone. Like for good."

"You were meant to." She averted the girl's eyes. "I'm the one who should be sorry. For putting you through that."

"It was awful. The weeks went by without a sign or clue or anything. I gave up." She shivered, looking down at her feet. "But Dad never gave up. He kept looking and looking. I told him to stop. To accept that you were gone and to move on. I'm sorry."

Lara looked at this young girl trying so hard to be strong. She had never considered the havoc she wreaked with her vanishing act. Ripples on a pond or dominoes falling in order, there were consequences. How to reconcile that?

She scrambled her brain for some way to explain but got cut short by the girl's embrace. "I'm glad you're back," the girl said.

Lara squeezed the girl and then shooed her off to bed, promising twice to not flee before morning. She watched Amy go up the stairs and then went back to the sofa. Admonished herself to get some sleep.

For once, she was grateful that her tear ducts didn't work anymore.

"WEREWOLVES are universal. From the ancient Greeks to Native North Americans, Asia, Europe, every culture seems to have some form of lycanthropy. But the similarity ends there. In some cultures, it's a curse given by a witch, or it's a gift from a shaman. Some people believed the werewolf was actually your soul, let loose to destroy your own kind." Amy paged through her notes. "Weird, huh?"

Across the table, Lara and her father stared at her like she'd grown two heads. He frowned. "Where did you get that?"

"The internet," Amy shrugged, like there could be some other answer. "I've been researching it."

"Wonderful."

The three of them sitting round the kitchen table. Cartons of Indian take-out spread out on the table top. Amy's favourite. She had called her dad at work and cajoled him into picking it up on his way home. A special occasion, she said. When he groused, she reminded him that it was Christmas and not to be a Grinch.

Despite the events of last night, the three of them had carried on like it was any other day. Gallagher, hurrying to get out of the house. Hollering at his daughter to get up and get her butt in gear. Amy grumpy and slow like every morning. Her dad reminding her that she had work today, nagging her not to be late. Lara, although still a little shaky, made breakfast. Amy marvelled at the normalness of it all, the three of them bustling through an eve-ryday routine. She said nothing to her dad about Lara's attempt to run away the night before. Neither did Lara, but she winked at Amy over her coffee. A silent nod of thanks for keeping a secret.

Amy had her dad drop her off at work and Lara stayed home with the dog. Coming home that afternoon, she found Lara flipping through the news, bored. They caught up, Lara eager to know what Amy had been up to these last three months. When dad came home, they unpacked the take-out cartons and tucked in.

Flipping through her notebook, Amy went on. "It's weird. Every culture has some version of a shapeshifter but there's no consistency to any of it. But maybe that's how it works, you know? It affects everyone differently."

Lara shifted in her chair, uncomfortable with discussing it openly like this. Like chatting about some flaw, like a stutter or a wart, as dinner conversation. "We don't have to talk about this," she said.

"Of course we do." Amy jerked her head up in surprise. "Not to be rude, Lara, but you're a lycan-thrope. How often does that happen?"

Gallagher sipped his beer. "It's not a freak show, Amy."

"I know. I'm just trying to find some answers to something that's kinda unprecedented. I mean, what is it? Is it biological, like a disease, or is it supernatural? What triggers it? Does the moon have anything to do with it?"

"It has nothing to do with the moon," Lara said.

Amy looked at her dad. "See, there's something. You have to understand something first before you can deal with it."

"Isn't it past your bedtime?" Gallagher groused.

She ignored him. "So how does it work? Can you switch anytime at will?"

"It's always there, just under the surface. I'm not sure how to describe it. It's like keeping a muscle clenched. All I'd have to do is let go."

"But there is a trigger?" Amy perked up.

"It runs off your emotions. Raw, primitive ones. Like fear." Here she shot a look towards Gallagher and looked away. "Some other emotion."

Gallagher coughed, watched his daughter take notes. Notes, for god's sakes.

"So what's the deal with the silver? When Dad cut you with it last night, you stopped convulsing."

"Silver can shut it down. If I do it before I'm too far gone." Lara pushed her plate back. "Why that works, I don't know."

Amy, tapping her pen against her lips. "Maybe it's a cure."

"There is no cure."

Gallagher squared Lara with a look. "We don't know that."

"Well there's death," she said. "That cure is garaunteed."

"Ivan Prall thought he had a cure."

"He was wrong."

Amy watched them, eyes moving from one to the other like a tennis match. Hearing the tension under their voices. There was more to the story. "Forget about a cure for now. We just need to manage the symptoms."

"What do you mean?"

"How does the silver knife work?"

"By drawing blood. Cutting the silver into the bloodflow shuts down the transformation." Lara held out her forearm, the scars crisscrossed over the skin. "If I catch it in time."

"Why silver?" Gallagher said. "Of all the weird things in the folklore, why does that one work?"

"It's pure," Amy suggested. "The ancients believed it could purify illness. Silver can prevent sepsis too."

"It's a moot point," Lara said. Impatient, having already run through the same arguments in her head for months. "Maybe it's a chemical reaction or maybe its a placebo. I believe it will work, so it does. There's no way to know for sure."

Gallagher sneered. "So what, we just give up?"

"No, we just face some simple truths. There are no real answers." She nodded at Amy's notebook. "It's fairy tales and conjecture. Nada mas."

He let it go. Lara reverted to Spanish when riled.

"It works in piercings," Amy offered, oblivious.

"Piercings?"

Amy clutched her earlobe although there was no earring to be seen. "It's the one metal that won't cause infection. Ask any tattoo artist."

"Again, fascinating but not that useful." Lara held a palm to the sky. "You see the dilemma."

"But in your case the silver only works if you cut before you're too far gone?" Amy chewed her pen then bolted up and tossed her notes onto the table. "I got an idea. Be right back."

She ran for the stairs. Lara frowned and rose to clear the table. Gallagher tucked the leftovers in the fridge and then leaned against the counter. "Why are you so quick to dismiss any idea that might help?"

"This part of it is new to you, John. You said yourself you hadn't thought about what to do once you found me." She ran the faucet, plugged the sink and looked back at him. "I've done nothing but think about all this for months. My expectations for a happy ending are a little soggy by now."

"And that's the problem. You've already given up." He brushed her shoulder, sliding more plates into the water. "Because you've been working the problem alone, with no one to bounce ideas off of. That's why the lieutenant insists we work in pairs. The open murder book will swallow a detective working solo. Simple as that."

"Facing reality is not the same as giving up."

She felt his hand on her back. "Hey," he said. "You're not alone. Not anymore. So give your old partner a chance to suss out the landscape, huh?" His hand slid down to her waist. "Listen, last night was weird. My bad. I wasn't thinking."

She turned the water off. "There were two of us there. Half of that bad was mine."

A tiny respite from the tough exterior and wary-looking glances. He scrambled for the right words to say but then Amy came crashing back down the stairs.

"Ta-da!" Amy bounded up, breathless. She held up a small metal bolt.

Gallagher squinted. "What is it?"

"It's a piercing stud. Silver."

"You want to give Lara a piercing?"

Amy scowled at her dad, turning to Lara. "Instead of cutting when the change comes on, this will keep the silver in your skin all the time. Or at least until it heals. Then we'll have to stud in a new spot."

"Let me see that." Lara held the stud up to the light. Over an inch long, thick.

Gallagher looked skeptical. "It's a bit big for an earring, isn't it?"

"Not her ear, dad." Amy beamed and patted Lara's stomach. "Your navel."

Even the dog hung its face in doubt.

Lara handed the stud back. "Your circus, kid. Let's give it a shot."

"ARE you sure that's sterilized enough?"

"It's fine. Don't block the light."

"So what do you do, just stab it through?"

"Dad, please..."

Lara Mendes lay on the living room floor, an old beach towel spread underneath her. She hoisted up her shirt and exposed her belly. The muscles taut, ribs poking up in ripples through the skin.

Amy sat on Lara's legs, holding a thick piercing needle still wet with rubbing alcohol. The silver bolt, likewise sterilized, was pinched in her latex-gloved fingers.

Gallagher kneeled over them, training a flash-light onto Lara's navel. "Where did you get that thing?"

"It's Gabby's."

"I shoulda known. And what exactly were two planning on doing with this stuff? Giving each other studs?"

Lara shot him a look. "John. Not now."

"Okay, hold still." Amy bent to her work, pinching up a wedge of flesh and threading the needle against the skin. The instrument shook, as did her whole hand.

"Ouch."

"Hold still."

"I am."

It was harder than it looked. Blood dribbled out and welled up in the navel and Amy couldn't see the point of contact. She pushed and Lara flinched but Amy couldn't push the needle any further.

"Is it done?"

"I can't get it to go through."

"Just push it," Gallagher said.

"I am!" Amy snapped. "Do you want to try it?"

"Nope. This is your idea." He grabbed a towel and smeared away the blood. "Lara, look at the ceiling and hold your breath."

Lara looked away, saw the dog watching them.

"Get a good grip," Gallagher whispered to his daughter. "Then give it all you got."

Amy held her breath too and stabbed. Lara gasped and her stomach caved in but the needle went through. "Okay," Amy panted. "Gimme the stud."

"That stings."

"Almost there," he said.

Amy lined up the stud, pulled the needle through and threaded the stud in. Gallagher dabbed the blood away and Amy capped the silver stud. She leaned back, holding her bloodied hands up. "There. How does that feel?"

Lara sighed, looked at them both. "Good. It feels good." In truth, she felt nothing but a sharp sting. No discernible change inside, no exorcism of the monster coiled in her heat. But Amy seemed pleased so she kept that information to herself.

24

GALLAGHER CAME TO WORK with a tray of tall coffee cups in hand, the fancy stuff that Detective Wade always went for. He was feeling magnamous and generous, perhaps a little guilty too. Wade was a decent guy who had tolerated his black moods and frequent disappearances with nary a complaint nor snide remark. Buying a round of coffee, even the froo-froo stuff Wade indulged in, wouldn't make up for all of it but it was a start.

Gallagher strode with an uncharacteristic light step. Despite the fact that he had left his teenage daughter alone with his former homicide partner, who had been presumed dead but was contrarily alive and cursed with lycanthropy, the day seemed especially fine. He ambled off to work with a lightness in his heart so rare he barely recognized what it was. It was Christmas too.

"What's all this?" Detective Wade looked at the tray in Gallagher's hand. Wary, he said "You need a favor, G?"

"My turn to buy the joe." Gallagher slid the tall cup onto Wade's desk and held the empty tray for a moment before flinging it like a Frisbee across the bullpen to Detective Kopzych's desk.

"Your turn was in November."

"Merry Christmas."

Wade plucked the lid off the cup and looked inside, idly wondering if it had been poisoned. "You feeling okay, buddy?"

Gallagher shrugged. "It's just coffee, homes. Don't go all weepy."

"Somebody got lucky last night." Wade wagged his finger, grinning wide. "Come on, muchacho. What's the poor woman's name?"

"Your sister." He looked over the mess of his in-box. "What fraction of the daily manure pile are we tackling today?"

"Rowe and Dorsey caught a floater on the riverbank over in Lakewood. They might need some help combing the weeds."

"Better than sitting here." He pushed the paper-work away. The desk phone buzzed and he banged up the receiver. "Gallagher."

"G, you got another hit." Taylor down in IT. "Pretty good match too."

"Dude, it's your lucky day. You can shut down the bloodhounds. I won't be needing it anymore."

"Now you tell me? Shit, man." Taylor wheezed into the phone. "You wanna hear this last hit or was this a monumental waste of my time and talent too?"

"Naw, let's hear it."

"Some lady reported that her dog was killed by something. A bear or a giant dog, she didn't know what. But it ripped her pooch to hamburger."

"Where was this?"

"Northeast Stafford. No Po."

North Portland. Close indeed.

LARA was going stir crazy, that was plain enough. She couldn't sit still and Amy watched her cross repeatedly to the bay window to stare outside. The spruce lined street and the telephone lines drooping from pole to pole in a cat's cradle of humming wire. Like a date abandoned on prom night, Lara would turn away and busy herself with some task only to return to the double-glazed glass again.

"Are you expecting someone?" Amy asked, looking up from her creaky old laptop propped open on the kitchen table.

"What?" Lara turned, her eyes a thousand yards away.

"You keep looking out the window."

"It's nothing." Lara strode to the kitchen and folded her arms. She put away the two dishes in the dryrack and wiped the counter with the cloth and folded her arms again. "Just cabin fever, I guess. No big deal."

Amy studied her for a moment and a curious study she was. Different from how she used to know her but it wasn't just the reedy thinness of her or the sombre hollows of her eyes. A twitchy edge underwrit Lara Mendes's every movement. Her eyes darted at any stirring and her head constantly cocked at an angle, as if her ear snagged on some sound only she heard. Or the dog. More than once she had caught Lara and the husky turn their heads to the door at precisely the same instant and pause. It was freaky. "What was it like? Being on your own out there."

"Harsh. Scary sometimes. Lonely."

"Of course," Amy nodded. "Still, it must have been kinda cool being totally free. No one to answer to. No commitments, no responsibilities."

Lara shook her head. "There was nothing free about it. I was living hand-to-mouth, scrabbling for any scrap. It's unbelievably hard, being that alone. There were more than a few nights I went hungry or slept out in the open." She swept her hand before her, as if dealing an invisible hand. "Freedom like that is a burden."

Amy mulled it over but had little notion of what it meant, neither precedent nor antecedent. She changed the subject. "Let's get out of here for awhile."

"That's not a good idea."

"Psshaw. We'll hit Mississippi Ave and go walking, get something to eat. I still got Christmas shopping to do."

Lara's eyes drifted to the window again, the yearning writ plain across her face but she sobered. "No. I can't risk being seen."

"What are the chances? Hang on." Amy ran to the hall closet, dug through it and came back with a fur trimmed bomber's hat. Dark sunglasses. "Wear this."

Lara took the glasses and headgear, turning them over in her hands. Before she could protest, Amy clapped her hands together like a little kid. "Try it on."

Humoring the girl, Lara went to the mirror in the hallway and pulled the hat on, pushed the glasses on her nose. Plain and anonymous. Any passerby on a cold street.

"See?" Amy plunged back into the closet and thrust a long coat into Lara's hands. "Your army parka looks a little conspicuous. Wear this."

Lara reminded herself that she was the adult here and the plan was foolishly risky but the enthusiasm of a young girl can be rolling tidal wave. Hard to push back.

A short trip, she comprised. Just enough to get some air and stretch her legs. No harm, no foul.

"Roosevelt was a good boy. He never did nobody no wrong. It's just awful." The woman's name was Maggie and she lived in a small but tidy bungalow on Stafford Street. She'd let Gallagher in and the two of them stood in her foyer, Maggie folding her arms against the draft whistling under the door. "Just goddawful it was."

"What time was this?" Gallagher had his notebook out but had yet to record any detail. "Roughly?"

"Past midnight. Closer to one, probably."

"And what did you see?"

"Roosevelt started barking something awful. He's a good boy, only barks when there's trouble. He *was* a good boy, I should say." The woman plucked a tissue from her sleeve, dabbed her nose and tucked the tissue back where it came. "I came down to bring him inside, hush him up. There was this goddawful roar, like nothing I ain't never heard and Roosevelt got real quiet. Then..."

Gallagher waited for her composure to return, watching her retrieve the crumpled tissue from her sleeve again. He patted his pockets for a tissue pack but had none.

"This thing swooped out of nowhere and just took him off. Roosevelt was there one minute and then this blur of something and then whoosh, my dog was gone. I went outside later, to call him. He was crumpled up against the back fence like a broken-up old toy." She started to cry again. "I didn't even recognize him at first he was so torn up."

"And the animal that took Roosevelt, you said it was a big dog."

"I don't know what else it could have been. I thought maybe a bear, but that's silly."

"Can you describe it?"

"It was big. Fast. That's all I saw."

"What colour was it?"

"What?"

"Anything. Light, dark?"

"I don't know. It was a blur and it was loud. Goddawful sound I never want to hear."

Gallagher peered out the window, looking over the yard. "Do you mind if I take a look at the spot where you found him?"

"Go ahead. You're welcome to see Roosevelt too, if you want?"

"He's still here?"

"Nobody's come to pick him up yet." She nodded towards the hallway. "He's in the garage."

Maggie led the way into the garage and popped the overhead light on. A Chrysler Reliant took up most of the space, asleep under a layer of dust. Maggie cinched her cardigan tighter against the drop in temperature and shuffled past the car to the stack of garbage cans. "Been two days since I called and it's damn outrageous it's taken you people this long, I don't mind telling you. Leaving me to sit with the poor dog and him two days dead."

"Animal services should have picked him up by now."

Maggie turned, looked at him. "Ain't you animal services?"

"No ma'am. I'm a police officer."

Her brow arced in a veneer of disapproval. "You forget your uniform this morning, young man?"

"No. I'm a detective. We get to dress a little better than the beat cops."

"Detective? Now that's more like it."

Settled next to the recycling bin was a plastic storage tub with a fitted lid. Gallagher pointed at it. "Is this it?"

"Yes." Maggie turned away, waving her hand as if to call it all off. "You help yourself, if you don't mind. I don't need to see that again."

She crossed to the single window in the garage and burnished a clear spot from the grime on it. Gallagher snapped off the container lid. A garbage bag folded inside. He folded back the plastic and turned his head from the rank smell that wafted up. Poor Roosevelt was a tangled mass of fur and pokey ribslats. What fur was left was dark with blood. It was hard to even recognize the carcass as canine.

Snapping on the latex gloves, he turned to the dog owner at the window. "It's awfully cold out here, Maggie. Why don't you go back inside. I'll put everything back as I found it. I'll call animal services and get them to come for Roosevelt right away."

"Thank you." She shuffled back to the door and stopped before going inside. "Terrible way to go," she said, nodding to the bin at his feet. "Man or animal, no one deserves to die like that."

He agreed and waited until she went back into the house. Turning back to the makeshift tomb, he spread out some old newspaper across the floor and lifted out pieces of the carcass. He laid them over the paper, the severed legs and crushed torso of exposed ribs, the head flopping loose like a rag. Laid out on the floor, he examined the wounds in the hide and the scoring on the snapped bones. A chill rippled down his backbone.

He'd seen marks like this before.

WINTER in Portland. What little snow there was slurred into a grey slush along the curb. The cold was damp and bone-seeping, not crisp like the open country but Lara Mendes breathed it all in. She passed faces along the sidewalk, looked up at the festive lights strung from lampposts and the tinsel garlands in the shop windows and realized again how much she missed her old home. A sharp tug at her heart over these simple things that she had exiled herself from. A girl half her age at her side, linked at her arm as she pointed out at this particularly window display or that cyclist outfitted in a full Santa costume, the red felt material mottled dark from the slushy streetspray. Portland with its fabled citizenry of artists, shamans, fools and iconoclasts, each denizen determined to outwit the last in eccentricity and all of it washing the streets in a miasma of gleeful oddity. Lara relished every step, awestruck at how homesick she was for a city she had so often complained about.

"Oh, I love this store." Amy pulled her into another oddly painted shop with a bizarre window display. Inside, the aisles were narrowed by racks of vintage clothes and the air cloyed with burnt patchouli. Amy flipped through the hangers and plucked out a shirt, holding it up for inspection. "This is cool. It would look great on you. Where's the change room?"

Lara removed her shades and looked the item over. Honestly touched at Amy's suggestions at first but now, the fifteenth or thirtieth time, she could muster no more sincerity. "I can't look at anymore, Amy. Why don't you finish your Christmas list. I'll wait outside."

The girl's face fell and she re-examined the item. "You don't like it? It's your color."

Lara unzipped her coat, stifled in the humid confines of the store. She peeled off her hat and shook out her hair. "I've hit my limit."

Amy wondered if she'd done something wrong. "You okay?"

"Yeah. I just need some air. You go on." She shooed the girl along and wound through the tight aisles for the door.

Lara stood under the canvas eaves of the shop and drew breath through her nose. The wind smelled clean after the suffocating reek of hippie perfume, steam-drying and mothballs. She watched the cars trundle past, tires splaying a brownish sludge onto the sidewalk. A car horn blared up North Mississippi, followed by the bellowing of some irate driver and Lara peered down the causeway to see a cab driver arguing with a bike courier. Some things never change.

Pedestrians moved around her, shoulders up against the cold and sidestepping the puddles of slush. Shoppers rushing home with their treasures.

"Lara?"

Lara froze, too afraid to turn and face the voice but it was too late not to. She had forgotten to put the hat and sunglasses back on before hitting the street.

"Lara Mendes?"

Lara turned. Charlene Farbre stood before her with a look of disbelief dropping her face. Detective Charlene Farbre, her old friend and colleague from Assault Detail. Lara scrambled for some ruse or lie but her mind tangled in too many threads until it was overruled by one simple urge. Run.

Charlene took a step closer but remained wary, as if some elaborate prank was playing around her.

"Lara, it's me, Charlene. My God, I can't believe it's you..."

Lara watched the woman's eyes search her own for some tick of recognition and Lara remembered that she looked different now. Some gaunt phantom of herself and this was what Detective Charlene Farbre was trying to parse.

"Perdón?" Lara blurted up without thinking. Then, rolling with the ruse, she said "No hablo Ingles."

Charlene leaned back as if she'd touched something hot. She reached out for Lara's arm. "Lara, stop. It's me. Where have you been? Everyone searched—"

"No me toques." Lara snatched her arm back but her heart stung at the hurt look on her old friend's face. She turned and marched away, bootheels clicking dully on the wet pavement. She didn't look back as Charlene called after her. Amy, still in the shop, would wonder where she'd gone. She'd explain later. Lara turned down the first corner and broke into a run.

Charlene Farbre stood on the slushy sidewalk calling out to an empty street. It didn't make any sense. The woman had looked so much like her missing friend and yet, not quite. Altered somehow. The Spanish had thrown her and all she could surmise was that this woman bore an eerie resemblance to Lara Mendes. But Lara was Hispanic...

Charlene trudged back to her car, wondering why on earth her old friend would pretend not to know her. Turning the ignition, she saw a young woman rush out of a store and look frantically up and down the street as if she'd lost something. Charlene hit the wipers to get a better look at the girl before she ran off in the same direction as the mystery woman. She knew this girl. Had in fact met her this summer. Her name was Amy. The teen-aged daughter of Lara's former partner in Homicide Detail.

25

LARA RAN FOR COVER, SHELTER, anything. She didn't know what she was running to until she saw it. A small clapboard church on Skidmore, the door illuminated by a single naked bulb.

The door groaned as she pushed against it. The nave was dark, the only light glowing from a dozen candles at the feet of the virgin. The smell of polished wood and candlewax was strong and it tripped childhood memories. For a tiny moment, Lara idly wondered if she would burst into flames stepping foot inside a church. She closed the heavy door behind her, took another step towards the pews and nothing happened. God was too busy to incinerate a tiny monster such as herself.

The pew was solid but comfortable. She studied the enormous cross suspended over the altar, the wooden figure twisted and bleeding on the crosstree. Coming back to Portland had been a mistake. What did she think was going to happen? A happily ever after with Gallagher? An insane notion. There was no place for her here. She should have ran the moment she spotted Gallagher. Further into the wilderness, deep and remote to someplace where there were no roads, no people, no life save that of rocks and trees.

She would go. There was just no other choice. The last two days had been so good. Some small scrap of normalcy. Not being alone. Being able to talk to someone without guarding her words. Sitting over a cup of coffee listening to John and Amy nanner across the breakfast table. The thought of leaving it behind again broke something inside her.

A noise rang out, echoing over the vaulted ceiling. She wasn't alone.

Four pews up the aisle before her, a figure rose and sat up. Some intransigent sleeping off a drunk on the church pew. The man leaned back and stretched his elbows on the backrest of the pew. His boots came up and propped upon the pew before him, crossed casually at the ankles.

"You see what I mean now," the man spoke. "Suicide becomes the viable option."

Lara slid down the pew as if pricked with a needle, deflating from a slow leak. She knew who it was before he even spoke. Who else could it be?

Grissom didn't look back at her. His head tilted up as he studied the cross in the sacristy. "Sorry it didn't work out for you. You almost smell happy to me."

Lara patted her pockets for a weapon but there was no weapon. Grissom didn't move, his feet up like he was at a baseball game. She watched his back. A clear, easy headshot. If only she had something to shoot him with.

"That was a hell of a shot you took at me." Grissom tilted his head slightly. "Silver-tipped bullets? Goddamn girl, where'd you get those? You got any idea how hard it is to dig those slugs out of your leg? I'm still limping."

She cast her eyes back to the door. If Grissom had a game leg, she could probably outrun him.

"I'm guessing your boyfriend there had the silver loads. He knows what you are, doesn't he?"

"Why did you follow me?" Lara kept her timbre steady. Don't show fear. "My answer hasn't changed."

"You know you can't stay here. I'm giving you one last chance to set things right."

She looked at the door again but said nothing.

"You got three options, honey. I'm offering you one. The second is to do yourself in, which I guess those silver-tips might come in handy. But if you stay here, I guarantee you you will lose control and the wolf will kill everyone you know."

"That's supposed to scare me?"

"Who do you think the wolf will go for first? Those closest to you. The scents she knows. You want that?" His boots thudded to the floor and he tilted off the pew and stood. He pivoted and finally looked at her. "There's a rest stop out on highway five, just outside of north Van. You meet me there tonight and we'll leave without rustling a leaf and your people will be safe. If you don't show, I can't guarantee their safety. Simple as that."

Lara felt every muscle constrict, like a spring coiling. Fight or run.

"It's unusual to hold out this long," he said. "To walk that thin line between wolf and human. But you got to go all the way, Lara. Become a true wolf. The pack needs you." Grissom made a slight bow and sauntered to the rectory door. He disappeared behind a curtain and then she heard a door click shut. He had limped the whole way, favoring his left leg.

GALLAGHER clocked out, wondering how long it would take Lieutenant Cabrisi to read him riot for his lax hours. He'd deal with it when it came. For now, he was fixated on the wreckage of the dog carcass and the fact that three calls home had gone unanswered. Lara wouldn't pick up but Amy was supposed to be home.

Cutting through the parking garage to his space, he heard the heavy door slam open behind him. Heels ringing smartly off the concrete.

"Gallagher?"

Turning, he saw Detective Farbre marching up. "Hey Charlene. What's up?"

"I think I just saw Lara Mendes," she said.

He froze, feigned surprise. "What are you talking about?"

"North Mississippi, just standing on the street. I swear to God it was her. Has she contacted you?"

"No." Keel this easy, he thought. "Are sure it was her?"

"I don't know. It looked like her, but different. Like she was ill."

"When was this? What did she say?"

"She spoke nothing but Spanish to me. But I swear to God she knew it was me. I think she's been here in town all this time, hiding."

"Why would she do that?"

"She was involved in Lieutenant Vogel's death. Maybe she's hiding something."

"You knew Lara as well as I did. Better even. Does that sound like her?"

"I don't know, John. The woman vanished into thin air three months ago and her skinny doppelganger shows up wandering the streets. I don't know what to make of it but we need to find this woman."

He started for his truck, keys jingling his hand. "Okay, we will. But right now I gotta run home. Keep me posted, okay?"

"Gallagher, what the hell?" Charlene's eyes bugged from their sockets. "Your missing partner is out there somewhere and you don't care?"

He climbed behind the wheel. "Course I do. But I got something right now."

She stopped the door from closing. "John, has she contacted you?"

"No."

She zeroed in on his eyes and he knew he had to pull this off but Charlene Farbre was a detective. She was lied to on a daily basis and her internal bullshit-detector was damn near faultless. The jig was already up. Charlene's face had gone from suspicion to hurt. "You know. How could you keep this secret? After all this."

Gallagher took a breath and squared her with a look of his own. "Charlene, please. I can't explain. Just stay out of it for now."

The look on her face was terrible. Shock, hurt, betrayal. He slammed the door shut, fired the ignition and pulled out of the parking space. He'd have to deal with it later. Could Charlene be trusted if he told her the truth? Could she help? Or would she, like any sane person, go running in the opposite direction?

Wheeling onto Multnomah, his phone went off. He fished it up, hoping it wasn't Farbre.

"Dad?"

"Amy, I've been calling the house all afternoon. Where are you?"

Silence on the other end. Ambient street noise in the background.

"Amy? What's wrong?"

"Lara's gone. Dad, I'm sorry. I've lost her."

"Okay, slow down. What happened?"

Twinkling lights whooshed over the windshield as he listened to Amy's rushed, fumbling train of events. He told her to calm down then asked where she was.

"I'm still here on Mississip, looking for her. Do you think she's at home?"

"Stay where you are. I'll stop at the house. If she's not there, I'll come find you. Go inside somewhere, stay warm. I'll call back in five minutes."

He hung up, pushed the accelerator and gunned for home.

AMY pulled the hood of her coat up as the snow fell around her. Trudging two blocks west and still searching for Lara, she stood under a streetlamp trying to decide whether to keep going or to double back, vainly hoping the missing woman would return.

"You'll catch your death out here in this damp."

Amy turned. A tall man in a dark coat stepped into the streetlamp's pool of light. He turned his collar up against the chill and smiled at her. "I hate winter in this city. Too wet, too damp." He nodded at the grey slush around Amy's feet. "Too goddamn mucky."

Amy didn't react. Chatty strangers were nothing unusual, especially on this street. The man didn't seem like trouble, didn't have the twitchy look of the crazy nor the unsteady stagger of the dead drunk. There was something about his face however, that kept pulling her gaze like a magnet. Not necessarily good-looking but something that drew her in.

The man tilted his face to the falling snow. "How many days until Christmas?"

"You don't have a calendar?" Amy said.

"I kindly gave up on 'em."

"Uh-huh. So how do you know what day it is?"

"Who cares what day of the week it is? Or the artificial number the calendar dictates. You need to know the season is all."

Amy scanned the street for movement but nothing moved. Even the traffic seemed to have given up and gone home. "Season, huh? Must be hell keeping a dental appointment."

He watched her eyeballing the deserted street. "Looking for somebody?"

Amy gave him a once-over. She had pretty good instincts for creeps and weirdos but the man didn't trip any of her Spidey-senses. Still. "My dad's picking me up. He's a cop."

"You're old man's a Johnny Law?" The stranger's brow arced in genuine surprise. "Well ain't that the drizzling shits."

Amy took a step back, a tiny Spidey-sense tingling like a finger plucking a piano wire. Maybe the guy knew her dad. Was in fact some perp that her father had busted. She peeled her eyes to the street, willing the old Cherokee to appear.

"What's your name?"

She didn't respond, other than to take a step away, her feet freezing in her boots.

"Will you give your old man a message for me?"

She stamped her feet. This was getting weird. Where was Dad?

The man just kept grinning at her. "You tell him you can't keep a wild animal. It don't work."

"What's that supposed to mean?"

"Means you can't take something wild and make it a pet. You keep it inside and it will sicken and die. Worse, it will turn on you."

"Uh huh," Amy said. "So that's like a metaphor for something? Clever."

"No metaphor, just a fact." The man stirred and looked behind him, as if sensing someone was there but the street remained empty. "You tell him."

LARA burst out of the church and stood under a streetlight. Her heart was beating faster and that eerie tingle had started buzzing through her spine. The first telltale signs of the change, tripped by Grissom's sudden appearance. She patted her pockets only to remember that she was wearing Amy's coat. No silver blade, no kill-switch.

Not now. She couldn't afford the risk of changing in the city. Too many people, too many dangers. She fought to breathe through it, knowing full well that panic only fueled the transformation.

It took a moment before noticing that the ache in her backbone had receded. Her heart slowed. The change dying off before it bloomed. The stud. Her hand went to her belly and she felt the silver piercing through her clothes. It was working. Amy was right.

Amy.

She ran back to the avenue, where the falling snow refracted the holiday lights. The traffic had reduced to a few vehicles slushing their tires in the muck and barely a pedestrian anywhere. Save one, a slight figure the next block over. It was Amy.

Lara quickened her pace, keeping the girl in her sights when a second figure emerged from the shadows. Tall, male, talking to Amy. A friend or some stewbum begging for change?

The man straightened up and turned in her direction, letting his face fall under the haze of the streetlamps. Lara's stomach dropped.

Grissom, bold as day, talking to Amy on the street. She started to run. Grissom nodded in her direction before exchanging a few words with the girl and then he limped away and disappeared into the night.

Amy looked up, spotted her friend and came running. "Lara, where did you go? You gave me a heart attack!"

"I'm sorry. I had to leave."

"Don't do that to me." Amy clutched Lara's hand, as if to keep her from disappearing again. "I don't need that kind of panic. Why did you book on me?"

Lara cut her off. "Why were you talking to that man? What did he want?"

"Him?" Amy leaned back in surprise. "Just some chatty weirdo. He doesn't like calendars."

"Did he threaten you?"

"No. He's just another bizarro. This street's crawling with them."

A horn blared, cutting short Lara's next question. The Cherokee rolled up out of the swirling snow and hewed to the curb. The door swung open.

"Get in," Gallagher barked.

26

THE DOG PRANCED AROUND everyone's knees as the trio tangled inside and kicked off their boots but received little more than a pat on the head. The mood was foul. Gallagher clunked the bottle of Jamesons onto the table while Lara filled a water glass. Amy scrounged a soda from the fridge and braced herself for the coming lecture from dad.

The husky's tail ceased wagging as he withdrew to his corner near the door.

Gallagher crashed into a chair. "Honey, can you give us a minute?"

Amy looked at her dad then to Lara. She had apologized for taking such a dumb risk, owning all responsibility and expecting to be shouted deaf for it. All he had said was 'it's okay' and then nothing. Not a good sign. Lara had said even less.

And now this. A stony silence before being asked to leave the room so the grown-ups could talk. So much like the last year her parents were together it was spooky. Well, she wasn't twelve anymore. "What's going on? You two are weird. More than usual, I mean."

"We just need to talk." He tilted his head towards the staircase. "Go on."

This wasn't fair and Amy refused to budge. "Do we really need secrets?" she said, looking to one and then the other. "After all this?"

"Yes. Now vamonos."

Amy folded her arms and looked over at the dog.

"John," Lara said. "Let her stay."

He grimaced but the somber look in Lara's eyes squelched his protest. "Okay. Let's pow wow."

They joined him at the table. He pushed the second tumbler towards Lara and said, "You ran into Charlene Farbre."

"How did you know?"

"She confronted me about it. I lied but she saw right through it."

"Who's Charlene?" Amy asked.

"Friend of Lara's," he said. "A detective. You met her last summer when Lara was in the hospital."

"Oh yeah," Amy nodded. "She was nice."

"That's why I ran." Lara swirled the liquid in her glass. "I tried to blow her off but..."

"She's tough," Gallagher shrugged. "Hard to bullshit past her."

Amy sat up. "Can't we tell her the truth? Maybe she can help?"

"It's too risky." Lara shook her head. "I've been missing for three months after an incident involving the death of a police lieutenant. Charlene's a good cop but she couldn't lay all that aside."

"Even if she knew the truth?" Amy objected.

"We can't take the chance," Gallagher said.

"It gets worse." Lara looked at the two of them and took a breath. "Grissom survived. He's here in Portland."

He nearly dropped his glass. "How do you know?"

"Who's Grissom?" Amy said.

"He cornered me after I ran into Charlene."

"But you shot him."

"I winged him. He's got a limp." Lara sipped her drink. "He must have tracked me all the way back here."

"Shit..."

"Who's Grissom?" Amy repeated, louder this time.

"The man you were talking to."

This time Gallagher's tumbler fell. Whisky puddled and dripped off the table. His eyes turned murderous, then they latched onto his daughter. "He spoke to you? Did he do anything? Threaten you?"

"No. I thought he was just another weirdo," Amy huffed, still in the dark. "What's the big deal?"

"Grissom's like me." Lara's voice was hushed. Ashamed. "He wants me to go with him."

"Where?"

"I don't know. Somewhere far away where there are others like him." Lara knocked back the glass, added "Like us."

Gallagher's jaw stiffened. "What did he say?"

"He expects me to meet him. Tonight."

"He thinks you're just gonna show up?"

Lara put her drink down. "He knows about both of you. Said there's a price to pay if I don't show."

The chair squeaked as Gallagher shot up and turned to the sink. His knuckles white. "Goddamnit, Lara..."

"It's not her fault, dad." Amy shot back.

"No? Then whose, yours? For taking a stroll down North Miss?"

"Enough John," Lara interrupted. "This isn't helping."

The dog raised its head, ears tuned to the hoarse voices. It rose to all fours and padded to Gallagher but he ignored it. Amy clucked and the dog came and she plunged her fingers into the nap of its hide. She looked at Lara. "What are we going to do?"

Neither of the adults said a word. The husky nosed Amy's hands, licking the palm.

Gallagher took up his emptied glass and refilled it and left the room.

Lara sat at the table alone, mulling over the havoc she had wreaked. Amy had gone to her room and Gallagher remained in his office. A nettle of guilt stinging its way through her guts. She looked at the clock above the stove. Ten twenty-two. Less than two hours before midnight.

Her parka hung on a hook in the hallway. The clothes on her back, no other belongings to pack. Everything else had been abandoned in the little shack back in Weepers. Doesn't matter now. She would ensure that the silver knife was there in the pocket and slip out the front door. Get away from this family as fast as she could and thumb or steal a ride and meet Grissom out at some deserted rest stop. When the opportunity arose, she would plunge the silver blade into his breast and drive it home into his stony heart.

Game over. That same blade would cut through her wrists and bleed out to its sordid conclusion. End of the line for the goddamn werewolves.

"Going somewhere?" Gallagher strode in clutching a canvass duffel bag.

Lara folded the parka over her arm. "This has gone too far. I've led him straight to you and to Amy."

He laid the duffel across a chair and unzipped it. "First thing we have to do is protect Amy. I guess sending her off to her mom's isn't an option, right?"

Lara shook her head. "He's already tagged her scent. He'll just track her there."

"Maybe he'll eat my ex-wife instead."

"That's not even funny," she said. "What about the precinct? Surrounded by police, even he wouldn't try that."

"That's a good idea. Tricky to do without raising a lot of questions."

"Maybe Charlene could help after all? Is there anyone else in the detail you haven't pissed off?"

"Not many. If I have to, I'll just sneak her in and plant her at my desk. Once she's safe, you and I need to hold up somewhere secure and we let Grissom come to us." Reaching into the bag, he unloaded gear onto the kitchen table. His service issue Glock and the big Desert Eagle. Spare magazines for both. The shotgun with a dark parkerized finish. Last of all, he placed three metal tubes onto the table.

One rolled away and Lara caught it, turning it over in her hand. "Flashbangs?"

"You remember Mockler from the tactical unit? I got him to swipe me a few."

Lara thumbed the release pin. "I don't know how effective these will be."

"Better than nothing," he shrugged. "If I coulda gotten my hands on real grenades, I would have. We'll have to settle for these." Gallagher reached for the Eagle, spun it round and pushed it forward butt first. "The silver tips only fit that piece. It's fifty cal, so I figure a headshot should be enough to put that thing down."

Lara took up the piece and tested the balance in her hand. Heavy, even with her left hand gripped underneath for support. She racked the slide and popped the round from the chamber. "How many of these silver rounds do you have?"

"What's in the magazine. Maybe a dozen more."

She held the cartridge up to the light and scraped her thumb over the shiny point end. Her thumb tingled against the metal. The bullet was enormous and the impact from it would be devastating, silver tip or no. "This ought to do a lot of damage." She snapped the slide back and slid the magazine out. The single round fitted back into the magazine and she snapped it home.

"It's not much of a plan," he said, loading the weapons back into the duffel. "But it's all I got."

"It'll do until we think of something else." Lara looked at the clock again. "We should go."

"SO I just twiddle my thumbs at the police station while you two geniuses go off hunting monsters?"

Amy didn't think much of the plan either and said so. Repeatedly. She tugged her boots on, dragging her heels the whole way.

"In a nutshell, yeah." Gallagher hefted the bag onto his shoulder. "C'mon, let's go."

Lara opened the door to the garage. "It's just for tonight, Amy. Just so you're safe."

"And what happens tomorrow?"

Lara shot Gallagher a look but he didn't know either. He shooed his daughter into the garage. "Let's go."

"See?" Amy blew the hair up out of her eyes. "You haven't thought it through."

In the garage, Gallagher passed the duffel onto Lara. "Hold this. I want to grab a few more things. Amy, open the roll-up."

The husky followed Amy as she tugged on the garage door. It rolled up with a squeal and stopped at her eye-level and wouldn't raise anymore. "Is the dog staying here?"

"What?" Gallagher said, rifling tools off the shelf.

"He comes with us." Lara ducked under roll-up door and opened the back hatch of the truck.

Amy scratched the dog's ear. "Wouldn't he be safer with me?"

"Not in the precinct." Lara looked over the street. The snow had stopped falling. "They wouldn't let him past the door."

"We need him with us." Gallagher followed them outside and tossed a box into the back of the Cherokee. "He's our early warning system."

"You mean he's cannon-fodder."

The dog, as if understanding the girl's words, raised its head to her and trotted away. Its nose jerked westward, as if yanked hard, and pointed at the darkened street. It bolted away, disappearing through a hedge.

"Now you done it," Gallagher gruffed. He whistled for the dog. "Here boy!"

Lara stopped cold, looking on in the direction the dog ran. "John, be quiet."

"What is it?"

Lara stepped to the edge of the driveway, eyes cast down the row of houses. There were neither cars nor pedestrians anywhere.

"Lara?"

A small sound reached their ears, like a soft popping noise. Amy squinted west, trying to see what it was. Something about the far end of her street seemed wrong.

It was the streetlights, winking out one by one like snuffed candles. Their street vanished into darkness at each popping sound. A tidal wave of nightfall rolling down the avenue towards them.

Lara took a step backwards. "Oh Jesus."

"Get in the truck."

From the darkness, the sound of the dog barking.

"The dog," Amy said. "We can't just leave him!"

"Get in the goddamn truck."

Amy felt herself tugged back just as the streetlamp overhead popped and the night swallowed them whole. She felt herself pushed into the vehicle but then the noise rang out and he stopped cold.

A roar. Guttural and unearthly and unlike anything Amy had ever heard in her life. It sounded furious, hatred dripping in every note.

Lara shook her head, breaking whatever spell that had frozen her limbs. Amy saw her rush for the back of the truck, where the weapons were stowed. Then all hell broke loose. Something enormous sprang out of the night, slammed Amy against the Cherokee as it flew past and took Lara down.

Amy hit the ground, heard her dad curse. Then more of the growling. Vicious and terrifying as whatever it was snarled and snapped. Too dark to see clearly, all Amy could make out was an enormous dark shape with Lara in its jaws. Jerking and snapping back and forth like a shark attack.

She watched her dad lunge at the thing, hitting and kicking and screaming at it to let go. Lara was hitting it too with one free hand, clawing at the monster's eye as if trying to rip it out.

Every limb, every joint in Amy's body trembled and when she felt something warm at her crotch, she realized she had wet herself. Her brain was screaming to do something but her legs wouldn't respond, her arms locked and immobile.

Then she heard Lara scream in pain. Amy scrambled for the duffel bag and tore out the big handgun, the one too big for her hands and she swung it up and fired. The shot went wild, cracking into the garage but the thing dropped Lara and sprang away into the darkness.

Lara lay sprawled on the snowy asphalt as if dead and her dad was already dragging her into the garage. Amy followed him inside and hauled down the garage door. Shot the bolt through the lock.

Lara was leaning up against the bench, one hand clutched to her shoulder. The front of her coat stained dark with blood. Amy peeled the coat back. "Easy, Lara. Let me see."

"Don't touch it," Lara wheezed, pushing the girl's hands away.

"You're bleeding."

Lara gnashed her teeth, lashed out. "Get away from me!"

"Dad. Help her!"

Gallagher shouldered in, looking over Lara's bloodied coat, the material ripped to shreds and tiny down feathers sticking to the blood. He spoke softly to her, telling Lara to stay calm.

Lara's quaking became violent, shaking her whole frame. Amy held her down. "She's going into shock. Do something!"

Lara growled, teeth clamped in fever. "Get away from me."

Amy watched the blood drain from her father's face. "That isn't shock," he said.

Bang.

The garage door rattled, slammed from the outside. Another hit and the metal crumpled inwards. The wolf at the door.

Amy felt herself shoved away from the door. Away from Lara. "Give me that," her dad snapped. She looked down, surprised to see the gun still in her hand. He took it from her.

Lara thrashed violently on the floor.

The door banged again. Hinges popped from their moorings as the metal creased.

"Oh Christ," he hissed.

She clocked the fear in his eyes. Something she had never seen before. He pulled her close, almost suffocating her.

When Amy looked back to Lara, Lara wasn't there. Her clothes hung shredded and webbed over something and it rose up on four limbs. Pale and prehistoric-looking. Outsized teeth in an enormous maw. Its coat pale and ghostly in the available light and when the wolf swung its massive head in their direction, Amy couldn't scream or whimper or even breath as if the thing had stolen the wind from her lungs.

The great lobo took a step towards them and Gallagher swung the gun up with its silver rounds of calamity and he drew aim straight between the wolf's yellow eyes.

Amy pushed his hand away. "Don't," she snapped. "Don't shoot her."

"Stop it."

"It's still her!"

The pale wolf came no further, its nostrils flaring at them. Gallagher aimed again but held off, counting off seconds as they stared down the massive thing before them.

The roll-up door exploded in a spew of metal and glass. The grey wolf vomited up out of the breach nose first and, with jaws wide, it lunged for the other lobo. The pale wolf swung about, locking its teeth onto the grey one's neck. The two monsters thrashed and jerked, crashing into the workbench.

Screws and pennynails rained down and Gallagher shoved his daughter out of the way. He aimed the gun again but the wolves were a blur of hide and teeth, now pale, now grey and he could find no clear shot without firing on the pale one. The noise of splintering wood and crashing crates echoed through the cinderblock garage and above it all the growls and snapping jaws and popping teeth. Amy covered her ears with her palms and screamed for everything to stop.

The pale lobo jerked free and dove through the wreckage of the door and bounded away. The grey wolf thundered after it.

Gallagher lurched to the crumpled door and looked out into the darkness, the gun useless in his sweaty grip.

There was only the empty avenue and the sound of the wolves trailing off into the dark streets of Portland.

27

THE DOG CAME BACK, LIMPING gamely through the hedgerow to heel at Gallagher's feet. He patted the Siberian down. It winced and lifted its hind leg. A splotch of blood but he couldn't see the damage in the dark. He told it to stay and ducked back into the garage.

Amy remained curled into a ball against the cinderblock, her face a chalked-out blank with saucer-sized eyes. He had to coax her up to her feet, rubbing her back and repeating softly that it was all over. When her eyes finally wheeled up to meet his, she stammered. "Dad? Lara, she... she..."

"It's okay. Just breathe, honey."

"But that thing went after her."

"Can you walk?"

He led her outside. The dog limped to Amy's knee and licked her hand. Voices bellowed in the darkened street. The neighbors stepping onto their porches and grousing about the racket and the power outage. For the moment, Gallagher was grateful for the extinguished streetlights.

"That other one, the wolf," Amy chattered through her teeth. "It went after Lara. We got to help her."

"I need to get you somewhere safe first," he said. He recognized their neighbor's voice across the street. Julie, a single mom who used to babysit Amy way back when. "You can stay with Julie, okay? I'll go after Lara."

"No." She wouldn't budge.

"This isn't the time, honey. I gotta go after her."

"*We* have to." Amy opened the passenger door on the Cherokee. "Let's go."

"Amy..."

"We don't have time, dad. Trust me."

No time to contest the point. Gallagher opened the back door and snapped his fingers. The husky hopped in and laid down on the backseat. He fished something out of the back, jumped under the wheel and tore out of the driveway in the direction the wolves had fled.

"Which way did they go?" she asked.

"There." He pointed west and then reached over and dropped something in her lap. "Take this. Keep it down but be ready."

Amy looked down at the thing in her lap. The nine millimeter. She ran her thumb over the safety catch to ensure it was on and laid it across her lap.

"Roll your window down," he said. "Keep your ears open for their sound."

North on 22nd with the cold air blowing through the open windows, Gallagher gunned up block after block without seeing any sign. Amy leaning one elbow out the window, ears cocked for any sound.

"Do you hear anything?"

She shook her head then leaned further out. Then her hand went up. "Stop the truck."

He pulled to the curb and killed the engine. Looked at her.

"Can you hear that?" she said, all but falling out the window. "I can't tell where it's coming from."

"Roll down the back window and watch the dog. He'll show you which direction." He rolled forward while Amy watched the dog crane its neck out the port side window. The husky snuffed and then darted for the starboard side.

"East," she said.

He took the next left, swinging onto Killingsworth. The dog slung its head out the window, nose twitching. Twenty yards on they could see the path of the wolves before them. Two cars lay crumpled like squashed soda cans, the wheels of the Cherokee crunching over the spray of glass on the pavement. The front windows of three, now four shops blown inwards as if hit by a truck. A man darted into the street, screaming holy terror and then vanishing between the parked cars.

They followed the path of destruction, weaving around an overturned dumpster knocked flat in the middle of the street. Amy raised her hand again and he stopped and they all listened. The noise was close, the sound of crunching metal and glass and above it all the awful noise of the things themselves.

"Scooch over. Get behind the wheel." He shifted into park and swung out of the cab. Throwing open the tailgate, he fished something from the duffel and stuffed into his pocket and came back. Amy slid behind the steering wheel. "Turn this around," he said, "and go back to the next block and wait. If those things come back, you get out of here and drive straight to the precinct. You understand?"

"What about you?"

"I'll be fine. This whole area will be overrun with uniforms in about two minutes. Go on." He stepped back and watched his daughter wheel the Cherokee around and trundle away. Then he turned and ran towards the sound of mayhem.

Two people were screaming inside the doors of a Min-Mart. The windows on the one side lay gaped in shards. A silver Audi lay dead in its tracks with its roof squashed in. A man in a Seahawks jacket lay face down on the street. Gallagher collided into a parked van, eyes on the downed man. Nothing lies as still as the dead and he knew within moments that there was nothing he could do for the prone Seattle fan. A car alarm was blaring and Gallagher strained his ears to hear anything beyond its insistent racket.

He ran, the gun locked in both hands. Two cars zoomed up behind him, the driver of one gawking at the destruction in the street but driving on nonetheless. Gallagher hollered at it to stop but his voice barely rose above the pulsing car alarm.

Coming on his left, a blur of red lurched into the street. A man in a filthy Santa Claus suit tottered and reeled, singing loud and out of tune. Auld Lang's Syne. Idly, Gallagher wondered if this Father Christmas had missed the date for the Santa Rampage or if he'd been rampaging the streets ever since. The thought was cut short when the first werewolf bounded into the intersection.

The pale lobo sprang out of nowhere, its ivory hide spackled with blood. The thing hammered directly into the path of oncoming vehicles. Horns blaring and brakes slamming, the cars swerved and fishtailed and crashed into other vehicles parked at the curb. The dull thud of metal on metal.

The second wolf, the grey, lunged after the first, deftly leaping over the crashing cars. It too was covered in blood and gore, its maw opening as it collided into the pale wolf. The monsters twisted and snapped, curling around and tumbling into cars. Each one chomping at the other's throat. The guttural roar of them was awful to hear, an abhorrence to nature and reason alike.

Gallagher swung the gun up, elbows locked as he drew a bead on the grey wolf but no clear shot materialized in that storm of clashing lobos. And then Santa man lurched forward directly into his line of sight. The man held onto his belt with one hand to keep the oversize red pants from falling down and blinked stupidly at the beasts before him.

A distraction. The wolves broke off and separated and Gallagher would have had his shot if it weren't for the man in the red suit. Saint Nick raised the glass in his hand as if in salute. The grey wolf swung round its head and lunged. A blur of red, the cheap red felt and the blood, as the grey lobo chomped down on the reveler and shook him violently to pieces. A flailing crimson doll in the jaws of the monster, the great wolf's head jerked and ticked as if trying to swallow Father Christmas whole.

Gallagher yanked the pin from the stun grenade and tossed it clattering over the pavement at the lobo. The pop of the flashbang only enraged the monster. It snarled and shook the man harder. There was a loud snap as his neck broke. Saint Nick's head was cleaved clean off and it rolled and tumbled through the slushy pavement towards Gallagher. He swung back to avoid touching the thing.

The pale wolf had vanished and the grey swung about looking for it north and south before it pointed its massive snout back and charged full bore at the man with the gun. Gallagher cursed, the thing steamrolling at him, hands raising the 50 cal too slow at the beast. It lunged and he fired. The round singed the razored back of the thing and blew out a shop window. The lobo sailed over and before he could tap off another round, the wolf bounded west down a side street.

With his heart clanging inside his ribs, Gallagher felt his legs give out and he sunk, one knee dropping to the dirty slush as he panted and blew. He scanned over the mayhem of the street. The glass eyes of Santa's head wide on him and he rose up and walked away.

HOMICIDE detail was quiet after the shift change, the night crew settling in while the day shift drifted out. Charlene Farbre lingered at her desk, scrutinizing the case file involving the death of Lieutenant Mike Vogel and another file about the disappearance of Detective Lara Mendes. The strange sighting of Lara and Gallagher's bizarre denial had eaten at Charlene's guts all day but she hadn't had a chance to open the file until now. Not that there was anything new to learn. She had assisted the primaries in both cases and contributed much of the material herself.

She clicked off the file and pushed away the murder book. She had debated the idea of bringing it up with the Lieutenant but held off. Accusing a fellow officer of misconduct was a can of worms no one in their right mind wanted to open. The blow-back could be devastating.

Stretching the kink in her lower back, she spotted Wade still at his desk. Charlene bit her lip then crossed through the bullpen. "Hey Rueben. Got a minute?"

"For you Charlene, always."

She nodded towards the empty cubicle beside his. "Where's your partner?"

"Keeps his own council these days," Wade shrugged. "Said he's got some family stuff to deal with."

"Has he been acting cagey with you lately?"

"Define cagey."

"I don't know. Out of character. Dismissive or secretive."

Wade leaned back and regarded her. He pulled up the spare chair and nodded for her to sit. "What's going on, Charlene?"

She sat, took a breath and sketched it out as briefly as possible. Her encounter with missing detective Lara Mendes (or her emaciated twin) and Gallagher's troubling dismissal of her questions.

Wade listened patiently. "You think he's lying to you?"

"I don't know what to think anymore. Three months ago I wouldn't have even considered it but Gallagher hasn't been the same since that incident."

"But why would he lie about something like that? He's spent every spare moment looking for Mendes. Long after everyone else gave her up for dead. If he found her, why keep it a secret?"

All Charlene could do was shrug. "I know it doesn't make sense. Do you think I should talk to the Lieutenant?"

Wade shook his head. "That's dangerous. Why don't you talk to Gallagher again?"

"I can't even get him on the phone. Have you even seen him today?"

"Nope." Wade leaned forward. "Do you really think he's lying to you?"

"I know he is." Charlene squared him up with a hard look. "I want to go to his house, talk to him there. He might be more inclined to talk outside of the office. And I'd like you to be there."

"Charlene..."

"We're just checking in with him," she said. "To see if he's okay."

Wade frowned, not liking the idea at all but before he could answer, two detectives ran past the desk. Charlene stood up and saw Detective Varadero pulling on his coat. "What's going on, Ray?"

"Real shitstorm up on Alberta. Some kinda dog attack. Two people down."

Wade rose out of his chair. "Dog attack?"

"Crazy, huh?" Varadero nodded at the TV screen suspended on the wall. "Fucking newsies are already on the scene."

The detective ran for the door and Charlene went to raise the volume on the TV. The news footage was an aerial shot of North Killingsworth, two cars steaming from crumpled hoods and the windows of storefronts destroyed. A figure on the ground. It looked like a war zone. The newscaster's voice boomed up.

"...conflicting reports of a pack of dogs attacking people. Unconfirmed reports say two people are dead. We also have reports of gunfire in the area..."

"Holy shit," sputtered Wade. He looked back to Charlene but she was already running for the door.

28

THE WOLVES HAD VANISHED, leaving no sign of their escape nor any track to follow. Gallagher had driven through block after block of empty streets, Amy watching shotgun, and doubled back for a second, third sweep. He had gotten out and trekked on foot with the dog, cutting for any trace of the monsters but found nothing. Of Lara, there was no sign at all, not even a hint from the husky. They had driven home, hoping she had returned on her own but the house was empty. Amy ran in for a spare set of clothes for Lara and they resumed their search. Amy had hung in there until close to four AM when her chin kept dipping. She laid down on the back bench to sleep while he drove on until he too gave up and sat parked on a low rise with the engine killed and the cold creeping into the cab.

The eastern break over the skyline was already graying in that eerie stillness before dawn and he looked at his watch and rubbed his eyes. He had lost her again. And to what this time? Had the grey wolf killed her? Was she injured and transfigured back into human form, slowly freezing to death in some ditch? Or had the pale wolf simply bolted for higher country like last time?

His daughter stirred, turning over in the backseat. He watched her sit up with that dazed look of the barely awake. She yawned. "What time is it?"

"Five-thirty. Go back to sleep."

"I'm freezing." Amy patted the dog beside her then looked out the window. "No luck, huh?"

"Nope. How's Tonto?"

"Who?"

"The mutt."

"Sound asleep." She ran her fingers through his fur and cast her gaze to the window. Snow, industrial buildings, a few trees. "Do you think she went back home?"

"Maybe."

"Let's go home."

His fingers folded around the key in the ignition but didn't turn it over. Going home meant giving up. Meant that Lara Mendes was gone again and finding her a second time would be a miracle.

"Dad?" Amy leaned forward and put her hand on his shoulder. "Sitting out here isn't helping anyone. Let's go home."

She squeezed his shoulder and he came to his senses. Sometimes he forgot how smart his kid was. Intuitive but sober for such a young person. He fired it up, slid into gear and turned for home. Then he stomped the brakes.

A figure stood in the middle of the road, clad in what appeared to be a tattered blanket. Her hair was wet, the lips blue.

Amy bolted out the door and the dog barked. Gallagher rushed out to help his daughter bring Lara into the backseat.

KILLINGSWORTH Street was a disaster zone. Uniformed officers taped off the area and assisted the detectives combing every square inch of pavement in an effort to unravel one simple question; what in the name of Jesus went down last night?

The skid marks of the crashed cars told a tale of slammed brakes but the statements of their owners was confused and contradictory. The civilians found cowering inside a Mini-Mart were similarly unclear and could confirm no part of any other story.

It was a giant dog.

It was a pack of pitbulls.

It was Bigfoot.

Detectives Lidia Summers and Trevon James were on rotation for active calls on the nightshift and therefore primaries on scene. Charlene and Wade worked support along with four other detectives; two from the Homicide Detail and two from

Assault. Together they worked the scene while more uniforms showed up to assist and the forensics van rumbled under the yellow tape and the techs got to work. Detective James examined the body of the Seahawks fan while detective Summers, drawing the short straw, sifted through the red costume of the decapitated Santa.

A uniformed beat cop named Martinez found the blown out shell of a concussion grenade. She circled it with a length of chalk and informed Detective Summers of her discovery. Summers cursed, wondering how much more effed-up this crime scene could get. Detective James sauntered over not a minute later to relate that the techs had dug a slug from a storefront. The crumpled shell fragment was, to the tech's estimate, a round from a 50 caliber output. At that news, Summers threw up her hands and declared quietly to her partner that she had no goddamn idea what had just happened here.

Standing well back from the string of yellow police tape lingered one onlooker who could have answered the detective's questions. Edgar Grissom cocked an ear to hone in on the police banter above the murmurs of the crowd. He smirked, watching the police grapple to form some cohesive chain of events that led to the mayhem. Bullshit piled atop road apples.

As stupid and impetuous as it had been to tear after the pale wolf out in the open like this, to cajole and fight and sink his teeth into her in the wide open streets of this city, Grissom knew he was safe. The little that he had observed from his short stay in the city of roses, he concluded that two out of three citizens were either batshit crazy or willfully, gleefully deranged. His full-fledged lycanthropic battle on the streets of Portland would garner no more than a shrug and a declaration of 'whoa dude...' from the average citizen. Even the tired looking police investigators seemed nonplussed at the statements stammered out by the shellshocked witnesses. Portland, Edgar Grissom concluded, was perhaps the safest city for a lycanthrope to call home. Set next to the precociously strange and the doggedly indifferent, a werewolf could settle in without fear of alarming the neighbors.

He hopped onto the hood of a parked Saab and knocked the slush from his boots and sat watching the street. His plan, simple as it had been, had not worked and he now forced to recalibrate his approach. The woman was under the protection of a family and he had to work around them or eliminate their protection before he could get to the female. Murdering them outright would be messy and lead to trouble. Especially since the man was a police detective. Simple plans wouldn't work. Grissom scratched the raw scab on his throat left there by the pale wolf's teeth and wondered if there wasn't some way to use the family against Lara Mendes. He looked at the blood on his fingertips.

"What the hell do you think you're doing?"

Grissom swung his head up to see a man marching on him with an outraged look on his face.

"Get the hell off my car, asshole!"

Grissom looked away. "Piss off, son. I'm busy."

"Get the fuck off it, man! Before you scratch the paint."

Annoyed, Grissom slid his butt down the hood and the tabs on his jeans screeched loud as they scored down the maroon paintjob. He hopped down and advanced smartly upon the apoplectic Saab owner but the man backtracked away, cursing something about finding a cop. Grissom leaned and spat in the snow and then walked away. Even he couldn't press his luck with so many uniforms about.

GALLAGHER shrugged off his coat and tossed it across the seat to Amy, then cranked the heater to full. The dog licked Lara's palm as Amy drew the coat over her.

Amy blanched at the dried blood caked over Lara's face. Leaning over the seat, she fished up the first aid box from the back and snapped it open.

The dog, forced into the footwell, looked at Gallagher and whined.

"I'm okay, Amy" Lara protested as she waved the girl away.

"Yeah, you're in great shape. Let me take a look."

Lara relented, too exhausted and cold to put up a fight. Amy peeled the coat off one shoulder and looked over her wounds. Claw and teeth marks up and down her shoulders and ribs but all of it scabbed over. The worst of it was a ring of puncture marks in Lara's neck that were still wet and leaking a thin serum.

"That looks bad," Amy said, unraveling a roll of gauze. "Does it hurt?"

Lara's teeth were chattering. "I'm too cold to feel anything. Can you turn the heat up?"

"It's on all the way." Gallagher tilted the rearview mirror so he could see her. "Let Amy wrap that up. Looks awful."

Lara pulled the coat tighter and relented to the girl wrapping the gauze over her neck wounds. She looked back at Gallagher through the glass. "How bad did it get last night?"

Amy bit off a strip of gauze. "You don't remember?"

"Not much. We fought. There were people on the street. Did anyone get hurt?"

"Two people. Dead," Gallagher said. "Not by you."

Lara shivered and clenched her teeth to stop them chattering. Amy reached over the seat to get the bundle of spare clothes and put them in the naked woman's lap. "Here, put these on. We'll be home soon."

Gallagher gunned for home but kept it under the speed limit. Cutting across Ainsworth, he wheeled onto the homestretch only to hit the brakes and pull to the curb. "Shit."

Amy collided against the seat. "What is it?"

"Company. You see it?"

Lara and Amy peered over his shoulder. Further down, a car sat parked in their driveway. Two people stood outside, looking over the wreckage of the garage door.

Amy squinted. "Who is it?"

"That's an unmarked police vehicle," Lara sighed. She looked at Gallagher. "Have they spotted us?"

"I don't think so."

Amy bit her lip. "What do we do now?"

Gallagher pulled away from the curb and swung a U-turn, parking on the opposite curb but he left the Cherokee running. "Amy, hop over the seat and take the wheel. Go wide around the block and don't come back until you see that they're gone." He opened the door and got out.

Amy clambered over the front seat. "Where are you going?"

"Gonna see what they want."

"Is that wise?" Lara leaned forward. "Let's just keep driving."

"They'll sit there all day. I'll get rid of them." He was about to close the door when the husky leaped over and slithered out of the cab. He tried to shoo it back inside but the dog scampered ahead before turning to look back at him.

"Get out of here," he said and closed the door. He watched his daughter take the wheel and drive away and then he walked for home with the dog heeling up smartly behind him.

"HEY partner. You should answer your phone sometime."

Detectives Wade and Farbre stood on the front stoop as Gallagher approached home. Wade offered up a friendly smile while Charlene was all business. Gallagher had doled out the good/bad cop routine so many times before but he'd never been on the receiving end. This ought to be good. Classic approach so he came back with the same. "Is there a problem, officer?"

"You missed some real fun last night," Wade said, keeping things breezy. "Down on Killingsworth. Shitstorm city."

"My loss." Gallagher looked at Charlene, found a frosty return.

"Where have you been?" Charlene said, cutting out the chitchat.

He looked at the husky with its tongue lolling. "Walking the dog."

"Without your coat?"

"Whoops." He looked at the detectives. "What do you guys want?"

"We need to talk, Gallagher." Charlene maintained eye-contact, like the bad cop does. "About Lara Mendes."

"You find her yet?"

"It's kind of cold out here," Wade said. "Let's talk inside."

"We can talk out here."

The smile fell from Wade's face and it was plain to see how much he hated all this. Charlene remained hard. She squared him up. "Where is she, John?"

"I have no idea."

"Hey," Wade cut back. "We're not on the clock here, bud. We just came to talk before something goes wrong. Charlene saw Lara Mendes yesterday. And she was with your daughter. You're not gonna deny that, are you?"

He looked at Wade and then to Charlene. "Every word."

Wade sighed, hating this even more now. Charlene stepped off the pathway and nodded at the ruined garage door. The aluminum panels busted in and torn up like a bomb had hit it. "What happened to your garage?"

"Forgot to open the door before I backed out."

The three detectives went silent in a deadlock of bullshit. The dog looked on, bored.

Charlene resumed, acid etched into her tone. "She has family, you know. A sister down in Albuquerque. Instead of keeping her all to yourself, maybe she'd like to know that her sister is alive."

"Have you talked to her?" he spat. "Because I have. I check in with Marisol every three weeks, keep her appraised of my search for her missing sister."

Wade winced, knowing full well that the missing homicide detective had long been given up for dead. Charlene didn't bat an eye and told Gallagher so. "You're digging your own grave with this, John. Bring Lara in. We can sort all of this out. I promise."

"Thanks for stopping by." Gallagher turned his back on them and unlocked the door. The husky rose and ran in after him and the door closed tight.

Charlene shook her head but Wade was already walking for the car, shivering the whole way. "I'm freezing. Let's go."

Wade started the car and cranked up the heat and pulled away. "So? What now? Talk to the Lieutenant?"

"I don't want to do that just yet." She looked out the window, watching the houses pass by. "I might take a page from G's book and do something stupid."

"I don't even want to know." He steered for the precinct. "How stupid are we talking about?"

"Like get my car and come back and park and watch the house. What's that on the stupid scale? A seven?"

"Nine. At least. You might want to go home first and put on your long johns."

BACK inside the house, the dog went straight to its bowl and the phone was already ringing. Gallagher finally let himself shiver and once the first one came, he couldn't stop. Standing in the goddamn cold being grilled by people he worked with. Fucking unbelievable.

He grabbed the receiver, guessing if it was Amy or Lara. "Where are you guys?" he said by way of hello.

"Howdy."

A man's voice. One he didn't recognize.

Gallagher frowned. "Who is this?"

"You're Lara's friend, right?" The voice on the other end was drawled and raspy. "We sorta met last night."

Gallagher let the clock run out, dead air hissing from the phone. "Who is this?"

"We need to talk, Mister Gallagher. My name's Grissom."

29

"WHAT DO YOU WANT?"

"I think you know what I want."

"Well you're shit out of luck, sport. So why don't you screw off back to whatever rocked you crawled out from."

Quiet. All Gallagher could hear was the man's breath rasping down the telephone line.

"You know how this is gonna turn out, don't you?"

"I know how it won't. You're going home empty-handed."

"Stop and think about what you're saying, Mr. Gallagher. You know what she is. You really want that? You know what will happen to your daughter. Your city." Another raspy sigh. "Hell, you saw that mess last night. Bad business. For everybody."

"So you want me to what? Just step away?"

"Exactly."

"Go to hell."

"You step away and let Lara come with me and you're daughter will be left...untouched. Think it over. That's the best offer you're going to get."

"You're a real piece of work, you know that?" Gallagher snarled. "You threaten me. Over the phone? Why don't you grow a pair and come talk to me. Man to man."

"Done," Grissom said.

Click.

More than anything, Gallagher hated being hung up on. Who doesn't? Like a perfect slap to the face that the slappee can't ever reply to except to stand there fuming uselessly with the dead phone in their hand. He hated it so much he almost forgot what he had done. Which was to cajole the bad guy, werewolf, killer dude into shading his doorstep.

"Shit..."

Toggling the kill button, he dialed his daughter's cell. It rang three times before clicking over. "Amy? It's me."

"Thank god. I thought it might be the police calling from the house phone."

"They're gone. Put Lara on."

"What's going on? Can we come home?"

"Just put Lara on."

A muffled sound, then Lara's voice. "What is it, John?"

"You need to drop Amy somewhere safe. A restaurant or somewhere with a lot of people. Then haul ass back here. Grissom's on his way."

"What? Get out of there. Now."

"No. This is ending right here. But the guns are still in the truck. Including the fifty with the silver."

"What are you thinking?" Lara yelled. "Don't go up against him. Just get out of there and wait for us."

Gallagher gritted his teeth. Why did no one listen to him anymore? "Lara, just do it. And be quick."

This time he hung up first. He expected it to feel satisfying but it didn't. It was just a shitty thing to do.

Returning the handset to the wall, he ran a quick mental inventory of any weapon in the house. Every firearm he owned was in a duffel bag in the back of the Cherokee. There was a police truncheon hanging off a peg in his office.

He went to go fetch the fuckstick when the living room window exploded and a hurled brick thumped across the hardwood floor.

AMY yanked the truck to the gravel spur and watched Lara fume at the cell phone in her hand. "What's going on?"

"Grissom's on his way to the house. Your dad wants me to get you somewhere safe."

Lara felt herself flung against the door as Amy spun the Cherokee in a hard u-turn. Horns blared as oncoming vehicles swerved around them. "Amy, slow down."

Amy kicked it. "You don't expect me to sit this out, do you?"

"No." There was no point trying stop the girl so Lara didn't even try. Flinging an arm across the seat, she checked the rear window. No flashing lights or sirens after Amy's reckless u-turn. "Watch your speed. Now's not the time to get pulled over."

GALLAGHER stomped towards the front door, ready to murder the sonofabitch who smashed his window. Like his home hadn't been wrecked enough in the last twenty-four hours. His hand reached for the knob when the whole door blasted open like a hurricane and kicked him back six feet.

That hurt. Gallagher looked up from where he'd landed. A blurry figure filled the frame of the blown door. Had to be Grissom. "Mister Gallagher," the man said, advancing fast.

A cacophony of barking zoomed over his shoulder at the intruder. The dog went berserk and tore after the intruder, lunging for the bastard's throat. The dog was flung back, crashing into Gallagher's legs.

Get the nightstick. He bolted for the back hallway, bounced off a wall and rebounded into his office. Tore the black truncheon from its peg, gripping the lacquered finish. Standard issue police fuckstick. He charged back out swinging.

Grissom ducked and said something he didn't hear. Keep talking asshole. He returned fast on the backswing and gave the stick everything he had. Bingo. It connected with the man's ear with a satisfying crunch. The son of a bitch yowled in pain but he coiled back and fired a knuckled jab straight into Gallagher's throat.

The pain was lethal but it was the panic of being unable to breathe that brought him to his knees. His windpipe rattled wet and sticky, slurping up air in sucking gobs. He keeled flat, cheekbone slamming the floor. The intruder came on and kicked his guts in.

Grissom squatted over him, one hand pressed to his ear and blood trickling through the fingers. "That fucking smarts."

All Gallagher could do was listen to the wet ripple in his throat. Wait for the stars to clear from his eyes.

"I'd heard you were the tough guy," Grissom said. He lowered his hand and looked at the blood on his fingers and returned the hand to the cauliflowered ear, as if to stop a slow leak. "But you look a bit slow to me, mister Gallagher. Old."

Gallagher's vision cleared but he wished it hadn't. Grissom was abhorrent, caught in some early stage of the morphing. Eyes a pinprick of black inside glowing irises. His teeth sharp and yellowed, crusty with tartar and the stains of god only knew what. Gallagher forced his throat to work, pushing enough air back out of his lungs to utter two agonizing syllables.

"Fuck you."

"Is that supposed to make me angry? Enrage me enough to kill you quick and easy?" Grissom sneered, lips peeled flat against those discolored wolf teeth. "Clever. But not today.

"I'm not gonna kill you, Mister Gallagher. But I will make this hurt." Grissom snatched an ankle and dragged Gallagher down the hall into the kitchen. "We're gonna go for a ride you and me. But first we need to leave a message for our little friend."

Gallagher wheezed, unable to utter anything more than the sucking rattle in his pipes as he was dragged roughshod onto the linoleum floor of the kitchen.

"Ahh... I love family photos." Grissom stopped at a wall of framed photographs hung in an artful display. Most of the snapshots were of Amy. Five years old and dressed in a dusty pink princess costume, a plastic pumpkin bucket clutched in hand. Amy at thirteen with a basketball tucked under one arm. Amy at age three, all cheeks and big eyes, nestled between her mom and himself. Smiles as big as day on everyone.

Grissom studied every photo like a patron in an art gallery then swept them all to the floor. Frames popping and glass tinkering as they broke. Grissom regarded the naked wall. "This will do," he said.

He squatted down, hovering over Gallagher again. "What do you think? Big letters, clear message. In blood too." He looked at his bloodied hand again but shrugged. "I got enough here to script something but I think this would really be more heartfelt if it was your blood. Lara will be able to sniff out the difference no problem."

Grissom leaned in close with an index finger raised as if making a point. Gallagher watched the fingernail mottle dark and elongate, growing in length before his eyes.

"Hold still now, this is probably gonna hurt." Grissom dug the claw into Gallagher's arm. Dark arterial blood circled his wrist and dribbled over the broken photographs of his daughter.

THE CR7 cruised up 22nd and pulled over behind a green Tercel. Charlene Farbre killed the engine and leaned back against the seat. From here, she had a clear view of Gallagher's house and any traffic coming up or down the strip. Returning to precinct earlier, she returned the unmarked car to the motor pool and got her own vehicle. It didn't look like an unmarked cruiser so Gallagher wouldn't notice it parked on his street.

A panel van squatted in Gallagher's driveway. Plain white with rust buckling the wheel wells and a roof cage for lashing cargo to. Backed in with the rear hard up against the wrecked garage door, back plate hidden. It looked like your average contractor's vehicle. She gathered up her notebook and marked the time when the headlights on the van shot on. The vehicle rumbled to life and trundled down onto the street. As it drove past her, Charlene tried to get a look at the driver but the window was too grimy to make out anything more than a silhouette.

She was mulling over following the van when another vehicle came up the opposite end of the street and wheeled into the Gallagher home. This one a Jeep Cherokee, maroon paint, maybe ten years old. The driver swung out and Charlene immediately pegged the diminutive figure as Amy Gallagher. The girl ran for the front door but Charlene focused her attention to the passenger following the girl up the steps. Not much taller, a slight build under a man's winter coat..

Mendes. It had to be.

Charlene dialed the precinct, spoke to the desk sarge. Two patrol units in the vicinity were dispatched to her location for backup.

The moment they stepped through the door, Lara knew they were too late. The splintered door
jamb and shattered hall table. Muddied bootprints
stamped onto the floor like some crazed dance
steps. Hovering overtop all of this was the smell.
Grissom's scent and the evaporating tang of
adrenaline left by Gallagher.

Amy tore through the house, screaming for her
dad. More wrecked furniture through the house,
more signs of a violent struggle. Then Amy was
shrieking for her to come quick and Lara's knees
wobbled suddenly, fearing the girl had found her
father dead in the mudroom. Staggering in, she saw
Amy kneeling over something on the floor. It was
the dog. Still breathing but knocked cold, the eyes
like whited slits.

The girl screamed, demanding to know where
her dad was and what had happened. Lara held the
girl tight, talking her down but they both saw the
dollops of blood on the tile floor like spilled paint.

Lara told the girl to see to the dog and she went
on to the kitchen, trying to piece together the order
of events. Grissom had kicked the door in and attacked Gallagher. The dog had gotten in the way
trying to defend him.

Then she saw it. A message scrawled onto the
kitchen wall in big crude letters. Almost childish in
its form, as if written by a hand unaccustomed to

writing. The ink was blood and it had already dried. Gallagher's blood.

COME FIND US

That's all it said. Lara studied those simple words and considered wetting a cloth and scrubbing it from existence. The girl didn't need to see this but it was already too late. Amy rushed in behind her, gasping at the blood on the wall.

"What is that?" Amy looked to Lara for some answer and then back to the blood smeared wall. "Did Grissom write that? What the hell does it mean?"

Lara scrambled for some answer that would make sense but there wasn't one. The racket at the door let her off the hook. Two uniformed police officers stormed inside, barking at them to get on the floor. On the heels of the uniforms came two plainclothes officers. Lara didn't recognize the man but the sight of the woman made her stomach drop.

Charlene strode in as the uniforms forced Lara and Amy to their knees. A cold edge to her tone. "Hello Lara."

30

INTERVIEW ROOM TWO WAS TINY. A table and two chairs, the beige walls. How many times had Lara been in this room before, questioning suspects, entering and leaving at will? Drilling shitbirds or empathizing with witnesses to chip away at the truth. It was completely different being on the other side now. Unable to leave, unable to breathe in this coffin of a room. It was effective. It wore you down. She gained a new level of respect for those hardened suspects who resisted the stifling closeness and maintained their stony denials or silences.

Cracking wasn't what had her worried. It was the tingle of adrenaline coursing down to her fingertips. What would happen if she couldn't keep her head? Keep that secret chamber in her heart clenched tight?

Charlene sat across the table, lobbing question after question at her. Where had she been for the past three months? Why had she fled? Why did she come back? What happened the night Lieutenant Vogel died?

Lara mimicked the flinty silence of every bad mofo she'd grilled in this room. Neither a *yes* or a *no*. Nada. No habla. She tuned Charlene out, focusing on the more pressing matters of keeping her head to prevent the lobo from ripping her old friend to fucking pieces.

Charlene blew out her cheeks in frustration. She pushed aside the file before her and changed tactics. "Lara, I have to apologize to you. I gave up looking for you because I thought you were dead. It was a shitty assumption and I'm sorry I didn't try harder."

Lara felt her resolve sift away like ash on a breeze. "It's okay. I would have done the same."

The harsh edge left Charlene's eyes. She placed a hand on the closed folder. "Leaving this aside for the moment, where is Gallagher? And that message on the wall. The tech's confirmed it was blood. His type. Who put it there?"

Lara resumed her silence.

Charlene frowned. "Lara, this is serious stuff. You gotta level with me. Please."

"Am I being charged?"

"You're being questioned."

"Then let me out of here. Charge me or let me go. Simple as that."

"You're a key witness into the murder of a police lieutenant. You're not going anywhere and you know that." Charlene dragged the folder back to the center of the table. "Give me something here, Lara."

Lara dipped her head and said no more.

Charlene wanted to scream. Instead, she gathered up the file and crossed to the door. "We used to be friends, Lara. For that, I'll try and help you any way I can. But you have to help me first."

She left the room. Lara concentrated on her breathing, trying to slow the beat of her heart. When she was processed through, the officers had turned out her pockets and taken her coat. They had also confiscated the silver stud in her navel, the small talisman keeping the beast locked up in her heart.

AMY had an easier time of it. Questioned by Detective Rueben Wade, she answered most of their questions without lying or omitting too much. Her dad had followed another lead in his obsessive search for his missing partner and came home with Lara Mendes. Of Lara's whereabouts or the particulars of her absence, she hadn't been told. Lara had encountered a man she called Edgar Grissom and this man had pursued her to Portland. Amy gave a description of the man, having met him once. This man clearly invaded their home and attacked her dad and what, she wanted to know, were the police doing to find him?

Wade reassured her that they were doing everything they could to locate her dad. In that instance, he had done the lying, unsure exactly what was being done to find Gallagher. He found it hard to believe that Gallagher, of anyone, could be abducted.

Wade then left the room and when he came back twenty minutes later, said she could go. He took her down to the lobby. "I might have a few more questions later. Just follow up stuff. Okay?"

"Where's Lara?" she asked.

"Answering questions, same as you. We'll look after her."

"Will you call me the minute you find out anything about dad?"

"I will." He patted her shoulder. "We'll find him, Amy. Just hang in there."

A standard issue response and Amy knew it. She followed Wade into the lobby, then stopped. "What about our dog? Is anyone looking after him?"

"The dog bolted, wouldn't let anyone come near him. I think Animal Services is trying to find him ." He patted her shoulder and looked over the precinct lobby. "Now, where's your ride?"

Amy startled when her mom came bounding at her. Of course they had called her mom. Cheryl was roughly the same height as her daughter and it was obvious looking at her where Amy got her looks from. Amy had inherited her dad's eye color but everything else was mom. Something she hated at times.

"My God, Amy," Cheryl blurted after squeezing her daughter so hard Amy was winded. "What happened? Were you hurt?"

"I'm okay, Mom." Amy pulled away. "Can we go?"

Pushing out the front door, her mother hooked an arm around her as they marched for the car. "Is there any word about dad? Do they know anything about what happened to him?"

Amy heard the tension in her mom's voice, how she was biting her tongue to keep from screaming. "Not yet. They promised they'd call when they do."

"You must be tired," Cheryl said. "Are you hungry?"

"I think I should stay at Dad's tonight."

"It's a crime scene, honey. You know that."

"What if he calls?"

"They'll either have someone at the house or they're monitoring the phone."

Amy sunk down in the bucket seat. "I need to get the dog."

"No. I'm not having that dog in the house."

"He can't stay there alone." Amy bristled at her mom's rules. "He'll stay in my room. You won't even know he's there."

Cheryl hated dogs, always had. "Okay. But just until we find someone else to take him until your dad gets back."

Until dad gets back. Like he had simply gone away for the weekend, fishing with his buddies.

THE house was dark when they pulled up. With the bay window smashed and garage door destroyed, the house looked like one of the foreclosures that dotted every neighborhood like rotting teeth. Police tape strapped the front door and garage.

Cheryl nosed up behind the Cherokee in the driveway and left the motor running. "I'll go in with you," she said, looking uneasily up at the dark foursquare with the green trim. She disliked going inside at the best of times.

Amy slid out of the car. "It's okay, mom. I'll be two seconds."

"We shouldn't even be here, honey." Cheryl called out, watching Amy dip under the yellow tape.

The place looked awful. Amy hadn't noticed how badly it had been trashed when she and Lara ran back in looking for her dad. Heartbreaking and unnerving to see your home beat up and left to die. She popped on the light and looked over the kitchen, calling for the dog. Passing through to the mudroom, she opened the backdoor and called out to the dark backyard. The dog slunk out of the shadows with a soft whimper and wagging tail.

She hugged the husky as it collided into her legs. Cooing to it, she examined the dog for injuries, running her hands over its legs and neck. The dog winced when her hand touched a spot on its ribs but she found no cut or visible wound. Bruised ribs, she guessed. "Come on, boy," she whispered to it. "You're coming with me."

The dog panted at her with those eyes and stayed close as Amy gathered up the big bag of kibble and hauled it out to her mom's car. She opened the back door and set the bag on the floor and knickered to the dog to jump in.

Cheryl turned in her seat to find the dog panting with its tongue flapping loose less than a foot from her face. Hot dog breath. "When we get home, there's a lint brush in the kitchen drawer. I won't have dog hair furring up my car."

"Okay, mom." Amy closed the door but then stopped, looking at the Cherokee. Patting her coat pocket, she remembered she still had the keys and marched for it.

"Where are you going?" Cheryl called.

"Hang on," Amy said, unlocking the truck on the passenger side. The black duffel bag sat crumpled into the footwell. The police had neglected to search the truck. Thank God. Slinging it onto her shoulder, she loaded it into the trunk of her mom's car and climbed back into the passenger bucket.

Cheryl looked at her. "What's in the bag?"

"Uh... Christmas presents and stuff," Amy said. "So no peeking, okay?"

Cheryl backed out of the driveway. Amy sighed and wondered how long this short string of luck would run.

GALLAGHER ran for his life. Feet stomping through ankle deep snow, bolting through the pines in some dark forest. Brambles tearing at his face as he ran headlong through the brush.

Something big and angry on his heels. Popping teeth and insane yellow eyes.

Heart jacking against his ribcage, he dove through the underbrush and came into a clearing. The night sky was clear and the moon full, its eerie light turning the snow blue. The lobo crashed from the pines and slammed him with the force of a freight train.

No defenses, no weapon. His hands useless against the powerful jaws of the wolf. It tore into his guts and chomped his right arm, snapping the bone. Its maw enveloped his ribs and shook him back and forth with feral savagery.

Whipped under that godless force, his neck snapped and Gallagher knew he was going to die. The monster would kill him and eat his flesh and there'd be nothing but scattered bones to find come the spring thaw. His shattered arm swung free on a hinge of tissue and when he felt a tug on his stomach he knew the lobo had gone for the belly and was dragging loose the purply ropes of intestines. The steam of his guts wisped up into the cold air but the pain subsided and he knew this was the end.

The jerking stopped. He didn't want to look down but couldn't help himself. The bony tips of his ribcage shone through the wet gristle of meat.

The wolf was gone.

Lara crouched in its place.

Squatting over him, naked as her birth and her wet hair hung over him, dripping with sweat. She was covered in his blood, as if she'd painted herself red with the stuff. She sklathed forward on her haunches and punched her fist under his ribs. A wet popping sound as she plucked her arm free with the raw meat of his heart in her fist. It beat once, twice and then went still.

He looked away, unable to watch as she devoured it. He screamed but no breath came out, no voice was raised under the blue of that killing moon.

The nightmares were back. Piggybacking the terror was a plunge of disappointment. He'd been doing so well since he'd found Lara. All these nights without the nightmares that robbed his sleep and left his nerves raw. Why now?

It all came back when the scream of his nightmare couldn't escape his throat. He couldn't open his mouth. Duct tape, sealed taut over his mouth. Blindfolded. The pressure of the fabric pressing down on his eyeballs. Trapped. His wrists burning under rope ties, arms bound tight against his chest. Ankles trussed.

He listened to the hum around him. The floor vibrated and rattled. A vehicle. Something big enough for him to stretch out in and judging by the vibrations of the floor, the vehicle was moving at a fast clip. Highway driving.

Grissom. The son of a bitch wasn't content with mopping the floor with Gallagher's ass, he had to kidnap him too like some hapless victim whose face adorned a thousand police flyers. The nightmares had returned but now he was the one who had vanished. The irony was neither funny nor poignant.

Worst of all, he had brought it on himself by daring the son of a bitch to come out into the open.

stupid

stupid

stupid

31

SAFELY INSIDE THE HOUSE, Cheryl had gone nuclear. Amy sat with the dog at her feet and quietly endured a barrage of rants and questions and more rants. Norm, her mom's common-law beau, stood off to the side and interjected now and then to calm Cheryl down. Amy had little use for the man, tolerating his mellow vibe but had to admit he had a way of talking Cheryl down from the ledge. Amy employed the same lifeless answers here in her mother's kitchen that she had used back in the precinct. Dollops of truth mixed into a batter of denials and shrugs.

The Siberian had saved her butt. Rising from its coil at Amy's feet, the dog had padded across the tile to Cheryl and, in what Amy could see was an effort to calm or silence the woman, had leaned its flank against her mom's knees.

It worked. Cheryl lost her cool and ordered the dog from her sight. Get out of jail, do not pass go. Amy clucked her teeth and the dog scampered back and she led the husky to her room. Even with the bedroom door closed, she could hear her mom turn her outrage against Norm until her shrillness subsided into sobs. She pictured Norm hugging her in his hippie way, cooing until Cheryl collapsed into his shoulder with full-body sobs.

Gross.

She fell onto the bed and wondered where her father was. Why did that guy take him? Lara had said that he was after her, not her dad. Where had he taken him? Rueben had assured her that they would do everything they could but they hadn't been able to find Lara when she was missing. Lara was the only one who could find him now and she was locked up inside Central Precinct.

What if dad didn't come back at all?

The dog had sniffed its way through the room and chose a patch of floor under the window to curl up in. It raised its head at the sounds of sobs coming from the bed. It rose and hopped onto the bed and lay back down, its chin draped over the girl's knees.

LARA tried to sleep. Stretched out on the floor of interview room 2, she closed her eyes against the fluorescents and fell asleep. She had seen plenty of suspects stretch out for naps inside the interview rooms and was always amazed how anyone could sleep in these rooms. Now she knew. Hours ticked by with no clock to tally their passing and nothing but walls to stare at. As a detective, she had assumed that any skel hard enough to nap in the interview room was guilty. Now she was sure of it.

She pushed herself up to a sitting position. A figure sat in one of the hard-backed chairs. Squinting against the light, she assumed it was Charlene or Wade but it was neither. A dark figure in a green rain slicker, the hood pulled up to shadow the face.

"Made a real mess of things, didn't you?" he said.

Lara rubbed her eyes to dispel the phantom. Just a bad dream.

A grimy hand reached up and pulled back the hood. Stringy hair and filthy beard, the eyes hidden under mirrored sunglasses. Ivan Prall's face was spackled with blood and when he leaned back, Lara could see the open destruction of his torso. Split down the middle, his guts tumbled out and hit the floor with a wet plop. The ropes of intestine lay coiled there and Ivan Prall reached down and scooped them back up. "Hard keeping this stuff in. You and that asshole gutted me pretty bad."

"Go away," she said.

"I never meant to pass this onto you. It was supposed to end with me when I killed the son of a bitch who cursed me." Prall shrugged and a tube of gut spilled out. "But we both know that didn't work."

When she and Gallagher were tracking Prall, he was on a mission to save himself. Ivan Prall thought that if he killed the lycanthrope that had infected him, he would sever some kind of spell and cure himself of his own lycanthropic curse. It hadn't worked and she and Gallagher had killed Prall, but by then it was too late for her.

"You know what you got to do," he said. "You should have done it a long time ago."

Lara pinched the skin of her arm. Wake up.

"How long are you gonna last in this fishbowl before you turn? How bad is it gonna get when the wolf is turned loose in here?" More guts tumbled as he spoke and he scooped them back up. "Where's your knife?"

"They confiscated it."

"Too bad. That woulda worked." He looked around the room, the table. "You could try bashing your brains against this hard corner but my guess is they'd stop you before you did any real damage."

"You want me to kill myself?"

"What other option do you have?"

Lara's eyes fell to the patchwork of scars on her forearm. How easy would it have been to just cut deeper? How many times had she wavered with the silver blade hovering over her wrist? Too late now.

"Have you killed anyone?"

She looked at him. "What?"

"As the wolf. You killed anybody?"

"No." She shook her head sharply but her brow furrowed, doubt creeping in. "I don't know. I don't remember anything when it happens so how would I know?"

"You'd know." Ivan Prall scratched his foul beard. "There may be some hope for you yet if that's the case."

"What kind of hope? A cure?"

"Your soul. If you ain't taken a life as the wolf, maybe you won't go to Hell."

She didn't want to have this conversation. Not now, not with him. But there was nowhere to go. In for a penny, in for the pound. "Is that where you are? Hell?"

"Yes."

"Good."

He slipped the sunglasses off and his irises glowed yet with that eerie amber, some vestigial remnant of the wolf still in there. There were tears too, dribbling from the corner of his eyelids. "It's awful. It's so goddamn awful..."

Wolves don't cry, she remembered. Prall himself had told her that. Apparently that rule didn't apply to the dead.

It was too much. This onetime lobo holding his guts in and crying into his rancid beard. Lara lay back down and turned her face to the wall and waited for it all to go away.

THE husky snored, crowding her space on the bed. Amy lay awake, watching the minutes click over on the bedside clock.

Dad had been taken.

Lara under arrest.

She was trapped in her mom's house.

Something had to be done. Amy stared up at the ceiling and formulated a plan, discarded it and formulated another.

She sat up, shook the dog awake. "Wake up."

Creeping downstairs, she set her things by the front door and scarfed down a bowl of cereal and fed the dog. A small whiteboard hung on the refrigerator door and she took the marker dangling on its string and tried to think of a note to leave for Cheryl.

"Honey?" Cheryl tiptoed into the kitchen, her arms folded against the chill. "Why are you up so early?"

"Uh, I got a lot of things to do today," Amy said. *Think fast.* "Thought I'd get an early start."

Cheryl squinted at the clock. "It's not even six. Is everything okay?"

"I couldn't sleep. Needed to do something, you know?"

Cheryl nodded and put her hand on her daughter's arm. Gave a little squeeze. "Your dad's going to be okay. I know he will."

"I know." Amy nodded to where the dog sat waiting by the front door. "I'm taking him with me. We won't be back until tonight."

"Oh. Be home for dinner, okay?"

"Don't wait for me. I'll fix something if I miss dinner."

"I'll keep a plate warm for you."

"Okay." Amy gave her mom a squeeze back. "Go on back to bed. I'll see you later."

Cheryl patted Amy's arm and yawned and headed back towards her room. Amy wanted to say something more. *I love you* or *goodbye* but she held her tongue, knowing it would alert her mom that something wasn't right.

She listened for the click of the bedroom door and then slipped on her coat. Hefting the black duffel over her shoulder, she led the dog out and closed the door behind her.

SHE got off the 24 bus and walked the last five blocks home with the duffel bag killing her shoulder. The dog trotted ahead, sniffing everywhere and marking territory. She was worried there would be a cruiser parked in the street to watch the house but the street was empty. Letting herself in, she left the bag by the front door and went to her room and dug out her backpack. She stuffed it with extra clothes, all heavy winter wear stuff and then took it out to the hall closet and tossed in extra hats and gloves.

Hauling the backpack and duffel outside, she loaded the gear into the back of the Cherokee. Some of the camping gear her dad had packed was still here. The rest of it, including the extra bag of dog kibble, had been unloaded just inside the garage and she loaded it back into the truck. The duffel and her backpack went in next.

The husky looked up as she came back into the kitchen and followed her into her dad's office. She rummaged through the desk drawers until she found his stash of emergency cash. Two hundred and fifty dollars, some loose change. She folded it into her pocket with her own cash and opened the bottom drawer of the filing cabinet. The dented license plate was stuffed in the back, along with its paperwork. She turned out all the lights in the house and went back to the garage for a screwdriver.

Ducking low behind the Cherokee, she removed the plate from the back and replaced it with the old dented plate. Never one to be above bending rules, her dad had once showed her the extra set of tags he had kept handy. He'd kept cagey about what exactly he needed these plates for but seemed pleased with himself for setting up tags that officially belonged to someone who only existed in a file with the DMV. Small mercies, she could use these false tags now.

She whistled and the dog hopped through the driver's side door and on into the back. Amy climbed in after and fired it up. The gas gauge registered full, to her relief, and she pulled out and drove away.

"RISE and shine, sunshine."

Lara sat on the floor as the door swung open and a detective entered. A man, moustache and gut of a seasoned pro. "Detective Mendes in the flesh. They told me they found you but I thought for sure they were pouring shit down my socks."

Detective Latimer. Veteran homicide cop and pillar of the detail. The few times Lara had dealt with Latimer, he was an asshole. Little had changed in her absence.

Latimer grunted as he sunk into a chair. "Do you know what I been doing since you up and vanished on us, Mendes? Cleaning up the mess you left behind. For months now. That was a helluva crapout you left us with. Meanwhile, everyone around here's been so *'oh where could she be?'* and *'we look after our own around here. Find her'.*"

Lara said nothing. Clearly Latimer needed to blow off steam. So let him.

Latimer was just warming up. "Me? I knew you were dead. You know how I knew that? Because no cop would just bugger off like some French back-packer on tour. Not after this shitstorm. If she's alive, I told 'em, she'd be back to help tie this up. No cop leaves their balls twisting in the wind like this." The blotchy patches on his cheeks brightened. "But low and behold, you pop up outta nowhere. And, this is the kicker, they tell me you won't talk. Izzat true? All this shit smeared over the detail and... YOU WON'T TALK?"

Latimer rose, grunting under the effort and he brushed his hands together as if they were soiled. "Sweetheart, you shoulda been dead. Cuz you're going wish you were after this is done."

"Feel better?"

"What?"

Lara craned her neck. "That little speech. Did it go as well as you'd rehearsed it?"

"Dig that grave a little more, Mendes. Your tombstone's all picked out and waiting."

Another shadow darkened the open door. Detective Wade. He held a clutch of papers in hand and pushed them into Latimer's chest. "Latimer, who'd you blow to swipe this file out from under Charlene?"

"I'm the one with the book collecting dust, not her." Latimer looked at the forms in his hand. "The hell is this?"

"Orders. You gotta take her to the hospital for an assessment before anymore questioning."

Another capillary burst on Latimer's nose. "I don't got time to babysit a doctor visit."

"Lieutenant's orders. Take it up with him."

Lara bristled at Wade's words. She rose to her feet. "Hey, I'm fine. No doctors."

"Out of my hands, Lara" Wade said. "They just need a doctor to check your pulse and officially declare you among the living."

A hospital. Doctors probing and prodding. How quickly before they found something out of order and called in some other doctor for a second look? Biopsies and tissue samples and then somebody calls the tabloids. "No," she said, trying to keep the panic from her voice. "I'm fine. Really—"

"Shut up." Latimer dragged her to the door. "A small reprieve before the guillotine. Let's get this over with."

Lara shot Wade a pleading look but all he did was shrug as Latimer escorted her away.

AMY smeared an arm across her brow. A cold sweat that she hoped the desk sergeant didn't notice. "Please. Detective Farbre knows me. She'll okay it."

The desk sarge shucked up his shoulders. "She's not available. Sorry."

"Then try detective Wade. He's my dad's partner."

"Honey, this is a busy place. Tell me exactly what you want and maybe I can help." He looked as exasperated as she felt.

"A woman was brought in last night." Amy sighed, going through it all again. "Her name is—"

A bustle at the hallway cut her short. Lara, escorted into the lobby by Detective Wade and another plainclothes officer. Amy darted past the desk towards them. "Lara!"

Latimer thrust out a hand. "Whoa, back up kid."

"It's okay," Wade said, waving Amy in. "It's Gallagher's daughter."

Amy slowed at the sight of Lara. Her hands were cuffed and her eyes look hollow. "Lara, are you okay?"

Lara startled. "Amy, what are you doing here?"

"She's fine," Wade said. "Detective Latimer here is just taking her to the hospital for a quick assessment."

"Hospital?" Amy looked at Latimer, then back to Wade. "You can't. I mean, can I talk to her for a minute?"

"Sorry, kid." Latimer pressed on, tugging Lara after him. "We got to go."

"Please. Let me talk to her."

Wade looked down at those puppy dog eyes and hated himself for caving. "Okay. Keep it short."

"I don't got time for this," Latimer sputtered.

Wade fixed the blotchy-faced detective with a stern eye. "Yes you do."

Latimer made no attempt to hide how much he hated this. He pointed to the bench. "You got exactly two minutes. Go."

"You look awful," Amy said as they sat down.

"I'm fine." Lara kept an eye on Latimer, hovering close by.

Amy lowered her voice. "We have to find dad."

Lara lifted the cuffs on her wrists.

"Where are they taking you?"

"They didn't say," Lara said. "My guess is Providence."

"You need to get away from them. I've got the truck packed, ready to go."

"Easier said than done."

"Not for you." Amy zeroed in on her eyes. "You're stronger than they are. If you choose to be."

Lara shook her head. "Amy... you don't know what you're asking. I can't just turn it on or off like that."

"You don't have a choice, Lara. Dad never gave up looking for you. Now we have to find him."

"Time to go, ladies." Latimer barked.

Lara felt her legs go numb. The girl was crazy, asking her to just wolf out and overpower cops, bust out of a hospital.

"I'll be parked outside the hospital," Amy hissed before Latimer broke in. "Find me."

"See ya, kid." Latimer nodded to Amy and led Lara away. Amy watched as they were joined by two uniformed officers who flanked the detective and his ward as they went out the door.

32

THE CORRIDORS OF PROVIDENCE Portland Medical were a miasma of smells that assaulted Lara at every step. Disinfectant and blood and body odor and desperation. A wall of scent that overpowered her like tear gas. The fact that she was this sensitive to it meant the wolf inside was uncoiling, the first uptick of heartbeat signifying what was about to unfold.

She was escorted to a small examining room, Latimer nodding for her to sit on the gurney. "Sit tight, we'll get this over with soon as possible." He unlocked the bracelets. "Then you're all mine." Latimer posted one of the uniforms to stay in the room and he and the other officer left.

Lara massaged her wrists and tried to breathe through her mouth. She could smell every sick person who had passed through the examining room. The remaining officer stood with his back to the door. There wouldn't be a better time but she hesitated over what she was about to do. Letting slip the wolf just enough to overpower her guards but not enough to take over. Like walking the edge of a knife.

She slid off the table. The officer raised a hand in warning. "Sit back down please."

"Officer, I'm sorry for this," she said. He was probably going to get hurt.

"Everything's fine," he said in an even tone. "Just have a seat, please."

Later, PO Pudowski would be unable to explain exactly what happened next. One second he was warning her to sit back down and the next he was face first on the floor with a knee driven into the small of his back. Despite outweighing his prisoner by a hundred pounds, Pudowski found himself tossed and folded like a dirty sheet.

"Sorry." Lara shackled the officer with his own cuffs.

PO Pudowski bucked and kicked and yelled his head off. Lara sprang up and planted her heel into the officer's back just as the door swung open.

Here they come.

Latimer was first in, the other uniform on his tail. She didn't bother apologizing to Latimer before grabbing his collar and pivoting on her heel. Airborne, the detective crashed into the wall and landed on the bed, tipping the whole thing to the floor.

The uniform shot an arm round her neck and hauled back. Lara's feet left the ground as she was tilted back in the chokehold. Her gut instinct was to bite down on the young man's arm. How bad would that turn out? Pudowski was scrambling up and she kicked her feet off of him and slammed the other officer into the wall. The chokehold slackened and she slipped out. He reached for his sidearm. She folded him in two and jettisoned him into Pudowski. They crashed over Latimer like tenpins.

Latimer cursed when he saw the open door. The prisoner gone.

Lara sprinted past gaping faces in the corridor and shouldered through a door. An empty stairwell, one flight down to where the exit door fed out onto the street. At the bottom she shrugged off her coat, stuck it under her arm and calmly pushed out to the street. Keeping an even pace, she struck north through a parking lot and didn't look back. Taking the air, she tried to pick out Amy's scent from the toxic stink of the city street.

AMY stood outside the Cherokee, one eye out for Lara and the other for parking authority. The only place to pull over was a no-stopping zone but it afforded a good view of the northeast corner of the hospital. But a pesky parking cop might be a problem if he issued a ticket to the bogus tags on the truck.

Of Lara, there was no sign. What if she couldn't find her? What if Lara couldn't even escape and was at this moment being prodded and examined by doctors aghast at what they were seeing?

The dog slung its head out the open window. Amy let him out and told him to stay. Maybe the combined scent of her and the dog would help Lara find them.

Then she spotted the ticket cop. He popped up between the parked cars to her left, issuing the notices and slipping them under wiper blades. Only a few minutes before he made his way to them. Another panicked glance at the hospital but there was nothing to see.

"Come on, boy." She coaxed the dog back into the truck, trying to stifle her panic and when she looked up, Lara was there. Amy couldn't stop the smile stretching her jaw muscles. "You made it! I was starting to worry."

Lara flung open a back door. "Get us out of here."

Amy hustled behind the wheel and pulled into traffic without looking. A car honked at being cut off and Amy ignored it, speeding up. The wail of siren froze her blood. An ambulance sailed past.

"Take a right up here," Lara said from the backseat. "Cut over to Halsey."

Amy checked Lara in the rearview. She didn't look good, doubled over with sweat beading her pale face. "Are you all right?"

"It's happening."

"Oh shit." Amy reached for something on the passenger seat and handed it back. "Here. Best I could do."

Lara took the bundle and unraveled it. A big carving knife. The tip broken off and the handle wrapped tight with hockey tape to form a sturdier grip. The tingle in her fingers confirmed that it was sterling. She had seen this knife before. Gallagher had told her it came from his dead mother's carving set. They had used it to gut open Ivan Prall.

She pushed up her sleeve and ran the edge of the blade into her forearm. Blood welled up under the silver and the effect was immediate. Her heart rate dropped, her mind cleared. The dog watched her with wary eyes.

She searched out Amy's eyes in the mirror. "Are you okay to drive?"

"I'm fine. Stay down."

Lara slid down in the seat, ignoring the sting from the blade in her arm. "We'll have to lose the truck soon. It won't take them long to flag your dad's vehicle."

"We're good," Amy said. "I swapped out the plates."

That took Lara by surprise. "With what?"

"Dad had bogus ones. They're issued to the city. Got the paperwork too, it's in the glovebox."

Lara felt her pulse slow even more and watched Amy drive. "Girl, you're awesome."

THEY stayed off the main corridors for as long as they could then Lara had Amy take the Vet Memorial across the river into Washington. On the north end of Van, Lara told her to pull over. Amy turned into an empty lot surrounded by hemlock trees and killed the engine and everyone disembarked. The dog scampered off, marking every tree in a ten yard radius.

Amy kicked at the gravel, watching Lara stretch. "How do feel?"

"Exhausted but I'm glad to be out of there." Lara looked at the girl. "Hey. Thank you."

"Did they keep you in that room all night?"

"Not exactly the Ramada. Weird being on the other side like that."

"Like a criminal."

Lara nodded.

Amy watched the husky bounding over the terrain. "What now?"

"Need to get my bearings. Then try to pick up their scent, determine which way they went. Is there a map in the glovebox?"

Amy rummaged the glovebox and came back with a map, unfolding it across the hood. Clicked on a flashlight. "How precisely can you track them? Is it a general direction or can you pinpoint the route they took?"

"They went north, I can you tell that. I should be able to follow their path. It just means stopping every so often to double-check."

"Cool."

"We're about here." Lara pointed at a spot on the map and trailed her finger up half an inch. "We need to find a bus station. Get you a ticket and you can head home. I'll call to update when I can."

Amy leaned back. "I'm going with you."

"It's too dangerous."

"No." Amy's features set to stone. "That asshole has my dad. I'm going with you."

"Amy, you were great back there, getting me out. And the plates and packing the truck with gear but this..." Lara stumbled, chose her words carefully. "You know what Grissom is. I can't bring you into this. Your dad would kill me."

"He'll be dead unless we get moving. Two are better than one. And I'm not some useless kid."

Lara steeled herself. "I am going to find your dad and bring him back. But I can't do that if I have to look out for you too. You're a crackerjack kid, Amy. No doubt. But you're sixteen and—"

"Seventeen," Amy cut in.

"I can't do it. I won't."

Even the dog sensed the standoff. It stood watching them, one forepaw lifted and waiting for something to happen.

Amy yanked open the truck's rear door and dug around and came back with the nine millimeter. "See that stop sign?"

The red sign leaned in the tall grass thirty feet from where they stood. Lara glanced nervously at the road. "Put that away, Amy."

"Three rounds in the 'O'." Amy planted her feet and brought the gun up in both hands. A tiny pause before she tapped off three rounds. The Glock bucking only slightly in her clenched hands.

Lara watched the puncture marks bloom inside the third letter of the stop sign. The smell of the gun drifted across the frozen grass.

Amy bent to pick the spent casings from the ground and slipped them into her pocket. "I know what we're going after, Lara. I know our chances aren't worth crap but I'm going with you. It's my dad who's in trouble and if you think you're gonna ditch me here, you got another thing coming."

Lara blew out her cheeks, cried uncle. "Okay," she said. "Let's find your dad."

THEY drove the rest of the night, travelling east through The Dalles then north, past the towns of Kennewick and Pasco. They had pulled over twice so Lara could recalibrate her fix on the trail. Amy had started to fade so Lara took over behind the wheel and Amy hunkered down in the passenger seat to sleep.

When she woke, the truck was quiet and still. The driver's seat empty. They were parked at a decrepit looking gas station. A light snow was dusting the few cars humming past on the road. Lara stood on a gravel spur, looking out across a vacant field of snow to where the treeline hemmed in the sightlines. A wall of pine and cedar and darkness. The dog was nowhere to be seen.

Amy swung out of the cab. "Why did we stop?"

Lara turned to look at her. "They crossed the border."

"How do you know?"

Lara kicked at the snow with her boot. "Because the border is twenty minutes north and their scent is already cold. They're still travelling north, up into the BC interior."

"So we cross the border too." Amy watched a tractor-trailer roar past. "It's Canada. How bad can it be?"

"Not if we get stopped. I have no ID on me. Your name has probably been red-flagged to border authority. And if they search the truck, we're screwed."

"Is there some other way in?" Amy nodded to the treeline before them. "It's not like we have to swim across. There must be some backroad we can take."

Lara shook her head. "There's no roads anywhere near the demarcation line. The border's patrolled constantly. More so on this side. We'd be spotted in a heartbeat."

They watched the road, neither one speaking. The dog trotted up behind Amy and nosed her hand.

"We'll have to chance it," Amy said.

Lara looked at her reflection in the windshield. "God, I look terrible. We should clean up first, try to look like tourists."

Amy opened up the back. "I packed us some clothes. Brought your toothbrush too." She nodded at the ramshackle gas station. The exterior door of the bathroom was filthy and chipped. "How disgusting do you think that bathroom is?"

"You don't want to know." Lara rifled through the bags, pulling out clean clothes. "So what's our story? Why are we visiting British Columbia?"

"To see family." Amy pulled out the small toiletries bag. "Tomorrow is Christmas Eve."

Lara's face darkened.

"You okay?"

"Yeah. It's just, I usually spend Christmas at my sister's. This will be the first time without her in five years."

Amy kept unpacking stuff, pretending she didn't see Lara quickly wipe her eyes. "Maybe when this is all over, you can call Marisol. Just to let her know you're okay."

"Yeah. Maybe."

The bathroom was cramped and it smelled and they jostled over one another as they changed clothes and made themselves look as normal and bland as possible. Just two gals travelling into another country for the holidays. With a cache of lethal firepower hidden in the back.

The husky was waiting patiently outside the door when they came out. They climbed back into the truck and drove for the border.

33

GALLAGHER AWOKE TO SILENCE. No vibrating rumble of the vehicle nor low hush of highway whipping past. He sat up, stiff from the hard floor beneath him and blinked his eyes against the gloom. His coat had been tossed over him as a blanket. The temperature had dropped and he wasn't in the van anymore.

His hands were free, the restraints gone. So too was the blindfold and the gag over his mouth. The floor underneath him was wooden and it creaked under his weight at the slightest movement. Slits of light broke through chinks in the wall and his eyes picked out the contours of a room. Bare walls and the old wood floor, dark joists strapped across the ceiling. The room smelled of must and dirt and rot. Where the hell was he?

He got to his feet and his head swam like a bad hangover. His eyes found the outlines of a door. He expected it be locked but the door swung open with a croak of rusty hinges. The glare of sunlight off the snow blinded him. The ground stretched out before him and ended at a wall of trees. Giant pine and cedar, a few spruce trees. His boots crunched the snow as he stepped out and turned back to survey the building he had awoken in. A ramshackle wooden house of blackened clapboard and grey cedar shingle. At least a century old, the timbers skewed and the beams tilted out of plumb. Crumbling slowly in on itself with the weight of the snow pushing the roof down. Hemmed in close behind the house stood the treeline, the heavy forest creeping in as if slowly swallowing the structure.

He stood on a road. Fresh tire tracks in the snow. A single vehicle had passed this way, presumably the one he'd been transported in. The treads snaked away as the road twisted around a bend. He followed the tracks, rounding the bend. More buildings came into view, lining both sides of the road. Some were houses or small cottages, others were tall with wide verandas. Storefronts with picture windows. All of them as old and decrepit as the one he'd awoken in. A crumbling pioneer outpost from the early part of the last century, left to molder against the wall of pines creeping in around it.

A ghost town.

THE border crossing was relatively quiet, even for this time of the year. Two pickups and a handful of tractor trailers snaking their way through the guard booths. Lara drummed the steering wheel and watched the vehicles inch forward. Not one had been pulled aside.

So far.

"I think we'll be okay," she said. "They're waving most people through without a fuss. Christmas, I guess."

Amy bit her lip and turned to regard the dog in the backseat. "What about the dog? What if they hassle us about him?"

"Just be cool and everything will be okay."

"This is crazy. Maybe we should turn back, try something else."

Lara took the girl's wrist. "You have to calm down. These people go on their gut instincts. Any paranoia or twitchy behavior will set them off. So be cool. Okay?"

Amy took a breath and counted sheep as they inched closer. Needing to distract the girl from her own demise, Lara asked her about basketball. Was she still playing guard? How had her team performed this year?

It worked. Amy launched into a breathless recap of their season and how she had improved her game but still had a problem fighting off the bigger players. Lara kept her talking until they drew up before the yellow swing arm.

The border guard peered at them with an air of practiced boredom. A woman in badly applied eyeshadow and plastic nails asked them where they were from and what their nationality was.

"American," said Lara. "From Portland." The key to bullshitting your way through was to cut as close to the truth as you can. A ruse Lara had gleaned from an endless parade of shifty smokehounds trying to eyefuck her in an interview room.

"Where are you headed?" the guard asked.

"Calgary."

The woman bent low to see Amy and then scanned the rear seat of the truck. "What's the purpose of your visit and how long will you be staying?"

"We're spending the holidays with some family. Coming back the day after Boxing day. So five days."

"Uh-huh. Is that dog registered?"

Lara just rolled with it, spotting a test when she saw it. "Yup."

The woman clicked her fake nails on the window sill. "What's his name?"

Amy gulped. The dog didn't have a name. Why hadn't they ever named the dog? How stupid had they been?

"Ivan," Lara replied without missing a beat. "He's not liking the drive at all."

The woman clicked her teeth. "They're like little kids in the car, huh?"

"Exactly." Lara smiled back. "What kind of dog do you have?"

"Sharpie," the guard said. "She hates the car too." She reached for her control panel and the liftgate swung up. "You have a Merry Christmas."

"You too." Lara waved and drove through the checkpoint, picking up speed as the dotted lines guided them onto the road into another country.

Amy gasped for air, realizing that she had held her breath the whole time.

The husky stuck its snout through the window, flaring its nostrils against a fresh blast of wind and scent.

Another hour on the road before stopping for gas. They bought a roadmap and sandwiches and let the dog stretch its legs Amy unfolded the map on their knees. "Where are we?"

"We crossed here in Boundary." Lara pointed at the map. "So we're about here. They're still north of us."

A dollop of tuna salad dribbled onto the map. Amy wiped it away and snaked a finger along their route. "There's a lot of wilderness here. And not too many towns."

"Mountains too."

"Can you tell if we're getting close?"

Lara shook her head. "He's got a day's start on us. Plenty of lead time."

"You need some rest. You're looking a little bleary."

"I'm fine."

Amy leveled her with a look. "Lara, you've been driving for how many hours? You're starting to weave all over the road."

Lara couldn't deny it. The last hour had been rough, her eyesight blurring the road ahead. Now with a meal in her belly, exhaustion set in to roost. "Okay. We'll find a motel somewhere and get a couple hours of sleep, then continue on."

"I don't want to lose anymore time," Amy said. "You sleep in the back. I'll drive for a while."

"You're exhausted too. We both need to be alert when we get there."

Amy looked at the map again. "Where's there?"

"There's only one highway that runs through these mountains." Lara traced her finger up the map to an open space of green. "They turned off the main road, somewhere up in here I think."

Amy lifted her gaze to the road. "What if we're too late?"

"Your dad's going to be okay."

"How do you know? He could be—" She cut off the thought before uttering it.

"Grissom wants me to find him. He won't do anything drastic until I do."

Amy took a breath to calm down. "What are we gonna do when we get there?"

"I don't know yet," Lara said. "One more reason to rest up and clear our heads."

Amy lowered her eyes to the map again. "Looks like there's a town up here. Not too far."

"Okay, let's crash there. Where's the dog?"

The tiniest crack of a smile lifted Amy's mouth. "You mean Ivan?"

"I know. My mind blanked out on names. Except for that one."

Amy stepped out and opened the back door, whistling for the mutt. The husky trotted up out of a ditch with its nose dusted in snow and leapt into the back.

THE crumbling shacks held little but musty smells and broken glass. The dry bones of woodmice strewn amongst the debris on the dryrot floors. Gallagher roamed from building to building, exploring the earthly remains of whatever town this was. He found a blacksmith's shop with an anvil and blast furnace still intact. Rusting pickaxes and spades piled into a corner, the wooden handles splintered and gone. He hefted the pick, the tool of a miner and guessed that this was once an outpost of the goldrush. One of a countless number of towns that sprung up overnight when some crazed hermit panned gold from a creekbed. Abandoned just as fast when the vein ran dry and no further ore could be picked or dynamited from the mountainside.

He ducked under the low lintel and stepped out to the road. His eyes cast up and down the drag, ears cocked for any sound but there was none. Where was Grissom? Did he dump him here and keep moving? Why bother abducting him at all? Cupping a hand over his mouth he hollered up a 'hello'. A bird startled from a tree and flapped away. Nothing more.

He explored more of the dead village, passing the barnboard wreck of a stable and the ruins of a church. The roof had caved in and the cross that had once crested the steeple lay poking up out of the snow.

The single tire treads wound past the ruins of the church and graded down the hill. There, at the bottom of the slope, was a vehicle.

A plain-looking cargo van, quiet and still on the incline. Rushing down, he jerked open the driver's door. Empty.

The keys, impossibly, remained in the ignition.

He turned the key but nothing happened. Not even a click. He turned it again and again. He popped the latch lever and climbed out. Threw up the hood and peered into the engine. The distributor cap was gone, the cables ripped out to leave the plugs exposed and useless. Searching around the van, hoping to find where it had been tossed but there was no sign of it. Gallagher spit onto the snow. The vehicle was useless.

Opening the rear door revealed little save the space he'd been confined in. There was a toolkit and a chainsaw. A red gasoline canister, three-quarters full. Trash and debris.

What the hell was the bastard up to? Grissom had transported him all the way out here to this ghost town and then crippled the van beyond repair. That meant that Grissom was close but had no further need of the vehicle.

End of the line. For everybody.

AMY awoke to a cold nose pressed into her cheek. The husky snorted and wagged its tail. Pushing the dog away, she sat up and looked at the window. Still dark outside.

Lara didn't stir in the bed next to her. She didn't wake, didn't even seem to be breathing she lay so still. Amy shuddered and got dressed quietly and took the dog outside.

She let the dog run and walked to the truck stop just south of the motel. Got coffee, eggs and bagels to go and headed back. Slipping back inside the motel room, she found the bed empty and the bathroom door closed. A hushed break from the other side of the door that sounded like sobbing.

Amy stood still, listening. "Lara?"

The sobbing ceased, replaced with the sound of running water.

Lara emerged from the bathroom, patting her face dry with a towel. "We overslept."

"Guess we needed it," Amy shrugged. "Is everything okay?"

"Yeah." Lara reached for her clothes. "Is that breakfast?"

"Greasy spoon fare." Amy handed over a cup of coffee and watched Lara dress. "Anything you want to talk about?"

"No. Let's get going. We'll eat on the road, okay?"

The highway was empty of traffic so she let Amy drive. A single vehicle passed them travelling south before the sky broke grey. Sunup still an hour away. Lara studied the map, trying to spot some area of terrain where Grissom might hold up.

Amy held the wheel. "Any luck?"

"No." Lara put the map down and watched the road. "They're close though."

"How can you tell?"

"It's hard to explain. I can just tell."

The Cherokee drifted over the yellow line. Amy corrected her course. "When you change into the, you know, wolf, do you remember anything?"

"Nothing."

"Nothing?"

Amy steered on. "I think when you become the wolf, some part of you is still conscious."

"Can't be." Lara watched the trees whip past. "It's an animal. Not even an animal."

"When we were in the garage and you changed then, you didn't attack me or dad. You...or it snapped and snarled but held off. It wanted to attack but something held it back. That was you."

"You're reading too much into it."

"No. There was something in the wolf's eyes. Some recognition or something." Amy glanced at her but Lara stared out the window. "I saw that other one up close, the grey one. There was nothing but murder in that thing's eyes. Hatred, savagery."

Lara stopped listening. Something was wrong and it was wrong immediately. She sat upright and looked back. "Stop the truck."

"What's wrong?"

"I lost them. Pull over."

Amy drifted onto the snowy shoulder and slowed. Lara jumped out before the vehicle had even stopped. Turning her nose to the road ahead and downwind the way they had come.

Amy leaned into the passenger seat. "What is it?"

"I lost the scent." Lara climbed back inside. "Go back. They must have turned off the road somewhere."

Amy cranked the wheel and doubled back down the empty road. "Where did we lose them?"

"I don't know. Keep your eyes peeled for a turn-off or side road."

Amy slowed her speed and they scanned the ditch on both sides. Trees and snow and rock. It all looked the same, with no break or clearing. The dog was on its feet now and Lara lowered the back window so the husky could poke its muzzle out into the wind.

"There," Amy said, pointing to a faint break of bare white in the roadside. A windrow of snow bifurcated with tire treads.

She turned into the break and plowed through the windrow. The side road, if it was a road, appeared as no more than a winding path of white cutting through the trees. Unplowed as it was, the snow was cleft with twin tracks that snaked ahead and vanished among the pine trees. "I don't know if this is even a road. Is it on the map?"

"No." Lara checked the map again. "This is just some old logging trail."

"Are you sure they went this way?"

Lara's nose quivered. "This is it."

Amy shifted into neutral, coasting over the snow and toggled the shifter. A short grinding sound before the four-wheel drive bumped in.

34

THE TEMPERATURE DROPPED WHEN the sun went down, sending Gallagher scrambling for shelter. One of the ramshackle houses had a fireplace and a few dry matches scattered on the mantel. He broke up what furniture there was for firewood and passed the night on the dirty floor. He didn't sleep but he didn't dream either.

When morning came his back was stiff and his mouth parched. A sour ache churned his stomach and he couldn't remember when he last ate. The ghost town looked as dead as ever in the grey light and he went back to the blacksmith's shop to rummage among the broken tools for a weapon. There was an axe with a heavy blade but the petrified handle split under the first test swing. Tossing it back with disgust, he quit the shop.

The treads of the van were still visible in the snow so he followed them. It would be miles of dense forest before any sign of life but it was better than staying in this hamlet of tombstone houses and dryrot history.

Keeping a casual pace he lost sight of the town and was enveloped in a bleary scape of snow and tree trunks with nothing but the tracks before him to distinguish anything. He'd not gone far when he heard something rustle the trees. Gliding invisible among the pines, matching his pace. Stalking him.

He should have looked harder for a weapon. Even a heavy stick would do but there was nothing in his hands and even less in his pockets.

Another few paces and the wolf appeared. It sklathed out of the trees and onto the road before him. Massive in its girth, the hackles raised and its chops slung open to reveal the rows of outsized teeth. He assumed it to be Grissom but this wolf's pelage was dark, almost black. It wasn't Grissom. Some other lobo.

A second wolf emerged from the treeline to his left and then two more on his right flank. Without turning around, he sensed the fifth one moving up behind him. Werewolves. A pack of them, like storybook beasts with their snouts curled back in snarls. Monstrous in their abhorrence, things that skulked the ragged periphery of the natural order. Blasphemous things all.

The monsters were enormous but seemed thin and ragged. Deep scars riven across their snouts and dorsals. One was walleyed, as if driven insane by its condition and another loped in a peculiar trot, one hind leg missing from the shank down.

His heart seized up at the sight of them, these things from his nightmares. His hands went numb, all the fight draining out of him. Encountering just one of these monsters had ruined his life but now this. A pack of them.

Just lie down and die.

Get it over with.

The wolves circled at a distance, as if sensing his defeat and waiting for him to give up the ghost. Sidling in a trot, muzzles low to the ground. Grouping and then fanning out.

A gap opened on his right flank and Gallagher moved, stomping through the trees, traversing uphill. The lobos sklathed forward and he clambered up a low foothill, keeping one eye on the pack as he went. For a moment he fooled himself that there was an advantage to this, moving uphill of the monsters but it was a pretense and no more. He was at their mercy and the wolves were simply taking their time with it.

Clambering up, he saw a dark maw opening against the snowy hillscape. The mouth of some cave or cleft in the mountain. He scrambled towards it. Shelter or a last stand. An Alamo.

The wolves closed in, bolting forward and running at a pass towards him without striking. Taunting him. Gallagher cursed them and flung a dead branch at the nearest one and clambered on with all he had. He heard their jaws pop at his heels, teeth snapping like death.

It was a mine shaft. The mouth of it framed in moldering beams, a few broken tools strewn aside like artifacts from some mad archeological dig. Gallagher crashed over the broken timbers and scrambled inside. Moving further in, his boots slipping on what felt like loose shale. Impossible to run, visibility swallowed in the gloom. He fell, a rattle of dry sticks against his knees and then he looked back. The opening of the mineshaft was an orb of white light in the pitch.

The wolves passed against the opening and passed again, dark forms against the light but they did not enter. After a moment they appeared no more and he knew they were waiting for him to come out again.

Gallagher stepped warily but there was nowhere to find a firm footing, his boots crunching over this pile of dry sticks that blanketed the entire floor of the mine. When his eyes adjusted to the gloom, he saw what he was treading on. Bones. The calcified ribcages and broken skulls and snapped vertebrae of man and animal alike carpeted the floor of the cave like some mass ossuary.

This was no shelter, no last defense. It was a killing floor. The wolves lair. No Alamo, no last stand.

Gallagher sunk down, rattling a slurry of drybones under him, and tried to remember the last words he had spoken to his daughter. It hadn't been goodbye.

THE road winnowed down to a treacherous slice of snow, little more than a gap in the brush. The wheels dipped and clunked over the snowcrust, jerking and popping the Cherokee's suspension. Amy's knuckles were white from gripping the steering wheel as she fought to keep the vehicle on the path.

"Easy," Lara said, one hand on the dashboard. Wondering if she shouldn't take the wheel.

"Sorry. It's hard to see the road."

"That's because there isn't one."

Amy slowed to a crawl and followed the path as it meandered through the thicket of snowloaded branches. The road vanished as she negotiated a hairpin turn. Then she hit the brakes.

An enormous tree lay across the path. The massive trunk four hands in diameter and God only knew how many tons of it. There was no going around it.

Amy looked at Lara. "Now what?"

"We weren't meant to drive any further." Lara studied the fallen timber and the snowbound path underneath it. The vehicle treads they had followed passed underneath the deadfall. "The tree was pushed down after the vehicle drove through."

"Grissom pushed it down?" Amy blinked at the massive thing.

Lara pointed to the sheared end of it, the sawdust splayed over the snow. "He cut it down."

"Okay. So what, we go in on foot?"

"Yup." Lara checked the road on her side. "But let's turn the truck around so it's pointed the other way. Just in case we have to leave in a hurry."

The tires spun in the snow and Amy cursed when she bumped up against a tree but got the Cherokee turned around in the tight space. She climbed out and let the dog out of the backseat.

Lara strode away from the stink of the vehicle to catch the breeze coming through the brush. The hair on her arms stood up and something cold fingered up her spine. Trouble on the wind.

Amy unloaded the weapons from the duffel. She checked the load on the Eagle and laid it aside and checked the Glock. This she stuck into her coat pocket and reached for the shotgun. Pumping it once to find it unloaded, she took up the hulls loose in the bag and loaded them into the chamber.

The dog was antsy. Nose twitching at the road ahead and pacing in a circle only to stop and sniff the air again. Amy turned, saw Lara acting strange too. Stock still and staring off in the same direction as the husky. "Lara, you okay?"

Lara didn't respond, didn't move.

"Is dad out there?"

Lara shook her head as if to clear it. "Yes. So is Grissom."

"I guess the dog smells them too. He's acting weird."

There was more than that on the wind. Exactly what, Lara couldn't tell but she didn't like it. Could Grissom's musk be that strong or was it something else? She looked at Amy. "I think you should stay here. Keep the truck ready to go when I get back."

"I'm not doing that." Amy went back to unloading their gear.

"Something isn't right here, Amy. Please."

"We've run this number already. I'm not staying back. Not if that bastard has Dad." Amy plucked a flashbang from the bag. "What's out there?"

"More wolves."

Amy stopped what she was doing. A heartbeat and then she hauled her backpack onto her shoulders and closed the hatch. She came round with the shotgun in one hand and the 50 .cal in the other. "I don't care."

The husky slunk between them and leaped onto the fallen tree.

"If you can smell Grissom from here, can he smell you coming?"

"Yes." Lara registered the weapons in Amy's hands. "Where's the Glock?"

"In my pocket."

Nodding to the Eagle and the shotgun. "Which one do you want?"

"What's the plan?"

"Find your father. Kill Grissom."

Amy held out the big handgun. Lara took it and chinned the Mossberg clutched in the girl's hand. "Are you okay with that?"

"The spread is lethal," said Amy. "If there are other wolves, I want a good shot at blowing them to pulp."

Lara scrutinized the girl's eyes. For the hundredth time she questioned the wisdom of bringing her to this place but there was no turning back now. She cinched up her coat and Amy did the same and they set out on the trail, the husky loping through the snow before them.

NOTHING passed before the mouth of the cave, nothing blocked the light coming in. Gallagher sat among the bones and scrambled his brains for a plan. He rummaged through the ossified remains, the bones tinkling like dry wood, until he found a thick stem of femur broken off at one end in a splintered point. Barely a weapon.

A shadow rose up before the mine entrance but the silhouette blocking the available light stood on two legs, not four.

"Come on out of there," the figure called out.

Grissom.

Gallagher held his breath, didn't move.

"The wolves are gone," Grissom hollered up, his voice ringing off the walls of the mine shaft. "Come out of there. We need to talk."

No sense in hiding. Gallagher made for the entrance, his bootheels grinding the skeletal twigs under each step. The splintered bone spur clenched in his fist. If he was lucky, he might get a chance to drive it through the son-of-a-bitch's eye.

Stepping out of the darkness into the pale light, he scanned the terrain. No wolves, just the man.

Grissom stood back from the entrance, raising his palms as if to prove there was nothing up his sleeve. "They're gone. I called 'em off."

Gallagher gritted his teeth. The last thing he wanted from this bastard was to parlay. "Where did those things come from?"

"All over." Grissom lowered his hands. "This country, some from the States. One of 'em came all the way from Mexico."

"And they're all like you?"

"No, they're nothing like me. They're true wolves now."

"True wolves?"

"True as can be," Grissom said. "They changed all the way, no shred of humanity left. They can't ever change back." He kicked at the snow with his boot. "So no, they ain't like me anymore. Or Lara. They've gone all the way."

Gallagher eyeballed the distance between himself and his abductor but there was too much ground to strike. Grissom was strong and he was fast. Keep him talking, draw him in. "What is this place?"

Grissom stuck his hands in his pockets, casual as can be. "Used to be called Blackwood back in the gold rush days. But you won't find it on any map. Quiet, ain't it?" He rocked back on his heels, friendly and gregarious. "That's what I like about it. Mind you, about two years back, we had some folks set up camp here, looking to build some half-assed hippie commune. They didn't last too long neither."

"Why was that?"

The man grinned. "They didn't cotton much to its true residents."

"You."

"Us," Grissom said. "The pack winters here. Come the spring, we'll move back north."

Another step closer. Grissom remained relaxed, like he was chitchatting on a streetcorner and didn't seem to notice that Gallagher was closing the distance. Gallagher kept jawing. "Why'd you bring me here?"

"Lara needs a little push. And I knew she'd come if I hauled your sorry ass up here."

"You think she's coming?"

"I know she is."

"So what then? You take her prisoner?"

"Won't have to." Grissom scanned the trees about, the mountain. "Once she's here, among her true kind, she'll stay of her own accord. Take her place in the pack."

Gallagher turned his head and spat into the snow. "Just like that, huh? You think she's going to settle in with you filthy mutts."

"Where is else is she gonna go? With you? We both know that ain't gonna work."

"Why? Why go to all this trouble?"

"Every pack needs a female." Grissom kicked at the snow. "Our numbers have been cut down. All males now. The pack needs to rebuild. That means breeding."

Gallagher almost dropped the spur, taking in what the man said. "Breed? Are you fucking crazy?"

"It's not easy, not with our kind at least. But Lara's strong. She can do this."

Gallagher gritted his teeth to stay calm. A half step. He ballparked the distance to six feet. Almost there, keep him talking. "And what happens then, when Lara joins your pack?"

"I think you know."

"You're going to kill me."

"Fraid so." Grissom shrugged, like it was all out of his hands. "See, Lara's got one last step to make to become a wolf. She's never taken a human life and that's where you come in. When the prodigal returns, you get to be the fatted calf."

Gallagher snarled. "Then I hope you choke on my bones you ugly son of a bitch."

"That's the spirit, detective."

"Course, that's assuming Lara comes at all. She's no dummy."

"Oh she's coming all right." Grissom turned and looked back towards the town. "In fact, she's already here."

Grissom's back was almost turned. No better chance. Gallagher sprang, slamming the man into the ground. The bone spur in his fist plunged deep into Grissom's neck. Blood erupted up over his hand, gurgling onto the snow.

The roar from Grissom's throat was an echo straight from Hell it sounded so inhuman. He bucked like a bronco, throwing Gallagher.

Gallagher rolled across the snow, sprang up only to be flattened by a ten-ton weight. Blood spackled over him as Grissom shoved his face into the icy ground. Hissed in his ear. "You're a tough old bastard, ain't you? Tough meat too but maybe we can tenderize that some."

Gallagher felt the blow to his skull, but only for a tiny moment.

35

THE DOG HAD PICKED UP THE scent, bounding ahead on the snow-packed trail. Lara trudged on, the hair on the back of her neck bristling at each step. Grissom and Amy's father were close but there was something else jagging her nerves raw. The vastness of the evergreens and the mountains, a steamy fog lifting from the snow. The absence of people and their stench. The immensity of sky plucked at some chord in her heart that was hard to deny. Had it been so bad, those days of exile with no companion but the birds? It would be so easy to shrug off her skin and slip into the wolf. Lara Mendes could be left behind like the husk of a moulting snake while her lupine shadow ran free.

The only thing spoiling the moment was the sound of Amy's boots grinding the snow.

The girl marched in silence, cutting a grim figure for someone so young. Armed with the pump action and a cast of pure murder in her eyes, she bore little resemblance to the seventeen-year old she had left behind in Portland. Maybe she was feeling the wild call to her too.

Amy sensed her eyes on her. "Are they close?"

"Very."

"So what's the plan?"

"Grissom will come out to talk. We demand he free your dad."

"And if he doesn't?"

"I'm going to kill him," Lara said. "Either way."

Amy narrowed her gaze on the woman. The cold frankness of her voice. "Is that necessary?"

"He won't stop until he gets what he wants. Either I give in or he dies. There isn't any other way." Lara marched on, the path rising uphill. "We have some element of surprise. He's only expecting me."

"Will that be enough?"

Lara's eyes dropped to the Mossberg in the girl's hand. "Are you prepared to use that? Because if you're not, I'll go on alone from here."

"I'm sure." A half-truth. Lara's demeanor had changed since they left the truck and it frayed at Amy's resolve. Lara seemed alien and distant, some stranger marching beside her in the middle of nowhere.

"Amy, if this gets messy I may change. You might have to get your dad out on your own." Lara stopped and took the girl by the arm. "Can you do that?"

"Yes. But I think you should fight it. There's something different here and if you change, I'm not sure you'd come back to us. Sounds crazy, I know, but..." Amy shrugged and left the rest unsaid.

They went on, cresting the hill and looked down at the tombstone shacks of the dead town. There was no sound as they approached, no winter birds flitting from the trees. Even the breeze held its breath.

Amy gripped the shotgun tighter as they passed the first of the abandoned structures. Leaning in the snow at odd angles, the rotting front stoops like broken teeth in a leering face. "What is this place?" Amy hissed.

Lara shook her head, her eyes peeled for any movement as the passed through the gauntlet of haunted houses.

A burst of movement. Amy brought the shotgun to her shoulder but lowered it as the husky came bounding back at a dead run. It circled around them, whimpering.

Amy thumped his ribs. "He's scared."

"He smells what's here." Lara stopped moving, listening. "Wolves."

"Grissom?"

"More than him."

Amy took a step backwards. "Oh shit."

Lara nosed Grissom before her eyes spotted him. The road, flanked by dryrot shacks on both sides, was empty and then it wasn't. The figure seemed to rise up out of the earth and there Grissom stood, straddling the road as if waiting on an old friend.

Amy brought the gun to bear and would have fired if Lara hadn't snatched the barrel. The girl shot daggers at the woman. "What are you doing? He's all alone."

"We need to find your dad first," Lara snapped. "Keep your cool."

Grissom watched them inch forward, unconcerned or unaware that he'd almost been shot. "What took you so long?"

It took all Lara had to keep the 50 caliber weapon pointed at the ground. Every instinct itching to just shoot the leering son of a bitch. "Where's Gallagher?"

"He's here." Grissom stopped and regarded her. His eyes slunk to the girl and his mouth stretched into a pervert's grin. "I'm surprised you brought the pup. Hello Amy."

"If you've hurt him I swear to god I will kill you." Amy felt all the blood rush to her head and her hands tremble in stifled rage. "Let him go. Now."

"Business first, kiddo." Grissom turned his eyes back to the woman. "You ready to join us, Lara? The pack's waiting on you."

"I'm ready."

Amy startled, chanced a glance at Lara. What if she was speaking the truth, unable to resist what was clearly calling out to her? That meant she had walked right into a trap and she wouldn't save her dad. He would die alone out here, at the mercy of the wolves. So would she.

"Let me see Gallagher first," Lara said. "I'll go with you, but after the girl and her father are safely away."

The grin on his face soured. "Let's drop the bullshit, okay? You know how this plays out."

Amy didn't want to hear anymore. She nestled the stock into her shoulder and leveled the barrels at Grissom's face.

"Amy, lower the damn gun," Lara hissed.

"Shut up." Amy kept her sights on the man. "Where is he?"

Grissom leered, nonplussed at staring down the business end of a twelve gauge barrel. Bending at the knees, he reached down and pulled up a rope hidden unseen on the ground. Trailing it up, the rope lifted from the snow and lead off behind one of the shacks. He tugged it smartly and something stumbled into the open.

Gallagher staggered in, kicking up snow with each step. Hands bound behind his back and Grissom's tether noosed around his neck. His face was bloodied and he stumbled as if drunk each time the cord was yanked. He dropped to his knees and hung his head as if shamed.

"Dad!" Amy bolted, pure instinct upon seeing her father in such a state. Her arm was snatched, holding her back.

"Stay where you are."

"What are you doing?" Amy pushed Lara off but couldn't shake her. "He's hurt."

"It's a trap. He wants you to run in."

Amy ceased but a wire burned hot in her brain. Wanting nothing more than to blast Grissom away but her only weapon was useless. The buckshot would flay her father at this range before hitting its target.

"Cut him loose, Grissom" Lara shouted. "He's not the one you want."

"Put the canon down. Come to me." Grissom gathered the slack rope into a loop. "Simple as that. Then he can go to the girl."

"Gallagher first."

"You got nowhere else to go, Lara. You're one of us now." He let the rope fall. "Can't you feel it? All around you, this place calling to you. It's home. Where you belong."

Amy held one eye on Lara, feeling a chill up her spine. The woman was trembling and her eyes flared up with that unearthly amber. She was feeling it. "Lara...?"

Lara swung the Desert Eagle up in both hands and pulled the trigger. The boom deafening. The shot was intentionally high but Grissom instinctively ducked all the same. "Now," Lara demanded.

The man's face darkened. Gallagher was still on his knees but his face tilted up at them, squinting at two blurry figures as if witnessing a mirage.

Grissom sounded. Some inhuman noise. A bark of command that brought forth the wolves.

They padded out from the shadows of the ghost town. Five in all. Outsized beasts from some childhood nightmare. Scarred and foul and mad-looking. Spittle ran from their chops as the wolves snorted up the smell of kin and fresh meat.

Amy's heart dropped into her guts at the sight of them, these monsters. She could smell them from where she slackjawed and the musky tang of them choked liked tear gas. She stumbled back, turning to Lara for a cue.

Her heart withered altogether.

Lara was on her knees, a blasted expression in her eyes. The gun barrel dipped into the snow. The proximity of the wolves, their scent and appearance, blew the wind from Lara's sails and expunged reason from her mind. Her eyes flared brighter and Amy knew the woman was beginning to change. To give in.

"Lara, don't!" She grasped her by the collar and shook hard. "Snap out of it!"

The lobos skulked in. One kin, one easy kill.

Grissom's voice echoed over the bedlam. "I was saving Gallagher for the big kill. Your first human,

Lara. Your baptism. But here you brought the girl. She'll do."

Grissom clicked his teeth and the wolves swung their muzzles in his direction. He uttered some obscene roar and nodded to the man in the noose.

The wolves surged forward in a primal attack. Their massive teeth ripped into John Gallagher and his blood bloomed red on the dirty snow.

36

EVERYTHING IN AMY GALLAGHER'S eyes slurred to slow-motion horror as she watched the wolves swarm her father. She heard him scream in pain, a sound she'd never heard before. A sound no child ever should.

Lara remained on her knees, lost in some private hell of her own. The big gun with the silver-tipped rounds lay useless in her hand, the barrel end filling up with snow.

Amy dropped the shotgun and snatched the Eagle from Lara's cold hand. Planting her feet, she raised the heavy weapon in both hands and drew the bead on the mass of roiling wolf flesh.

Boom.

The recoil knocked her shoulders back. A wolf cartwheeled under the impact, its hind quarter destroyed. It let out a diabolical cry and the pack reared up en masse and charged at her.

An enormous lobo with white flecking thundered up fast, its jaws opening wide to swallow her whole. She corrected her aim and blasted the round straight down the monster's gullet. Its spine exploded outward in a spray of gore that showered the wolves behind as it tumbled grotesquely over the ground.

The pack broke ranks, scattering confused against the destruction that had downed their frater. They thundered past and snapped and roared at the girl. Amy tracked the darting targets with the muzzle and blasted another round. It went wide, strafing the trees.

The crack of gunfire jerked Lara from her spell. She saw the bloodied mess of the lobo before her, the lone girl fighting off a pack of lycanthropes. She snatched up the discarded shotgun and fired from the hip. The wolves roared at the sting and she pumped the slide and fired again.

The banshee of the wolves was deafening, their attempt to regroup fouled by the blasts of buckshot and silver caps. They broke and scattered for the trees, leaving only the fading sound of their pads thundering into the wilderness.

Lara swung the Mossberg round but Grissom had vanished. All that remained was the dark form of Gallagher sprawled in the snow. He didn't move.

The dog rose up from where it had hunkered down during the racket of gunfire. It bolted for the prone form on the snow and when Amy and Lara caught up to it, the husky was licking the bleeding wounds.

"Dad?" Amy dropped and touched his cheek. The eyes half-lidded. "Dad, wake up!"

Unconscious. Blood seeping through his coat. Lara hauled him up and peeled back the parka. "Help me get his coat off."

The girl didn't move, didn't react. Shock numbing brain and limbs alike.

"AMY!" Lara snapped. "We need to check his wounds. Help me."

Amy moved robotically as the shock tried to freeze her blood. She tugged the coat free and they laid it under him . There was more blood staining the shirt and Lara tore this away to expose the wounds. Smearing the blood away revealed the angry puncture wounds left by the wolves' teeth.

"Oh God," Amy gasped at the rows of teeth marks. "They bit through the coat..."

Both knew what that meant. Neither gave voice to it. The dog lapped at the blood. Lara pushed it away. "We need to stop the bleeding."

Amy slipped off her backpack and dug through it. Tossing a small first-aid kit to Lara, she rooted out two rolls of gauze, some tape.

"You packed all this?" Lara said, watching Amy pull more supplies from the backpack. "Smart girl."

They worked fast, cleaning away the blood and patching the wounds as best they could. Laying his arms straight, Amy cinched the coat over him to keep him warm and Lara bent to examine the wound on his leg. A noise filtered through the trees, stopping them both.

The awful howling of a wolf, out there in that chaos of wilderness.

Lara was on her feet with the gun sweeping the treeline. The dog froze with one paw raised, ears cocked.

"Are they coming back?"

"I can't tell." Lara lowered the barrel. "We're wide open here. Get him inside."

They dragged him over the snow to the nearest tinderbox shack and laid him out on the bare floor. Amy pushed back the panic bubbling up her gullet. "Is he gonna be okay?"

"There's no major bleeding, no arteries severed." Lara cinched his coat tighter. "We need to keep him warm, in case he goes into shock."

Amy cradled her father's head in her lap and smoothed the hair from his brow. His skin was cold against her palm. "We have to get him out of here." She rubbed the heel of her palm into her eyes and looked at Lara. "We have to get him back to the truck."

Lara shot to the door and surveyed the dead town. "We wouldn't get very far."

Not the answer Amy could stomach. "We can't stay here. Those things will just pick us off. We can carry him. Or drag him or whatever."

"Catch your breath."

"No, goddamnit! We found him, now we have to go."

Lara stayed her vigil at the door, unable to look at the girl.

Amy loathed being ignored.

Easing her dad's head to the floor, she sprang at the woman. "We can't wait here to be slaughtered. Help me carry him!"

"Stop!" Lara barked back. "We need a plan."

Amy saw Lara's hands tremble. Something was wrong. "You're stalling. You're feeling it. Aren't you?"

"What are you talking about?"

"The wolves. They're getting to you."

"Don't panic on me." Lara bit down her own rage but the look in the girl's eyes unnerved her. The betrayal and revulsion laid bare in those young eyes.

"Why don't you go to them? If that's what you want, just go. Let me take my dad and leave." Amy shook her head and snarled. "The only reason we're here is because of you."

Lara snapped. What broke from her throat sounded neither English nor human. A guttural animal noise. A flash of amber flared over her irises and Amy took another step back, suddenly regretting what she had provoked.

THE sound of their voices wormed into his unconscious brain but what had truly awoken him was the goddawful smell. Gallagher's eyes opened to an extreme close-up of teeth and his heart jumped until he realized it was only the husky. Lapping his face and assaulting him with dog breath.

He pushed it away and tried to sit up but the pain zapped him with its voltage and he lay still until it ebbed away. He studied the dark ceiling above and listened to the voices in the room until his foggy brain could stitch together a few broken pieces of memory. Grissom outside the cave. Wanting to kill Grissom. A rope around his neck, pulling him along like a mutt on a leash. Ho ho, the irony of that. How clever.

After that, nothing. A black hole. Had he been shot?

The voices again, somewhere out of his range of vision. He clenched his teeth and hauled himself up into a sitting position, the agony sharp enough to make him vomit. He caught his breath and squinted at the two figures across the room. Lara. She had come for him, like he knew she would. But who was the other one?

He blinked at the smaller figure clutching a shotgun. It couldn't be Amy. Lara wouldn't be that stupid or careless to bring his daughter out here. And yet, who else could it be?

His voice didn't want to work. Too parched or too raw or maybe it was injured. He tried again, forcing it up but all that came out was "Why?"

The women turned. First Lara then Amy. Of course it was Amy. They rushed to him, both talking at the same time. "How do you feel...lie down...don't talk...does it hurt?"

"Why?" His throat reduced to spitting out single words. He looked at his daughter. "Why are you here?"

"Easy," Amy said. "You're hurt."

He grabbed at Lara, wanting to shake her violently. "Why did you bring her here?"

Lara didn't answer. She pulled his hand away.

Amy zoomed into his frame of reference. "Dad, slow down. You've been hurt."

"What?"

"You've been hurt," Amy repeated. "Be still."

The pain hadn't gone away, his anger had simply overruled it. He looked down and saw the blood on his clothes. His coat had fallen open, along with his shirt. Gauze bandages taped over his ribs. Still no cognizant memory of how he'd been injured. "How?"

Neither Amy nor Lara spoke. How many times had he seen his daughter cry? He knew the facial tics when the floodgates were threatening to open up.

Jesus, how bad could it be?

Lara softened her tone. "Do you remember anything?"

"Grissom. A rope around my neck." He shrugged. Even that hurt.

"You were attacked," Lara said, then stopped. Reluctant to spit out the rest.

His daughter's voice was a hoarse whisper. "Grissom set the wolves on you. You were...mauled."

He didn't want to believe it but the blood and the pain said otherwise. Shards of memory floated back like smudged Polaroids tossed into the air. The stink of the lobos and the sting of their teeth. He had been bitten by the wolves.

bitten

infected

cursed

The truth of it punched him down and he boiled it back up and spewed it out in a banshee wail so anguished and abrupt that his daughter and old partner backed off. When the dregs of it ran dry, Gallagher hung his head and wished it all away. After all this, coming so close, only to be trumped and doomed in one razor cut.

He felt a hand on his cheek. Amy, tipping low to find his eyes. "Dad," she spoke in a gentle hush. "It's okay. We'll figure it—"

"Don't," he cut her off. "Don't even go there." Gallagher pushed her hand away and coiled up. Said no more.

Lara watched the exchange. The sting in the eyes of the girl and the withdrawal of the father. She knew what was wringing out his insides because she had experienced it. But she had suffered it alone. "John," she said. "Snap out of it. I know what you're going through but we don't have time right now. Accept it and deal."

His eyes flashed venom. "Accept it? Like this is a case of the clap? Whoops?"

"That's exactly what I mean." She tapped the watch on her wrist. "We're on the clock right now."

"Get away from me."

It was his turn to be shaken senseless. Lara snatched him up and rattled him so hard he felt the meat slur from his bones. "You don't have time for this, John. Your daughter is here and the wolves are out there." Her tone softened as her rage ebbed off. "I'll help you through it. Just not now."

He pushed her hands away and croaked into a sitting position. He shook his head and spat onto the floor. "How did you get here?"

"The truck," Amy said. "But it's back down the road about a quarter mile. Grissom blocked the way in."

"Who's got the fifty cal?"

"I do." Amy pulled the Eagle from her pocket.

"How many silver rounds left?"

Amy slid the magazine out, eyeballing a hasty count. "Half the magazine. Four."

He looked at Lara. "Where are the wolves?"

"They scattered." Lara turned to the open door, the breeze blowing in. "They didn't go far."

Gallagher rattled up the Mossberg and thrust it into Amy's hands. "Take this and make for the truck as fast as you can. Take the dog with you."

"What about you two?"

"Lara and I will make a stand here and kill as many of them as we can."

"No," Amy gritted. "We're not doing that."

Lara agreed. "That won't work, John."

"It's you they're after, not her." His tone harsh, accusatory. "Amy's fast. She can make it."

"And what if the pack splits and some of them go for her?"

His face darkened. She was right and he hated her for it. Amy put it to rest. "Forget it. I'm not leaving. Think of something else."

No one spoke. The dog paced near the door, unable to sit still.

"There's gotta be something." Amy's frustration bubbled up. She kicked at a broken floorboard. "We have weapons. There's three of us against five of them."

"Six," Gallagher said. "I counted five wolves, plus Grissom. Twice our number."

"It's five," Lara corrected him. "Amy took out one of them."

His eyes brightened on his daughter. "You did?"

Amy shrugged. No big deal.

"Good girl." He pushed himself up. "Where is it?"

37

THE CARCASS LAY IN THE SNOW where it had died. The three of them looked down at the wet mass of blood and fur.

"Hell of a shot," Gallagher had limped out of the shack despite their protests, slow and unsteady but determined to walk. "Score one for the visitors."

"We're still trailing." Amy turned away from the gore at their feet. "Three to five."

"Are you two done with the basketball analogy?" Lara frowned. "Because I'll go wait over there until you are."

The dog sniffed at the carcass warily. It snorted then withdrew, keeping clear of the dead thing. Gallagher watched the husky as it raised its snout to the air. "What we need is to even up the numbers. All the way."

Lara knelt over the carcass, studying the glassy eyes. "How so?"

"By incinerating them. Come over here."

He pointed down the grade. "There," he said.

The road inclined down past a few outbuildings to where the white cargo van squatted in the snow. Lara arced an eyebrow. "Was that your ride?"

"Yup. Not a pleasant one."

"Why didn't you just drive away?" Amy asked.

"Grissom disabled it. But the gas tank is at three-quarters. And there's a canister in the back."

Amy scowled. "So it's useless."

"Just the opposite," Lara said, seeing what Gallagher was hinting at. "It's a bomb, waiting to go off."

"You want to blow it up?"

Gallagher nodded. "We rig it to explode, get the wolves to close in and ka-boom."

"That would even the odds," Lara agreed.

He looked at Lara. "We keep the van between us and them and then blow it when they're close enough."

Amy wasn't buying it. "What if they don't go anywhere near it?"

"We lure 'em close."

"With what? Us?"

Gallagher turned back the carcass in the snow. "These things aren't used to losing, are they? To something fighting back."

"No," Lara agreed. "They're top of the food chain."

"Maybe we can rattle their confidence first. Confuse them." He turned to Lara. "There's a chainsaw in the back of the van. Can you get it?"

Lara's skepticism was palpable, her words almost moot. "What for?"

He smiled. "We're gonna cut the head of that thing."

"JUST give it a sharp tug. When it catches, throttle it up and start cutting."

Lara gripped the chainsaw in one hand, the other tight on the rip cord. She looked down at the carcass. The wolf's tongue splayed out of the open maw. "I don't think I can do this."

"You have to," Gallagher said. He would have gladly sawed the bastard thing up but his injured left arm was too weak to hold the chainsaw. "There's nothing to it."

Lara stalled. This thing wasn't her, she knew that, but she recoiled at the thought of dismembering it. With so blunt an instrument as this.

"He's right," Amy said. She stood with arms folded, a hint of suspicion lingering in her gaze. "I know it's gross but you have to be the one to do this. Cut any ties to these...things."

The contempt dripping off Amy's last word left Lara wondering how much the girl resented her for putting them all in this situation. This was a test. Beheading the dead wolf no more than a line in the sand. What are you, Lara Mendes? Woman or wolf? On which side does your allegiance fall?

She yanked the cord hard and the engine fired up and sputtered out. Another pull and it roared to life and Lara throttled the gas. The chainsaw roared, lethal and powerful, in her hands. Tilting it down, she bit the buzzing blade into the grey pelage and the blood flew, spewing out a fine mist across the snow like red spray paint. Amy stepped back to prevent being misted by the blood.

The action slowed as the blade sunk into the neck meat and she sawed the blade back and forth, pushing it deeper. It snagged on the bone and sputtered out. Placing her boot on the thing's jaw, she worked the saw free and pulled the cord again. Another stab into the carcass but slow and cautious against the vertebrae to avoid another choke. The buzzing vibration numbed her hands but she kept sawing down and then the blade slipped through into the snow. The severed head of the wolf tipped over like a split pumpkin.

"You'd make a hell of a lumberjack." Gallagher reached down, clutched the wet pelage and hoisted the wolf's head into the air. Gore dribbled down the exposed meat and bloomed against the snow, the head twisting slowly in his grasp. "Heavy son of a bitch too."

Lara hit the killswitch and dropped the chainsaw in the snow. Amy's face paled to a shade of seafoam green. "Sick," she said.

THE husky usually heeled up beside Gallagher but with the gory mass in his hand, the dog kept its distance. Dogs can display a variety of facial expressions; warmth, anger, playfulness. Disgust is nigh impossible for a canine's limited range but somehow the Siberian conveyed its revulsion with crystalline clarity.

The head plopped into the snow as they approached the van. Gallagher flipped open the small fuel door and spun the cap off. Lara threw open the rear doors. "How do you want to rig this?"

"Keep it simple," he said. "I need some cloth or rags. Then we splash out a gas trail to a safe distance up the hill."

Lara turned to Amy. "Toss me the backpack. Then get the canister from the back."

Amy handed her the pack and went to the backdoors. Lara dug out a roll of gauze and unfurled it. "Will this do?"

"Perfect."

Amy returned, loosening the cap off the red plastic fuel container. Gallagher soaked the gauze in fuel and fed one end down the van's tank, letting the other trail down the side of the van. "Can you tell where the wolves are?"

"North of us." Lara nodded towards the road leading out of the ghost town. "They'll come that way."

He looked off in that direction and then crossed to where the decapitated head lay upended in the snow. Nudging it with his boot, he flipped it right side up. "Trail out the gas around this thing, then lead a trail of it up the hill."

Amy gathered up her backpack while Lara poured the gasoline over the ground, trailing out a path back up the road. When the canister ran dry she tossed it into the trees and the three of them crossed to the broken veranda of the nearest house.

Amy called the dog to her and rubbed her hands down its back. "Now what?"

"We wait."

Amy looked up at the paling light over the tree tops as the last of the daylight faded away.

NIGHT fell and draped all with inky pitch and then the moon rose over the treeline. The sky was clear and filled with stars. The moon burned cold in the night sky and burnished the snow around them with a pale blue glow.

The three wayfarers sat hunkered on the broken steps, shivering as the temperature dropped. Amy looked up at the riot of stars and studied the moon, how it hung there like a paper lantern in the dark. "Look at that. Full moon."

Lara and her father glanced up but made no reply, their eyes dropping back swiftly to the road before them.

"Kinda funny, I guess." Amy craned her neck, wondering if staring at the full moon could harm one's eyes. "Now, of all nights. Will that affect the wolves?"

Lara looked up at the sky again. "It's giving us plenty of light."

"Will they howl at it?"

"I honestly don't know," Lara said. "These aren't typical wolves."

Amy blew into her hands. "I'm cold. I wish we could start a fire."

"Try moving around. Get your blood pumping."

Amy got up and stomped her feet. Lara watched the girl pace around and stop to stare up at that big moon and pace around again. She turned to Gallagher, who sat quiet and huddled up with his arms crossed over his knees like some gargoyle on a perch. His eyes fixed on the road outbound before them. She put a hand over his arm. He was quaking underneath. "Hey. Are you all right?"

"I feel stiff." He raised his good hand, clenching and unclenching a fist. "Like every muscle is seizing up on me."

It was the paralysis that was working through his limbs. It would worsen until his entire body was paralyzed in a death-like rigor that would leave only his mind free. Lara had undergone it after being attacked and remembered it as the most terrifying experience she had ever suffered. Ivan Prall had called it a baptism. She related none of this to him, only squeezing his arm and saying "You should get up and stretch."

Gallagher watched his daughter pacing the snow and then leaned in to Lara, speaking in a hush. "How long do I have? Before this starts affecting me?"

"I don't know. I think it effects everyone differently."

"Then these fucking wolves had better hurry up before I keel over." His eyes went back to the road. "How stupid is this plan?"

"It's going to work. Don't second guess it."

They both watched Amy pace the ground in a circle. "All that matters now is her," he said. "Whatever happens here, she has to get out."

"I know."

"Promise me, you'll get her out of here."

"Don't talk like you're saying goodbye." She shivered and folded her arms tight around her. The tone of his voice scared her and she didn't need that hanging over her. Not now, not with what they had to face. "It's not fair."

"You're right." Gallagher studied her profile as she kept watch. "Sometimes I forget that you got your battle to fight. I'm sorry."

A breeze blew the snow up, kicking white pixies between them. She touched his arm again, sought out his eyes. "So am I. I never meant to put your family in danger."

"We're here now, we'll finish this." He coughed, wincing as a flash of pain shot through him. "Jesus. How bad does this get?"

"Bad."

"I don't know if I can deal with this."

"You have to." She brushed away the snow nesting on her eyelashes. "I did it. So can you."

"I'm not so sure. You survived this, managed it. I don't know if I'm as strong as you are."

She thought he was pulling her leg but saw neither smirk nor wink in his eye. She leaned her head against his shoulder and meant to say something reassuring about their predicament but when she spoke, something else tripped from her lips.

"I love you, John. Whatever happens now."

"You better." He leaned in and kissed the crown of her head. "Cuz I love you back."

"Heads up." Amy stopped pacing. "They're back."

Lara shot to her feet. How had she missed it? The wolves slinking back without her detecting it first?

The road before them was a pale band of blue bookended by dark trees. The wolves no more than shadows without origin creeping into that open sea of blue haze.

Gallagher rose and fought to keep his balance. All three watched the lobos advance. They had divvied up the weapons. Amy refused to take the pump action but Gallagher insisted. It packed a punch and his hands were shaky. He took the smaller caliber service issue and Lara wielded the canon. The husky spanned the road before them, back and forth with its tail slung low.

Amy glanced quickly at the other two. "Do they see us?"

"Yes."

"Amy, over here." Gallagher motioned to a spot beside him. Amy planted herself behind them. He swapped the Glock to his numbed hand and dug into a pocket for the lighter ensconced there. Their collective gaze fixed onto the wolves, waiting to see what they would do.

The pack trotted near the dead vehicle and the lead animal halted and the others heeled. Their snouts dropped to the snow in unison, tails lowering as their noses picked out the unnerving smell near the van.

The severed head stained the snow and the wolves approached it cautiously, circling it with their noses slung low. They closed in on it and prodded it with their snouts and backed off in a start and circled round. One lobo shot its head skyward and throttled up a mournful howl to the moon. The pack howled up after it until the sky reverberated with their baleful cries.

Gallagher dropped to one knee, the disposable lighter in hand. Stretching out before them, invisible in the snow, lay the trail of gasoline snaking back to the vehicle.

"Fuck you pooch," he said and flicked the lighter to the fuel.

The flames whooshed up and fled down the road in an arrow of fire, zigzagging towards the pack of monsters. The wolves stopped howling and veered backwards. Any animal, even unnatural beasts such as these, instinctively fear the flame.

The fire snaked down the snow in a headlong rush as it closed the distance. Then it sputtered out. The flames roiled up less than twenty paces from their target and winked out in a hiss.

As quick as it had started, it vanished. Their plan evaporated the instant the flame died.

"Oh God."

The wolves charged. A rampage of snarls and rage. Three weapons came up like a firing squad at an execution. The crack of the hammers was deafening and gunsmoke filled the air.

The wolves scattered, veering off the main road to the shadows but still they came on. A hellish noise of popping teeth as they rushed forward, invisible in the darkness. Booming towards them on both sides.

Gallagher barked at them to move back. "Get inside. Now!"

They careened up the tilting veranda of the desolate house, retreating to the door when the first wolf sprang. It shot up over the railing, splintering the balusters. Its jaws sprang open as it hurtled towards Amy. Lara and Gallagher turned and fired and the thing bucked backwards and skittered for cover but already the others were charging in.

They slammed the door shut, shot the bolt through. Something hammered into it from the other side and the bolt held but the top hinge plate tore from its desiccated casing. A massive and foul snout shot through the gap, the snapping teeth wet in the pale light. Gallagher jammed the pistol barrel under the thing's jaw and fired. Blood geysered up out of the nose and the snout withdrew.

The east window exploded in a spray of glass and splintered muntin, another wolf bulking the frame as it dove inwards. Amy pivoted on one heel with the Mossberg leveled and blasted a hole in the damned thing. The kick knocked her back but she recovered, racked the slide and fired again. The monster retreated. Lara pushed over a dusty hutch to cover the breached window. It tilted forward as another of the lobos tried the window, forcing its way in and Lara fired at it. Blood sprayed across the sash.

The door bucked again, Gallagher shouldered it back. The west window exploded as another wolf sought entry. Splinters of wood rained down from above. Gallagher looked up to see cracks in the rafters as something traversed the decayed roof over their heads.

Another blow against the door jostled him back and he all but tripped over the chainsaw left on the floor. He blinked at the tool. Blunt and close range but probably more effective than the nine millimeter in his hand.

He cursed, looking for a way out but there wasn't one. How long could they hold them off in this tinderbox shell? Three doomed piggies with the wolf blowing at the door and their ammunition going fast. And out there, at the bottom of the hill, lay the trap they had abandoned, rigged but yet to be tripped.

There is a way out. Simply a question of how badly you want it?

He snatched up the chainsaw, flipped the toggle and yanked the cord. He called his daughter to him and she backed towards him, the shotgun trained on the window. "Amy, bolt this door after I go, Understand?"

She saw his hand draw back the bolt on the lock. "What are you doing? You can't go out there!"

"I'm gonna buy us a little time. Just lock this af- ter me!"

"Are you crazy? No."

"We can't hold them off much longer." He squeezed her arm. "Trust me. Okay?"

Amy shook her head, refusing to cooperate. He pulled her close and kissed her brow. A roar at the window broke the spell as another lobo fought its way inside. Amy swung the barrel up and blasted it full in the face.

With his daughter occupied, Gallagher slipped out and shut the door behind him.

38

A WOLF WAS WAITING FOR HIM. As if knowing that one of them would rabbit. It squatted there in the snow and sprang up at him with its jaws open.

Gallagher throttled the gas and swung the chainsaw up to block those awful teeth and cut deep into the lobo's maw. The Husqvarna sawed through the yellow teeth, splicing deep into the bone. The wolf shook its head in a frenzy to extricate itself and it ran off.

He ran through the snow, the impact of each step jarring his wounds, the pain hot. The wolves came after him, pounding at his heels until he stopped and swung the chainsaw. The whizzing blade caught the fur of the closest lobo and the others backed off. And then it was a game of keepaway as the wolves chomped and he swung the buzzing saw at them. The lobos darted and feinted and he throttled the chainsaw to keep them back, moving downhill one step at a time.

The van squatted in the snow, the fuel door propped open just as they had left it.

THE husky skittered along the floor. It barked and snapped at the wolves erupting through the windows and then cowered under the blasts of gunfire. When the wolf burst back into the window, popping the casing out with its bulk, the husky leapt and sunk its teeth into its neck. Jerking violently back and forth, trying to rip open the tough hide but the monster swung its head round and clamped its teeth onto the dog's flank.

Amy shouldered the pump action but held off the shot, screaming at the dog to get out of the way. She saw the wolf bite into the husky and the dog yelped, hit the floor. It scrabbled away leaving a smear of blood behind. Amy unloaded the charge and the wolf screamed from the blast of buckshot to the face. She pivoted back to scream at her father but he wasn't there. The door cracked open.

Lara spun at the dog's cry and fired. The trigger piece locked, the gun jammed. The piece was hot as she hammered the slide to spin out the jammed round before the lobo crashed inside. Then she heard Amy scream for her father. Her eyes took in the girl and the open door but no Gallagher. He simply wasn't there. Had he been snatched away?

"Where is he?" Her voice shrilled with panic.

Amy turned and her mouth gaped but no words came. The terror in the girl's eyes was raw.

The husky limped forward, dribbling blood from its flank, and pointed its nose to the door. It bolted forward, hopping in a peculiar limp past Amy's knees as it shot out the door.

"No!" She grabbed at it, hollering for the dog to stop but it sped past leaving her with a handful of bloodied mane.

Amy spun back to Lara for help, for anything. All she saw was the wolf bursting through the window like a hurricane, taking Lara down in a flurry of teeth.

LEVIATHAN teeth chopped at Gallagher's heel and he swung the roaring chainsaw but the monster dodged and parried. The wolves were playing with him now, matching his pace with unhurried grace, each lobo watching for an opening to take him down.

He felt a slick warmth run down his belly and he knew that the gauze had ripped away and he was bleeding anew. How long before he lost too much blood to keep up the pace? The van was close. The trap.

An unnatural roar blew hot on his ear. The crazed looking wolf with its walleyed stare pounded in recklessly as if it meant to run him over and he brought the burring saw teeth hard onto its snout. It cried out and he throttled it harder, exulting in the demon's pain.

He sprinted for the van. Triumphant. Overconfident.

The scarred lobo with the disfigured snout came in like a shot on his starboard flank. It took him down hard and its teeth sunk into his ribs. It shuddered him hard, the way it would a fieldmouse and then let go and he spun crazily through space and slammed hard into the panel side of the cargo van.

Thumping onto the snow, light spots in his eyes. His injured left arm folded underneath him like jelly and bent at an angle it was never meant to. The bone shattered. The sunspots faded and he realized he had landed beside the van. Snapping jaws clarified before his eyes and he saw the pack surround him.

Easy pickings. No more challenge than a broken rabbit. The damned things almost leered at him with perverse lupine grins.

"Fuck you, hoss," he hissed at the nearest wolf. "This ain't your show."

He dug into a pocket and came back with the cheap plastic lighter. Next to him, the open fuel door and the rippling stink of gasoline. The petrol soaked rag of gauze. One flick and it was all over.

Light 'em up.

The wolves closed in.

Amy.

He thought of his daughter. He wished he could say something more to her. What was there to say? Goodbye never works. He wished this didn't have to happen, that none of it had come to pass. He wouldn't be around to see his daughter grow up. All those clichéd milestones. Graduating high school, maybe college. Dinners when she'd come home for the weekend. Walking her down the aisle to some putz he would never approve of but would fake for Amy's sake. Kids. Grandkids.

There was so much left to do. All he had left were seconds.

She'd be okay. Amy was smart, tough when she needed to be. More than that, she was wise. Wiser than she should be for a kid her age. That happened to kids of divorce; they got wise or they got troubled. Amy would be okay, even after all this crazy bullshit. He trusted her in that.

But before any of that, he had to do what was required. To underwrite that future.

The lighter wavered and he couldn't stop his hand from trembling.

Do it. Now or forever.

Movement snagged his eye and something shot through the legs of the wolves surrounding him and collided into him. For a flashing moment he thought it was one of the pack but it was too small. It licked his face with a coarse tongue.

The dog squirmed up against him, wagging and whining as it licked his chin. The mangy Siberian he had pulled from the pound all those months ago. Of all the times...

"No!" He pushed it away. "Get outta here! Go!"

The husky slunk its head low, confused and cowed, but it wouldn't leave.

He swatted its rear, trying to make it bolt away but the stupid dog wouldn't run and now it was too late.

The wolves closed in. No way out now.

He pulled the dog in and draped his arm round it. Cursed it for being so goddamn thickheaded. The plastic lighter flickered in his hand and the flame blew. Gallagher pulled the dog close and buried his face into its neck.

It was bright and it was hot and the flames ate the breath from their lungs.

And then it was over.

THE weight of the wolf pinned Lara to the floor. She kicked at it like a mule. Two battles, fighting off the wolf with its teeth in her and holding back the wolf inside. The lobo within clawed at the door of her heart but she wouldn't let it out no matter how much her nerves screamed for release. Capitulating to the lupin now would mean the death of them all.

The wolf bit down, its yellow eye walled up at her own. She caught a glimpse of Amy hammering the butt of the shotgun against the monster, trying to crush its skull. Feeling the impact of each blow through the teeth in her shoulder but the lobo refused to let go. She twisted under it, gaining some wiggle room and drove her thumb hard into the wolf's eye. It popped with a wet smack.

The thing reared back and shook its head as if trying to dislodge the crushed eyeball. Then an awful noise broke against the timbers of the house. The howling of the pack, savage and unearthly. A war cry. The wolf lunged away, crashing through the door as it escaped.

Lara felt herself jerked upright, Amy pulling her to her feet. The girl was in a panic, barking at her to hurry. "Slow down," she said. "Where's your dad?"

"He's out there. He ran outside." The girl's eyes were crazed with urgency as she pulled Lara to the door.

The pain in her shoulder clouded everything. The girl wasn't making sense. Why would Gallagher run outside? It didn't make any sense.

They hurtled down the broken steps, lurching onto the snow. Further down the path they saw the wolves congregated before the crippled van. Then a glimpse of Gallagher, clutching the husky to him and then it all flashed out in a ball of fire.

The shockwave knocked them back. The fireball mushroomed bright against the winter sky. Tiny comets of flaming shrapnel zipped past their ears.

Lara turned her eyes from the light of this artificial sun, disbelieving what she already knew was true. Gallagher had sprung the trap.

He was gone.

She reached for Amy. The girl's face blanked in shock, her lips worked up and down without sound until a single word tripped out.

"Dad."

The girl stumbled for the inferno, repeating the word like a mantra. Lara pulled her back and Amy fought to get away but she held fast until the girl collapsed into her.

A cry of anguish erupted from the bonfire. A mass of molten flame stumbled from the blaze and careened over the snow this way, now that. The wolf a shimmering mass within a rolling ball of fire. It staggered on, howling as it went and Lara blocked her ears until the monster fell into a heap and howled no more.

The burning vehicle popped and blew, smaller eruptions that flung more shrapnel through the air and these flaming missiles struck the dryrot shacks of the town. The desiccated wooden frames went up like stacks of kindling and the fire reached out its greedy fingers to touch the next one, a daisy chain of flames winding its way through the ghost town.

"We have to go." Lara pulled the girl up but Amy wouldn't budge. Still in shock, Lara doubted the girl could even hear her. "Please, Amy. The fire is spreading."

Amy flailed and pushed away, saying she didn't care and then she lay down on the snow and hugged her knees.

Lara watched the girl shudder with sobs but she had made a promise and pushed down her own grief. She snatched Amy up and jerked her clean to her feet. "We're getting out of here. If I have to carry you, I will."

The girl lowered her head and took the woman's arm, letting herself be led away. Lara turned them away from the burning wreckage and guided the way out. The heat rolling off the burning shacks singed their faces as the fire raced from ruin to ruin. She quickened the pace, startled at how fast the decayed outpost was going up in flames.

An ungodly shriek rang out, stopping them in their tracks. They turned. A ball of fire broke from the inferno and shot towards them. Flames riffled and trailed like a comet's tail as the burning wolf thundered at them. Its boiling eyes locked on Lara and Lara alone.

Even through the flames, Lara deciphered those ravaged eyes. Grissom.

She blanched. Only enough time to push Amy out of the way before the fireball slammed into her, impacting with the force of a runaway train. The woman and the wolf tumbled over the ground. Flames hissed against the snow and teeth popped in the woman's face. Her hands singed holding back its jaws. The wolf savage and driven mindless with pain, its sheer strength overpowering her.

She could not win this contest, doomed if she tried. Lara dug deep and unclenched some small part of her heart and allowed the wolf a little space. Just enough to stretch its limbs and give her its strength. Like walking on razorwire; too much and she would lose control, too little and the burning lobo would snap her neck in two. It was already too close, the beast blowing hot on her face.

It flared up in her eyes, a guttural sound rumbling in her throat. Power hummed her veins and Lara Mendes dug her fingers round the wolf's throat. Its windpipe collapsed under her grip and she didn't let up until the monster choked and rolled away.

The wolf scrabbled madly over the snow, its hide billowing up greasy black smoke. It jerked and reeled in spasms, morphing with the roll of tremors. Fur and blood flew off with each paroxysm until the wolf shed its skin to lay bare the man.

Amy rolled onto her knees, eyes saucered at the struggle, then the transfiguration. The man lay in a wreckage of twisted limbs and charred flesh. She looked away. Lara gasped for breath like an asthmatic. A volcano trembling to erupt.

Amy threw her arms around the woman and pulled her close. The way one would to a child suffering a fit. "Easy," she cooed. "Push it down."

The woman shrilled at Amy to get away from her. She shrugged and shirked, trying to slip free but Amy held on that much tighter and whispered into her ear. "You're bigger than it. Push the wolf down."

Tremors rippled through her stem to stern. Lara bit down, folding the wolf back into its place in some dark and unmapped chamber of her heart. The wolf bansheed for release but she choked it back until the lobo capitulated and sank with a low tail.

Amy felt Lara go limp. The struggle was over, Lara had won.

"*Bitch.*"

A garroted voice, gurgling out that single word. Grissom clawed at the frozen ground, a charred husk of a man reeling under the eye of the moon.

"Bitch," he gibbered, smoke puffing from his lungs. He dragged his broken frame forward. "You were supposed to be our bitch..."

Amy felt Lara shudder and held her tight until the last tremor passed and she hissed at Grissom. "Shut up. Just shut up and die."

Grissom rolled over onto his back. Eyes open the night sky, a last tendril of smoke issuing his lips. "You were the one. You were sup save us..."

Amy gritted her teeth, willing the man to die. She dug through the pockets of Lara's tattered parka until she came up with the big gun and its calibers of silver tipped catastrophe. She gripped the piece in both hands and leveled the barrel at the burnt man.

Her arms trembled under the weight of it. The man was a monster. A killer. She screamed at herself to put him down but the man's eyes rolled up to meet hers and her finger froze on the trigger piece.

A hand touched her arm. Lara teetered up on shaky knees. "Give me the gun."

Amy didn't respond, didn't move. Her arms locked in place.

Grissom swiveled his eyes to Lara. "You betrayed the pack..."

"I'm not like you," she said. "Never was."

Boom.

Amy pulled the trigger and Edgar Grissom's head erupted in a vomit of gore over the snow. The upper half of his skull splayed out but his jaw remained whole. It gibbered open and shut as if there were some last words to say but nothing spilled out and then the jawbone stilled.

The moldering cottages around them burned in a riot of orange and yellow flames, the dried up mining town giving up the ghost to the fire and the heat of it melting the snow around them.

The woman leaned on the girl and they turned away and tottered back the way they had come. No father, not even the dog.

THEY said little on the drive home. Stopping at a gas station, they cleaned up as best they could before crossing the border. Despite having to work the holiday, the border agent was cheerful and seemed to sense the grief rolling out the window of the Cherokee. She waved them through, wishing them a merry Christmas.

Traffic was light as they came back to city. Amy shrank down in her seat as the familiar sights zipped past the window. It didn't look the same. Never would.

The Cherokee rolled to a stop outside of Cheryl's house and Lara killed the engine. Amy looked up at her mother's house and listened to the truck tick and sputter.

Lara grasped for something to say but there were no words that fit. All she could do was reach out and take the girl's hand.

"What happens now?"

"I don't know. I can't stay."

Amy nodded and Lara felt her heart sink even further. After all the girl had been through and now she had to abandon her.

Amy wiped her eyes. "Where will you go?"

"I'm not sure. Maybe south."

"Will you stay in touch?"

"Of course."

Amy scrounged a pen from the glove box and scratched out an email address on a scrap of paper. She handed it over and swung out of the cab. "Goodbye, Lara."

"Goodbye, Amy."

Amy closed the door and watched the truck roll away and then she turned and went up the steps.

39

New Mexico - One month later

THE BUS RIDE WAS LONG and tedious and Amy tried to sleep through most of it. Twenty-six hours on the road from Oregon to New Mexico, with stopovers in Boise, Twin Falls and Salt Lake City. She slept coiled up in the seat with her shoes off and her head vibrating against the window. The stir of the other passengers woke her and she squinted out the window at that unending flatland. A line on the horizon, low hills in the distance and sky. She had never seen anything so barren.

"We're here," said the man next to her. He straightened up and ran a hand through his hair. "About damn time too."

Amy watched the desert scrub give way to flat-topped buildings and grey strip malls as the bus wheeled through the streets of Albuquerque. She slipped on her shoes and silently thanked God the bus ride was over.

The bus trip was her brilliant idea but her mother had flat out refused to let her go. All kinds of terrible people travel by bus, Cheryl argued. It's no way for decent people to travel she declared and refused to buy a ticket. Amy packed her gear and paid for the ticket herself. Cheryl had insisted on driving her to the station and on the platform she slipped an envelope into Amy's pocket as they said goodbye. Amy didn't touch it until the bus had pulled away, opening the envelope to find a modest stash of twenty dollar bills. The note read: *Walking around money. Call if you need anything.* She smiled at that.

She stepped off the bus and collected her backpack from the luggage compartment. The sky overhead was blue and the air dry, so unlike the constant dampness of home. Shouldering the pack, she looked over the people milling through the bus station for a familiar face.

Lara Mendes cut through the foot-draggers, her face beaming with a big, big smile. The backpack slid to the floor and they embraced and held on and when they pulled back, both wiped away tears. "It's good to see you," Amy said. "You look great."

"I'm so glad you could come, Amy." Lara leaned back to get a better look at the girl. "Did you cut your hair?"

"Nope."

"Well, there's something different about you. Come on, let's get out of here." Lara took the backpack and led the way out of the station, asking how the trip was. Amy told her about the cranky man who complained at length about how federal taxation was killing America.

"Sounds brutal."

"I told him I was running away from home. Pregnant."

"Did that shut him up?"

"No. He wanted to save me."

They turned up 2nd Street to a gravel parking lot.

"Oh my God," Amy said. "You still have the truck?"

Lara unlocked the Cherokee and loaded in the backpack. "I should probably trade it in for something else but, I don't know. I'm kind of attached to it now."

Amy bit her lip to stem the tide rising up in her. Seeing Lara after all this time, and now their old truck, brought it all back. When she climbed into the passenger side and closed the door, it hit her even more.

Lara saw the girl struggling. "You okay?"

"It's just the truck. It smells like dad."

"I know." Lara turned the ignition. "The dog too."

Amy laughed.

AMY watched the streets roll past the window. The flat-topped buildings and dust-blown exteriors, all the signs in Spanish. "How do you like living here?"

"It's all right," Lara shrugged. "It's got good parts and bad parts, like any place. I'm settling in."

"What's your place like?"

"It's small. But nice." Lara turned off Third Street and headed west on Gold. "Have you heard from Charlene lately?"

"She stopped by last week," Amy said. "Not officially or anything. She just wanted to see how I was doing."

Before saying goodbye that last time in Portland, the two of them had discussed the police investigation that would follow. Amy would stick to the story she had initially told Detective Charlene Farbre; that her dad had located missing homicide detective Lara Mendes and the two of them appeared to be working some private investigation. As to Lara's escape from police custody, Amy would claim total ignorance. She told Detective Farbre that, following her father's abduction, she had stayed at a friend's house for a few days.

After dropping Amy off at her mother's house, Lara had made one last stop before leaving Portland for good. At a payphone on Fremont, she called Charlene Farbre and told her that John Gallagher was dead. Sketching out few details, Lara told the detective how the suspect involved in her own disappearance had abducted Gallagher and she had gone after them but she had failed to bring him home. The suspect's name was Edgar Grissom. Both the suspect and Gallagher had perished in her attempt to free her former partner. The detective had insisted that she turn herself in immediately but Lara appealed to Charlene, an old friend, for clemency. The phone call was the best she could do right now but asked that Charlene go easy when she questions Gallagher's daughter. The girl knew nothing of this. Lara had said goodbye and ended the call.

To her credit, Charlene had done what had been asked and kept Amy out of the investigation as much as possible.

"I feel kinda bad for Charlene," Amy said. "Left with all those questions, not knowing what really happened. Must be frustrating."

"That's police work. She's used to it."

The truck rumbled along and Amy sat back, listening to the familiar hum of the engine. She watched the buildings as Lara drove out of the core and she watched the people on the street go by. Everything seemed so flat here, the houses and the horizon.

She chewed her lip trying to think of some polite way to broach what was on her mind. There wasn't one. "What about you? How are you coping with, you know, your situation?"

"I'm good." Lara cracked the window down to let in some air. "I mean, it's still there. It's always there but it's under control. It's gotten a lot easier to manage, to tell you the truth."

"Have you had any, like, episodes?"

"One. But that was my doing. I drove out to the desert one night and let it happen. I just wanted to see how much control I had."

"Oh." Amy couldn't help the surprise in her voice. "What happened?"

"I ran the desert. But I was still there, you know? Still present. When the sun rose, the lobo came back to the truck and it was all over." Lara wheeled onto another street. "I caught a cold from it."

"A cold?"

"You wouldn't believe how cold the desert gets at night. And there I am, in my birthday suit and sweating like you wouldn't believe. Hurrying to get my clothes back on. I'm lucky I didn't catch pneumonia."

Amy smirked and Lara slowed the vehicle. She swung the Cherokee into the driveway of a modest ranch style home. A rabbitbrush hedge framed the yard. "Is this your place?" she asked. "It's nice."

"This is my sister's house." Lara swung out of the cab. "Come on, I want you to meet her."

Amy blinked. "Your sister?"

Marisol Sparks was a few years younger and looked nothing like her older sister. Five foot nothing with a big smile, her hair cut short in a bob. Marisol came out of the kitchen wiping her hands on a towel and threw her arms around Amy. Kisses on both cheeks. "Finally I get to meet the famous Amy," the woman said. "I've heard so much about you. Come in, come in." Amy took another step inside the door when Marisol suddenly hugged her again. "Honey, I'm so sorry for your loss. I've said prayers for you and your dad."

Caught off guard, Amy glanced at Lara but her friend just beamed like a proud aunt. Marisol chased them inside and shouted into the living room. "Jackson, come say hello to tia's friend!"

A small boy with big eyes peeked around the corner and studied the guest but came no further. Marisol said something to him in Spanish but the boy clung to the wall. A quick wave was all he offered as a greeting.

"He's shy around strangers," Lara said. "Give him a few minutes, he'll warm up to you."

While Marisol hurried back into the kitchen, Amy took Lara's arm. "Is this safe? I mean, staying with your sister?"

"Yeah, everything's fine."

"What did you tell her? About your disappearance and stuff?"

"I told her everything. Are you hungry?" Lara shrugged out of her coat and hurried for the little boy watching from the doorway. Amy watched her go, unsure she had heard Lara correctly.

Marisol had prepared dinner, something special for her sister's friend. Amy had never had chile rellenos before and helped herself to thirds. Jackson warmed up to her over desert and had brought out his favorite toy, a Spiderman figure, and showed Amy all the tricks it could do. Marisol asked after Amy's mom and how school was going, her plans for the future. So warm and welcoming, she seemed to Amy like an aunt she had never met before. Amy asked if Marisol's husband, who was serving overseas, was coming home any time soon.

"They're supposed to rotate him back home in April." Marisol ruffled her son's hair. "We're counting the days. Right, honey?"

"Seventy-two," Jackson said loudly.

Lara beamed. "Can you believe how smart he is?"

Amy wanted to help with the dishes but Marisol would hear nothing of the sort, insisting that she and Lara catch up. Amy rubbed her belly, regretting having thirds. Lara leaned and squeezed Amy's hand. "How about you? How are you coping?"

Amy shrugged. "I dunno. It still doesn't seem real, you know? That he's gone. Sometimes I forget that he's not here. I'll think of something to tell him, something funny I heard, and then I'll remember that he's gone."

Noise tumbled from the other room. Jackson playing Spiderman. Amy flushed, went on. "It doesn't seem to get any easier. I mean, you hear people talk about closure and stuff. I keep waiting for that to happen or at least not hurt so bad when it comes but..."

"Closure's a myth," Lara said. "I don't why people talk about it like you can put your grief in a box and be done with it. It doesn't go away, it just hurts less each day." She nodded towards the kitchen, the sound of dishes clanking in a sink of water. "We lost our dad when we were kids. I was twelve, Marisol nine. I still miss him."

"Do you still think about him?"

"All the time."

Amy spun her teacup around with one finger. "Maybe it would have been easier if there'd been a funeral. Something to mark the occasion. But we had nothing to bury."

"Maybe." Lara pushed her chair back and rose up. "Grab your coat. We'll get going."

"Where to?"

"We'll drop your gear at my place, then take a ride. There's something I want to show you."

THEY climbed back into the truck after saying goodbye. Marisol made Amy promise they'd be here for dinner tomorrow night. She was planning something special. Amy demurred, said "Don't go out of your way for me, Marisol. Please."

"Who do I have to cook for?" Marisol replied. "Please. Just be here at four tomorrow. On the dot."

Five blocks west, Lara pulled up before a small Santa Fe with vigas extended from the façade. The interior was small and barely furnished. "It's not much to look at, is it?" Lara said. "I kind of like it Spartan like this."

"It's cute," Amy said as she got the tour.

Two bedrooms off the back. Lara showed her into the smaller of the two and laid her backpack on the bed. "This is the guest room. Again, not much to look at." The bed pushed against the wall was small, the dresser secondhand.

"Stop apologizing." Amy looked out the window. "I love it."

Lara ended the tour in the backyard, "This is the nicest part of the house." In contrast to the interior, the yard was a riot of cactus and shrubs, ironwork furniture and ornaments hung from branches. A clay chiminea bookended by two log benches.

"It's beautiful," Amy said, trying out a chair. "Where'd you get all this stuff?"

"Most of it was left here by the previous tenant. Kinda hippyish but I like it." Lara crossed the yard and leaned over the fence and called to someone on the other side. "Hey Nestor, come say hello."

An older man appeared from the neighboring yard. Grey moustache and deeply etched lines in his face. He propped an arm over the fence. "You must be Amy," he said, extending a hand. "I'm Nestor."

Amy shook the man's hand, feeling his callused palm.

Lara patted the man's arm. "Nestor's a master woodworker. He's done some work for me. His stuff is amazing."

The old man looked at Lara. "Have you shown her the piece?"

"Not yet."

Nestor nodded and turned to Amy again. "Let me know what you think after you see it. If it doesn't meet your approval, I can do another."

"I'm sorry," Amy said, cocking a brow at Lara. "See what?"

Lara frowned. "It's supposed to be a secret, Nestor."

"It is?" Nestor shrugged and tottered away. "Whoops."

"What's he talking about?"

Lara shooed her back inside. "Come on. I'll show you."

Back in the truck, Lara steered out of the neighborhood and drove for open country. Amy watched the houses flit by, giving way to vehicle yards and empty lots and then these too vanished until all there was to see was the flatland of the desert. The blacktop before them a postcard of a high lonesome highway vanishing against the horizon.

"I've never seen anything like this before," Amy said. "It's wild."

Lara propped an elbow on the window sill. "It's big. All that sky. Keeps you humble."

"So what's this big secret?" Amy couldn't stop grinning.

"Patience, young Jedi."

"Ah come on."

Lara pointed towards the arid land to the west. "See that foothill over there? The one closest to us. It's there."

The Cherokee slowed and Lara swung off the main road onto a dusty track, the truck dipping as it rode over a downed cattle guard. The track led up the incline of a low hill, bouncing over dips and bare rock until they pulled onto a plateau. Dust wafted from the tires and Lara asked her to wait for it to disperse before opening the doors.

They went on foot from there, Amy's shoes gritting over the sandy rock face. From atop the hill, she beheld a vista of the Chihuahuan scrub below and beyond that the sprawl of the city. It was colder up here, the wind sharper.

"Watch your step." Lara jumped down an edge where the rock face dropped. A bench of flat rock led out to where the hill inclined steeply below them. "There it is," she said.

At the far edge of the bench was a cairn of stones piled into a mound like the forgotten resting place of some lost pioneer. Jutting up from the mound of stones stood an archaic-looking headstone, some dark plank of hardwood framed up against that big sky and flat landscape. The edges of the milled wood were already pumiced raw from the windblown grit.

Amy squinted at it, thinking Lara had taken her to some odd tourist spot. "What is it?"

"Go see." Lara shooed the girl forward.

The inscription was hand carved. What she read there took her breath away.

JOHN WILLIAM GALLAGHER
Father
Friend
Lawman

Amy blinked at the tombstone in its berm of rocks. The air felt thinner than ever as she read the inscription a third time.

Lara came up alongside. "Well? Do you hate it?"

It was a minute before Amy found her voice. "You did this?"

"Nestor carved the headstone. I planted it here." Lara looked down the slope. "Your dad had said, on more than a few occasions, that he loved Clint Eastwood movies and stuff. So, mira." Lara glanced up, tension wrinkling her eyes. "So, do you hate it?"

"I love it." Amy threaded her arm around the woman's elbow. "He would too."

"I'm glad."

"This is a beautiful spot. How did you find it?"

"That night I tested myself, I came up here. Or the lobo did. Somehow I remembered it. I drove the truck up here afterwards and hunted around until I found it. And then, without really thinking about it, I just started collecting rocks and piled them up."

"And the headstone?"

"That didn't occur to me until later. I kept coming back here, just to sit and be alone. But the pile of rocks never felt like it was enough. So I had Nestor carve up an old-fashioned gravestone."

The wind kicked up. Icy gusts finding the gaps in their clothing. "It gets pretty cold up here." Lara cinched up her coat. "Whenever you want to go, just say so."

"Can we stay a bit longer? I just want to sit awhile."

"Of course." They sat on the bare rock. Amy tucked her feet under her and Lara studied the clouds in the sky.

"It really is a beautiful view," Amy said. "Do you come out here a lot?"

"I do. That's why I placed the headstone facing east."

Amy tilted her head, not following. Lara nodded at the skyline before them. "That's due west. And up here, the sunset is spectacular."

Amy smiled and settled in. After a while, she huddled closer to Lara for warmth and they watched the sun slant towards the earth, burning the undersides of the clouds a soft shade of pink.

"How long were you planning on staying?"

Amy tilted her head. "Dunno. A week. If that's okay with you?"

"Make it two. I could use the company."

The story begins...

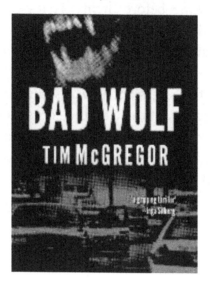

Detective Lara Mendes finally joins the Homicide detail only to find herself partnered up with a cop no one likes. John Gallagher is a veteran homicide detective who loves stomping bad guys but hates partners, especially green ones. The transition, needless to say, doesn't go smoothly and when the rotation says they're up, their first homicide is a doozy.

Human remains found on the river bank, mutilated and partially devoured. Their investigation reveals a pack of feral dogs stalking the streets of Portland, led by a suspect who believes himself to be a werewolf.

But there's a catch. The crazy werewolf suspect? He isn't crazy...

ABOUT THE AUTHOR

Tim McGregor is a novelist and screenwriter. The Bad Wolf Chronicles is his first book series. His produced films can usually be found in the bargain DVD bin. Tim lives in Toronto with his wife and children.

Made in the USA
Las Vegas, NV
11 March 2023

68928375R00252